BEHIND THE
THE
Broken

BEHIND DARKNESS DUET BOOK ONE

BEHIND THE
Broken

CHLOE C. PEÑARANDA

LIMITED DIGITALLY SIGNED 2024 FIRST PRINT

LUMARIAS PRESS

Behind The Broken
Copyright © 2024 by Chloe C. Peñaranda
All rights reserved.
This is a work of fiction. Names, characters, places, and incidents either are the product of the author's imagination or are used fictitiously. Any resemblance to actual persons, living or dead, events, or locales is entirely coincidental.
No part of this book may be reproduced in any form or by any electronic or mechanical means, including information storage and retrieval systems, without written permission from the author, except for the use of brief quotations in a book review.

Published by Lumarias Press
www.lumariaspress.com

First Edition published February 2024

Jacket design © 2024 Lumarias Press
Case Art © 2024 Katerina Zaitseva (@lepra.art)
Edited by Bryony Leah
www.bryonyleah.com
Interior art by @pandacapuccino & @elizianna.the.one

Identifiers
ISBN: 978-1-915534-13-2 (eBook)
ISBN: 978-1-915534-12-5 (paperback)
ISBN: 978-1-915534-11-8 (hardback)

www.ccpenaranda.com

Content Warning
While not dark romance between the main couple, backstories and plot elements touch on dark themes including:
Violence, death, murder, gun violence, loss, deep grief, suicidal ideation, human trafficking, explicit sexual scenes, mentions of captive abuse.

Playlist

Train Wreck
James Arthur
Bruises
Lewis Capaldi
Another Love
Tom Odell
Slayer
Bryce Savage
Fire on Fire
Sam Smith
Don't Blame Me
Taylor Swift
I'm yours
Isabel LaRosa
Him & I
G-Eazy, Halsey
To Build a home
The Cinematic Orchestra, Patrick Watson
Chandelier
Brooklyn Duo

FULL SPOTIFY PLAYLIST:

Dedication

We're all different kinds of broken; be proud of your sharp edges, and aim them to your enemies.

CHAPTER 1
Rhett

When I thought of the last time I'd hold my fiancée's hand, I imagined the diamond ring I'd adorned her finger with just hours ago would be clasped through mine, our skin aged and worn, not coated in the blood of our youth.

The countdown to the last time I'll hold Sarah Carter is drowned out by the laughter and drinks of the best night of our lives. Two loves completely oblivious to our rapidly draining time together.

That's how life is, I suppose. Unknown. Uncertain. And complete fucking hell.

"My mom is going to freak out!" Sarah gushes, hardly able to put her hand down from staring at her ring. The relief I got it right for her lifts my heavy shoulders after six months of planning. "My sister won't be surprised—she's been close to pushing you along herself. Oh Rhett, it's just perfect. You're perfect."

Sarah stops walking, grips the folds of my coat, and pushes up on her tiptoes to kiss me. *Fuck*, I love this girl. It may have taken me some years to finally commit. I can't be certain where the fear came from. It doesn't matter now. She'll be mine forever.

Her lips are soft but cold from the winter that dusts light snow around us. It's her favorite season, and last Christmas I made a promise to myself that the next I'd ask her to marry me. So here we are, on Christmas Eve, and nothing about today could be more perfect.

Breaking apart, I tuck a lock of her blonde hair behind her ear before dusting the snowfall from her cheek. "Let's go home and get warm," I say, cupping her frozen face. "The best of our celebrations has yet to happen."

I kiss her once, firmly. She gives a soft moan at the back of her throat that has me aching to be back at our small apartment in a quiet pocket of Philadelphia. It's nothing high-end or lavish. Sarah is just finishing medical school to become a doctor, and I'm about to start my second year of SWAT training to advance to FBI after another two years. This path of fate became my only way out of a situation that would have turned me into everything I fight against now.

There's one cloud of burden that will never leave me in our relationship, and perhaps that's a lot of the reason I waited so long to propose. There's a side of my life Sarah can never know about. My uncle, who I lived with until I turned sixteen, is the leader of a notorious crime syndicate across several states. When I grew old enough to understand his "work" I was horrified, though I could do nothing. It's a helplessness I carry with me now, knowing he's still out there, likely furious the *heir* to his empire escaped him and has remained out of his reach and network for eight years. When I was young he'd use me to smuggle drugs on occasion. I came to learn that was one of the tamest crimes he carried out. Reprehensible, unspeakable things.

I killed the name I was born with, and I didn't mourn that boy. It was for him I became Rhett Kaiser, the man who would fight to stop the types of villainy my sick uncle endorsed.

"Are you sure we can't take an Uber?" I murmur, wanting nothing more than to shed our thick clothing and feel her skin pressed to me instead.

She shakes her head, taking my hand again. "The night is beautiful. It's only thirty minutes." As Sarah admires the snow I can hardly stop myself from admiring her.

The night isn't too chilly thanks to the buzz of alcohol coursing through both of us. The extra bottle of wine gifted for our engagement by the fancy hotel restaurant I booked went down quickly in the high of our excitement. It took many months of saving to get here, but this is worth it.

"Thirty minutes less I could be spending between those thighs," I say, leaning down to her ear. Her body gives a delightful shiver.

"I'm sure you'll find the time to make it up," she says, batting long lashes up at me, and maybe I quicken our pace a little. "We can take the shorter way." She beams, pulling me across the street toward a narrow alley.

My unease rises at the lack of streetlights and the darkness it will encase us in.

"I don't mind the usual route," I say warily.

"You've filled my head with other thoughts now, so I do." She casts a wicked smirk over her shoulder, encouraging me along.

Well, I won't argue against getting home sooner for that.

I grip her hand a little tighter down the eerie path. Normally I'd flow with conversation, but I can't explain the need to keep my senses on high alert. As sharp as I can while the alcohol dulls them. It's too painfully quiet, and the regret that begins to tighten my gut will come to haunt me for the rest of my days.

I should have listened to my instinct. We're borderline drunk. I have no gun. Not that I'm in the habit of carrying my police firearms around on a regular night, especially if we're drinking, but my sudden urge to have one inspires a ringing in my ears.

"You're going to cut off the circulation in my hand soon," Sarah says with a giggle.

"Sorry," I say, trying to relax my nerves.

There's nothing around. No one. I'm taking my new fiancée home and we will most certainly not be getting much sleep tonight. Sarah Carter will be my wife someday.

Soon, I decide. Why wait when no tomorrow is promised?

No hour is granted . . .

No minute is gifted . . .

It takes less than one.

Less than one minute to walk straight from a dream into the scene of a waking nightmare.

They come out of nowhere. An ambush of too many hooded figures. All I can do is push Sarah behind me, but the barrier of protection my body gives is cut down in seconds.

Sarah's cry pierces the night, driving a spear of icy terror through my chest.

"Don't fucking touch her!" I yell.

A dark chuckle answers me, followed by a decent punch to wind me in the gut, then another across my face. I tackle the guy in front of me, barely registering the pain of each punch I deliver to his face, losing count after four. Someone tries to pull me off, but these thugs are amateurs. Kneeling, I hook my arms around him from behind, throwing him over my shoulder before I stand and crack the heel of my shoe into his skull. It knocks him out.

"A pretty thing you have," a man's voice coos.

I spin with such fury in my bones to find Sarah pinned to the wall, whimpering softly and trying to shrink away from the finger he strokes along her wet cheeks. I see white. Lunging for him, the alcohol slows my senses. *Why did they give us that bottle of wine? Why did I drink it? Why? Why? Why?*

I'm so, so sorry.

I don't reach her. She's right there and I can't fucking save her.

Three men drag me down, taking turns at kicking and punching, and the pain should be excruciating by now—bones are certainly broken—but my adrenaline is coursing so hot I can only focus on one thing.

Her.

"Please," I beg, holding my hands up in pathetic surrender.

If I were sober . . . if I had my gun . . . I would have killed them all by now. I know no fucking morals in this moment.

My vision comes back around as I roll onto my knees, coughing and spitting, the coppery tang filling my mouth.

"Rhett," Sarah cries softly.

My chest is about to explode. I can hardly look up with how badly I failed her. But we're going to make it out of this, and I will spend my life making it up to her.

"We're going home, baby," I promise.

"You shouldn't lie," the same man taunts, stepping away from Sarah to stalk in his arrogance toward me.

I begin to commit every detail of him to memory. Dark, rugged hair, brown eyes, then a scar that's an easy identifier across his left cheek, above light shadow a few days overdue a clean shave.

"I'm going to fucking kill you," I snarl.

I don't care what it takes. I will end them all if it means getting my fiancée out of here.

"No, I don't think you will," the man sings. Two others hold me down as this one approaches, punching me with better force than the others. "It's too bad I won't get to kill you . . . yet. We're to deliver a worse punishment for your desertion."

"Please stop hurting him," Sarah sobs. I've never heard her so terrified, and it's all my fault.

"It's okay, Sarah." I try to console her, but they're weak, miserable words.

My blood runs cold when the crook's words finally register. He can't mean what I think he does. Yet as I manage to straighten despite the pain throbbing across my face and pounding in my head, the slow, sinful smile he wears only drags me into a waking hell.

"Did you really think you could escape him, Everett Lanshall?"

I can't believe it. After all this time I allowed myself to think I'd really done it—that my uncle couldn't find me and had given up out of boredom. I'm useless to him. But I should have known that isn't what matters to him—not really. Even after eight years he won't let go of someone who made a mockery of him by escaping.

"What do you want?" I ask, close to begging now it's all I have. "Whatever he's offered you, I can do more."

The man chuckles. So fast that all I register is the click of the safety, a gun is pointed at my head and Sarah's cries turn frantic.

"Please!" she wails.

That sound will haunt me in the depths of the hell I'm about to meet.

"Just let her go. I'll come with you," I plead in defeat. That's all that matters. Not my life, nor their plan to drag me back to my uncle for torture.

"That wasn't my instruction," he says with no remorse.

Something about the sinister amusement that comes over him freezes every nerve cell in my body.

It happens too suddenly.

The end of my fucking world echoes in the blast of a bullet.

My eyes fall to his aim . . . to Sarah. Her wide blue eyes swim in an ocean of agony, locked on me. Her hands clutch her abdomen and crimson begins to flood her pale skin. A roar tears from my throat as I pull free from those restraining me. I scramble to Sarah's side in time to catch her fall.

Panic seizes me. "You're okay, baby," I say, but it's a lie. A dark fucking lie, and the blood that pours too fast doubles my vision.

"Rhett," she says through tight, wheezing gasps. "I-I'm scared."

"Shh, I'm right here. Right fucking here. Stay awake for me, Sarah."

Her eyes flutter, fighting the pull under.

This can't be happening. No no no, this isn't the end, when minutes ago it only felt like the beginning.

Dipping into my pocket, I dial two numbers before the cell is ripped out of my hand and thrown against the wall. Rage shakes my whole damn body.

I'm seconds from lunging for the bastard's throat when Sarah's grip tightens on the arms I'm cradling around her.

"Don't leave me," she whispers. So weak.

"I won't," I promise quietly, cupping her cheek and blinking back the flood in my eyes at the ghostly fear flashing over her beautiful face. "I'm so sorry. I'm so, so sorry."

Sarah's eyes fall closed, and if hearts can cleave, mine cleaves so tangibly, the pain ripped free in a cry I barely hear. Her hold slackens on me completely, and I rock her as if this is all some sick, twisted nightmare.

"Don't sleep, baby," I plead. Hollow words that will never be heard. No one is coming. This is all my fault.

My breathing calms with deep gulps of her scent.

Then the next thing to detonate is my fury.

One second I'm holding Sarah's lifeless form; the next my hands are wrapped around the throat of the nearest man. Tighter and tighter, until my patience snaps along with his neck, to get him out of my way. The next man pulls out a gun, but I'm so far removed from any fear—anything of humanity at all—that I grip the barrel as he pulls the trigger, bending his arm back, and the bullet flies skyward as his bone breaks. I pull him to me, using my finger over his to fire the next bullet, which hits the last man, and all that is left is their leader.

I use the man in my arms as a shield to advance. He takes three bullets before I toss him aside, close enough to grab the gun aimed at me and push my final mark with feral force into the wall.

"Holy shit, dude. I'm sorry, I'm just the messenger. I-I can help you find him—j-join you!"

There is not a damn chance in this hell I would trust him.

"You're on borrowed time, as I need you to do what you do best and deliver a fucking message," I say, not recognizing the person who spoke with such sin and promise. Ripping the gun from him, I strike it across his temple, and he cries like a child, crumpling to the ground. I kick him. Again and again. A note of me is sickened by what I'm capable of, but I had everything taken from me this night and my vengeance knows nothing but violence. I can't stop. Not until he's lying in a bloodied heap, barely able to breathe through the blood he chokes on.

I commit his voice to memory. His face. I will find him again and his death won't be quick, certainly not painless.

"Tell Alistair Lanshall," I seethe, dipping each word in a promise that will see us both burn in the flames my uncle ignited, "when I come for him, he'll get the monster he wanted to create."

The man crawls on all fours before clawing at the wall to stand.

Now my adrenaline turns cold. I plummet to frozen before I become numb. Turning around, I focus only on Sarah's face—so peaceful and beautiful and perfect. A face that deserved so many more years than what she got. An innocent whose only mistake was falling for me.

I take her in my arms, not really feeling the air or the gravity or my broken bones, carrying her in a shuffle that begins to ache until stabbing pain from my injuries takes over my whole body. I keep going. Walking. Shuffling. Slowing. Until the streetlights glow again, and with the light, reality crashes my knees to the icy ground. I might call for help through my cries, hoping someone will hear me and maybe, by some miracle, it isn't too late.

It's taken losing everything to turn my soul black. And it will take becoming everything I've tried to deny I am . . . to seek my revenge.

CHAPTER 2
Anastasia
THREE YEARS LATER

The last year of university should be devoted to studies, having fun with peers—the final push before we're thrown into the world. Not for me. My father is a senator in the upcoming presidential election that is about to bulldoze my life. Dramatic, maybe. But it means more public appearances and people might start to recognize me. For someone who hates attention, I won't deny, the thought of moving states and adopting a temporary alias is appealing.

"He's kind of hot," my best friend Riley says, leaning against my long window frame.

I know she's eye-fucking the new security guard my dad is seeing out since I refused to. The idea is ridiculous—that he would assign me a personal guard to follow me at school, out shopping, everywhere!

"Stop lusting after him." I scowl, picking up a small cushion and throwing it at her. "He's not going to be around for long."

"I don't know, Ana. Your dad sounded *very* stern on the need for one. And after hearing all his reasons, I can't say I don't agree the protection is a good idea."

"Don't side with him!"

Riley holds up her hands. "There's a lot of creeps and bad people out there! Once you start becoming a public figure there will always be a risk to you. Politics is not an amateur's game."

I groan, flopping onto my bed. Sometimes I wish I wasn't the daughter of a hopeful new president. That I was no one at all.

"I don't like him," I mutter, recalling the guard I met named Victor. He was handsome, I guess, with dark brown hair and eyes to match, an easy kind of attractive, and only six years older than me at thirty so he wouldn't look so out of place on campus. How considerate of my father.

"What is there not to like?" Riley asks, throwing herself down next to me. We stare at the red velvet canopy of my four-poster bed.

"He just felt . . . weird."

"You *felt* him?"

My cheeks flush. "I don't mean like *that*. I just . . . I can't explain it."

It's probably irrational. Simply my bitterness not letting me see anything nice about him.

"It's only until your father is in office, right? You might get to ditch him for the last semester."

So six months of being awkwardly trailed by some secret service guy. Great.

"Anastasia, can you come speak to your father, please?" my mom calls through the door.

My eyes pinch shut with a moan.

"I should be getting home anyway," Riley says, slinging her satchel over her body. "We have that summer assignment due."

"That paper was optional for extra credit." Something I quickly decided I'd forgo to spare the suffering. "And don't pretend like you haven't already finished it." I smirk, following her out my room.

"It needs revising," she argues.

Riley is top of our class in postgrad English literature. She's incredibly smart and an invaluable hand to hold while I've struggled through many of our classes over the years. Literature wasn't my first choice, but my parents never supported music as a real opportunity beyond high school.

"You mean you need to make sure it'll pass with a higher mark than Nolan Flynn," I tease, pushing her arm.

The name triggers a furrow of her brow that's more adorable than menacing on her delicate face. With blonde hair and moss-green eyes, she's so beautiful that even after five years of friendship I'm often in awe of her. My hair is a chestnut shade of brown, but my eyes of bright hazel are my most complimented feature.

"He surpassed me the last two papers of the year," she grumbles.

I find their rivalry highly amusing. It's a silent kind of classroom battle where it's like they've both pinned each other as their competitor, but they rarely speak a word to the other.

"You should just fuck him and get your frustrations out already," I say, smiling deviously at her open-mouthed shock and flushed cheeks.

"I would rather fail a whole semester."

I gasp. "Wow, your competitiveness runs deep. It would make for great sex."

Riley whacks me with her satchel and we both burst into

laughter. Until we come to the grand foyer, where a glance sideways at my father's office sours my mood.

"You should take your own advice," Riley says low, mindful of the passing staff. "Take your frustrations out on your new guard. What a scandal you would incite."

I roll my eyes, pushing her out the door. "I'd rather get blackout drunk and end up dancing on some sleazy bar top."

Riley giggles as she leaves, and my mood plummets the moment she's gone. I drag my feet to my father's ridiculously large and lavish office. Though it's nothing compared to the Oval Office he's said to be the favorite of the presidential candidates to be instated in this election. My hands wring together at the thought of moving. I decide I'll get my own apartment when that happens. I love our home, but I hate all kinds of formal political appearances and I've avoided them as much as I can throughout his campaigns. They'll be unavoidable if he becomes president.

"Anastasia, thank you for coming." My father greets me warmly, pushing up from his tall leather seat.

I gravitate toward him, naturally stepping into his waiting arms as he kisses my head. My relationship with him is perfect, and despite my own feelings I'm so proud of him for coming close to achieving his dream.

I realize we aren't alone when he releases me. My father's close friend and business partner, Gregory Forbes, is seated on one of the side sofas. He'll be vice president if my father takes office. Instinctively I survey the room as if I'll find his son.

"Liam is in the games room." Gregory smiles at my observation as he stands, buttoning his suit jacket. "Our visit is short. We were just discussing the final security measures for the both of you. Things are about to get a lot of more intense with paparazzi and tabloids for the big run of the campaign."

I almost smirk, imagining Liam putting up even more of a protest than I am.

"I just wanted to let you know that Agent Victor Ross will be starting next week," my father informs me.

"Semester doesn't start for another two weeks," I argue.

"I think it's in your best interests to get aquatinted before then. Get used to his presence."

I can't hide the line of protest on my face, but my father only smiles at it. I won't get myself out of this one. Even the agent's name sounds old, strange. All I can hope is we'll work out some agreement that he'll stay the hell away from me and make himself invisible.

"Is that all?" I ask.

"Yes, darling. Dinner is at six o'clock with the Van Der Laizes, remember."

"Yeah, yeah." I wave him off as I leave through the side door.

When I get to the games room Liam is lining up his next pool shot.

"Playing against yourself is just sad," I say, heading for the other pool cue.

He sinks his shot with ease. "What's sad is our fathers believing we're incapable of protecting ourselves."

I huff in agreement, deciding to aim for the stripes. There are more of them, but he didn't give himself too much of a lead.

"Any plans on how to ditch the bodyguards? Run them out of their jobs? I can be down for some criminal activity to make them quit."

Liam chuckles, running a hand through his black hair that often falls over his eyes when it isn't formally styled. Paired with his deep green eyes and tall, strong physique, he's any woman's dream. I tried flirting with him once, but it was then I learned he's hung up on someone he refuses to speak about.

"I have a hit man set up already," he says, sinking another ball and lining up for a second shot.

"Ironic. That protecting you from an assassination will make them a target."

He gives a wicked side-smile as he straightens. It doesn't last long. His smiles never do, and often his eyes are disconnected, distant, when he thinks no one is looking. I know he doesn't have the best relationship with his father. When I see them together Liam's posture always changes—it's straighter, firmer . . . as if one wrong slouch will disappoint his father.

I've known Gregory for a few years now. To me he's kind and generous, but never have I seen him display that side of his personality to Liam. His son has never liked to talk about him.

The clack of the white ball hitting my shot breaks the silence, and I smile in victory when it sinks. I survey for my next, saying, "What do you need one for anyway? You don't get up to much."

"I'm leaving for New York. He's sending two guards with me."

I lean on my pool cue with the weight of sadness. Liam's company can be prickly—he's often sarcastic and grumpy—but he's familiar. One of the very few friends I have.

"What are you going there for?" I quiz.

He looks hesitant to tell me the truth, and that only twists inside of me.

Liam shrugs. "Work stuff for the campaign. I won't know specifics until I get there."

It seems too vague, but I know his tells by now, and pushing him on it will only turn him guarded.

"Maybe I can ditch this postgrad year and come with you," I say wistfully.

"No," he says too sharply, but he wipes it from his expression. "You're too smart to throw all you've worked for away. Your parents would lose their minds."

They would never allow it, but I'm a grown adult at twenty-four and they never let me feel the independence of one.

"Why does that sound like motivation?" I sigh.

We share laughter and then lose ourselves for a while in the game of pool that evens out, right before we compete to sink the black and Liam ultimately wins. We're on our second glass of whiskey stolen from my father's cabinet. Liam's older than me at twenty-six, and it isn't that we're not legally allowed to drink, but daytime drinking is frowned upon by our parents as if we're still minors.

"So much for not being here for long," Liam says, now reclining effortlessly on an armchair. His white button-down shirt is open at the first few holes, tucked into expensive tailored pants.

He's dressed smart-casual while I'm lounging in leggings and an oversize white jumper, my hair pulled into a messy bun. I needed to shower and dress for dinner soon since we're to host one of the wealthy families endorsing my father's election.

"When do you leave for New York?" I ask, swinging my legs from my perch on the pool table.

"Next week," he says, eyes casting off to the side as if he's traveling there this very moment.

"You have to send pictures," I gush. I've never been to New York and I can't deny I'm envious of his trip.

"I'll try."

"That doesn't sound promising. Of course, you'll forget about me the moment you're out there with all the freedom and parties and women while I'm here under lockdown."

"That's an exaggeration for me and dramatic for you," he muses.

I release a long sigh, taking another drink of whiskey. It burns, pinching my face on its way down down my throat. When the door swings open I push the glass behind me discreetly. I don't expect Liam's older brother to wander through.

Liam straightens in his seat, tracking his brother, who keeps his sights on me as though I'm the only one here.

"Hey, Ana," Matthew greets.

I can never be sure what it is about Matthew Forbes that makes me uncomfortable. He's always been kind, harmless. Yet I'm always glad we've never been alone in a room together.

"Are you shipping off to New York too?" I ask him.

He comes around, leaning on the pool table to face me. "I'll be traveling back and forth for a while."

The conversation turns tense, or maybe it's the air charging that makes my skin prick.

"I should get ready for dinner," I say, hopping off the table, but I don't want to leave Liam alone.

Matthew reaches for my glass with a finger of whiskey left. He drinks it unashamedly, keeping his brown eyes on me.

Liam looks like their father, but Matthew, I assume, must take after their mother, with the same deep red hair. If I didn't know them, I wouldn't guess they were brothers from how different they are.

Liam stands then, clearing his throat. "I'm sure we're just about to leave."

Matthew sets down my glass, casting his brother a bored

look, and I don't know why it flares in me. Like he's always seen his younger brother as lesser when it is so far from the truth.

"Let's go, son," Gregory interrupts from behind me.

Even I tense at the intrusion. I can't explain the dynamic between the Forbes, but what I do feel is protective of Liam when it's as if his father has always favored his older brother. I can't fathom why.

Liam only nods, casting me a smile, but it isn't like those he gives when we're alone. As he heads out the door without another word, Matthew pauses close to me.

"It was good to see you, Anastasia," he says, and I think it's my own discomfort that hears something seductive in it.

Blowing out a breath of held tension when I'm alone, I head to my room. Next week will be the end of my unsurveilled freedom, and if I'm going to suffer, misery loves company, and this guard isn't getting an easy job.

CHAPTER 3

Rhett

Listening to a grown man plead on his knees, hardly able to stand the stench of urine when he pisses himself, isn't how I intended to spend my evening.

I have a dinner reservation, in fact.

Keeping my gun aimed at his head, I check my watch. *Shit, I'm going to be late.*

"P-please, man. I have a wife and a kid," he blubbers like a child.

My eyes narrow on this low-life excuse of a man. His colleagues are all dead, and the three women they kidnapped—likely days ago, from the looks of them—were ushered out by two from my team.

"You lived as a sadistic, vicious man," I say coldly. "Even if you did have a child, which you don't, Derrek Finley Spencer, they would be far better off without such a poisonous influence in their lives."

The sound of the gunshot rings out and his body hits the

ground. I don't linger around the scene, fitting my gun back into my concealed belt under my suit jacket. I examine myself. I kept clean of blood, thankfully. Rushing home to change would suck.

At the table in the abandoned warehouse where we tracked this movement of hostages to, I make quick work of filtering through their papers, collecting what I can, along with a briefcase full of cash. It's dirty money, but we use it toward resources to help our victims and fund our work. Cleans it right back up if you ask me.

Jeremy, a younger member of my network at only nineteen, comes rushing back in to take over for me. "Shit, dude, that was awesome!"

I cut him a warning look. He's too spirited sometimes, and though it's a triumph this round, I try to drill home that there is nothing to be celebrated. Not when a takedown like this is only a drop of antidote to the thick vines of poison that grow through many cities. My uncle is one of those at the very top of such sinister corruption involving those in high places with enough money to kill their problems, feed their evil desires, and take without a care.

I got out and only wanted to live a peaceful life with my fiancée. My Sarah. I would have taken down crime legally and earned my rightful place in society. Then he came for me. As if his leash on me had only extended for a few years of delusional freedom, it became clear the moment he killed Sarah that the only way to cut free from him was to cut him down.

There's no legal way to find him. No righteous path that will stop him. I have to do this *my* way. *His* way. Not better, but far fucking worse.

He's a very powerful man, however. A master of hiding behind so many people. Over the three years since I started my network, Xoid, we've managed to disband many of his criminal ongoings, but I've never found *him*. I've hunted his movements through the dark web, killed those I could find, and sent my messages in blood and body parts that I'm sure he received—if not directly, then he heard of them. He knows I'm coming, yet he's too much of a fucking coward to face me. I won't stop until I find him.

"Clean up the mess, take everything you find here back to the den, and get to work on our next lead," I command firmly.

"Yes, sir." Jeremy salutes.

I resist the urge to groan.

He's harmless, and I won't deny his spirit is a relief. I wouldn't wish it shattered or for anyone to live a life so numb. I don't mind this fractured existence though. I have a purpose to fulfill, and that's all that matters. I don't deserve anything more when a beautiful, innocent soul was taken far too soon by such monstrous hands because of me.

I head out, slipping into my black SUV. It takes ten minutes breaking speed limits to park outside the expensive hotel. I pass off my keys to the valet, and when I see her in the restaurant I ignore the waiter to take up the seat opposite the stunning dark-haired woman.

"Make this worth my time, Allie," I say, picking up the glass of water and taking a long drink.

She rests her chin in clasped hands while her large brown eyes sparkle at me. "I've tried. You always refuse me." She pouts.

Her flirtations are adorable but not serious.

"You said it was urgent," I press. Time is precious with my kind of work.

Allie became an unexpected member of Xoid. From a high-profile family of lawyers, her role is of the utmost secrecy and discretion. Only a few know of her in the network, and only I know her full name. She's incredibly smart and from her connections is able to get information in some places out of our means.

"You once mentioned you traced a trafficking lead that hinted it was tied to someone *very* high up," Allie begins.

"Yes," I confirm.

"Well, I think you could be onto something. Something really big," she says. It's not often Allie wears such a ghostly expression.

I lean in closer as she takes a sip of red wine, her tanned skin furrowing at her brow.

"Who is it?" I ask, but I know it's never that easy.

"I don't know. When I hacked into the stream of communication I was swiftly kicked out. I only got a few code sentences that made no sense, but I figured it out. I've seen it before—when they swap the letters of the vowels. There's a hit for a kidnapping that you're going to be interested in. The reward is enough to make any saint a sinner."

I hook a brow for her to continue, raising my hand at the waiter who was about to ask if I want to order. I can't stay long.

Allie waits until they're gone to whisper, "Anastasia Kinsley."

I lean back in my seat, mulling over the family name I've heard before. "The presidential candidate?"

"His daughter, more specifically. I searched the database. There are others with the same name, but none that could warrant such a prize. She's to be taken alive, so I would assume ransom, but with what they're willing to pay out that doesn't make sense."

"She's an easier target to get than a running president, but it's meant to lure him out as a perfect target," I conclude, puzzling it over in my mind. "Who would want Archibald Kinsley dead?"

"It's politics. The list is long. There was also another name, Rhett." She tries to hide her wince, and because of that I save her the bother.

"Lanshall?"

She nods and my fist tightens. My uncle is an arrogant son of a bitch. It will be his downfall to use his true name for his dealings. He could have found me anytime—I wasn't hiding and I've waited three years for it—yet it seems the rat is trying to outrun the flood of rage coming for him.

"Shit," I mutter, downing the rest of my water.

"Sure you can't join me for a meal?" she asks just as the waiter brings over a delicious-looking ravioli. "You look like you could use a moment to unwind."

That would seem laughable at the best of times, but with the bombshell Allie just dropped, my mind is racing faster than it has done in months. There's no chance of it calming.

"So this woman is in danger, and it could lead me to Lanshall?" I ponder, swirling my fingers around the rim of my glass as if it might untangle the mess of my thoughts.

"It might be worth looking into, yes," she says.

My eyes slip to her as she finishes her next mouthful. Her expression gives off a hint of triumph.

"You wouldn't be telling me this if you didn't know of a way in," I assume.

Her smile is all beautiful victory.

"How many years have we worked together?" she muses.

She is a fucking diamond. It's baffling to me that someone so stunning and smart is still single. I don't doubt men throw themselves at her feet even if she walks past oblivious. If I weren't so fucked-up and dangerous, perhaps I might ask her out. But that life is not for me. Not since Sarah. I don't date, I don't flirt, though occasionally I've given in to a night of sex and nothing more. I won't cross that line with someone like Allie though. She's too precious to me, and she deserves far more.

"You deserve a raise," I say, doting on her.

"You don't pay me."

Allie won't accept anything for the help she offers. She comes from a ridiculously wealthy family, and we met when she hacked into one of my servers—one of her only accidents—and I went looking for her thinking she was a threat to our network. We never use her full name, and this restaurant is hours away from where she lives.

"You deserve the world," I say.

She gives her best attempt at being flattered.

"As it so happens, I heard the president is doubling down on security for the upcoming election. I can't say if he's aware of the threat made against his daughter or if it's just normal. He's hired her a personal bodyguard already, but I did some digging into him."

Allie reaches down into her bag and then slides a brown file across to me. I flip it open with racing curiosity, but it quickly turns to trembling anger when I read about the dark dealings this guy, Victor Ross, has been involved in. Trafficking. My favorite kind of monster to kill slowly.

"You know what you have to do, right?" Allie says quietly.

I do, though I'm conflicted with what it will mean. This isn't the kind of work I hoped the rest of my year would entail.

"Thank you, Allie. You're invaluable to all of this," I say, standing. I slip five hundred-dollar bills under her glass as I lean in to kiss her cheek. "Have another glass of wine. And that raspberry cheesecake you came here specifically for."

Before she can protest the money she spies, I slip away.

My determination fixes in place when I begin to calculate my next move outside the restaurant. I think of who I could assign to this task, but it feels too valuable, too important. Pulling out my cell, I dial an old friend who's more like a brother to me. He picks up on the third ring.

"I have a feeling this isn't a catch-up call," Xavier groans into the phone. He's a prolific FBI agent in the position I should have joined him in had the devil not set other plans in place for me by crafting me a spot in hell.

"Another time, soon," I promise. It's been too long since we saw each other when he was relocated to Washington, D.C. a year ago. It almost seems like fate now.

"Just get out what you're going to ask for, you damn bastard," he says.

It's a lighthearted comment when he knows exactly the kind of work I've built over the years instead of following him the legal way. Sometimes we consider ourselves opposite sides of the same coin. He's never judged what I do even though it's against every legal responsibility he has.

"I need credentials. Stellar ones."

"Rhett, that's some serious fraud shit you're asking of me."

"I know. But it's really important."

"Are you close to finding him?"

Xavier Leith knows about my uncle. He knows everything.

"I think so."

I don't want to get my hopes up, but Alistair Lanshall's death is ironically the only fucking thing keeping me alive, driving toward something before I fall to the same fate as Sarah. I don't deserve my life when hers was stolen.

"What division?" Xavier asks.

I know what I need is no small ask. In fact, it's damn near suicide if I'm caught.

"Secret service."

Xavier groans into the phone. "Do I even want to know?"

"Probably best not for now."

"All right, man, I'll see what I can do, but I can't promise."

"Thanks. I owe you one."

"You owe far more than that, Kaiser," he sighs. "But if it helps you catch the son of a bitch..."

I swallow hard, filled with gratitude. I don't deserve the loyalty of him or anyone else who's stuck by me since I became such miserable company and a constant danger. I don't like having to ask for favors, but some things are quicker or more out of my depth, so I have to bow the need for help.

I will do whatever it takes to plummet Alistair Lanshall into the deep grave I've been digging for him since Christmas Eve three years ago, dead or alive, through whatever means will grant the most suffering.

Though it will still be only a fraction of what I live with every day.

CHAPTER 4
Anastasia

Being told my new guard has arrived and I'm supposed to greet him, I purposely take my time getting ready after my long gym session of letting my anger out on the treadmill and the punching bag. It's close to my favorite method of releasing the emotions that always run too high within me.

The idea I have to be followed by a guard everywhere I go beyond this house is as ridiculous today as it was a week ago when my father dropped the news.

Not to be negotiated.

I tie my hair in a high ponytail with the front sections loose. Then I dress in a red bodysuit with tailored, high-waisted, slim-leg black pants. I opt for flats. All I'm supposed to do is show him around the house and to his room, which is annoyingly opposite mine. Planning to ditch him afterward to go to a pre-semester mixer, I slip what I need into my pockets—things like my cell, some money, and of course the red lipstick I'm wearing, which is sure to need topping up after a few drinks.

Making my way leisurely to my father's office, I smile to myself, hoping my tardiness makes Victor Ross irritable from the start. If I have to endure this, I can at least have a little fun.

I hear his voice in conversation with my father as I approach, and though I've only met him once, it sounds different from what I remember.

I knock before entering, and both stop their conversation as I do. The agent has his back to me, but he is most definitely not Victor. The dark hair I expected to find is such a light shade of blond it's almost white. He stands from the chair opposite my father to turn to me and I find myself staring at the most beautiful man I've ever seen. Seriously, who looks like that and ends up standing across from some senator's adult daughter as her bodyguard? He wears all black. Even his shirt beneath his suit, his watch, his cufflinks—everything solid black, making his hair even more of a stark contrast.

His eyes are an icy blue and his facial structure is sharp, making him appear lethal, yet so damn attractive he feels like a trap. The final edge that tips him closer to *dangerous* is the scar that starts on his right temple, hidden by a curl of silver and trailing a jagged line that breaks off into two, one scar narrowly missing his eye and the other continuing to the hollow of his cheek.

"Anastasia, I'd like you to meet Agent Rhett Kaiser, your personal guard for the next six months." My dad introduces us. "Agent Kaiser, this is my daughter, Anastasia Kinsley."

"A pleasure to meet you." Rhett extends his hand, but I'm delayed in my confusion and distraction at the deep, entrancing voice.

My hand slips into his, tingling with warmth, and I realize we haven't stopped looking at each other since I entered.

I pull out of his firm grip, snapping myself out of my stupor to cast my father a frown. "What happened to Agent Ross?"

My father grimaces. "Unfortunately, he was involved in a fatal accident just a few days ago. We'll be sending our condolences to the family. He was a great man."

I don't know why my gaze shifts to Rhett at the news. His face is near impossible to read, a perfect sculpture of cool indifference, but his hands ball into fists—only for a single tight flex before he relaxes. When he looks my way I quickly avert my gaze, not knowing what it is about him that's kind of frightening. But not in the way I thought he could hurt me.

"It's just as well Agent Kaiser came highly recommended and was available for immediate placement. He's been very eager to meet you."

My spine stiffens. I guess taking the role of babysitting me in my boring postgrad university life is an easy payout for anyone. It's no wonder he was eager to take it.

"Right, well, can we get this tour over with?" I sigh. I want to get away as soon as possible, not understanding my nerves around this man. Unlike when I met Victor Ross, I'm intrigued by Rhett, and perhaps that's what scares me.

"You'll have to excuse my daughter. She can be . . . spirited," my father says with a warning look.

I don't hide my displeasure.

"A fiery spirit should never be excused," Rhett says.

My sour expression relaxes at the unexpected comment.

"Anastasia will show you around, Agent. I look forward to seeing you again at dinner this evening to discuss more."

That was our cue to leave, which I take eagerly before my dad reads the guilt on my face. I don't plan to make it back in time for that dinner.

I become hyperaware of Rhett trailing me closely—too close.

"You're already taking this *personal* guard thing a bit too literally," I say.

"How many paces should you like me to stand, Miss Kinsley?"

The way he addresses me breaks a shiver. The title, the low tone he speaks in. Is he trying to be seductive?

I cut him with a warning look regardless, at which a smile hints at the corner of his mouth.

Deviant asshole.

"At least three," I say.

"Of your leg span or mine?"

Considering the height of him, I don't have to look lower to gauge how much bigger his strides are compared to mine when I only meet his shoulder.

I stop walking to face him, folding my arms with the irritation he's stirring already.

"Did you really just use a cheap excuse to look at my legs?"

"My eyes have been trained on yours the whole time. I don't need an excuse. It's my job to ensure every part of you"—to make his point, his blue gaze slips down my body, and I damn myself for the disruption in my stomach at that slow assessment—"remains intact."

"You're to keep those eyes on the invisible, nonexistent threats *around* me, not on me, Agent."

"On you, around you—my full focus is entirely yours."

He's making my goal of trying to drive him to quit easy. It's like a silent challenge sparked between us just now. I smile sweetly, pushing down the unwelcome giddiness in me before turning into the next hall, not bothering to account for him keeping up.

I point and explain all of the main rooms: games room, cinema, pool, gym, dining room, kitchen. He barely gets a glance at any of them before I'm moving on, but much to my ire he doesn't seem fazed by my lack of enthusiasm for him or the tour.

We get to our rooms, and I awkwardly stand outside mine and cast a hand behind him.

"That's your room," I explain to his patient, calm stance.

"Aren't you going to show me inside?"

"I think you're capable of figuring out a room on your own. There's a bed, and you have your own bathroom."

Rhett has this annoyingly devious look about him that always seems to be debating if he should incite argument out of nothing more than amusement.

"Give me your phone," he says, holding out his palm.

"What? No."

"I need to place my number inside, just in case."

My jaw locks in defiance, but I decide it isn't worth being petty. I fish it out of my pocket, unlocking it before I hand it over.

He taps for a few seconds longer than I think necessary, and I come close to snatching it back.

"So, this is what you didn't want me to see—"

I do reach then, nearly grabbing his whole hand and pulling him to my chest too when I rip the phone back.

The screen only displays his new contact info.

"Now I'm *really* curious as to what you're hiding in there," he muses.

"Nothing," I snap.

Rhett's barely-there smile is becoming a trigger to my volatile thoughts. He dips a hand into his pants pocket before unlocking his phone and handing it out to me.

"If you will, please," he says at my hesitation.

It's open on the dial screen.

I take his phone with more reluctance than necessary before adding my number.

"If that was all, I have something I need to do," I say.

"Then I'll see you at dinner, Anastasia."

"Just Ana," I correct before I can stop myself. My full name sounds too formal.

"Ana," he repeats after me, and from his mouth it sounds enticing.

I need away from him, so I spin on my heel to march off.

"Where are you going?" he calls after me.

"You're not on duty yet, Agent. That's none of your business," I say without looking back.

Every time I lay eyes on him I can't explain the conflict inside me trying to gauge him. It's like he can protect someone from the world, but also tear it apart in his wake.

I rush out of the foyer after checking my mom and dad aren't around to question me. It's easier to plead forgiveness later when they insist having dinner with my new guard was more important than a party. I beg to differ. In fact, more so than before, I'm longing for the distraction from a certain stunning blond man who is to become a regular presence, too close for comfort. Something in the gleam of his stupidly attractive eyes tells me he won't commit to the three strides rule.

Plucking the keys to the matte-black Porsche from the garage wall, a little flashy but my favorite to drive, I fold inside as the door finishes opening and speed off. I'll leave it at the party and Uber home. I smirk to myself. Perhaps I'll ask Rhett to retrieve it tomorrow, make his pretty face useful for something.

I can't erase him from my mind and it's sparking my frustration. I press on the gas, surpassing the speed limit just a little.

My hands tighten around the wheel. *Stop thinking about him. He's just a man, no better than Victor Ross.*

The moment I think it my mind scolds the lie. Though there's a note of guilt in me for ever thinking badly of the sense I got from Victor now he's tragically gone. I spent the week determined to prove to my father I don't need a guard and would make the poor guy quit by becoming his problem.

Yet now Rhett Kaiser may have just become mine.

CHAPTER 5
Anastasia

Music blares in the part of the house where I'm dancing with Riley. I need the noise to drown out my thoughts, and, tipping back another shot of *something* handed to me by someone I recognize from a class last year, I realize I need the alcohol to numb my body.

I'm not usually the partying/drinking type. I swear. It's all the shifts in my life from my father's campaign, my upcoming postgrad year, and my new unwanted bodyguard. Everything that makes me feel out of control. But this—small rebellions like this night—is my taste of freedom.

Riley takes my hand, trying to pull me from the dancing, but I resist.

"One more song!" I whine loudly over the music.

"I have to pee!" she yells back, giggling into me.

"Go—I'll be right here." I spin away with my hands in the air, at which she laughs some more before maneuvering herself out of the small crowd.

This house is massive, yet so many have shown up for the mixer that I wonder how much of the university is here. After the next song finishes, Riley still isn't back, and dancing alone just isn't as fun. I'm about to make my way to the kitchen for another drink, or outside since some fresh air to cool the body heat sounds amazing, when a hand snakes around my waist.

I peer back, and the quick acknowledgment I'm *disappointed* to find a sandy-haired guy instead of a silvery blond shocks me. *No. No way am I allowing Rhett Kaiser to have this kind of influence already.* The guy pulls me tighter to press his mouth to my ear.

"You must know you are the most stunning thing in this place," he says with suggestion.

I shiver at it, debating if I want to indulge his flirtations.

"No, I don't. Please go on," I purr, turning in his hold.

Lust is painted in his eyes, nothing more.

"I could show you," he says, leaning in closer. His warm breath fans across my face, smelling of cheap beer. My flirty edge dissipates in the cloud of it. I push on his chest, but he takes it as teasing, gripping my hips tighter and grinding his hardening dick against my thigh in time with the music.

"I'm not interested," I say.

My sights won't fully focus from the alcohol, but I know he's pretty in the way he's used to getting what he wants. He eases a cocky side smile before leaning in, his mouth to mine again.

Panic surges in me. I plant both hands on his chest this time and push with all I have. All his gloating falls to a disgusted frown, but it's nothing compared to my repulsion at his lack of taking a hint.

"An average kiss from an average man won't improve my confidence."

"What a bitch," he scoffs.

Ah, bruised egos always shine true colors.

"That wasn't very nice," a low voice cuts in.

My stomach flips. I just can't be sure if it's excitement or the slam of shock.

Rhett's hand clamps around the guy's shoulder, and his anger fades when he looks up at Rhett, who is at least a head taller than him.

"Sorry, man," he mutters.

Rhett's eyebrows twitch together. "I'm not the one you offended."

The guy turns his head back to me with a muttered apology I barely hear. It doesn't seem good enough as he hisses at the pressure Rhett adds to his shoulder.

"Stop," I say, growing irritable over the scene he's making.

"She didn't hear you," Rhett says, ignoring me.

"I'm fucking sorry. I didn't know she was taken."

"I'm not," I say immediately.

Rhett lets him go, even giving him a pat as if they've turned into old friends. It's almost chilling the way he moves. Speaks. Looks. Everything about him screams danger, and it's utterly compelling.

No. It's sinful and infuriating.

Rhett Kaiser is here. Why the fuck is Rhett Kaiser here?

My mind buzzes with alcohol, but I need more to drown in the denial.

"I must have missed my invitation." Rhett's low, smooth voice creeps over my nape in the kitchen.

He's more than three paces away as he wanders around the island. He draws so much attention to himself—giddy eyes from the women and wariness from the guys—though he seems oblivious to it all when his focus is either subtly on his surroundings or on me. A blush threatens to warm my face, and I take another long drink of my vodka and lemonade.

"You weren't invited. How did you even find me?" I glare at him.

Rhett eyes my cup. "How much have you had to drink?"

My smile isn't friendly. "I'll tell you only if you plan to catch up. A hint though. You have a lot of catching up to do."

As I pick up the vodka bottle again, he swipes it from me.

I wait for him to take a drink straight, just like the challenge in my stare encourages. Instead he sets it aside and I frown deeply.

"Did you only follow me to kill the mood? You're not even supposed to be guarding me yet, so leave me the fuck alone." I reach for the bottle again but lose my balance as the last drink hits me all at once.

A warm, strong hand catches me by the waist, only long enough for me to straighten before Rhett rips his hand back as if I'm made of fire. I shouldn't be offended by how quickly he distances himself. He's my damn guard, and it's highly inappropriate to think of him like any other guy who would have slipped their hand to my ass if the opportunity were there.

A feminine groan on my other side draws my delayed attention. "The line was so long!" Riley complains.

My struggle to get her face to focus makes me relieved Rhett prevented me from getting another drink. I'm going to suffer tomorrow.

I blink a few times and find Riley combing her fingers through her hair. I forget all about my stupidly overprotective bodyguard and grab her with a gasp.

"Riley O'Neil, did you fuck someone in the bathroom!?" I accuse playfully in her ear.

"No!" She bursts into fits of giggles. "But almost. And it was outside the bathroom, actually. The line really was long."

"Who!"

She shrugs. "Some guy from last year's literary studies." Riley looks off to reconsider. "Or was it creative writing?"

"At least one of us saw something of action tonight," I complain. I don't really mind.

Riley's eyes widen when they look up behind me, then I remember who must have caught her attention.

Rhett leans with arms crossed against the island, looking so bored yet intimidating anyone would question why he's here at all.

"Who is that?" Riley gushes in my ear.

"He's, uh, my new guard," I say vaguely.

I shake my head when I understand her confused look. She was there when Victor was assigned.

"I'll explain later?" I plead. I don't want to talk about him. Actually, I hoped she'd help come up with a way to ditch him.

When I survey the party in the living area it seems Rhett isn't the only brooding face in the room with eyes pinned on us.

"Nolan Flynn is basically eye-fucking you," I say, dragging her back to dance.

Riley isn't impressed. "Nolan Flynn looks like he wants to end my existence."

"I bet he gets off on trying to best you."

She whacks my arm but steals a glance behind us to where Nolan stands. He has dark brown hair and wears round glasses that are highly attractive on him, complementing his brown eyes. He's tall with a slimmer build than Rhett.

Dammit, Ana, stop thinking of him.

My traitorous eyes don't listen as they try to find him, but all the bodies are becoming a blur, and the music blends to a consistent thump and nothing more.

"I think I've had a little too much to drink," I confess. It's never a good time of the night when my mind starts to scold itself for the overindulgence.

"Agreed. You didn't turn down a single shot tonight. I was starting to get concerned."

"It's been a long week," I drawl.

Some hot guy hovers behind Riley, placing his hands on her hips, and she's into it. I understand when I catch her mouthing the words "bathroom guy." Before I know it, I'm left awkwardly dancing as she turns to him and they kiss.

I find Rhett by the side of the room with eyes like a hawk on me. My alcohol-clouded mind finds his scowl to be a challenge as I twist through the bodies toward him.

"Dance with me," I say loudly over the music.

"Not going to happen."

I don't listen, grabbing his hand and pulling, but I underestimate how strong he is, because he doesn't budge an inch.

"You're not very fun, are you?" I pout.

He answers by regarding me with a stony expression. *Ugh, could I have been landed with a more uptight ass?* Rhett is twenty-something going on forty with the judgement in his eyes.

I'm starting to nurse a headache and my bed sounds like the best thing in the world right now, so I head back over to Riley, but she isn't where I left her. It takes a little wandering before I hear elevated voices down a hall and distinctly recognize one of them as my best friend.

Riley is adorable yet kind of frightening when she's angry. Right now she's pissed as hell, but so is Nolan Flynn in heated conversation with her.

"Everything okay?" I say tentatively, as if they're a grenade and my interruption will pull the pin.

"Fine," Riley snaps, not really at me, as she storms toward me and grabs my hand.

I cast Nolan a glare before I'm pulled away, though his gaze is fixed on Riley's back. I don't know what he's done, but if she's pissed, so am I.

"Want to tell me what that was about?" I ask when we're back in the main room of the house.

She rubs her temples. "He thinks he knows what I want when he's really just an arrogant dick out to ruin my life at every turn."

I hook a brow. Oh . . . *oh*.

"Sounds like jealousy to me."

I hold my hands up at the lethal look she cuts me with.

"Yeah, jealous I can have a sex life *and* best him at finals when the only time his dick is wet is in the shower."

We both burst into laughter. Childish, overactive laughter from our sorry, drunken states, and the last vodka I had really starts to weigh on me as I lean into the wall.

When we collect ourselves I sigh deeply. "I'm going to go out front and call an Uber. Want to ride with me?"

"Jacelyn is sober and she's driving my way. I can ask if she has a spare seat—"

I pull her arm before she can go looking. "No. I'm in the opposite direction from you anyway. There'll be an Uber soon, I'm sure."

"Okay, but if the wait is long, come back inside," she says, hugging me.

Nodding, I make my way out a little clumsily through the crowds.

When the night air hits me it's both bliss for my lungs and suddenly freezing. I didn't think to bring a jacket. I rub my arms, patting my pockets for my cell and blinking in panic when I don't feel it.

A hand enters my vision, holding exactly what I was looking for, and I reach for it in confusion. Tapping the screen, I confirm it's mine when the wallpaper displays a picture of me and Riley from last Christmas. I smile at the memory, even giggle at the antics we got up to that night. I look at this photo every day, yet right now the full reel of that night decides to take me away from gravity. My footing stumbles.

"Ana," Rhett says, slightly pained. I realize his arm is around me. He's so warm but stiff, as if he wants to let me go but doubts my stability. "Where are your car keys?"

For a second I'm once again irrationally insecure over why he can't stand to touch me, but his question steals my focus and I try to think. Patting the pockets at my hips again, I feel the small distortion.

"Aha!" I say as if it's a grand discovery. My hand struggles before retrieving the fob. "Are you suggesting I drive under the influence?" I accuse, pointing it at him.

His stern face doesn't flinch as he snatches the key and begins to lead me down the garden path. He finds the Porsche easily, and if I were in my sober mind I might be unnerved.

Rhett opens the passenger door, waiting. I fold my arms.

"How did you get here?" I ask.

"Uber."

He's so cold and grumpy that it's dampening my night.

"Sounds more appealing than a car ride with you." Unlocking my phone, I barely get to open the dial screen before it's plucked from my grip.

"Get in the car, Ana," he says in a rather hot command. Especially in the way he uses my name.

I do want to get home. Sleep sounds so good right now, but at the same time a headache is beginning to form, which turns my stomach, and I fear the motion of the car.

Why did I drink so much?

It's been so long since I've been this irresponsible.

"You have ten more seconds before the alternative is throwing you over my shoulder and walking."

My eyes narrow and my arms fold. "It's a forty-minute walk."

Those blue eyes swim with a dark challenge and his silence enforces it.

He wouldn't . . .

Rhett leans down a fraction and my adrenaline spikes.

"Okay!" I concede.

So he's a man of commitment, no matter how absurd.

Getting into the car, Rhett starts the engine while I tug at my seat belt. It keeps jamming.

Stupid. Damn. Belt.

With a long sigh, he reaches over before I can react, fastening me in. While I would protest to being taken care of like a child, his proximity and the sexy way he did it flushes my body.

Get a grip, Ana.

My feet slip out of my flats as I tuck my knees up, settling as comfortably as I can and leaning into the door.

"You're lucky I'm not concerned for you sitting against all car safety regulations," he grumbles.

"Because you're an excellent driver? Is there anything you're not good at?"

"You haven't discovered anything I am good at yet. Thanks

for ditching me earlier. You missed out on an incredible dinner, by the way."

I rub my stomach with the thought. *Shit, I haven't eaten.* I blame that for making my drunk situation worse.

"Do you always drink so much?" he asks. If I didn't know any better I'd think he was genuinely concerned.

"Not really," I say sleepily.

"What happened tonight?"

I shrug, slipping my eyes closed.

"There were a lot of people, music, I don't know. After the past week and meeting you, I just needed the thoughts to stop and my body to relax."

"Did meeting me upset you that much?"

"This whole situation is stupid. I don't need to be the talk of school with a bodyguard trailing after me like some precious princess."

"You're only worried what people will think?"

"I don't want the attention," I confess, not sure why it feels safe to open up to him.

"I'll try my best to not make it so apparent, I promise."

I don't expect the soft sincerity. My head tips back against the seat to look at him, focused on the road he's speeding through.

"You're the opposite of a person who can blend in," I observe. "Agent Ross was far more qualified for that—handsome, but very ordinary-looking."

Rhett's knuckles flex around the wheel and I wonder if I've offended him. I notice several pale scars across the tanned skin of his knuckles and think about asking what caused them, but I should start at the beginning if I'm going to figure him out.

"How did you get handed the shitty job of babysitting some

senator's daughter anyway?" I divert. Then I add, "How old are you?"

"Twenty-eight. And I requested the position."

"Fieldwork getting boring for you?"

"Something like that."

I hum, and when we pull up around the glowing fountain in my parents' front yard I don't want to get out. I've gotten warm and comfortable in the car.

Rhett doesn't linger for a second, cutting the ignition and getting out. I manage to unclip myself with a reluctant groan, and then, when my door swings open, I scowl at Rhett, hugging myself at the sudden wrap of cold.

He hesitates, jaw locking, but offers his hand to help me out. A crash of embarrassment at his clear discomfort makes me refuse. I get out, albeit a little wobbly, and push his chest to get around him. I'm about to march inside when my impulse to spin around wins.

"What is your problem?" I demand.

"I have a problem?"

"Clearly. You can barely stand to be around me, and god forbid someone tries to attack me and you have to touch me."

He seems taken aback that I even noticed his clear distaste. It makes me question why he would desire a position that requires being close to me.

Rhett takes a tentative step toward me and I blanch.

What is he doing?

Oh no, I've provoked something.

I don't know what, but when the distance closes more I'm too rooted in intrigue to move. When his hand meets my waist and slips around my back I think I stop breathing. Then he leans down to my ear and my heart races too fast.

"It's my job to protect your body. There is no obstacle to that. No one will get within ten feet of you before they hit the ground, and I will take pleasure in it for them ever even thinking of harming you. That's my promise, Miss Kinsley. I'm yours."

He lingers, not releasing me immediately, and my brazen, alcohol-infused mind wishes he would draw me even closer to bring our bodies flush.

A succession of snaps breaks my inappropriate thoughts, and Rhett backs away swiftly, but his hand switches to curve back around me as he scans the area with a lethal focus. His other hand lingers under his jacket.

Holy shit, was he armed with a gun the whole time?

I should have expected it, but somehow it slams the reality of who Rhett is, what he's trained and willing to do in the face of any live threat, into me at full force.

"Let's get inside," he says, keeping a laser focus on our surroundings while guiding me in.

He relaxes indoors. I do too. Neither of us speaks on the way up to our rooms through the huge mansion, but I can't stop thinking about his hand on the small of my back, likely just waiting for my balance to topple at any second.

"I think I'm going to be sick," I murmur. The walls are tilting.

"You're already in trouble with your parents. Best not give them more reason if you're sick all over the hallway," he says, pushing me along faster.

I get to my room and run to the bathroom, heaving the moment my knees meet the ground, and I brace myself on the toilet seat. I throw up alcohol and party snacks until it pains my chest.

I'm leaning my forehead on my arm to catch my breath when

I flush. I think I'm alone until I see Rhett's shoes and his knees, crouching by me.

I wanted to get my guard to quit, and I might have just succeeded with this epic first impression.

"Regretting your decision to take this job yet?" I mutter, unable to peel my head up.

"Not even slightly."

I huff, finding the will to straighten up. He's holding a glass of water and a hand towel.

"This isn't part of your job. Which, I repeat, hasn't even started yet."

"It started the moment I met you. And your body is in danger of alcohol poisoning—I'd consider that my concern."

"You're not getting paid yet," I point out.

He merely prompts me to take the glass and towel. I do, sitting back against the vanity unit and gulping the cool water greedily.

"I'll consider this an induction."

I give a breathy laugh. "You'll quit soon."

"If that's what you think. It's not me who needs to get more comfortable with this arrangement."

Whatever. He's bound to get bored, or I'll test his limits too far and he'll request a transfer.

"You can go. I'm safe now, Agent. Mission of retrieval successful." I loll my head against the cabinet to look at him again. "How did you find me?"

"You must have mentioned the party to your parents. They seemed to realize that was where you'd gone."

I rack my brain, almost certain I didn't tell them about it for the very reason I was sure they'd refuse to let me go with tensions about my *safety* running high.

He stands and I snuff out the inkling of disappointment that he's actually leaving. There's something relaxing about his company even though it's tense, often scarily so, and pretty cold.

"The number of accidents you could get into in your state from here to the bed requires me to stay," he says.

My skin flushes, and I give a sheepish smile. The buzz of excitement is wearing off, leaving me in a sorry, sad predicament.

"Day one and you're already taking this role far too seriously," I say, pushing myself up.

Looking in the mirror, the thought of removing makeup feels like too much of a burden. So I only brush my teeth before heading into my room and fishing out some short pajamas.

"If you don't want to be scandalized too, you'd better turn around."

He already has, occupying himself with various items and photos on my dresser.

For a moment I scan the beige walls of my room with more scrutiny than ever. My mom decorated it with some purple accents on the bedding and decor, and for the first time I realize there's very little in here to leave a true impression of who I am. I've never had the heart to tell her the color doesn't feel like . . . me.

I change quickly, my nerves building even being naked for a moment with him in the same room. My pajamas are only a thin-strap tank top and shorts, and right now that feels as good as underwear. Before he can turn around I fold myself under the duvet.

"Perfectly safe and cushioned against accident," I sing. My bed has never felt so comfortable.

"You play violin?" he asks, holding up a photo frame.

I can just about tell from the vague shape in my blurry vision that it's a photo of me at my parents' annual Christmas party seven years ago. The first and only time I performed to people, and right after I was sick from the nerves. But at the same time, it's something I yearn to do again. I've just never gathered the courage when in the moment it was magical.

"Kind of. I used to. Only to myself now." I grow nervous at the personal things he wants to know. "It's not in your job description to study the unimportant details about me."

"I want you to stop mentioning my job," he says. "You're a person above anything, and not what I expected."

That clenches my stomach with a want to ask what he means by that. What was he expecting? I must already be a disappointment, not the proper, easy person he wanted to be in charge of protecting.

"You're wasting your time," I sigh, cozying into my pillow. "You'll be gone soon. Even if you stick the full six months, it's not worth the extra homework when we'll never see each other again after that."

I listen to him approach the door, but just before he leaves I shiver at his parting promise.

"I'm not going anywhere."

CHAPTER 6

Anastasia

Whoever is pounding at my door is asking for my wrath. It only amplifies my splitting headache. I groan, calling out for them to enter, ready to unleash my irritation.

When Rhett appears, my composure dissolves.

Shit. Last night. I was embarrassingly drunk.

My sober self is mortified as I recall the patchy events of getting home with him. What did we talk about? What did I say to him? Oh fuck, I don't want to ask.

He's carrying a bottle of water and something else in his hand.

"Your father needs to see us," Rhett says tightly. Something is wrong. He's almost *angry*.

"What's wrong?" I ask, rubbing my eyes as I push myself up.

He comes over to my bed and I hug the covers to my chest, aware of how little I wore with a creeping heat over my body.

While my hair is a tangled mess from the ponytail I pulled out in my sleep and my makeup is smudged—I must look a hideous sight—he's nothing short of devastatingly put together. It's easy to admire him in a plain black T-shirt and black pants. No color.

Only now I discover Rhett has a tattoo. Something part of a bigger picture—a smoke-like texture and the body of a snake, perhaps—that begins at his elbow and coils around well-defined muscle before disappearing under his short sleeve. Though more casual than I saw him yesterday, he still radiates authority.

Setting down the water, aspirin, and a cereal bar, he barely looks at me before heading out.

Did I do something really wrong last night? What if I made a move on him?

"Thanks," I call as he meets the door.

He pauses only to force a smile.

I flop back down for a moment, becoming riddled with all kinds of anxious thoughts about what could have caused his tense mood around me.

Not wanting to piss him off even more, I drag myself out of bed and head for a quick shower. Today is certainly one for leggings and an oversize jumper. The freshen-up does wonders for me. I eat the cereal bar, take the meds, and swipe the water with me, leaving my hair in long, damp waves that reach my waist.

It's not often I head to my father's office with unsettled nerves. He can be strict and firm, and he has all the qualities to make a great leader, but with me he's always so soft, letting me get away with more than he probably should sometimes. Our relationship is solid.

I'm not uneasy about facing his wrath for sneaking out last night . . . but have I succeeded in forcing Rhett to transfer already?

I shouldn't care. Once he leaves I'll forget him quickly, but I realize if I have to have a personal guard, maybe I don't mind it being him over someone else who might give me the creeps like Victor.

Rhett is already in the office, looking concerned and not at all pleased to see me.

"Have fun last night, my dear?" Dad asks. It's delivered with sarcasm and disappointment.

I wouldn't usually regret being rebellious, but something causes the air to hang thick with tension. Mom stands by my father too, her delicate brow pinched at what he's holding.

This can't be good.

"I'm sorry. It's my last year at the university and I didn't want to miss anything," I try pathetically.

"I hope it was worth it," Dad sighs. He lays the tabloid down.

I approach, making out two vague figures in a dark photograph. My heart speeds up when the recognition comes to me along with a fuzzy memory. I pick it up, trying to see something other than what is blatantly obvious. Me and Rhett, intimately close, his arm around me. I shiver remembering the warmth of his breath across my ear after I got out of the car.

The heading slackens my jaw.

AMERICA'S SWEETHEART: PARTY FLING OR SWOON-WORTHY NEW BEAU?

SPOTTED: HEIRESS ANASTASIA KINSLEY WITH HOT NEW DATE.

The daughter of presidential candidate, Archibald Kinsley, was last rumored to be dating the son of her father's competitor for running. So who is this new hottie seen outside the Kinsley estate with...

It goes on to speculate who Rhett is. Why they haven't seen him before. How good we look together. When to expect to see us again next.

I'm going to be sick.

"One photo and they come up with *this*?" I cry, outraged.

Shit. This is bad. Really bad.

"I warned you, we're under a microscope right now. They're looking for anything to fill the papers with regarding our family and my running." My father sighs.

"This is my life!" I throw my hands out, pacing as I pick at the skin becoming raw around my thumb. "And that is not true. He was merely helping me out the damned car."

I scowl at the paper. Though it's a small white lie about why he got so close, these vultures have twisted an innocent interaction into something wildly outlandish.

"I know. Agent Kaiser explained. But you have to understand it's out of my control how they've made this look," my father says, pained.

"It doesn't matter. They'll see he's just my bodyguard soon enough, and that their speculations were grossly off the mark."

It will all be fine. I try to breathe and tame my heart, barely able to look at Rhett, for now his distance this morning makes sense. He's angry with me for risking his job.

"I'm afraid it's not that simple," my father says, apology written in his voice.

My mom comforts him with a hand on his shoulder, giving me a wince of a smile.

"What do you mean?" I dread to ask.

"We had a meeting with our press team on how best to approach this rumor the moment they flagged the tabloid. I'm afraid if Agent Kaiser continues as your personal guard as planned, it will only make this situation a scandal rather than an innocent new relationship."

I catch on to his meaning. "That I'm sleeping with my guard?"

The room is suddenly too small. I hate the speculation, that my name is no longer my own, but rather it belongs to tabloids who will do with it what they want.

"So my only solution is to let him go. A shame considering he's the best in line for the role and the closest in age to fit in with you and your peers. Or . . ." My father trails off, hesitating. I've never seen him almost afraid of giving me the alternative.

"What?" I all but snap, not meaning to, but I'm trembling with anxiety.

My gaze slips to Rhett, who doesn't look so angry and firm anymore. He's looking at me with something else—a softer care. He keeps scanning me from my hands to my face, and it's he who delivers the alternative with a straight face.

"I pose as your boyfriend while being undercover as your guard."

"It was Agent Kaiser's idea," my father adds. "And, I must say, the more favorable option. Not only does it mean we can keep the most competent man for the job, but this way your classmates don't have to know of your guard. That's what you wanted."

They can't be serious.

I look at Rhett, but he gives nothing away. His face is tight like he doesn't enjoy the idea any more than I do, but there isn't another option. I wanted him gone, but this facade is his idea, and now I'm twisted with guilt that maybe he needs this job. The pay or whatever. If I choose to let him go I'll only be assigned someone else. There's no telling how much *less* I'll want their company.

"It's only for six months," my father goes on, coaxing me. "But it is your choice."

He'll take whatever decision I make, but the opinion of the room leans heavily toward the boyfriend ruse.

"Whatever," I say, shaking my head. "It's not like I have a third choice to abandon the need for a guard altogether."

This has gone from bad to so much fucking worse. I don't need protecting. I can damn well do that myself. Leaving without another word, I head to change into my sportswear of a crop top and high-waisted leggings. In the gym I start on the treadmill to warm up, putting in my AirPods and blasting music until the world fades away. I run faster, past the burn screaming at me to stop. After fifteen minutes I slip into boxing gloves and take out my frustration on the punching bag.

I'm not naïve or weak or incapable of looking out for myself. I don't need some tall, muscular, stupidly attractive guy posing as my *boyfriend* to protect me from invisible threats.

I don't know how much time has passed when I gasp with fright before I land my next punch. Rhett has managed to sneak around me, holding the punching bag as if he's waiting for me to continue so I can pretend it's him I'm taking my anger out on.

Removing the gloves, I pluck my AirPods out and scowl.

"We're about to be forced together for four to six hours of the day—the least we can do is enjoy our own space and time while we can," I say bitterly.

Rhett has changed his attire too, and I don't dare rake my gaze over him in black sweatpants.

"Or . . . we can put a little effort into how we're going to make this thing believable," he says.

"If you're suggesting I sleep with you—"

"That's not going to happen," he says sharply.

I pressed an unexpected nerve. Most guys would jump at the chance. What would a harmless fling do? I'm back to swimming through pitiful, insecure thoughts in my mind. Perhaps I'm not his type at all.

"Good," I say coldly.

I wander over to the mats, beginning to stretch my aching muscles.

"It's just a performance, that's all," he says, watching me attentively.

"Are you sure you can handle that? You barely want to touch me as it is. What a jackass boyfriend you'll seem. Should make our 'breakup' in six months very believable, I guess."

He comes around the mat after removing his shoes. My stomach tightens in anticipation.

"Lie down," he instructs.

I want to tell him to leave me alone, but it seems he's trying painstakingly to be nice to me. So I do as he asks.

"Not going back on your word already, are you?"

This earns the largest part of a smile I've seen from him so far.

"Lift your leg as high as it can go."

With growing concern about where this is going, I do so hesitantly.

"Do you trust me?" he asks before inching forward on his knees.

"I think I should ask you the same thing," I say, observing how tense he looks at being so close.

He sighs, attempting to relax, before his hands wrap around my calf and he leans into me gently. I'm pretty flexible, and if I'd known what he was going to do I might have protested, but he keeps testing me, and my knee comes close to my chest, which brings *him* close to my chest.

"Like I said, unexpected," he says. The gravel of his quiet voice pools warmth in my lower belly.

He isn't even *trying* to be seductive. He's so close I think he might feel the hard thump against my ribs soon. The curls of his silvery hair tip over his eyes with the lean, and I want to reach up and trace the scar that strokes like lightning down the right side of his face.

"How did you get that?" I ask quietly.

Rhett releases the tension on my leg, sitting back on his knees. I think he's going to retreat from me entirely—it's like he's always holding a shield ready to use against anything that might make him vulnerable. Instead his hand curls around my other leg, guiding me to stretch in the same manner.

"It's a reminder I was helpless once, and that I'll never be again," he admits.

Our faces come intimately close again, and I'm greedy to take in the details at the opportunity. How striking his blue irises are, the darkness of his brows in beautiful contrast to the silver-blond tone of his hair. His cheekbones, which are high and sharp. Another scar, far more faint, which runs across the corner of his mouth, and I wonder if they would feel as soft as they look.

Rhett lets me go again, and I shoot up with the inappropriate thoughts that flush my body.

"I'm done here," I say, swiping up my water bottle.

"Ana," he calls as I make to leave. "We should get to know each other—just enough to have a story and make this believable. It's not ideal, and I shouldn't have gotten close to you like that for them to have had the opportunity to take the photo."

He's taking the blame? Now I'm battling guilt. *I* was the poor drunk who could hardly walk straight. *I* was the one who pushed him about his job.

"That's a good idea," I agree.

"Join me for dinner this time?"

"Here?"

He debates for a short pause.

"Let's go somewhere else."

"Not a date though," I tease.

It seems to lighten the mood. "Of course not."

Maybe this can work. If we can find a friendship after the rocky start to our meeting, perhaps the time will fly by for both of us, and this way my father is right: there'll be no gossip around the university about the precious senator's daughter needing a full-time bodyguard. My mood brightens as I head out to change, growing giddy at the idea of dinner with Rhett.

CHAPTER 7
Rhett

Why did I suggest going out for dinner? I wasn't thinking right. Staying in this impressively huge manor to eat instead would be less . . . *intimate*.

It is not a date.

Yet when Ana meets me in the foyer looking like a fucking goddess, I turn irrationally sour at the thought of her leaving this house looking like that with anyone else. I wasn't thinking when I blurted the suggestion of the boyfriend facade after her father presented the damn tabloid to me. I severely underestimated how eager the press were already with their campaign starting to get serious. I need this placement, and I haven't even begun trying to get intel on the whole reason I'm risking life and limb to be here, yet it's already being sabotaged by the savage media.

At first I hated the thought of having to pose as some rich woman's guard for this. I expected someone pretentious and insufferable, but I'd tolerate it if it would lead me closer to Alister fucking Lanshall.

Anastasia Kinsley is . . . very unexpected. A fiery spirit for sure, and someone who is not going to make this side of my mission easy by any means. But I'm addicted. In a way that terrifies the damn life out of me. There was a moment I thought for the first time I might quit, find another way to get what I need. But this woman has already become my problem, because I can feel an obsession growing from the roots of intrigue with every new thing I learn. She plays violin. I want to know for how long. Who for. Where? Why? I want to know what she fucking felt while doing so, and that is a dangerous line I will not cross.

"I hope you picked somewhere nice," she says. I don't think she even realizes how effortlessly she could seduce a man with that tone and those stunning hazel eyes.

She's wearing red, a color that is my fast favorite on her. A dress that drapes like a crimson waterfall to mid-thigh and scoops low on her chest. I've held diamonds worth millions, but it's nothing compared to the thrill of wanting to stake my claim on something far more precious, like her.

I won't. Ana is not a pursuit. But she will make some guy rich beyond his means someday.

"Did you not learn from the party that the nights are growing cold with the fall?" I say.

She clicks her tongue. "Right, let me grab a jacket."

Her heels clack across the marble and I have to force my eyes off her as she walks.

When she returns her smile disrupts something in me. It's distant, still mostly dormant, and I won't allow it to awaken me no matter how much some quirks of hers try.

The night is still and peaceful as we cross the front of the house. This estate is almost the biggest home I've been in. The only one to top it was the house of one of my uncle's most elite drug cartel bosses. I gained a nasty scar across my side and lost two great men that night we raided it. But we stopped a whole load of dangerous shit from hitting the streets that had already taken the lives of many kids.

"Do you have a preference of car?" I ask as we step into the garage, glancing over the impressive range of sports cars and jeeps.

"You did look particularly good in the Porsche," she says.

I slip my gaze to her in amusement, but she avoids my eye as if she didn't mean to say it.

She suggests, "Or we can take an Uber so we can both enjoy a drink to take the edge off."

"What edge might that be?" I ask, genuinely curious.

I notice how often she fidgets, as if nerves are eating her apart inside. She'll pace or damage the skin around her thumbs or her eyes will tunnel a million miles away. I just can't figure out what causes it. How to help it.

Touching Ana is something I try to avoid doing. Though it should be innocent, like helping her balance at the party, I retreat to the fact I *enjoy* my hands on her. There are seconds when I want to linger or feel more of her, and the guilt tearing me apart inside feels like a betrayal to the fiancée I lost because of who I am.

I won't allow myself to enjoy this.

"I don't drink," I say.

She looks adorable, pinning me with accusation. "I don't mean get wasted. Just a glass of wine or two."

I pluck the familiar key from yesterday. "Porsche it is."

"Killjoy," she mutters.

I open her door, attempting but failing to keep from trailing my gaze over her legs, which are unfairly attractive as she folds herself inside the car.

In another life . . . *Shit*, the things I want to do to this woman. I internally groan as I head to the driver's side.

I've already seen her beyond her drinking limits, and nothing about that display was off-putting. She gave me only a taste of her fire and I crave to see the blaze she can become; would gladly go down in the flames. Ana's attempts to push me away may very well be the thing that pulls me so much dangerously closer.

"Did you always want to study English literature?" I ask. The silence with her is peaceful, but I have a hundred questions that thwart my attempts to believe I don't care.

"No. It was either that or medicine. I was terrible at science in high school."

My chest squeezes. Sarah was so close to reaching her full qualification to become a doctor. She loved helping people, with such a kind and gentle nature that wouldn't harm a thing in the world. And how despicable it was that this brutal world harmed her. No—*I* harmed her. I fucking killed her.

"Are you okay?"

Ana's careful voice makes me relax my tightening grip on the wheel. Part of me wants to call this night off. How can I be taking another woman out for dinner? Even if it's just friendly. I can't get rid of my guilt that this is wrong. Not the company —*me*. I shouldn't be cheating on Sarah.

"Why only those two choices?" I ask tightly, needing the distraction.

"My parents. In fact, my father was very in favor of a political major, but that was never a consideration of mine. So English lit it is."

"What do you want to do after?"

"Teach, perhaps. I don't know really."

Ana would make a wonderful teacher. She would be stern yet playful. Patient yet firm.

"What about you?" she asks. "Did you always want to join the police and end up in the secret service babysitting a senator's daughter?"

"Right down to the very specifics," I muse.

She chuckles quietly, and I capture that sound like treasure.

"I wanted to join the FBI, actually," I admit. A few truths feel right to share. How much of a lie I am to her is starting to weigh on me.

Her father has unknowingly placed his daughter in the hands of the leader of a notorious dark network attacking crime the very *illegal* way. It doesn't matter if the guys who die from our work are corrupt; we're all criminals to the US justice system.

"How come you didn't progress there instead?"

It's been a long time since I've met anyone who's asked about my past. I'm not prepared to be slammed so hard with my failure. The memory of the night that changed the course of my life surfaces so raw I almost stop the damned car.

"You don't have to tell me," she says softly. "But I'm quite a good listener if you ever want to."

I ease at that. She doesn't need to care, nor be patient, but here she is, and it's so damn nice that my instinct is to push her away before she can offer me more.

"We're here," I say, hating how dry I sound, but I can't help it.

Ana looks out at the small restaurant wedged in the middle of fancy high-rise apartments. Tucked away and hidden, most would overlook it since you have to go downstairs to get inside.

She says nothing as she unclips her belt, still staring at it, and I wonder if I've ruined the mood of the night already. Before she can open her door I've slipped out and come around to her side.

I grit my teeth, despising myself as I hold out my hand to her.

Once again she seems to notice.

"You don't have to make yourself suffer my touch," she says, more lighthearted than the last time, as if she's accepted my distance.

She doesn't know it's because I *want* to touch her. So fucking badly that I hate myself for it. But if this ruse is going to work, I have to get the hell over it. I need to touch her and not feed the craving inside of me. Touch her and keep cold to it.

When Ana refuses my hand and gets out, the impulse overcomes me to slam the door shut and step into her. She gasps, parting full red lips that are so sinful she doesn't even know what she's doing to me with no effort at all. Her scent is becoming a natural attraction. She wears something floral with notes of spice that reflects her perfectly. A delicate rose on fire.

"No man who wouldn't beg on his knees for your touch deserves you. Don't forget that."

"What are you doing?" she breathes, pressing a hand to my chest as mine slips around her waist.

"Practicing," I say. "We should set some basic expectations about how we should be seen in public, wouldn't you agree?"

I can handle this. No feelings. No attachment.

"Yes," she says.

"Good. Now come, or we'll lose our reservation."

I slide my hand down to hers, interlocking our fingers so effortlessly.

"May I ask why here?"

"I looked up the best Italian restaurants in the city."

"Have you been stalking me to know Italian food is my favorite?"

Her excitement makes *me* giddy like a damn girl. She isn't far from the truth. I don't think she'd appreciate knowing that when I took her phone to insert my number I hacked into it. I need her location at all times in case she tries to ditch me like her father warned.

"I asked around. The answer was unanimous." This isn't a lie. It's how I knew what she'd like to eat.

"I've never heard of this place."

It's small, intimate, an authentic Italian, and I didn't stop beforehand to consider it would be low-lit with soft-playing music. I try not to let my regret for this location arise.

"It was hard to find, but their reviews knocked everything else out the park."

Ana leans into me, a soft push. "Who would have guessed you'd be a hopeless romantic?" she teases.

I tense. This isn't a date. I'm not trying to be romantic.

"Relax, Romeo. We're just two friends having delicious food."

I want to tell her how much that means to me. I want to tell her why I can't touch her the way she deserves to be worshipped. I can't without exposing every sin that I am.

We're seated at a table in the corner. The place is fully booked but not overly loud. We eat and talk and laugh. I can't remember the last time a night felt so . . . *good*. The kind that passes time like it's too precious. I found out she has a fear of public speaking and performing, but at the same time she longs to overcome that because she enjoys it. Her life's a paradox to conquer. She's so fascinating. Ana is modest about her violin playing, but I don't believe her. I can picture her, how exquisite she would look standing by a grand piano as her accompaniment. Fuck, my mind even wanders deplorably to that image and how I don't think I'd survive the sight of her splayed *across* the glossy black top. She loves animals and begged her parents for years to get a dog, but they never caved.

"I wanted to move out for my last year of university, but with the campaign, my father insists I stay home until it's over. If he takes office I don't plan to go to the White House with them," she says, taking a sip of her red wine.

I could listen to her talk about herself for hours. Weeks. This night isn't enough when, with everything I've learned, I've become greedy for more.

"Would you stay in D.C.?" I ask, so relaxed in my seat as I watch her finish off her tiramisu. The soft sighs she gives at each bite drive me wild.

"I'd like to go to Colorado, actually. I've heard the scenery there is beautiful."

"Not a city woman then?"

"It has its perks," she says. Then her eyes drift sideways as she envisions her dream home. "I'd like a house with a wrap-around porch overlooking mountains and forests."

"With a swing." I paint it in her fantasy.

She grins, and it's the most breathtaking sight.

"Yes. And a big garden for the dog."

"Labrador?"

"Or a poodle."

"A Labradoodle then. You don't seem the type to choose."

Ana tilts her head with amusement. "Two days and you think you have me all figured out."

I smirk. "Not even close, little bird. But I have six months—there's no need to rush."

"You are absolutely a hopeless romantic, Rhett," she teases. "In a completely platonic way, of course."

I huff a small laugh. She doesn't even know why I'm guarded against the idea of romance and physical touch, but she's so damn considerate. She doesn't deserve to be a means to me getting what I want. Maybe she'll never have to know. After the six months I can merely disappear and she'll live her life to the fullest.

"I lost my fiancée three years ago," I say. I never intended to expose the deepest wound in me, but I feel like I owe her something for just being . . . *her*.

Ana straightens in shock, but I smile, and it's genuine, just like the sadness that clouds her face.

"She was killed, and I haven't found the man yet. I just wanted you to know . . . if I ever seem distant to your touch during the displays we have to put on from next week, or if I get sharp about your safety, you deserve to know there's a personal reason."

"Rhett, I . . . I'm so sorry," she says with such sincerity it's the first time I've ever appreciated the condolence.

Her hand reaches for mine placed on the table and I don't flinch away. I have to become comfortable with it if this is to be believable, but what's slowly killing me inside is how easy it is. How much I want this, the first touch of warmth strong enough to be felt through the ice.

"I guess I can *try* not run you out of your job and make this work," she says.

She's incredible. How easily she can disperse a cloud of sorrow so delicately.

I squeeze her hand. "Nah, don't change for me. I'm looking forward to you giving me hell. It keeps things interesting."

Her smile is one of wicked beauty. "Very well. You have yourself a deal, Agent Kaiser."

The way she addresses me like that is sexy as hell. A title that might have been mine in an alternate fate.

I pay our bill after much protest from Ana and link hands with her on the way out until I've closed her car door. When I take off I throw away all caution—*I have to get used to this*—and take her hand again while I drive.

"Thank you." She breaks the silence. "This was really nice."

"No need to thank me. It's just my job."

She gives a soft chuckle, which I smile at.

The phone in my pocket vibrates in a specific three-interval buzz, so I know who it is. It brings back the reality of why I'm here, holding this stunning woman's hand and pretending I'm the best man her father could choose to protect her.

I may have fraudulent credentials and a black soul thanks to how I ended up in this position, but one thing will stay the fucking truth. Anastasia Kinsley is mine. Her safety, her well-being, her damned happiness. No matter what else I have to do, perhaps even use her for, she is under my full protection now, whether she likes it or not.

CHAPTER 8
Anastasia

The first day of classes always wracks my nerves. I opt for a black fitted skirt, over-the-knee boots, and a tucked-in white blouse. I leave my wavy brown hair loose, but I debate pinning it back until I have no time left to scrutinize myself.

It feels like this year everything will be different. Having already been plastered in a tabloid against my will, I can't help the surge of anxiety when I'm out in society that makes me feel like there's always a camera watching, waiting for the next snap so the tabloids can spin their own narrative about my life.

I hiss when my thumb stings, and I realize I've broken skin with my fidgeting. Cursing, I suck on my thumb before I can get blood on my top. What will the tabloids decide that was from? *America's hopeful sweetheart wrestles grizzly bear.* Okay, that's a stretch, but so is assuming one close hold, *albeit kind of intimate-looking*, merits a full-blown relationship with my guard.

I sigh. This is going to be a long semester.

Rhett is waiting for me in the foyer, looking too good to be a postgrad student at their wit's end wondering why he didn't just take his graduate diploma and run. His black T-shirt hugs his toned torso, and it should be criminal how, paired with a leather jacket and black jeans, he's the lovechild of Damon Salvatore and Geralt of Rivia. He's immune to any color. Rhett finishes talking on his phone, hanging up the moment he sees me, and slides it into his back pocket without taking his eyes off me for even a flicker. I shouldn't get giddy over that small, insignificant detail.

Over the past week we've met every day. Just for a few gym sessions, and for the more thorough tour I denied him on his first day. We've agreed on what's appropriate and what he's comfortable with for our ruse. I've learned a few more things about him, such as how he has a best friend called Xavier that he hasn't seen in a while but plans to soon now he's in Washington, D.C. He wants to become FBI, but working through the secret service is an easier path after losing his fiancée.

My heart hurts for him so badly I don't know how to express it, other than to show him I don't expect anything from him, and that he can push me away anytime he needs to, so long as he doesn't lock me out for good.

"You ready?" he asks, taking my hand to try to make it as natural of a reaction as possible. It's too easy, and even still, my stomach flutters each time.

"As I'll ever be," I sing.

The morning is bright, but the sunshine is a mockery with fall coming in. It shivers a chill over me as we cross the front lawn to the garage.

We choose the jeep for school. Or, rather, I don't have a say in the matter when Rhett comes to the conclusion it's the *safest* of my father's collection.

"You look beautiful." He leans in to say this as he opens the car door for me.

He's too damned good at his role. I wish he wasn't. Wish chivalry were dead to him, as this kind of attention doesn't exist in the men I've dated. It would make it easier to remember he's just. My. Guard. Or perhaps I could cling to his fairy-tale ways as a separation from reality. He wants to impress my father—nothing more. Wants a good report card. If he were a real boyfriend I'd get my own door, he'd call me pretty maybe once a month, he'd never notice a haircut, he'd buy me flowers on the anniversary I'd have to wait to see if he remembered—he wouldn't, of course—and we'd live a very mundane vanilla life.

I know that's a grasp of desperation. Somehow I don't think there's anything *vanilla* about Rhett Kaiser.

The peaceful car ride is over too soon, and then I'm staring up at the giant university building for the first time in my final year. *You chose to do this, Ana.* Clearly, I'm a sadist for academic torture. It's both exhilarating to be coming to the end of my studies and daunting I'll have to face the world without the yearly routine to keep me on *some* kind of path. I often find it hard to see what lies beyond all this. So, naturally, I've avoided paving the steps beyond my institutional bubble.

Like clockwork Rhett is out of the car and helping me out, the gentleman act not failing to stop my heart for a moment.

People don't just glance as we pass; they stalk Rhett as if he's a shiny new toy or the menu for lunch, and I really can't blame them. He has a unique look about him, with the silvery hair and clear blue eyes, and he's so tall and built like stone that it's impossible for him to blend in. But as his hand is laced in mine their judgment trails over me too, evaluating our match, trying to figure out if he's too good for me. The stares are loud, and I don't realize I've been fidgeting until he brings our hands to his lips and kisses my knuckles.

"What's wrong?" he asks over my skin.

"Nothing."

Truly, there isn't. It's just my simple, overactive, irrational nerves acting up.

He pulls me to the side, up against a wall, and plants his other hand by my head, creating a cage of safety. Rhett's thumb brushes over the raw, torn skin of mine.

"How can I help this?" he asks.

I'm a little stunned. Nervous habits aren't a risk to my life—not really. He can't sense the dangerous speed of my heart too, can he?

"It's nothing," I insist, growing irritable as a natural defense mechanism.

Rhett searches my eyes, seeming to read that I don't want to talk about it, so he nods and continues to lead us.

"How do you know your way around?" I ask.

"I memorized your schedule, then the layout of the campus."

"That was unnecessary. I could have guided us."

"I have a job, remember," he says teasingly. "I need to know every possible exit and route to your classes."

"That's a bit extreme. No one is going to assassinate me."

"You underestimate the cruelty of the world, little bird."

I swallow any argument at that. He's been dealt the worst of life's cruel hand, and I promised not to protest any of his safety measures.

"Ana!"

I jump at the excitable squeal of my best friend. Spinning, my hand leaves Rhett's to embrace Riley, who bounds over. She casts one knowing look over my shoulder and I loop her arm to walk slightly ahead of Rhett before he can see her suggestive smile.

I told Riley over the phone all about our forced *arrangement* after the student mixer party. She found it hilarious and claimed she'd gladly switch places—which, if we didn't look the complete opposite, would have been a ruse to my ruse I might have explored. It reminded us of an old friend, actually. Her name was Nina Temsworth and she looked so much like me that people would mistake us for sisters often. She skipped town five years ago, before we were all to start this very course. It wasn't out of character for her to disappear since her father was a deadbeat drunk her mother left her when she was only five. We always thought she'd come back, and to this day I miss her and still hope she does.

Riley and I chat about the party and the week that dragged after it. I can't talk so openly with her when most of my week consisted of Rhett being too nearby. At the lecture hall his phone vibrates in a familiar pattern.

"I have to take this. Save me a seat," he says, leaning in to press a kiss to my temple, all for show, while surveying the room filling up with students.

First-day enthusiasm buzzes through the room, but it will slowly die out throughout the semester. Students are like any new bloom, so flourishing and promising at first sight, but inevitably they wither under the changing pressure of coursework, like the seasons.

I nod to Rhett and watch him leave before Riley pulls me up the steps to find our seats. This class is on poetry, and I wonder how Rhett is going to pass the time in his boredom.

"Hey, Ana," a smooth voice says to my other side, breaking my conversation with Riley.

His name is Adam, and last year we had something of a fling before I found out he was seeing some other woman at the same time. I wasn't his girlfriend, but it still hurt.

"What do you want?" I ask sourly.

The theatre is hardly packed full, and he has no shortage of friends to bother with his company. His arrival at the same time as me is damn convenient.

He holds up his hands. "I know we had a rough time last year, but I was thinking of you over the summer."

I raise a hand to my chest, faking endearment. "Out of the two fuck-toys you had, I was the one who lingered on your mind? I'm flattered."

"You were more than that. You know that, don't you?"

"If I was, you wouldn't have needed to place your dick elsewhere."

He tips my hair over my shoulder, admiring my neck, and though I stiffen I don't give him the satisfaction of a reaction.

"The seat you're in is taken," I say. "You'll want to move before he gets back."

Adam's brow hooks. "Didn't realize you'd moved on so fast."

"You know, I thought the same damn thing six months ago. Leave me alone, Adam. I'm not interested."

"Arrogant of you to think that's what I came over for."

My anger turns hot with the embarrassment he succeeds at surfacing. Did I mention Adam Sullevan happens to be the son of my father's main competitor in the running for president? You may think rivalry for each other runs in our blood, but in truth our fathers have a great respect for each other. Too bad Rolf Sullevan's son didn't grasp that concept.

Riley leans over me. "Adam, everything she's said can be condensed to two words: Fuck. Off."

I love my best friend. She's so quiet and ridiculously intelligent, but her pissed-off side is my favorite when it often comes so comically sudden. I, on the other hand, am usually the one who gets into more trouble than it's worth.

"Everyone is saying you're the first daughter. I have to say I'm surprised. For a long while it was my father who was favored to win this election."

"Tides can change." I brush him off. Is he only here to rattle my nerves?

I screwed Adam Sullevan one too many times before I realized how much of a pretentious, arrogant asshole he is.

"Hmm," is all he says, looking me over as if I'm hiding a whole conspiracy in my ponytail.

"Everything okay, baby?"

Rhett's voice is music to my ears in this moment. I look up to find him towering over Riley, who stands to let him into the row. He doesn't even need to speak to Adam; Rhett's stare alone causes him to rise from his seat, and he backs out without a word after lingering a look on me.

When Rhett sits, he makes the theater seat look far too small for a person. Luckily, no one sits behind him, and I doubt they will now.

He brings his mouth to my ear. "Is he a problem?"

"No," I say quickly. I don't need Rhett to place a target on Adam. He's harmless, really.

"An ex?" he presses.

"Sort of," I confess.

To my surprise, as the lecturer enters and dims the lights for us to watch their introduction presentation, Rhett's large hand slides over my thigh. It's possessive, meant for the eyes of Adam and the others who keep glancing this way. And it's so damn attractive that I can't take in a word while his thumb brushes over the bare skin between my skirt and boot.

In Rhett's other ear he wears an AirPod. I figure he's listening to music, but from the glances I steal, sometimes his distant expression flexes around his eyes and I think he's concentrating on a podcast or an audiobook. He props one elbow on the arm of his chair and holds his chin, and occasionally his fingers flex faintly on my thigh and his thumb stalls his relaxing strokes.

I have another class right after this one, which passes by just as quickly before we break for lunch. In the line for food I stare between a caesar salad and a chicken sandwich for far too long.

"Like I said, not one to choose," Rhett says.

I shoot him a look. He's right, but I won't let him gloat about it. Why is decision-making over the smallest things often so damn difficult? The main component in these dishes is the same, so it's mostly of case of do I want bread or leaves? Put that way . . .

Rhett reaches over me and picks up both before guiding me without any chance to protest over to the next options, a firm hand on my waist.

"I won't eat both—that'll be a waste," I say.

"We'll share. Half and half or whatever other ratio you choose. But please do so before lunch ends."

I whack a playful hand to his chest and he vibrates with a low chuckle.

Now, do I want Gatorade or water . . . ?

Rhett picks them both within a few seconds.

"That's just creepy. I didn't even debate that one out loud."

"You think I haven't noticed that all you've drunk this week is blue Gatorade and water?"

I blink at him. I wouldn't have thought he'd notice at all, and the fact he did warms my chest. "Fine. But you can't possibly know what sweet I want," I say, eyeing the assortment of cakes, candy, and chocolate bars. I want far more than just two. I've always had a sweet tooth.

"Hmm, you got me there. I'm going to take a wild guess you'll choose the peanut butter cups, Twizzlers, or chocolate chip cookies."

"Very good guesses." I approve. I reach for the Sour Patch Kids, hesitate, and pluck the cookies instead.

I slip a sheepish look to Rhett, who can hardly suppress his grin—the kind that feels rare on him and stops my thoughts for a moment. He grabs my abandoned Sour Patch Kids before nudging me again and paying.

"If you're adamant on spending your salary on feeding me, maybe I should pick more things."

"I might have to ask for a pay raise," he says as we get to the table where Riley sits with two other girls and one guy from our major.

"Ana, I've been dying to catch up on your summer!" Kayley says. Her attention drifts to my side, as do all the eyes at the table.

"Oh, this is Rhett. He's a new transfer, and I guess the answer to what I got up to this summer," I lie easily, chuckling awkwardly.

They can hardly suppress their admiration of the tall, stunning man next to me. Even Jack ogles him, and he has a boyfriend at another school two hours away.

"Can confirm," Riley says, helping to ease the anxiety my lie is obvious. "I've been fighting for her attention all break."

Rhett's hand takes mine on my lap, stopping me from fidgeting as his fingers lace through mine and he squeezes. He's talking to Jack now and absentmindedly slips the open sandwich pack to me.

We end up splitting *almost* half of our food. Except for the sweets—I eat most of both.

To my surprise, Rhett manages to pleasantly ease in with everyone. Either he's a spectacular actor, considering the grumpy guy of few words I first met, or he's a natural in college social settings.

When everyone else is chatting to each other, I lean in to him to talk between us.

"You never went to college, did you?" I ask. His age and where he's at in his job suggests he missed out on this experience.

"This is my first time," he says.

"Glad I could break your college virginity."

"I can't say I'm envious though."

"Two hours of deep-diving into classic poetry isn't your thing? Never would have guessed."

His hand on my thigh gives a light squeeze, shooting tingles through me. I have to refrain from wiggling in my seat at the reaction my body gives to that small movement, like some touch-starved creature.

Rhett's blue eyes flick up subtly before dropping to his classic all-black wristwatch. I don't mean to speculate, but I realize I'm greedy for details of his personal life when I notice it's a *very* expensive brand that would easily cost him a year's salary. I follow what drew his attention and find one of the campus security cameras in the corner.

"You finished?" he asks.

I nod and he gathers our trash before taking my hand to guide me up.

"We still have ten minutes," I protest.

"And I haven't had you to myself all day," he says charmingly. My heart speeds up at that even though I know it's only an excuse for those at the table.

It works. Though Riley is in on our ruse, even she doesn't hide her adoring puppy eyes at his comment.

His arm curves around my waist, and I wonder why the sudden closeness until I look up and see who's heading our way.

Adam Sullevan.

It seems convenient timing that Rhett would choose now to leave.

"Hey, little A," Adam coos. I hate when he calls me that. Even when he thought it was sweet during our fling.

Rhett says with a bored drawl, "Of all the things I had to learn today, what you name your dick I would pay to erase."

I bite my lip, shocked and suppressing my sudden amusement that Adam's two friends fail to hide.

"We didn't get a chance to meet," Adam says to him tightly. His smile reminds me of someone eyeing a target and wondering how much of Daddy's money it will cost to get rid of it.

"Rhett Kaiser, Ana's boyfriend, and about to be your problem if you don't move out the way."

Adam huffs a bitter laugh. "Easy there. No harm done. I don't tend to care where my seconds end up."

My fingers tighten on Rhett's, and I push with a hand wrapped around his bicep when he seems to contemplate lunging for Adam right there. The bastard chuckles as we pass and my cheeks flare. I can't deny the comment stings, and humiliation threatens my composure. Usually I wouldn't care, but Rhett hearing it makes me want to rip my hand from his.

I let go of him as we enter the hallway, quiet while students are finishing lunch. I don't want to go to my next class. I head for the exit instead.

"That's not the way—"

"I'd like to go, if that's okay," I say.

Rhett hooks my arm. "Don't let him win."

My teeth ground. "I'm just not feeling well."

Perhaps it's childish and cowardly, but I know Adam is in the last class of the day and I can't suffer his antagonizing eyes on me.

"I'm sorry," Rhett says. "I should have gotten us out of there sooner to avoid his path. I didn't realize who he was before."

My brow furrows. "You couldn't have known." Did he find Adam's name and look him up? I can't decide whether it's weird or touching if he did.

Rhett's jaw shifts. He takes a long breath and scans the hallway. "You know I'm not opposed to skipping out on a few hours of tedious lectures."

I smile, letting the tension disperse as we head out. "I'm in the mood for ice cream."

"I think you're past your sugar allowance for the day."

"There is no such thing." I wave him off.

"Let me guess, mint chocolate chip or something strawberry? You seem like an opposites type when it comes to sweet things, if lunch is anything to go by."

My lips part. He's right, but I don't want to stroke his growing ego about figuring me out. Rhett may not be an academic setting type, but he's too observant and analytical for his own good. I suppose it makes sense with his work.

When I look up as we reach the car and he opens my door, Rhett's eyes dipping to my open mouth makes my words stall. Then his alluring irises pierce mine, unscrambling them from my mind.

I get into the car without saying anything.

"An interesting first look into college life," he says, taking my hand as he drives. "How are you feeling about it?"

I blow out a breath. "I thought I'd feel sad about this being my final year, but I think I've been ready to leave for a while."

"How so?"

"The mundane. The drama. It's like college is supposed to define us."

"It's supposed to shape your future."

"Exactly. One shape. Maybe room for a little molding with the major I have, but it's always felt very . . ."

"Restrictive?"

I smile out the window. "Yes."

"So why the postgrad year?"

Rhett's asking questions I've never faced before. They live within me, but I fear them connecting with the answers.

"Is it pathetic to say I didn't know what else to do?"

"I don't think so."

He sounds sincere, curious.

I elaborate. "It just seemed like an easier thing to do when I didn't want to face the world yet. I want to move out, but the thought of picking a career path and potentially having it set my life . . . I guess I wasn't ready. Maybe I won't ever be and I just need to suck it up. Everything just feels so . . . beige. Unexciting."

Rhett is silent for long enough that my overactive brain starts doing somersaults.

So I add, "I know what you must be thinking—poor rich woman doesn't know how she'll keep herself entertained in the real world."

"I'm not thinking that at all."

My teeth grind in anticipation. I wish I didn't care to know his thoughts, but I want them so badly, as if they'll shine a light on something I haven't wanted to admit before.

"It's okay not to have your life figured out at twenty-four. Hell, you can change your mind at thirty, forty, and never touch your PHD again."

"Of all the bad influences you could have on me, my father hearing that might be what gets you fired."

His mouth curves with a faint devious smile. "I mean it. Your parents can't hold you in a cage forever. Break it if you must."

His tone feels personal. "Did your parents set expectations for you?"

A muscle in his jaw flexes and he doesn't answer right away.

"I was raised by my uncle after ten. He tried to shape me into what he wanted."

"But you chose differently?"

His fingers tighten on the wheel and his discomfort rises in a guarded expression. His past isn't something he likes to talk about, and that makes me . . . sad.

"Just don't let anyone tell you who you are, Ana."

CHAPTER 9
Anastasia

Having to prepare a debate only two weeks into the semester should go down as a criminal offense in the society of lecturers. As I pace in the cinema room I try to imagine it stretches back further, littered with classmates all watching me try to explain why I think Shakespeare's writing is universal and timeless against someone else arguing it isn't. I try to memorize my responses to what they could put forth in their case, but I keep stumbling and become riddled with the anxiety they might catch me unaware and I'll be standing there flustered and fumbling like a fool in front of everyone.

It's ironic, really. I've watched my father excel at this, and even in just a few short weeks I'll be flying to Cali with him for the big presidential debate.

Tunneling away as I recite my statements to myself, I'm not aware I have company until I catch glimpse of a ridiculously tall and broad figure leaning against the top entrance. My heart takes a moment to fall back to my chest after lunging up my throat.

"Sorry. I didn't mean to scare you," Rhett says, not apologetic in the slightest as he fights the amusement edging his mouth.

"Do you need something?" I bite out. He deserves my snipe for the fright.

"I figured you might want at least one face to fill your imaginary audience." He pushes off the wall, coming around the back double seats and sitting on the edge of one.

The sheets in my hands are already a crumpled mess, and his presence only rushes my nerves.

"I don't," I say, dismissing him.

"If you can't say it to me, how are you going to focus in a full auditorium?"

"I don't need the reminder I'm a flailing mess."

"Not what I meant. Haven't you done this before?"

"Yes. It doesn't make it any easier."

I chew at my thumb as I begin to pace again, reciting in my head instead of aloud and trying to block him out.

"What are you so afraid of?"

"I don't know. Nothing really, I've just never been able to prevent the nerves." I laugh resentfully at myself. "Would you believe I actually enjoy this kind of thing? That I want to perform and be able to talk in front of people. I think I'm actually pretty good at it. Yet I get so sick every time I try . . . It's infuriating."

"Do you want to know what I believe?"

"I have a feeling you're going to tell me."

"I believe that what we find most frightening are the things we desire the most. That life gives us nerves and fear as a challenge because nothing achieved easily will grant the same triumph as overcoming everything that tried to stop you."

My arms drop in surprise at his words. They repeat in my mind and I absorb them as something . . . comforting.

"Who knew bodyguards came with wisdom these days?" I muse.

"Your father paid for the latest model."

I smile to myself, watching the ground and his presence became less intimidating. With a deep breath I march over to him, thrusting a sheet at him, which he hooks a brow at before taking it.

"You can be my debate partner instead of just sitting pretty."

Rhett reclines back on the deep seat, hooking an arm behind himself as he reads over the lines. My cheeks flame, acknowledging the minute I spend checking him out while his body is stretched out, straining the fit of his black T-shirt, is a beat longer than appropriate.

"Shakespeare?" he quizzes as I make my way back down to the front.

"You can't give me life advice and not know who Shakespeare is."

"An ancient King of England, right?"

I snap him an incredulous look, but the bastard hides his deviant smile behind his paper.

He recites, "'William Shakespeare's work is exclusive and bigoted.' I'm against his timelessness?"

"Yes. I'm arguing his work resonates in our present time and reflects our future."

"You enjoy this kind of stuff?" he asks, genuinely curious.

I shrug. "I like his work, sure."

"I mean in general, literature, what you study—do you enjoy it?"

No one has ever asked me that before. My parents ask if I'm

doing well, what I plan to do next. I realize no one, not even myself, has ever questioned my enjoyment of what has been the driving aspect of my life for the past six years.

"I enjoy . . . some of it?" Why do I find the question so strange? Nerve-wracking. As if it could expose a lie I don't even know I'm harboring.

I shake my head to dispel the confusion and divert the topic.

"What do you do for fun, Agent?" I ask, folding my arms.

Rhett's hand drops from holding up his paper. He sets it aside and pushes himself to sitting, staring off as if he's thinking about it. "I'm pretty good with a gun," he says.

"I should hope so. Can't have you misfiring on the job."

His mouth twitches with a smile, but it's like it loses an internal fight to become whole every time.

"I used to enjoy sports," he reflects. "Hiking, kayaking, anything with a ball on the ground or in my hands. My fiancée hated most of it, but it was amusing to make her trudge along."

The melancholy that fills his irises as he stares at the wall pinches my chest. I don't expect the honesty, the mention of his lost love.

"You don't participate in those things anymore?" I ask carefully.

He takes a deep breath to swallow his pain. "I've become dedicated to my work over the past three years. There's little time."

I shouldn't want to insist he *make* time. That I'll go with him. The want to voice it pushes so strong, but it lodges in my throat as if that token of bonding would push us toward a line we can't get close to. Certainly can't cross.

"Want to hit the gym?" I ask suddenly. "It's not those sports, but I could use the distraction from Shakespeare and the fact my debate partner is Adam Sullevan."

Rhett's eyebrows pull together with that. "What's the deal with that guy?" He follows me out, leaving my papers behind.

"We had a fling last year. He was never my boyfriend, and I guess I was naïve to think someone without a label might not fuck someone else. He's the son of my father's competitor. We never should have hooked up."

"For what it's worth, he's a damned lucky bastard, but a fucking fool too if he had you and pulled that bullshit."

I smile to myself, not quite believing that's true, but I appreciate his attempt to lessen the blow of my ugly situation.

"It doesn't matter. I'm not wounded by it. Though it's added this edge of a competition now, like we've become part of our fathers' campaign as something personal."

"He's lashing out of nothing more than his own insecurity. It's why he'll take any moment to gain a reaction from you."

"So you're a people analyzer too?" I hook a brow at him.

He doesn't deny it, and I wonder if that comes naturally in his line of work. I should be uneasy at how observant he is, dissecting people like onions, layer by layer, and before they know it he's seen their core. I'm determined to keep my layers intact. Add extra layers. Rhett Kaiser is not getting close to any kind of nakedness with me.

"Meet you down there in ten minutes?" he says as we reach our doors.

I only nod and my heart skips at his small smile before he disappears into his room.

In the gym, I'm sitting stretching when Rhett strolls in ten minutes later than he said we'd meet. Not that I'm counting. Okay, maybe I am. He's wearing all black as usual, casual sweatpants and a T-shirt, and it's incredible how he can make something so plain look so devastating.

"Do you think you could teach me to fight?" I blurt when he's close enough. "You have that training from your work, right?"

Rhett assesses me, folding his powerful arms. "Why do you want to learn to fight?"

I've been debating the ask since I've never had the opportunity to learn so readily here without my parents finding out and wondering why.

"I just don't want to be defenseless."

With his silence he presses for my elaboration. Pushing myself up, I begin to stretch my arms and avoid his gaze.

"There's really nothing more to it. Never mind. It doesn't matter anyway now I'm constantly under surveillance."

"I can teach you," he agrees.

Not the easy acceptance I was expecting. While he doesn't seem satisfied with my poor reasoning, he brushes it off, heading to the mats.

He says, "You seem to have a great form when you attack the punching bag. Is that all you've practiced with before?"

I nod, slipping off my shoes to join him.

"I punched someone for real once," I admit, flushing before adding, "I broke my hand and had to tell my parents I stupidly fell."

I think he'll be amused. Mock me. In contrast, his eyes narrow a fraction and an unreadable emotion twitches his jaw.

"Show me," he says, stepping closer.

"You want me to hit you?"

"Yes. With everything you have, exactly as you did it that time."

Beginning to second-guess my want for this, I nervously adopt a braced stance to throw the punch. I'm putting a whole lot of faith in him knowing what he's doing, as I'm sure to break bone again if he lets my fist strike the barely cushioned steel of any part of him.

Here goes nothing.

I swing and connect with his palm as he catches my fist effortlessly.

"You're bending your wrist. Keep it straight," he instructs, fixing my error.

Taking a deep breath, I try again. This time he steps around me like a graceful cat. I expect some sort of impact from him as my balance wavers. The opportunity is right there. Instead his hand presses to my abdomen in the same breath before I can stumble. Rhett doesn't linger, but his touch ignites my skin. *Maybe this isn't a good idea*, I think when my slutty side decides to taunt my body with a flush.

"Your stance is good, but it could be better," he says, in a low tone that isn't helping my *situation*. "May I?"

I can only nod. *Keep it professional, Ana.* Rhett closes the distance, angling my hips and gently kicking my feet until I've shifted into a position that satisfies him. Innocent on his part. Absolutely scandalous in my mind. It inspires the want to know if he'd take this sort of control in the bedroom. Position me where he wanted me.

"Try again," he says close to my ear.

I take a deep breath to slam shameless Ana back in her cage. Then I throw my fist out with the release, and it feels good. Like sealing shut the door to that side of me that was clawing wild with Rhett nearby. Now all I need is a key to keep her locked away for the next five months.

Focus.

Rhett's hand comes under my elbow before I can retract it. He's so fast, so careful and attentive in the way he corrects me, piece by piece.

"Make sure your first two knuckles are aligned with the bone of your forearm," he instructs, showing the path of alignment with the tips of his fingers. I stifle a shiver.

His hand slips over my abdomen as he says, "Again."

I don't expect his precision and elegance in teaching. I thought he'd stand by and watch me flail around while ordering corrections from the sidelines, silently thinking I'm a lost cause.

I throw my punch again and his hand gently lowers my elbow.

"Contract your abdomen when you exhale as you deliver your blow. It'll have more impact."

He steps away and I'm flushed, though not with any exertion. Coming back around, he braces himself this time.

"I'm going to respond, but I'll stop the moment you say."

"Okay," I say, already a little breathless.

His silvery hair hovers over eyes that lock on mine, so focused and waiting for me to move.

With nothing to lose, I attack. Knowing he'll catch my fist, I throw out my other hand, which he blocks effortlessly. Spinning me, he presses my back to his front, but I lean in a side-lunge, bringing my elbow up. He anticipates that too, grabbing my forearm and pinning it across my body. He's too tall, too strong, and this idea was completely futile. Still, I don't give up just yet, managing to duck and twist out of that hold and rip my arm free. Rhett lunges for me this time, and in my surprise I'm taken off my feet, nearly thrown over his shoulder until he stops.

He could have thrown me like a sack of flour, and the worst part is I think I would have enjoyed it. *Traitorous mind.*

When he sets me down I catch my breath, pacing away with a hand on my hip.

"This was a stupid idea," I mutter.

"It's smart to want to defend yourself," he argues.

"What does it matter when I'll always be weaker, smaller?" I exasperate.

Turning back to him, I watch his expression fall quietly *angry*. I think I've messed up, said something to offend him, as he comes closer.

He asks, so low and careful, "Has someone hurt you before? Or placed you in a position that you thought they would?"

My lips part to spill the truth, but I shake my head before it comes out.

"No. It's nothing. It was nothing."

I don't expect him to take my chin when I try to look away. The intensity of his blue eyes pierces through me as if he'll be able to find the memory himself.

"If you don't want to tell me then fine, but don't say it was nothing when that's not true."

I swallow hard. "It was over the summer, not long after my ... *breakup*, if that's what it was, with Adam," I confess. Needing a distraction, I equip myself with the boxing gloves and take to the punching bag. It might not train me against someone who can attack back, but it's something.

"At a party, one of his friends approached me and said he'd heard from Adam how *good* of a lay I was. I told him I wasn't interested and thought that was the end of it. I didn't see him for an hour after that. I didn't drink a lot—I swear I don't always test my limits like how you saw me. I went to the bathroom, and before I could close the door, there he was." I push harder, punching and kicking, practicing all I can from being self-taught. "He forced his way in and locked the door behind him. I'd never felt fear like that before. The music was loud and I didn't think anyone would hear me if I shouted for help, so I tried to stay calm and reason with him. He thought my refusal was funny, then my insistence to leave turned him . . . aggressive." The backs of my eyes prick with tears. I haven't told anyone this. Not even Riley. It seems insignificant. "He touched me where I didn't want to be touched. I didn't know the first thing about how to fight him off even though he wasn't as tall or as built as you, and maybe I could have if I'd known the right maneuvers. So after that night I spent a lot of the summer here. I won't feel that helpless again, even if I only know the basics."

I stop attacking the punching bag, catching my breath as I unstrap the gloves and toss them to the ground before slumping down.

"What is his name?" Rhett asks with a note to his voice that chills me.

"Isaac Neil. He's in my classes, but he hasn't bothered me since."

"How did you get out of there?"

"Adam, actually." I huff a humorless laugh at the irony. "Isaac had only been in that bathroom with me for minutes that felt like far longer. I got that single punch to fend him off, but by my luck, that night I ended up breaking my fourth metacarpal. Adam saw him barge his way in and broke the lock before he could retaliate. Adam took me to the hospital, then home, and we never spoke again—until now."

"You never told anyone?" Rhett asks, his tone turning soft as he crouches beside me.

I shake my head. "My father had enough going on with the campaign stuff—something like that would only stress him out, and maybe he'd worry about some rumor leaking, so I told him it was a stupid drunken fall. Adam agreed not to do or say anything when I asked him not to, and I didn't tell anyone. I just don't want to feel like that again, that's all."

I dare a look, but Rhett gives very little away as he watches me.

"Your punch is strong—it just needs fine-tuning so you don't break bone again. It will always hurt to throw one. You just need to make sure it's worse for them than you. We can fit in an hour here as many days as you like. I'm all yours."

That brightens my mood, lifting all the heavy tension, and I smile. It seems to relax him when I do, and I push back up, feeling so much lighter now that's out to someone.

"I'll grab us some drinks," I say, heading out so we can get an hour of practice in today.

"Ana," he calls.

I swivel back to him.

"It's incredibly brave that you attempted to punch him at all. You have great intuition and an admirable will."

I don't know why his words impact me so strongly. I give a nod of gratitude and scurry out to the kitchen. Until I realize it isn't just his words—it's that Rhett Kaiser has never looked at me like everyone else. As Anastasia Kinsley, daughter of rich parents and a likely president, he looks at me like he sees potential, something invisible I've given up believing exists in me. He looks at me like he's waiting for me to take off a mask I've long forgotten I'm wearing.

CHAPTER 10
Rhett

Ana falls asleep curled up on the wide beige leather seat opposite me on the jet. I can't take my eyes off her, and if she knew I was watching her she'd find it creepy as fuck. Hell, *I* find it creepy as fuck, but I can't stop. It's not just because she's stunning; my mind is a lattice of thoughts of her, and it's becoming an irritating yet addicting fascination.

Her father and Gregory Forbes chat between themselves down the opposite end of the senator's private jet. Occasionally I catch Forbes' eye on me, which sparks my interest on *him* even more. Wandering eyes are curious. And curiosity is always sparked by one's personal secrets and desires. I have my team looking into him around the clock, but maybe I'll get a chance myself this weekend now he's drawn my intrigue.

After another half hour Ana shifts and the blanket falls from her shoulders. I reach across before I know what I'm doing, fixing it back over her. I'm taking this damn babysitter job far too literally. My fingers brush her brown hair while I'm so near.

Everything about her is temptation, crafted just to test me, and the will I thought was unshakable in me has begun to crack. *Oh little bird, you don't want that wall to come down.* Something tells me she'd survive the rubble, but not the thing that would lay its claim and devour her beyond it.

Ana is not something I can taste and get over. I know that if I got one taste of Anastasia Kinsley, there would be no escaping her.

The senator calls my name and I internally groan. I should be glad for an opportunity to speak to him, analyze him, get close to him and anyone he's with. But it breaks a peace I haven't felt in a very long time as I selfishly bask in watching Ana.

I head down to them, taking up a seat beside him.

"I wanted to ask if you'd read over the protocol for the time we're in California," the senator asks.

Three times. It wasn't exactly a meticulous code of instruction. I have to be close to Ana at all times, of course, but while we've only had one plainclothes guard trail us in D.C. without her knowledge, the senator hired three for her here since the press and the audience for this event will be hungry and demanding. On top of that, I trust my two men from Xoid more than the senator's security. They'll have eyes on us.

"Of course," I reply.

He offers me a miniature whiskey and a glass with ice. It irritates the fuck out of me, the implication I'd even risk a drop. Five feet or thirty-three thousand feet in the air, I will not drink in Ana's company.

"No thank you, sir," I decline politely.

"We have another five hours before we land—consider this time off. I insist."

There's no time off. Ana is my twenty-four-fucking-seven priority.

"I don't drink."

"At all?" Gregory inquires.

"No."

Once a year, but semantics.

"I'd like to know how else you cope with the shit and the stress," the senator chuckles.

I weather the storm instead of drowning it.

That isn't what they want to hear, so I merely join in with their amusement. So far Senator Kinsley has turned up clean, humble, and harmless. I won't give him a full badge of innocence just yet. Politicians often have hidden corners of dirt.

"How are you feeling about the debate, sir?" I ask.

I've never really paid attention to elections in the past. This is all new and kind of intriguing to me.

He sighs as Gregory smirks. "It's been a close running—it will be until the very end. I'm prepared and confident, of course, but I have to admit, Sullevan is some competition. I'd be lying if I said I don't think he can smoke me."

It makes my lips twitch to hear him speak so casually and, interestingly, so fondly of his competition.

"Are you acquainted with Sullevan?"

"We went to the same university, actually. Not that close, but I remember some great frat parties where we bonded. What are the odds we'd be the last two going head-to-head for presidency twenty years later?"

Improbable odds indeed.

His wife is sleeping another row back. This event requires them all to come for press opportunities. Meaning Adam Sullevan will be there supporting his father, and I'm not looking forward to seeing him around Ana. In fact, that's far too tame of a description for the anger rattling me. Now I know of their past, I can't decide if he's a threat or just a thorn in our side. What's her problem is mine. Her fears, her troubles, her minor inconveniences—they're all *mine*. Adam's an arrogant son of bitch for sure, but he also helped Ana when she was in trouble over the summer. Which reminds me, I have a hit on my list. I won't take Isaac Neil's life and he has Adam to thank for it, for stepping in before he violated my little bird past the limits of my mercy. But Isaac owes at least a finger, maybe two, depending on how he apologizes, for touching what isn't his.

"I'm sure Ana will want to make use of the heat over there," the senator says.

He doesn't need to mention it. I've already been reeling, trying to prepare myself for seeing Ana in a bathing suit as she's mentioned the beach several times. *Fuck*, this woman riles me with that image alone like a boy about to see pussy for the first time.

Her father speaks again while I run through deplorable thoughts of his daughter in my mind.

"And I hope she'll spend some time with Adam. As far as I last knew they were somewhat close, and now she never speaks of him."

So he doesn't know just *how* close they've gotten. That fact never fails to fan an irrational jealousy in me. I can't desire Ana. So I take a match to that dark feeling and try to come to terms with another man's hands on her. I might even have to witness it right in front of my fucking eyes if she decides to get flirty somewhere the press won't see. Or reignite what she had with Adam Sullevan while they're sleeping in the same building.

Suddenly the torturous cage of my mind is rattling violently at the image of our rooms side by side, hearing him fuck her through the walls, and what if I snap when right now, with the mere taunting illusion, I want to break his damn neck before they can get that far?

I don't realize my fingers are close to warping the leather that's likely worth a significant portion of my salary even at Xoid.

"She said they drifted apart and they're now focused on their studies," I lie. "I'm sure they'll relax in Cali."

It's clear the senator thinks fondly of Adam. Maybe he even favors their match. And once again inside me is the bitter acknowledgment of how *good* he is for her in status and image. It's disgraceful of me to be glad things ended. Though he has some groveling to do for hurting her, and I haven't forgotten.

The moment we hit the ground I'm fitting my earbud in and on two jobs at once. Ana is damn adorable with her grumpy expression awakening as she fits sunglasses on her face and scowls at my smirk.

"You should be well-rested—you slept like a log," I comment in the car.

It's just us, with Gregory and Archibald in the car ahead, and for once I'm not driving.

Ana yawns. "I'm disappointed, actually. I planned to make the journey insufferable for you with no escape."

She's a devious little thing.

"You did that by falling asleep."

Her head lolls against the seat toward me and she pushes her sunglasses on top of her head. "My dad talked your ear off the whole time, didn't he?"

My grimace must tell all, and she laughs.

"We're on vacation this weekend. I'll make it up to you, Agent."

I wish my dick wouldn't jerk at the sultry lilt she always uses with that title.

At the hotel, which is likely the most elaborate venue I'll ever stay in, I lead Ana up to our rooms, which are side by side. Pacing every square inch of hers and deeming it safe, I unlatch her side of the door that connects our rooms.

"What happened to privacy?" Ana protests.

"I haven't demanded you keep it open, just unlocked."

"You could walk in anytime! What if I'm naked?"

I do *not* need that image planted in my head and I'll certainly need to jerk off in the shower tonight to relieve the pent-up tension she's surfacing in me. Ana smiles coyly, knowing exactly what she's doing with her taunting flirtations.

"I promise no surprise visits unless I hear you scream. So be mindful of that when you're thinking of me tonight."

Her lips part and I leave her room with a smile of satisfaction. In my own I unlock my side immediately, and as if she was waiting for it, Ana enters seconds later.

"I will *not* be thinking of you."

"What *will* you be thinking of?"

A stunning pink colors her cheeks. "Nothing!"

Call it intuition, call it primal need, but it's like I can practically taste the lust surfacing in her. Ana shifts on her feet as if desire is pooling out of her right now and, *fuck*, the things I would do to her in another time. Another life. Why has such a stunning, enticing creature been put in my path like she was crafted just to test me?

"Whatever you say, little bird, but my warning still stands. If I hear anything from your lips that I can't immediately distinguish from you being in trouble, I'm not knocking before I rip open that door."

Her lips press together, and what I wouldn't give for her thoughts right now when those hazel eyes spark with a hint of challenge. My cock hardens at the thought of her *wanting* me to watch as she touches herself. I might very well walk over hot coals for that.

"I'm going down to the bar," she says.

"Probably a good idea when you're going to be up for ages after that rest."

"You should stay and catch up on yours."

"Not happening. Don't waste your time suggesting a moment without me again, Miss Kinsley. I'm by your side every second you do or don't want me to be."

"Fine."

"Good."

She spins back into her room, closing the door. I take a long breath as soon as she's gone, running a hand through my hair and pacing to the window. It's going to be a long fucking weekend.

CHAPTER 11
Anastasia

I sip my second martini while Rhett sits by me with a glass of ice water. Admittedly, I'm still riled up from our last conversation in our rooms. The thought of Rhett bursting through the adjoining door all threatening and hopefully shirtless, *no pants*, in the middle of the night, only to find me legs spread, fingers deep in myself, aches between my legs even now.

It's sinful and wrong. He's my guard. A professional appointed by my father. Yet that only seems to entice me the more I remind myself he's forbidden. A walking temptation, the devil himself latched onto my side. There's something so twisted with me.

I can hardly look at Rhett, but for the sake of our ruse his chair is intimately close to mine, our thighs near touching.

"Does your father know you beat Adam at your college debate?" Rhett asks. He doesn't hide his satisfaction, which blooms in my chest.

"I didn't mention it," I say. It was a very close result, the votes cast by our classmates for whichever side they were more compelled toward. But still, it felt damn good to beat him.

"Why not?"

I shrug. "He has a far more serious and real one tomorrow. He didn't need to hear of my child's play."

"Of course he should," Rhett says, sounding almost angry. When I turn my head our faces are in close proximity too. "Your wins matter, Ana, however small. And you were incredible in that debate."

A flutter erupts in my stomach at his sincerity. My parents sometimes ask about my schoolwork, but in the grand scheme of what my father does for a living, all that matters to them is that I pass. They mean well. They try to appear supportive. I've long convinced myself I don't need my triumphs celebrated.

I take another drink. "There was one class, Roman studies, where I passed with the highest mark in my class. Even above Riley and Nolan, our class whizzes. I told my parents and they merely smiled and said, 'That's great, honey.' I didn't expect much, but I was proud of myself for it. That's all that matters, I guess."

At the time, their lack of enthusiasm and understanding of what it meant to me stung, but I couldn't expect them to praise me for something that wasn't a grand achievement really. I quickly let it go.

"They should be so damn proud," he says with a furrowed brow.

I huff a laugh to brush it off. "I don't think I've heard that before, actually. I know they love me and they encourage me, but they've never said they're proud, and I've always just thought I'm not there yet. I haven't done anything that life-changing or amazing to be proud of yet."

"I don't believe that even for a second. I'm proud of you just seeing how you conquered that debate despite the nerves I watched tear you apart before it. Do they even know about that?"

"They had to console me after a breakdown performing my violin at the Christmas party when I was seventeen, but I think they assume it's something I've grown out of despite me still refusing to play again every year."

"Ana." His hand takes mine before I can reach for my glass again. He searches my eyes as if he doesn't know which words he wants to follow up with, but something disturbs him. "I see you."

I've never felt such an impact from three small words. Seven letters that fill a void I didn't realize was vacant in me. A sentence so short, but I long hear to it again. What is he doing? Nestling into parts of me I can't afford to find comfort in, because Rhett is a temporary placement in my life.

I swallow hard, bringing the martini glass to my lips. "Are you sure you can't join me for a drink? You're too serious all the time and I'm trying to enjoy my buzz."

He takes his hand back, but his expression gives so little away, and I hate the sinking feeling in my gut. It's better this way. Rhett is a mere want, a stroke of silly desire any woman would crave. Just as I think this, a dark seed of jealousy at the thought of him with someone else grows a dangerous root.

"Hey, Ana. I was wondering when I'd run into you." Adam's voice breaks our tension from behind me.

I swallow my groan as he leans on the bar beside me and orders a whiskey on the rocks. "Can't say I gave you the same headspace."

He smiles arrogantly. "Will you be at the beach tomorrow?

There's a volleyball tournament going on. Excellent press opportunity."

"We were just planning our day around it," I say sweetly.

Adam's gaze flicks over my shoulder to Rhett, then back to me. I don't like the way he clearly has observations he's leaving unspoken.

"Speaking of press . . ." Adam drawls, picking up his glass.

I swivel to follow his line of sight. Sure enough, our fathers have come down to the bar and there are now a bunch of reporters being kept back by security. The other patrons in the venue take notice of the presidential candidates, then a few linger looks on us as if they're only now realizing who we are. The attention pricks over my spine and I resist the urge to shrink into Rhett like a human shield.

"Want to head back up?" Rhett asks close to my ear. I shiver at his warm breath caressing my nape.

Nodding, I don't bother finishing my martini before we leave.

"See you tomorrow, A," Adam calls.

I don't look back.

Rhett leads me with a hand on my back, but as soon as we're near them, the reporters start following with their cameras like snapping piranhas, and their questions are fired at us. What interest am I in any of this?

"Anastasia, can you pose with your boyfriend for a photo?"

I freeze, wondering what Rhett makes of all this. It's *not* what he signed up for when he took the job. Guilt wracks me to think the facade of being branded his girlfriend could be upsetting him, just like how he once struggled with touching me. Always reminding him of his lost fiancée. Does he resent me for it?

"Just one photo, Ana!"

"We don't need to," I say to him.

"Do you want to?" he asks.

"It'll keep them satisfied. But you're more important."

His brow flinches at that and I can't read his deliberation.

"I know what I signed up for," he assures me.

I nod, but it doesn't untangle my sorrow for him. We turn, allowing them to snap the shot of us together, but I feel so terribly stiff, not knowing how to react when Rhett doesn't want this.

"Relax," he says in my ear.

"How long have you been dating?" a reporter asks.

"I— Uh, around six months now, I think," I answer like a stumbling idiot.

Rhett's hand tightens on my waist. "We met over the summer," he adds. "It was hard to entice a date out of her, but she fell for my charm eventually."

Is that so? Okay, Mr. Charmer.

"You can't really blame me when his pretty face is the best of his chat-up lines."

That earns some chuckles and a daring squeeze from Rhett that sparks a thrill straight between my legs. Some of the tension in my body dissolves under the desire he ignites so easily in me.

"Can we get a kiss?" another asks. Everyone turns eager, hungry for it.

Shit. I hadn't thought about that, and every reporter is suddenly desperate for the chance to snap that first shot. I look up at Rhett. He's turned taut against me.

"They've got enough," I say quietly to him. I take his hand, ready to dismiss the request that was crossing a line anyway.

Rhett becomes immovable, and I still. He's warring with himself in those ocean eyes as they search mine. Then his smile lights up my chest. It's not fully there, but it's enough, as his arm curves around me tighter.

"You don't have to do this," I whisper when his lips hover over mine.

"I want to," he says. "Fuck, I want to."

His hand cups my jaw, and I'm not prepared for the need that detonates between us. My body curves into him as my mind is lost to him.

Maybe he feels a fraction of it too, because his arm presses me tighter to him and our kiss doesn't end quickly, nor is it chaste or just enough to satisfy the picture op. It turns to something that drowns out the clicks and murmurs behind us with the blood rushing in my ears. Rhett kisses me hard and passionately, and I open to the sweep of his tongue against my lower lip. His hand clenches my nape as if he's refraining from devouring me right here, and I become lightheaded.

He pulls away suddenly, holding my eyes with bewilderment as if he doesn't know what came over him either. Then he masterfully composes himself, plastering on his fake smile before taking my hand. We give a short wave goodbye to the press before slipping into the elevator.

The silence is charged with all that was cut off so abruptly between us. I can't be sure if he's just as affected when any slight glance I steal reveals his typical stone-faced exterior. *Shit*, it upset him. Of course it did. Should I apologize? No—that would make this torturous climb of twenty-three floors even more awkward.

"They can be, uh— I mean, they don't have a care for modesty or boundaries," I say.

I should have stayed silent.

"We didn't talk about needing to kiss every now and then to keep it believable. I'm sorry if I stepped out of line."

"You didn't," I say quickly. "It was fine. Nice, actually."

What the fuck, Ana? I want to slap myself. I want to slap *him*, unfairly, but it's true. I want to slap him in this moment for making me feel like a girl hanging out with her crush for the first time.

"Nice?" He quirks a brow, finding amusement in my flustered choice of words.

"Your ego doesn't need more than that."

He gives a light chuckle edged with darkness. "Your body told me everything I need."

"We had an audience and a show to put on."

Rhett pushes off from where he's leaning back against the wall. I don't expect him to erase all personal space in front of me and I tip my chin back.

"What about now?" he says in a low, husky tone. "I've never done anything *nice* in my life, Miss Kinsley. Don't make me prove it to you."

This man is all dares and challenges. His mood switches give me whiplash. Yet at the same time my adrenaline races with pleasure for it. The uncertainty of him. How it's like he's always one push away from erupting and I hold the detonator.

The elevator opens behind him and two men shuffle in. I almost relax, thinking he'll put some distance between us with the company, but Rhett doesn't move. Instead his eyes turn dark and a smile tugs his mouth as it slants, inching closer to mine.

Heart slamming in my chest, my eyes flick up just as the numbers switch to our floor and the elevator dings open again. Rhett's lips barely graze mine before he takes my hand and leads me out.

What the fuck was that?

In a daze, I only follow until we reach our rooms, where I

watch Rhett pace mine in silence. At my door he turns back, wholly unfazed, as if nothing in the past twenty minutes happened.

"Remember, little bird. Scream only if you need me."

If the bed were on fire I'd throw myself into it right now. There's no winning against Rhett Kaiser when he's so insinuating with his words that leave me speechless. He takes his leave in triumph.

I strip for bed and debate sleeping naked. Cali is hot as shit, and Rhett fucking Kaiser has only heated my skin more now I can't stop thinking about him just beyond that door. He's always slept across the hall at home, but there's something more enticing about being in a hotel room. Like all rules are on the table and—

Shit, am I really debating sleeping with my guard?

It's completely inappropriate, not to mention shameless, that I even think he'd be interested. It would just be sex. No strings attached. But then I remember how he could hardly stand to touch me when we first met. He's getting better. He had to *force* himself to for this job, and that weighs in me with disappointment. Of course he wouldn't want to fucking sleep with me.

I huff out of nothing more than sexual frustration and throw myself onto the bed. Before I know it I'm slipping a hand down my body, squeezing my breast in the other, and for just one sinful night I imagine it's his hands over me. I picture him naked right beyond that wall, pumping himself to thoughts of me too. I'm so damn wet at the thought of one sound too loud exposing me. His warning wasn't a tease—I have no doubt he'd burst in without a thought and find me spread out on this bed touching myself.

Would he join? Take over? *Fuck*, I want it so badly I'm

becoming a puddle, biting my lip hard to suppress my moans as I circle my clit. Curving two fingers into myself, I wish I had a toy to help, but I quickly scratch that thought when the image of Rhett's wicked face between my thighs drives me toward my climax just as fast. Tasting me, slipping his fingers inside me. I know I'm punishing myself as I'll have to face him tomorrow, after this, but right now I'm so close to crying out his name as it tips onto my tongue.

Waves of bliss crash over me and I throw my head back with a silent cry. When my trembling subsides I lie there panting and gathering myself, wondering how I came to be this lust-crazed fool for someone I can't have. There's a line between us and I have to reinforce it, then set fire to it. For good measure I'll even throw gasoline on it to make sure there's no way of crossing it.

I will do that. Tomorrow. But tonight I'm not finished sating my fantasy. Not when Rhett Kaiser is lying unaware—or perhaps all-knowing—on the other side of that door and I'm the most turned on I've ever been in my life.

CHAPTER 12
Anastasia

I'm not used to the Cali heat that has my skin slick on the ten-minute walk to the beach from our hotel. Desperate to take my thin top off, and even more so for Rhett to shed his, we reach the busy sands and I'm giddy on my feet from the excitement.

"Do we need to find a bathroom?" Rhett asks.

I tear my gaze from the crowd for the volleyball tournament down the beach.

"What? No."

"You can hardly keep still."

"You're keeping *too* still," I counter. Then I pull him along from our joined hands.

No one has recognized us yet, and I plan to enjoy that for as long as possible. We get ice cream—the only logical thing to do when it's hotter than Satan's balls and your fake boyfriend refuses to even pretend to look happy. The ice cream doesn't help his naturally stern expression, but he looks adorable, his large hand making his cone look child-size.

"You're wasting your ice cream," I point out. It melts as he watches the volleyball game from our table in the shade. Mine doesn't get the chance to drip a single bit of mint chocolate chip deliciousness before I'm making my way down the wafer.

"You're wasting it by not finishing that one fast enough."

I toss the point of the cone into my mouth as I contemplate his half-eaten strawberry scoop. "We didn't agree to share. I ate all of mine."

He merely holds it out to me, and it would be a shame to let it go to waste.

Rhett has a big appetite and frequently finishes off anything savory I don't want. I tackle the desserts. It's a win-win unspoken agreement.

"You know, most would wear light colors in the heat. You can't be comfortable," I comment on his plain black T-shirt and the shorts that still manage to look expensive. He wears Ray-Bans that add *danger* to him and his expression basically repels company.

"If you want my clothes off, you're going to have to do better than that."

I refrain from launching the ice cream at him.

"If I wanted your clothes off, Agent, they would be off already."

"Confident, are you?"

I shrug. "We'll never know."

My ice-cold lemonade goes down a treat as we head closer to the volleyball. It's rather casual. The nets are generally for the public along the beach, no arena, and onlookers are cheering from the tapes set up around them for the games. It's nothing serious, just for charity, and the air is buzzing with friendly competitive spirit.

I spot Adam heading down the beach, walking next to some guy I've never seen before. They're the same height, both shirtless and impeccably toned. His companion has such a pretty face it's strange to feel envious of the long lashes, soft, kind features, and tousled brown hair.

"There's America's darlings," Adam's irritating voice drawls when they're near enough.

I scowl as it pulls unwanted attention to us, and he smirks. *Deviant bastard.*

"Adam told me all about you," Adam's . . . friend? says. "I'm Nathan."

"Don't believe a word of it," I mutter.

Nathan only chuckles as if our feud is genuinely playful. I've never seen him before, yet from their close proximity and the attentive gazes Nathan casts to Adam, they seem very well-acquainted.

"This game is almost finished—what do you say?" Adam encourages.

I skim my gaze from the beach back to him. Does he mean us against him? No. No way. I am *not* seeing myself front-page on some tabloid tomorrow with a sand facial.

"Come on," he says, louder now, and with the last match finished the crowd starts to find something else for entertainment. "Our fathers get their turn tomorrow. Let's not give them all the press this weekend. One game of pairs."

The onlookers agree, of course. Small murmurs of, "She won't do it," and, "Sullevan would win," boil me over.

"What's the loser's punishment?" I ask.

Now we're committed. *Game. Fucking. On. Sullevan.*

His smile curls with wicked deviance. "Losers swim out to the buoys."

I'm a competent swimmer, but I'm not fond of the sea. If I lose and become a sea creature's snack I'll never live it down.

"Deal."

The crowd cheers, and it erupts over me like I'm only just realizing what the hell I've signed up for. Winning a sport I'm not all that familiar with is one thing . . . but the audience is what shakes my nerves with regret.

"You sure about this?" Rhett asks.

"Please tell me you're good at this. I'm counting on you for victory."

He smiles in amusement. "Watch and learn, little bird."

I bite my lip and his eyes drop to it with his vanishing smile. He reaches out, and my heart tumbles until he takes my lemonade and finishes it off.

On the sands I hesitate with the want to take my top off. Would it be inappropriate? I only have on a bikini top, but I trust its support. I think. It's too damned hot, and with the game I could pass out from the unnecessary layer.

Fuck it.

I fold out of my top and toss it by our bag, leaving myself in only small denim shorts and red bikini top.

When I look up Rhett is shirtless too, and we both stare stupidly at each other. He's sculpted by Greek gods; those muscles seem to come naturally to him. It's completely unfair. But I'm stalled on his tattoo, which I discover is in fact a large serpent engulfed in smoke that coils around his large bicep, ending in a vicious, open-mouthed snake head across the right side of his chest. It's so beautiful I want to run my hand along it and discover the details, then I want to explore the rest of *him*.

"Done gawking, little bird?" he teases.

I roll my eyes. "If you are."

He stops me from passing him with a hand on my waist. The bare-skin contact flutters between my legs.

"Not even close," he says huskily.

He's playing his part for the crowd too damn well. People are already taking pictures, and I become hyperaware of our performance. *May as well take advantage.*

My hand trails up his abdomen, holding his blue eyes as they darken, right until I touch the serpent's fangs.

"If we lose, you're making the swim carrying me on your back."

His mouth twitches. "There's no outcome of this where you don't win then, Miss Kinsley, smart girl."

I don't know why that skitters pleasure through me. I need to rally my focus to be of *some* help in this sport, though I expect Rhett to take charge, and I wish I were a mere spectator watching him in action. He's being eye-fucked by so many men and women as the crowd grows thicker.

"Come here," Rhett calls to me.

When I turn back he's crouching by the beach bag holding a bottle of sunscreen.

"I put some on at the hotel an hour ago," I say.

"Not on your back now you're topless."

I can't protest. Then I realize what this means and my stomach coils. He squeezes some onto his hands and I turn, pulling my hair over my shoulder, out of the way. The moment his hands are on me I'm resisting the urge to melt to a damn puddle. I shouldn't find it so sensual, but it's like he's working his fingers so slowly and smoothly on purpose just to rile me. His hands are . . . *Shit*, I slam away thought after thought of what I want them to be doing to me. I almost moan when he massages my shoulders, down my spine, and under the strap of my bikini. His palms run up my sides and pull me gently into him.

"All done," he mumbles in my ear.

"You're determined to get top marks on your bodyguard report."

"Of course."

I turn around to do the same for him, and he squeezes out a healthy amount to cover the large expanse of his back before he tosses the bottle back into the bag.

"You're going to have to kneel," I say, shielding my eyes from the sun to look up at him.

"For you, anytime."

It's harmless flirting, but my body doesn't grasp the difference, and watching Rhett Kaiser lower in front of me sparks something powerful and pleasurable in me.

"Wrong way," I say.

His hands grip my hips unexpectedly. Then he leans in and my heart near slams out of my chest when his lips press near my belly button. Desire pools at my core.

"I know," he says, and he turns around.

I'm dumbstruck. Caught completely off-guard by the simple yet *sinful* act he so casually pulled out of nowhere.

I survey the gathering people again and find a group of women with eyes trained on us. All scowling at me and gawking at Rhett.

"Let's go, Kinsley!" Adam shouts from across the net.

I snap back into myself, rubbing the sunscreen into both my hands before they're upon Rhett. Then I'm lost in the contours of him. He looks impeccable, but he *feels* . . .

Stop it, Ana. Stop lusting after your damn bodyguard.

I speed up my work because I risk delaying this stupid game

by taking too long. My fingers skim over slightly raised skin so often that I become transfixed by his beautiful imperfections, wanting to know who or what hurt him with every single one.

"All done," I say as I finish on his shoulders, but my hands linger.

Until he stands and I have no choice but to let him go.

"Thanks," he says.

He looks like he might kiss me for show again. The press have made their way over and I can hear their completely shameless asks, but we're pulled away from the opportunity.

"Sullevan versus Kinsley!" someone shouts.

Fuck, this is a bad idea. I wonder if our fathers would say as much if this harmless game could be twisted into something political that could get nasty. So far everyone seems amicable, and I try to relax.

When we're on opposite sides of the net, Adam and I decide who gets to begin with a good old-fashioned game of rock, paper, scissors. I beam triumphantly at my clenched fist and knock his pathetic scissor fingers away.

"Muscle memory, I guess," he says with a wink.

My mouth drops open because there is no fucking way he's insinuating what I think he is. Suddenly it's not the California sun burning my skin. I flick a look to Rhett, who must have caught onto his meaning with the scary glare he pins to the oblivious Adam, and now I wish it was quicksand beneath me to drag me away.

A referee blows a whistle and throws me the volleyball, which I nearly make the embarrassing first impression of *missing*. I hand it to Rhett, because I wasn't kidding when I said I fear eating sand for dinner.

I brace as Rhett does and try not to get distracted by how

sexy he looks throwing the ball in the air, all stretched-out torso and a look that could kill with the volley he sends over the net with a powerful hit.

Then it's all sand, volleyball, and crushing Adam fucking Sullevan no matter what.

Any time the ball comes to me I mostly act as a boost so Rhett can step in and shoot it with impressive force over the net. We score twice. They score once. I didn't expect to lose myself and enjoy this as much as I am. I like working out, but I've had little time and opportunity for sports, save for the occasional family tennis match or badminton on a day out.

Rhett and I move like magnets. We communicate with few words but a lot of gravity. Sometimes our skin grazes and it sparks through me. We're sweaty and focused, and it's so exhilarating I don't even care about the score anymore. I jump for joy and we double high-five when we score, but even when Sullevan gains points our spirit doesn't break. Rhett often throws me a grin that takes my breath away for how rare the sight is. It's like he's forgotten the world that weighs on him in this carefree time, and it's precious.

We have five minutes to even the score with Adam now in the lead, and that'll bring us to a tiebreaker. I push the ball into the air and Rhett hits it across, but Nathan dives to catch it, and Adam jumps to slam it over the net directly in front of me. All I can do is brace for the force of the ball hitting me.

It doesn't.

Rhett saves me from the blow that would have no doubt hurt like a bitch, but it costs us the game when he hits it down under the net.

"Thanks," I breathe.

"Anytime. But we lost."

I click my tongue. "I hope those shorts are waterproof."

The whistle blows and the crowd erupts. I don't care, or really pay any attention, as despite the loss I can't wipe the grin off my face. My fingers unhook the button of my shorts and Rhett's gaze dips down.

"Wet denim is *not* comfortable," I say, shimmying out of them and jogging back to throw them with our things. When I return, Rhett hasn't moved an inch.

"Never seen a woman in a bikini before?"

His blue eyes snap to me. "You're not just any woman," he says, taking my hand as we head to the water.

People follow, but I hardly pay attention. I sigh contentedly at the first feel of the cool water lapping past our ankles.

"It's pretty far. You sure you have the stamina?" he quips.

"It's you who needs to worry about stamina. I'm just hitching a ride."

It takes straining on my toes to reach his shoulders, until he crouches enough for me to jump up and hook my legs around his waist. Giggles erupt out of me as he grips my thighs and hoists me up his back. Then he walks deeper into the water. His skin is heated and slick against mine, and his hair smells so damn good. I'm thinking inappropriate things again, but it's hardly my fault this time. Okay, it *was* my impulse that made me jump on his back, but I don't actually expect him to swim the whole way with me.

Rhett is a surprisingly powerful swimmer considering the additional cargo.

"I'm only doing this so the sharks will eat you first," I say.

He huffs a laugh. "I'm only agreeing because it's my job."

After a few more strides I let him ago. At least I try to, but

Rhett catches me around the waist before I can get even a foot away.

"What are you doing?" he asks.

"I didn't seriously expect you to carry me the whole way. What am I to do if you pass out?"

"I won't."

"I can't risk that. Good bodyguards are hard to come by these days."

"You're finally admitting your want for me?"

No. I will not—shall not, cannot—admit any want for Rhett Kaiser.

"You might be mildly better than whatever forty-year-old will likely have to take your place."

"Fair."

"Race?"

"There's no chance of you—"

I splash water in his face before I'm swimming away harder than I ever have before. I used to do laps in our pool frequently and pretend there was a shark on my heels to surge my adrenaline faster. It's not far from the truth now, when the thought of Rhett catching up gives a similar effect.

He grabs my ankle when I'm just shy of reaching the buoy, and I barely get to scream before I'm dragged underwater. Rhett's strong arms pull me up just as quickly, and I clamp myself around him, pushing the hair out of my face and laughing like a child being caught. Saltwater stings my eyes, and it takes a moment to blink his face into focus.

Distant cheering breaks out on the shore, and I see the crowd of people watching our forfeit. Rhett holds the buoy as we float, watching me with a softness I've never seen before. I do something so impulsive. Unwarranted. With him this close I don't know what comes over me, but I bring my head down and kiss him.

Immediately I realize what I've done and pull away, but his hand reaches around my nape to hold me there. Then he's kissing me back. I'm sliding a hand into his hair and moaning softly into his mouth as my fingers tighten.

"Ana," he groans, pained, against my lips.

My heart slams in my chest. "Sorry," I say, a little breathless from the unexpected kiss.

I have no excuse for it. No press to blame.

"Race back?" I say, needing to get the hell away from him.

"Ana—"

I let go of him before he can finish and focus all my efforts on the burn of swimming back, trying not to give in to the desire to drown instead to avoid the awkwardness of what I've done.

CHAPTER 13
Rhett

The hotel is buzzing for the presidential debate as I guide Ana into the auditorium and find our seats. I'm too focused and alert on our surroundings. There's not a single set of eyes that land on Ana that I don't know about. But I have other plans for this event that make my skin itch at the thought of leaving her. Once the debate starts she'll be safe here, in a room completely surrounded by security, and Rix will have eyes on her for me at all times through the camera feeds.

Ana is damn impeccable in her tight formal black dress and the contrasting red heels that match her belt. She's nervous, scratching at her fingers, and I take her hand absentmindedly.

"He's going to be great," I say in her ear.

She nods. "He's been working so hard on this."

Ana's admiration and pride for her father is priceless.

"Hey, Ana," a man says on her other side, taking up the vacant seat next to her.

Now I really don't want to fucking leave.

"Matthew!" she says in surprise. "I didn't know you were flying out for this. Is Liam here?"

Liam and Matthew Forbes. Gregory's sons. This guy is older than me at thirty-one. I already know everything I need to know about him from Xoid.

"No, he's still in New York. I had some free time and thought this was worth seeing in person."

Ana isn't fully comfortable with him. Friendly, familiar, sure. But she doesn't realize she's leaned closer to me a fraction as if anticipating Matthew will invade her space more than she'd like. That's enough for me to not trust him.

Matthew's eyes flick up to me then, and they dampen enthusiasm. The feeling is more than fucking mutual. I don't like the way he looks at her. Ana is a sight worth any jewel, but he has an attention for her as if she's here for his bidding.

"This is Rhett Kaiser, my boyfriend." She introduces me.

Damn right, I am.

"So I've heard," Matthew says.

"And this is Matthew Forbes," Ana says to me.

I have to act like I don't know this guy's social security number and the brand of shoes he buys as I give a tight nod in acknowledgment. Luckily, we're spared from conversation as the announcer walks onstage and the cameras start to roll.

Again, I don't want to leave, but I can't pass up this opportunity. Everyone is in this room. Sullevan, Forbes, Kinsley. All the security is locked down around us. It's the perfect chance for me to see if there's anything of remote interest in Sullevan's room.

Ana checks her purse for her phone, confused as she remembers putting it in there, but she didn't notice me take it right back out before we left.

"Damn, I must have left my phone. I wanted to get photos," she whispers.

"I'll be right back with it," I say quietly, pressing a kiss to her head. Before she can object I'm slipping away.

Last night I left my room for a half hour to swipe the master key card I need to access any room I want. I have Sullevan's room pinned—two floors above ours—and I head up, fitting my modified AirPod in.

"Cameras?" I ask Rix. He's Jeremy's older brother and my best security hacker.

"Cut in the elevator, about to hit the hallway."

It will look like a mere glitch, nothing suspicious. I don't know what I might find, so I can't risk leaving any trace of me being where I shouldn't. As far as security will see, I left that auditorium and hit a blind spot before heading to the bathroom for a damn long piss.

"Have you noticed anything through the feeds over the weekend?"

"Nope," he says, sounding like his mouth is half-full. "They've been relaxing almost as much as you have."

I make no comment. The game this afternoon was unexpected. The feel of having Ana wrapped around me, back then front, is something I can't stop thinking about in *very* sinful ways. How pretty she would look held in my arms, pressed up against a wall while I devoured her. Ana's body . . . *Fuck*, I can't shake it from my mind. "Perfect" doesn't cut it; seeing it isn't enough. I need to touch and claim every piece of her and it's been driving me to madness. The things I would do for a taste.

The elevator chimes and I adjust my hardening dick with my drifting thoughts.

"904," Rix says.

"I know."

The key card works, and I take the black handkerchief from my suit pocket to open the door. The penthouse is more lavish than our rooms, which are already pretty damn expensive. The senator has multiple rooms, and I gravitate to the office-looking space that could double as a meeting room. Papers litter the table, and I'm careful as I drift around, looking but not touching yet. Naturally, it's all shit to do with the debate and Sullevan's campaign.

"What's the guy Matthew's deal?" Rix mumbles between eating.

I stiffen. "What do you mean?"

"Does he have a history with her or something?"

"Why do you ask?"

"He seems . . . close."

"What the fuck does that mean?"

"Woah, shit, I just mean she seems stiff. It's nothing though. Just a graze here and there. I can't tell if he actually means it."

He fucking means it all right. This asshole has a thing for Ana, and that wavers my focus. No. It drives me to want to scour this place faster so I can get right back down there.

"The room has a safe, usually located in the bedroom," Rix informs me.

When I get there he recites the hotel-given code and I unlock it. Inside is more paperwork, a gun, and a credit card. Ironically, the paper is the most valuable thing in here. Certificates of authenticity for jewelry that could sell for a healthy early retirement. I take pictures and send them straight to Rix.

"Get me a trace on these. Allie might be of help here."

Rix scoffs. "I'll get the trace. Her rich-people connections are a cheat."

Their rivalry is all friendly competitiveness. They don't even know what the other looks like.

The next paper I find is the deeds to a small, secluded mansion back in D.C.

"I need a check on a home too. Looks like it belongs to Rolf Sullevan."

"You got it. Uh-oh . . ."

"What?"

"I swear I only looked away from her for a second. Little bird is flying. Let me just find— *Shit*."

"Rix."

"She's knocking on your door."

Dammit, Ana.

I shove the papers back and swiftly head out, counting on Rix to be cutting the cameras as I head down two floors.

"She's in her room. I imagine getting to yours through it."

"Goodbye, Rix."

"You're welco—!"

I pull out the earpiece and pocket it just as Ana comes back out. She's holding her phone and does a double-take when she sees me. Well, shit. Time to wrangle my way out of this.

"Ana," I drawl, shaking my head. "We need to have a chat about how not to leave the highest-security room without me."

"I'm not without you—that's the point," she quips. I find her fire intoxicating. All poised and breakable on the outside, but it's what's on the inside that sinks its claws into me.

"You're missing your father's debate."

"I'm sure I'll get to watch the recap. I'm only really here for family press photos. United front and all." She folds her arms as I approach.

"I'm supposed to be protecting you, so why did you leave in search of me?"

"You were taking too long. Where were you?" Ana pointedly holds up her phone. I don't know why I find this dance amusing.

"Again, it's my job to know *your* whereabouts. And you like to make that difficult." I close in on her personal space and she backs up in surprise until I have her against the door with a hand by her head. Though it catches her off-guard, she's not so easily distracted.

I come up with the best excuse I can in the moment.

"I went to the bathroom, then there was a lonely woman needing help with her bags out front and I stayed there until her Uber came."

I've lied and killed my way out of so many problems that my list of sins is sure to earn me the role of right-hand man to the devil. But I don't like lying to Ana. It unsettles me. Irritatingly. Infuriatingly. Something I find as easy as breathing now torments me with the want to take my lies back and show her all my dark and bloody truths. I'd watch her run, only to chase her and find some sadistic thrill in it all before she caves to me.

"How chivalrous of you," Ana says. She tries to hide the note of jealousy, but it's too fucking bad I find it sexy as hell.

"Damsels are my weakness." I play along.

"Then you're out of luck here," she says, pushing my chest and walking away. I could fall to my knees for her right here. "I'll leave you to damsel-watch in the foyer."

CHAPTER 14
Rhett

Ana is studying in her room when I'm called to meet her father. Senator Kinsley won the presidential debate in Cali last week and his campaign has been thriving since. I haven't stopped thinking about that trip. Specifically, the image of Ana in her bikini and how irresistible she looked playing volleyball. She looked so good I'm envious not to have been a spectator instead.

When she kissed me in the water I came close to abandoning all thought and reason with her. If she hadn't swam away so fast . . . I don't know what I might have done. We didn't speak of it, and I hate that I'm tormented with the thought she either regrets it or it meant nothing. I can't decide what's worse. I need to be keeping Ana at arm's length even though my resistance is weakening. She's pushing every boundary and moral I set against her, shortening the distance I should keep from her. I can only hope she's come to her senses again. A little bird would not survive in my world.

Senator Kinsley is sitting behind his desk focused on his computer when I'm granted permission to enter. I don't hold the best respect for anyone in politics when I've seen the most vile side of corruption through these very roots. I'm starting to admire Ana's father, but perhaps my admiration is swayed by her influence. So I'm praying my work here over and above protecting his daughter won't turn up anything that'll make him my enemy.

"The fall charity carnival is happening next week. My campaign team will have a stall, and we think it would be good for our image if Anastasia attends. To show participation, community, and kindness."

In other words, he wants to use his daughter once again to make himself look good.

It's not often the running presidents' children are active in their campaigns, but Ana and the annoying thorn that is Adam Sullevan are of ideal age and have been making a great impact already. I can see why continuing their involvement has the potential to sway people's votes. Anastasia is in every way fit to be America's Darling, winning hearts with her smile, her charm, and her easy nature that makes everyone fall.

"Have you asked her, sir?" I hedge.

She doesn't like attention or spotlight. This carnival might be okay since she won't be placed on a stage or have the focus on her. And she'll have me.

"Not yet. I wanted to get your approval as her security. To keep her *relatable* to the people, we're hoping you'll be comfortable being her only guard."

Comfortable? I'm fucking ecstatic that he trusts me so highly with his daughter.

"Of course. Anastasia's safety is my highest concern and greatest privilege."

The senator smiles—a smile that dances the line between personal and professional, and I should be rejoicing. Everything is going to plan. It's slow work, but if I manage to find what I need it'll be fucking worth it. Without sounding like a sad, pining fool, part of me already finds this whole thing worth it to have found a small light in the darkness that's shrouded me for three years.

The senator's intercom buzzes and his assistant's voice chimes through. "There's a delivery for you, sir."

His ruddy skin pulls together on his brow. He wasn't expecting the interruption.

"You'll have to excuse me, Agent Kaiser. I'll only be a moment and then we can straighten out the details."

I nod and watch his back as he leaves. The moment the doors click shut, I glance up at the security camera in the corner of the room just as the green light tuns off.

"We've only got six minutes at best," Rix says in my ear.

"I only need three," I reply, already around the other side of the desk, filtering through the files. One cabinet is locked. "Make that four."

Bending, I make quick work with my lock-picking kit.

Twenty seconds. Not my best.

The victorious click is fucking music to my ears.

I find a lot of highly confidential shit. Presidential schedules, voting predictions, contacts. Nothing that stands out as nefarious, however. I'm growing beyond frustrated to be continuously turning up nothing.

"Three minutes, Kaiser," Rix warns.

"Self-proclaimed best hacker and you can only stall the cameras for six minutes?"

"Self-proclaimed best lockpick and it took you thirty seconds?"

"Twenty. Your counting needs work."

He grunts down the phone. "Try finding someone else who can even hack into them in the first place. It took me well over a week!"

That's torture to someone who can typically hack a surveillance system within an hour.

I smirk, only teasing him as a distraction from my adrenaline. Keeps me focused. Pulling out a folder for the probable vice president, Gregory Forbes, I take my phone out and snap a picture of his profile, then one of his background. We've already looked into him, but I can't shake my suspicion.

"Uh-oh, never mind the cameras. Little bird is flying, and she's about to bust your ass in twenty seconds."

Shit. I slam the drawer shut and just manage to lock it again in time.

Ana stumbles as she enters, and I'm just coming around the edge of the desk, perhaps marginally too far around it for her not to speculate, when she catches me.

"Finished your studies?" I ask, leaning against the other side of it and folding my arms.

She's too damn observant—an invaluable asset, albeit a hindrance to my sleuthing—and for a second I think she's about to ask what I was doing.

"Where's my father?"

"He stepped out."

Ana looks across to the other door, and I want desperately to know what she's thinking. Puzzling.

"He must really trust you," she says, but her tone doesn't release me from suspicion. "He doesn't even like me lingering in here alone."

"Have you been saying nice things about me?"

She huffs a playful laugh, enticing me with those stunning hazel eyes. "I'm not to make your job easy, remember?"

"I'm still waiting for the challenge, little bird."

She bites her lip, and the thoughts I've had of her because of it are thinning my resistance. My fingers clench around the edge of the desk. How pretty she would look bent over it with her ass bare for me. Something tells me she'd enjoy the depravity, that she'd fuck me hard with all the passion she bottles up inside.

I stand straight, subtly adjusting myself at my sinful thoughts. Letting her hear them would likely have me transferred.

She says, "The worst is yet to come, Agent."

I fucking bet. She's going to drive me to madness. Perhaps I'm already there, though I'm supposed to be fully committed to my alternate mission here. Yet she occupies more of my headspace that I care to admit. I worry about her. I've made the mistake of *caring* about her. More than what's necessary in my post as her guard.

"Do you have something in store for me today?" I ask.

A flush colors her cheeks and I want to trace my fingers along it. Every thought I have of her isn't without a crash of guilt from the ghost of my past, but I decide I deserve the pain. Maybe I even enjoy it. I haven't felt this alive in three years. So I feed my insatiable hunger over her piece by piece, like sadistic torture.

"Not exactly. I came to ask if you want to watch a movie with me. If I have to keep reading about the history of the American language tonight I might go insane."

"We can't have that," I say, gravitating closer. "As your guard, I insist you take the night off to avoid risk."

She doesn't know what she's doing to me with those eyes. Holding me as if she's casting some damn spell in them and has me at her utter mercy.

"It's my turn to guess," she says in a tone so low and seductive but just subtle enough. "You look like an action movie kind of guy. Does it count as training if you watch crime in movies?"

I chuckle. Fuck, I want to pull her to me with the way she riles a thrill in me.

"Does it count as experience if you watch sex in movies?"

"I don't think anyone would have a good sex life if their expectations were based on movies."

I change the subject, at risk of getting rock-hard. There would be no disguising it in these suit pants. She's a sinful temptation.

"It's fall. Are you afraid of scary movies? I promise to check under your bed before you sleep."

She gives an adorable scoff. "I'm surprised you don't already."

I ease a devious smile, which makes her lips part and her eyes widen a fraction.

"No, you don't . . ."

I merely shrug, not bothering to confirm or deny.

Just then the senator returns, doing a double-take at the sight of Ana before his cheeks split with a father's grin. "I'm glad you're here, Anastasia," he says, sitting back in his chair with a new set of papers I try to catch a glimpse of. Rix might have better luck through the cameras if he manages to hold a feed. "I was just talking to Agent Kaiser about you attending the state fall carnival where we have a campaign booth."

She crosses her arms. "What if I don't want to go?"

"I won't force you, but it would be very advantageous to have you seen more. Appeal to the people. This campaign will be tight and we could use all the help we can get."

Ana relaxes with a sigh. She doesn't want to go, not if she's to be a public figure there, but her close relationship with her father has always been evident. She wants him to win this election no matter what it means for her.

"Fine. I'll go. But only because I'm craving cotton candy and popcorn."

I don't know when it started to happen, but my heart reacts to this woman's every whim.

Her father promises to brief her on what to expect before the carnival next week, and we leave, heading for the cinema room. It's impressive, with four large single seats at the front and two doubles at the back. I flash the thought of how perfect she would feel curled up against me on those particular seats, but we both come around to the front. Ana presses a button on the wall that begins to roll down a projector screen before she plucks the controller and tosses it to me.

"I get to pick?" I ask.

"We'll be here until morning if I try," she teases.

It's strange that I enjoy that about her. Her indecisiveness. She has a wild side that's caged in this life, just waiting to be set free. All she needs is the right encouragement.

"If you fall asleep you owe me," I say, choosing a horror movie called "Insidious."

"Owe you what?" she asks, flopping down after retrieving two blankets and throwing one at me.

"I haven't decided yet."

"That is not how it works."

"Do we have a deal?"

She rolls her eyes, getting comfortable, and she's the most adorable sight I don't want to tear my eyes from. Ana looks beyond sexy in a dress. She's breathtaking in her style for college, but this version of her in an off-the-shoulder oversize sweater, leggings, and fluffy socks, with her hair piled high messily, is so irresistible I have this pathetic desire to hold her.

"Fine, but if you fall asleep I'm blowing your salary for the month at the carnival."

I chuckle. "Deal."

About halfway through I win. When Ana's eyes close for too long I turn down the volume of the movie. I knew she wouldn't last the moment she sat down. Her fatigue was obvious. All the reading she did in her studies tonight finally caught up with her.

I sigh as I stand. She looks comfortable as hell, but I can't leave her here, and those chairs are certainly not big enough for me to enjoy a decent rest like her. Scooping her up with the blanket, I make it up the second step before she moans in protest.

"I wasn't sleeping," she mumbles.

"You're still sleeping," I counter with a smile.

She peels her eyes open then. "I want to stay. The movie isn't finished."

I pause next to the two-person seats, debating. I really shouldn't. My guilt aside, she's the probable president's daughter—a job. I'm a lie to her, and I've already crossed a few boundaries I swore I wouldn't.

"Rhett, please." She pouts.

Internally groaning, I cross the small space and set her down, but she doesn't let me go.

"You're very comfortable despite looking like a boulder."

"A boulder?"

"A nice one."

Ana scoots up the deep couch before patting the space next to her. "I won't scandalize you. Promise." She smirks at my hesitation.

It's official. Anastasia Kinsley is going to be the fucking death of me.

I stretch out beside her, and this position is far more comfortable than the single seat. I keep a gap between us, but Ana makes that difficult when her head angles down toward me while she curls up. A little while later, I can't help but notice her subtly drawing the blanket to her eyes every time the music turns suspenseful. I smile stupidly to myself, and before she can do it again I decide to be cruel and snatch the blanket from her.

Ana gasps, shooting upright, and her fright turns to a scowl as I hold the blanket out of reach. She tries again, planting a hand to my chest as I remain reclining, but my arm is too long for her reach. When she straddles me, not giving up in her defiance, I realize my error in provoking her.

My hand holding the blanket slackens. The other grips her hip as if she might lose balance as she all but presses her whole body to mine to snatch it back. With her victory our position seems to crash us back into reality. She looks down and our faces come so close.

I can't stop the compulsion that steals me in that second. The drug I've become so silently and unwittingly addicted to that now it's right in front of me, how am I to fucking resist? There's no willpower in the world that can stop the hand I slip over her jaw, bringing her head to mine in a collision that's as euphoric as it is a lashing of punishment. For wanting her. For caving to her.

Ana moans in the back of her throat and I turn wild for her, deepening the kiss to taste more. Her slender fingers on my chest clench my shirt, and I explode with the need she has for me too.

There's nothing searching or tender in the kiss that's unleashed between us. It's more than I've fantasized about, and if this is what she's giving now, holy fuck, I won't survive having all of her. But she's mine. Even if I can never fully have her, Ana is mine. It's a twisted contradiction, but I don't fucking care. I'll taste her now and find the damn will later to resist.

Her hips grind against me, and I know if I don't stop her I'll be too far gone in a few minutes. *Just. A little. More.* My cock is fucking aching, and Ana becomes breathy, chasing her pleasure against me.

"You can use me," I say huskily, removing my hands from her hair to plant them on her hips and press her tighter to my erection. She whimpers, her brow pinching in desire, and she's so damn exquisite.

I can give her this. It will be enough just to watch her climax against me. I already have my place staked in hell, and she's worth damnation.

"Rhett."

Fuck. The little breathy moan of my name nearly makes me come in my pants like a teen.

This isn't for me. This is for her.

"Just like that, baby," I whisper across her exposed collarbone before planting my lips there. Then my teeth.

She cries out, and I have to lift a hand to her mouth to suppress it.

"Shh," I say, returning to her neck now I've found a favorite spot. "If you can't do this quietly I'll have to punish you."

Her hands tighten in my hair as her movements turn more desperate. "Please," she begs. The most perfect sound.

"Please, what?"

"I need it."

"Then take it, baby. It's yours."

I suck on her neck and she bites down on my hand, which only drives me to the brink as well. Her hold is as painful as her bite, and I love this wild unleashing of her. She moves those hips like a damn goddess, finding the spot that knocks her sensitive clit just right each time. Her rhythm is mesmerizing. I resist the urge to slip my hand down to her pussy. No—she began chasing her pleasure against me, and now she's going to work for it.

"You can do better," I whisper against her neck. "You can take it harder."

I aid the press of her against me, delirious with the wave of her movements under my palms.

"Oh god," she rasps.

"You're using my cock, Ana, not his. Say my fucking name."

"I'm going to— *Rhett!*"

"Good girl," I praise, circling an arm around her as she begins to tremble, and I claim her mouth against the shattering cry of her climax.

Maybe there is a god to pray to, since Ana's orgasm is as close to a religious experience as I'll ever come.

Ana catches her breath with her head buried in my neck. This small, tender moment in the aftermath I want to hold suspended in time.

"Are you okay?" she asks.

My fucking heart.

"You are perfect," I whisper. Even though it makes me sick with resentment for myself that I'd think this of another woman.

There was once something perfect in my life, a person who was mine, and she's dead because of me. Above my guilt that I feel anything but glacial vengeance and grief, I'm unexpectedly terrified for Ana. I shouldn't have let this happen. But I don't regret a damn thing when it brought her this pleasure. I can give her that. Nothing more.

"Can I take you to bed now, little bird?"

She nods, not removing her arms from my neck, nor her legs from around me. So that's how I lift her, keeping the blanket wrapped around her. She's so fucking precious in my arms. I hope her parents have gone to bed, because this looks highly inappropriate for an agent and their daughter, even if she does appear to be sleeping with her cheek pressed into my shoulder. No one spots us, and I take her right to her bed, where she finally lets go.

"No regrets?" I ask, wary of how uncomfortable she's starting to look.

"I feel like I should be asking you that," she answers quietly.

She deserves an answer, but I don't have one. I'm already harboring too many lies from her, so I could at least be open about my damn feelings. But I don't want to feel anything. The past three years have passed angry and numb and vengeful. Now there's a warmth threatening the promise I made all that time ago, that I would never allow myself to find happiness again. Especially not while Alistair Lanshall lives.

"Good night, Ana," I say, straightening away from her—but as I turn I don't miss the drop of disappointment on her face. It lodges like a bullet in me.

Good. I want it to fucking hurt. One day I'll get to explain everything to her—who I am, what I've done—and she'll be glad she was spared from falling for a monster.

CHAPTER 15
Anastasia

Ever since what happened in the cinema room last week there's been a distance between me and Rhett. He still takes my hand—like now, walking to class. He's still charming in ways that would make any woman swoon. But he's back to touching me as little as possible when I believed he was starting to relax around me.

I shouldn't have risked that for a quick thrill. Even though he kissed me first. If I'd stopped it, perhaps there wouldn't be this tension that I can't fully shake.

At first I felt guilty, but as the days pass I begin to grow frustrated. Angry. It was the best orgasm of my life and he's acting like it was nothing. Discovering the words that can come from his mouth . . . *Oh boy, I'm in trouble.* It was only a sample of his dominance, his possessiveness, and now I'm pathetically yearning for it again, but the line between us has thickened more than before.

When we sit in the lecture hall for first class I cross my legs the opposite way from him, not realizing it's always felt more natural to be turned toward him until now. He doesn't try to place his hand on my thigh, and that only riles me more. I occupy my hands with books to avoid holding his until midday, and when it comes to lunch I barely speak to him, only picking an apple and a bottle of water before paying for myself and heading to sit with Riley.

It may be childish, but if he's going to treat me as merely his thing to guard, I'm going to act like it. Rhett sparked something inside me only to become the reason it's quickly dying out with his coldness.

"Are you going to the carnival tonight?" I ask Riley, taking a bite of my apple. I'm not really hungry with my storm of emotions.

Riley eyes the space beside me. Her observation that something is wrong isn't subtle. She reads my eyes, but even though I'm turned away from Rhett I don't want to explain.

"Yeah, a few of us were thinking of going. You're still going, aren't you?" Riley answers.

I nod. "I might have to do a few jobs at my dad's stall, but then I plan to ditch. Can I text you to hang out?"

"Of course! We were going to meet up to participate in the corn maze around five."

I turn giddy at the thought, glad to have my friend to bring back some excitement. I love the maze. The panic of getting lost and the puzzle of finding my way out with the map.

"I'll meet you there then," I agree.

Rhett doesn't speak the whole time. He keeps his AirPod in on one side as usual, and now and then he glances at his watch or at the security camera. It's starting to become weird.

If he wants hell, it's about time I give him some.

I leave the cafeteria, heading to a theatre hall. Just outside I spin to him.

"I have to chat to a professor about something. Stay here," I say.

"Not happening."

"I wasn't asking."

Rhett's eyes twinkle with their first hint of amusement in days, and I'm ready to claw them out.

"It's private."

"What could you possibly need to say about literature assignments that I can't hear?"

"That's none of your business. My life and prospects are not a show for you to observe."

"Ana—"

"Stay here, Agent Kaiser. I won't forgive you if you follow me in."

I push through the door without another word, and when it closes behind me I wait. Mercifully, he doesn't follow.

The room is empty, and I shoot up the stairs and exit out the back. I plucked the spare jeep key this morning, and I'm so twistedly thrilled just imagining Rhett's anger when he realizes I've left him without a ride.

My adrenaline pumps hot and fast, as if he's chasing me at this very moment, and I run across the parking lot before throwing myself inside the jeep and speeding off. I check the mirrors even when I'm a long way away from the university as if he'll come speeding to catch up in another car. I wouldn't put grand theft auto past him for this.

I don't go home. Instead I drive to a quieter part of the city twenty minutes away. When I pull up at the side of the road, only then does my breathing start to calm. I get out, slinging my jacket on and making a note that I would appreciate a scarf, maybe some gloves, with the temperature lowering in the fall.

This spot I only know because of one person, Nina Temsworth, and she's gone. It overlooks the city, and I enjoy the view knowing how bustling it is down there. I sit above it all in peaceful observance.

Missing Nina is like a passing season; it always comes around. And I'll always have hope she'll come back and I'll forgive her for leaving without a goodbye. I would understand no matter her reasons when her life was so difficult.

I can't stay here for long because of the carnival later, but I only want to make Rhett angry—even though it's a different kind from what's upsetting me. I want to be patient with him, or at least understand if he wants nothing more from me, but he's so damn confusing, hot-and-cold, it's messing with my head.

Somewhere along his line of duty I've grown attached to his presence. I could have lived with it only ever being in friendship . . . until he kissed me. For real this time, in the cinema room. Why did he have to do that? Now I don't want to imagine the end of his post, saying goodbye. I can't imagine him as just a friend who might text or call to check in once in a while when I'm no longer his problem. It *hurts*.

A car passes behind me. Then it stops. There is no way he could have—

The door slams shut as a clear announcement that it's who I imagine it is. I turn around. Rhett has never looked more pissed off than now, as his Uber leaves and he storms toward me.

"How the hell did you find me so fast?" I accuse.

Rhett's expression is so scarily furious I should be afraid. He marches forward like he won't pause and will instead slam into me. Yet as much as I back into the hood of the jeep and he erases all personal space, all that drums in my chest is thrill and anticipation. He plants his hands on either side of me, leaning in so close.

"Did you think that was daring, leaving without me?" he asks in a tone that makes my whole body shiver and tighten. "Did you think it was smart? Amusing?"

"I thought it was about time you worked for your damn job."

There's nothing kind in his slow smile and the way he searches my face. As if contemplating how to devour me.

"I see how it is," he says, toeing the line between danger and seduction. "You like games; I like to win. You like to run; I love to fucking chase. Keep trying, little bird. I'll happily indulge in your fire. Cause me pain and watch as I take it with pleasure."

"What do you want from me, Rhett?" I snap.

"Everything. I want absolutely everything from you, and I can hardly stand it."

I shake my head. "Then stop pushing me away."

"Life's true cruelty is always having something we want desperately that was never meant to be ours."

"You can't say that when you're not even trying," I grind out the last word, pushing his chest, but he catches my wrists, pulling me to him and not letting go. Our stare-off radiates with hate. "You're a fucking coward, Rhett Kaiser."

His eyes flex and his jaw shifts, but I don't think I'll ever be afraid of him no matter how frightening he appearance or how hard I push him to brink of snapping, and maybe that's why I do it. I'm so desperate for him to break to find out what it would take to tend to the pieces.

"Careful, Ana."

"Or what?"

He lets go of my wrists only to slide his palms across my

cheeks. "Every time you run you get closer to learning why you should never stop."

My retort dies under the ringing of my cell. I push Rhett, who yields as I fish my cell out of my jeans pocket. Seeing the FaceTime ID, my mood switches with whiplash as I gasp.

"Liam!" I squeal, glad to see a friendly face right now.

Rhett frowns down at my hand, and I scowl as I pace away to talk.

"Hey, Ana. I warned you I wouldn't be good with pictures, so I figured this would make up for it." He flips the camera to show he's standing in Times Square.

"Can you order my kidnap? I want to be there too," I whine.

Liam chuckles as his bright, handsome face comes back onscreen. "The new guard that bad, huh? I hope you're making him work hard."

My eyes flick up to Rhett, who's leaning against the jeep watching me. He gives no reaction, but my cheeks heat. He certainly went above and beyond in his *job* the other night.

"He's . . . fine. But the idea I need one is still ridiculous," I mutter under my breath as I try to gain enough distance to talk privately.

"Agent Victor Ross, right?"

"No, uh, there was an accident. I got a replacement."

Liam frowns deeply. "Who?"

Rhett calls over quietly. "We need to go. The carnival starts in two hours."

I internally groan. "I have to go. My dad is using me to 'appeal to the people' at the fall carnival tonight."

Liam grins at my ire, running a hand through his dark hair. "Go charm the masses, beautiful. You could single-handedly win the country's heart if you really tried."

I scoff. "Yeah, right."

When we hang up, his absence sweeps in with a lonely echo.

Rhett drives us home. For the first time I leave the car before he has the chance to slip out and make it around to my door. Locking myself in my room, I read for the first hour, get sour at the carefree, adorable romance in the fiction that usually has me swooning, and spend the rest of the time getting ready.

Knowing there could be photos, I keep scrutinizing myself in the mirror. I wear fall colors: a tight deep maroon skirt with black tights and over-the-knee boots, a long white coat, and a scarf and hat to match my skirt since the night will be cold. Should I put more makeup on? I only touched up the little I wore for classes, but wondering how I'll look in pictures is driving me to overthink.

A soft knock sounds at my door. When I don't answer and Rhett doesn't stroll in as he usually does anyway, I frown. I must have really pissed him off earlier.

I swing it open, and the guy on the opposite side winces at my scowl of a reception. My face smooths out.

"Miss Kinsley, I have to take you to the carnival," he says politely. A man in his late thirties, I would guess.

"Where's Rhett?"

"Agent Kaiser was called away for a few hours. He said to tell you he'll meet you at the maze at five o'clock."

He . . . left me? Even if it is only for a few hours I don't know why my stomach sinks. I'm annoyed with him, upset with him, but I need him tonight of all nights.

I realize I've made a mistake all at once. I let him in, close enough to become something comfortable, when I knew it was wrong. Both for his job and his life. I'm wrong for him. Not able to ever make up for the loss he suffered, and I should know better.

I shut my door and head out. I don't need Rhett Kaiser. I ride in the back of the large SUV with black-tinted windows feeling more than ever the pressure of who I am because of my father. My thumb bleeds into my mouth as I chew on it, watching out the window, switching to the other when it stings too badly.

I do not need Rhett Kaiser.

CHAPTER 16
Rhett

I don't want to be here. I don't want to be anywhere that isn't by Ana's fucking side. But the window of opportunity is too small and too rare to pass up. I have to make peace with the fact that while I'm not with her to protect her, following this lead is every bit to do with her safety as much as my vengeance.

"What's taking so long?" I hiss into the earpiece. Disguised as an AirPod, I wear it pretty much at all times, but it's altered to an impressively high spec for communicating with various channels so I can tap into people in my network.

My guise is shed and I'm clad like an assassin: masked, hooded, and crouching just beyond the front lawn of Rolf Sullevan's estate—the one I discovered the deeds to in his hotel room.

"Sorry, man, pizza came," Rix says, out of breath as if he just rushed back. "Before you send someone to cut my balls off, I've been waiting on a bypass window in the server anyway."

My patience is paper-thin, and that makes me a danger to anyone in my path.

"How much longer?" I grunt.

"Two minutes, give or take. You remember the blind spots in case I get kicked out?"

A branch snaps behind me and I have my gun pointed at the intruder in a breath.

"Fuck. Shit. It's me!" Jeremy whisper-yells.

When he gets close enough I grab the front of his jacket.

"You didn't think to tell me your brother was coming before I blew his fucking brains out?" I hiss into the earpiece.

"That little shit," Rix mutters, his anger making it clear his little brother didn't tell him either.

I speak to the teen with a lethal warning. "You ever pull this kind of shit again, you're off the whole damn network."

"Okay, okay, but you're going to be glad I came," he says, hardly fazed by me. I can't decide if it's irritating or admirable. Perhaps I've been too easy on the kid.

"This is it. Entry in about sixty seconds," Rix informs me.

I pull out my phone, tapping into a secure and invisible tracking app I coded myself. It's been in Ana's phone since the minute she gave it to me. I knew the little bird would try to fly from me at some point. It thrills me to no end she's growing the courage to leave her cage daringly, but she's never getting away from me.

As expected, she's nearing the carnival. It kills me not to be with her when she's trying to disguise her nerves for the event, but I won't be long. We found this secret manor a week ago, but it's always closely guarded. Until tonight. Rolf Sullevan has left the State and we've discovered this place will be vacant tonight.

Jeremy says, "So I was actually following a lead I didn't think would go anywhere, so I didn't bother telling you guys. You said the senator doesn't know about the threat to his daughter, but he does. He met with someone tonight. Not secret service or any of the other official organizations. This guy was part of Ketos."

I curse. Ketos is a highly advanced private investigation group. They're morally grey in their methods, a highly guarded organization. Almost like us. Except while they only bend the laws, we break them, set fire to them, and dance in the ashes. I've worked with them before, but they're an untrustworthy bunch and think far too highly of themselves.

"Why would he not report it to the secret service?" I wonder.

"Green light. You have fifteen minutes. Maybe twenty, but best not push the devil's luck," Rix says.

I pull my mask on fully, not taking any risks. We keep silent, but to his credit, Jeremy is laser-focused on my signals. It takes me thirty seconds to unlock the back door. *I'm losing my damn touch.*

"Oh, did I mention the two dogs?" Rix informs me casually.

"No, you didn't," I grumble under my breath.

A low growl vibrates the silence, standing the hairs on my nape.

"Let me get that for you," Rix says, and low light floods the room.

My eyes drop. The two tiny dogs that look more like naked rats start wagging their tails.

"Aww!" Jeremy gushes, leaning down to them.

Rix chuckles in my ear. "Think you can handle them, boss?"

"Where am I going, Rix? I don't have time for this."

The sooner I get to Ana, the better.

"Second floor, third door on the left."

I leave Jeremy occupied with the dogs while I head up. In the office I survey for where to start. The desk would be too obvious, too risky, for anything nefarious. The walls are all lined neatly.

No shelves, only evenly spaced backlit panels glowing blue. My hand runs along them, tapping each one, until . . .

Bingo.

One is hollow. My fingers brush along the gaps and find a trigger. It pops out the panel, which I slide to reveal a safe fitted behind it.

"Any guesses on Sullevan's lucky six numbers?" I mutter.

"Could be any of a million combinations. Where's Jeremy?" Rix answers.

"Step aside. You know I can best you at getting into that thing." Jeremy saunters into the room carrying both chihuahuas. He coos at them before setting them down, turning from a boy to a focused machine like the flip of a switch as he reaches into his pocket, producing a small kit, and bends to get to work.

"How long do we have?" I ask.

"Ten minutes is pushing it," Rix says.

I pace, trying not to watch the kid at work when I'm bound to snap with impatience and nerves.

It takes him six minutes to delicately remove the keypad and rewire it before victory clicks loud. I spin at the sound, eyes fixed on the space when the door opens. There are two guns this time and some jewelry boxes. Jeremy opens one large black velvet box and whistles.

"It's gotta be worth over a million." He inspects the waterfall of diamonds on the necklace.

There are three other boxes inside the safe, but what I'm interested in is the brown folder underneath them. My gloved hand reaches in, pulling it out and flipping it open. It's pictures. I've seen some dark and haunting shit in my career, but it never gets easier to see. Beaten women, frightened children. People being herded and photographed like cattle. I want to burn this whole fucking house to the ground.

"Trafficking," I say to Rix.

"Shit," he mutters. We were hoping for something like drugs, but this isn't so surprising.

Under the photographs are names, dates, locations. It's a damn gold mine. An itinerary for this stem of a far larger operation.

"This is a stopover house." I relay what I can find at a glimpse, but I take photos.

"You gotta get out of there, man," Rix warns.

A key slips out of the envelope and my heart drops to my fucking ass. *Are there victims in the house right now?*

I check my watch. Half past four and I promised my little bird I'd meet her at five.

Shit.

"I can't hold the cameras any longer before it trips an alarm," Rix stresses.

I take pictures of the jewelry and send them to Allie.

"Close it up," I say to Jeremy.

He nods, swiftly rewiring and screwing the keypad back into place after I return the documents.

I keep the key.

"Blind spots, you fuckers, now!" Rix snaps.

I pull Jeremy into the hall, sprinting into the main room just as the green lights of the cameras come back on and Rix cuts the lights again. We stand deathly still in a corner the cameras can't see.

"Fuck. Shit. Motherfuckers," Rix curses colorfully in my ear.

"What is it?" I hiss.

"You got company. A black SUV—driver and passenger from what I can see."

Jeremy may have been a great help with opening the safe and getting the intel, but right now I'm livid he's here at all. I don't care about the danger to myself—I don't doubt my ability to get out of here even if it comes to a confrontation. But accounting for his safety is enough to let damning fear trickle in.

"Follow me and do exactly as I say," I tell him.

He nods sharply.

Crouching, I dart to the kitchen island, making my way around it before slipping over to the back glass sliding doors. We're able to leave, and we got what we came for. Yet as Jeremy slips out, I close the door and lock it.

With me still on the inside.

The teen's eyes widen in protest, but I signal for him to get the fuck out of here just as the front door swings open, the lights flip on, and I dip into the next camera blind spot.

"What the fuck do you think you're doing!" Rix yells in my ear.

The key I found in the safe weighs too heavy in my pocket. I can't leave if there's a chance it leads to somewhere captives could be held in this house.

"Your vigilante savior bullshit isn't going to gain you a sweeter setup in hell, you know," he grumbles. "Staircase down. Take a left, then a right."

On the lower level is a huge room with a bar and every gaming setup imaginable. But this open rectangular room is fully covered by surveillance.

"Can you cut it?" I ask quietly. My adrenaline is coursing so fast it heightens all my senses. I'm acutely aware of the murmur of voices above. I think of Ana to calm me down. I'm going to make it in time for her.

Just wait for me, baby.

"They'll know this time. They'll be delayed in their alert, but if I do this, they'll know someone stopped their feed, and when they look into it they'll likely find the other twenty minutes missing,"

Well, shit.

We've never been discovered before, but we've had some pretty close calls. It's worth the risk.

"Do it," I order.

Rix gives a long, reluctant sigh and I wait for the green light to disappear from the camera across the room. The moment it does I'm tracking through the room. There has to be a hidden door.

"Try the old-school music box. I swear it's always those things in the movies," Rix says.

If I didn't need him I'd end the call.

I don't take his suggestion. Instead I head around the bar, hunting for a trip switch or something. The line of alcohol is all more than half-consumed. *Where the fuck is it?* My sight sticks on the bottle of whiskey, and I don't think twice as I swipe a glass and press it to the release.

"Not quite the time, man," Rix comments.

Nothing comes out. Reaching up, I pull the whiskey, and sure enough, a latch somewhere comes open.

"Holy shit, these guys have style!"

"Rix . . ." I warn.

The only thing these motherfuckers have are corrupt souls that need cutting out of this world.

Down the passage is a bolted iron door. I heave it open and

light floods into the dark space. It appears empty. The smell is damp and pungent, and I stuff my nose into my elbow while aiming my gun. There are several beds and only one tall rectangular window for light. There's no doubt this place has held captives before. At least my mind can settle knowing there aren't any here right now.

I'm moving to leave when a slight shift has me spinning, gun aimed, and a whimper follows my sudden movement.

"Shit! There's a girl," I hiss to Rix.

He rounds off his own venomous curses and thoughts as I ease toward her slowly, tucking my gun into the back of my pants and holding up my hands.

"You're safe now, I promise. I'm going to get you out of here."

She curls into herself more, dressed in dirty, torn-up wears, far too lean to be healthy.

"What's your name?" I try.

She doesn't speak, and the terror in those brown eyes is something that will haunt me forever. It's hard to say from the malnourishment, but I don't think she could be any older than Ana now I'm closer, and my mind tortures me with the image of her here instead since she looks somewhat familiar, with brown hair too.

"We have to leave now. Can you trust me?"

I hold out a hand, and it takes some patience, which I'm near trembling to sustain knowing whoever is upstairs could come down at any moment. She finally takes my hand and the relief drops in me.

Closing each door exactly how I found it, we make it back to the first level.

"You're about to run into them," Rix snaps. "Next right."

That'll lead me away from the back door I came through, but I trust Rix knows there's another exit.

"That little shit," he says, but the panic in his voice spikes in me too.

"Jeremy—where is he?" I dare to ask.

"About to get himself killed, and I'd like to do that myself," he snarls.

Commotion sounds toward the kitchen, and I pinch my eyes closed just for a second to collect my sanity.

"What was that?" an unfamiliar man's voice echoes.

I pull the woman into an open room as they come running past, and then we slip back out and come to another door.

"Head toward the bushes at the end of the property and hide. Wait for me and I'll come for you," I instruct her.

While seconds ago she was reluctant to take my hand, I have to pry it free now.

Shouting starts and a clamor erupts behind me.

"He needs your help, man!" Rix shouts in alarm.

"Now!" I bark at her.

She takes off with a whimper and I run back inside.

When I get to the kitchen I point my gun at the nearest guy, but Jeremy is under the threat of the other's gun.

"I could shoot both of you before you could pull that trigger," I say with a deadly calm. "Or you can let him go and no one needs to die tonight."

It's a lie. While my mask is still on, they've exposed Jeremy, and I can't risk him being found by these shitfaces.

Both of them only smirk, and I'm seconds from pulling the trigger until pain lances the side of my head. It explodes through me and I hit the ground, fighting for consciousness, not fast enough to avoid the next fist across my cheek from a third guy we'd failed to account for in the car.

Those are all the hits he'll get in tonight.

My fist connects with his face with far more force. I'm prepared to fight him, but when I get up he's out cold. I look up just in time to see the gun pointed at me and I twist, hissing with the fire that tears over my bicep, narrowly missing the plunge of the bullet.

Motherfucker.

Now I'm beyond pissed.

I don't spare a second, aiming my gun and firing a shot between the man's eyes.

"I-I'll fucking kill him!" The one holding Jeremy quivers.

I lean on the island, pretending to catch my breath.

"Please—I'll do anything," I pant, clutching my bleeding arm. It's a bit deeper than a scrape.

The man slackens his hold on the kid, just enough to let me know he thinks we'll come to some truce.

I don't give mercy to his kind of people.

Once I have my opening I fire at his shoulder. When Jeremy leaps out of the way, his shrill cry is cut off by the next bullet to the man's chest.

"Get the fuck out of this house," I snarl at Jeremy.

He doesn't hesitate, scrambling out, and just as I instructed, the girl is shaking behind the bushes. Jeremy removes his jacket and slings it around her.

The closest hospital is an hour away. It's five o'clock.

In the car Jeremy sits in the back with the woman, and the first yap I hear has me glaring in the rearview mirror.

"You stole the fucking dogs?"

She's holding one in her lap and it seems to bring a small comfort.

"There's no way I was leaving these adorable guys behind to the monsters! I'm naming them Frodo and Sam. They're part of the Xoidship now."

For the small smile it brings to the hollow woman's face, I can't be mad. Besides, two little ankle-biters will be Rix's problem more than mine.

"I'll have to drop you off at the apartment. Rix will pick you up to go to the hospital," I say.

Jeremy only nods. He knows he fucked up in there even in trying to help. I'm livid. I didn't intend to spill blood tonight, but I risk unleashing it too harshly right now. Ana is waiting for me, so I need to rally some fucking composure before then.

I'll find out more about the woman later. And hope to all hell there's something of a lead in what we found from the storm that just erupted tonight.

CHAPTER 17
Anastasia

When we arrive at the carnival I don't expect the cameras to target me so soon. I haven't left the car and we've only been parked for five minutes. I don't know if I can get out when my hands are trembling and my throat has seized tight.

"Are you ready, Miss Kinsley?" my temporary guard, Weston, asks.

I swallow hard. *Get yourself together, Ana.* When I nod, he gives an encouraging smile before slipping out and coming around to my side.

Voices erupt. Clicks happen in succession. I don't know where to look, but I stay close to Weston, who forces them out of my way.

"Anastasia, what do you think of your father's views on tax breaks for the middle/lower class?"

"Miss Kinsley, are you aware your father supports the shift of—"

Most questions become a blur. I'm not obligated to answer

any of them. I won't. My role here is just to smile, be present, and be captured participating in the mundane.

Weston escorts me to the stall plastered with my father's face. It's unnerving. Slightly creepy, actually. I've seen his setups before, but this is the first time I've been around it all without him, and his team begins looking at me like I'm supposed to lead something.

"Ana, we're so glad you could join us here," an older woman I know, Delores, says warmly. She pulls me into an embrace and my nerves from the parking lot begin to ease. The photographers aren't allowed past the carnival entrance en masse. Apparently, they need a special badge, so there are far less lingering cameras this deep in.

"Would you like a cookie, dear?" Delores asks, holding out a plate of sugar cookies with "President Kinsley" written on them.

"No, thank you. Do you want me to give these out? I could use a walk," I say.

She beams brightly. "That would be wonderful!"

And so off I go, circling the fairground with a bunch of small American flags in one hand while I clutch the cookie plate in the other. It isn't as awkward as I thought it would be. People are so welcoming, stopping me and engaging in pleasant chatter that isn't like the pressure-filled questions from the paparazzi.

I crouch to a young girl after speaking to her father. "I love your bear," I say, nodding to the pink bear she's clutching. It makes a smile break on her face.

"Daddy won it for me!"

Flicking my gaze up, I see her father doting on his daughter with loving eyes. I hold the cookies out to her and she swipes two eagerly.

"Just one, Mary," her father scolds playfully.

"One for Mommy! She loves cookies."

When I straighten, her father's face turns pained.

"We lost her mother just over a year ago," he explains quietly.

My stomach sinks deeply. "I'm so sorry to hear."

"It's not been easy. No loss is, of course. But single parenthood has been particularly difficult."

My heart cracks for the beautiful small family.

"Hey, Dad, can I hang out at Trevor's tonight?" An older teen boy comes up to us.

"Sure, son. I'll pick you up tomorrow?"

I smile at Mary as they finish talking and the boy leaves excitedly. "You have beautiful children," I say.

"Thank you," he says proudly, scooping up his daughter.

"Is there anything you need?" I feel the sudden urge to ask.

"Unless you can change the underfunding of schools," he muses.

"What do you mean?" I ask, genuinely curious as guilt grows that I have no insight.

He smiles as if he understands the divide between us, but it doesn't make me any less ignorant. "If I didn't have to work so much to keep a roof over our heads, I'd homeschool. There aren't enough resources and teachers are underpaid. I don't even know what I'll do for Nicolas's college fund. He's a bright kid."

"I'm so sorry to hear. Thank you for sharing with me."

I can't make promises, but meeting this humble and bright family ignites something within me. It doesn't feel right that parents should have to worry about the quality of their children's schooling. I stare after them until I lose them through the bustling crowds, unsure of why a new spark of purpose is awakening inside me or what I'll do with it yet.

Smiling, I head back to the campaign stall.

After an hour of playing carnival games with kids, chatting to more parents, and meeting people from school, I check my phone and realize it's already five o'clock. My heart sinks at the blank notification screen. Rhett hasn't even texted once. Gritting my teeth, I banish him from my thoughts since it was so easy for him to abandon me in his.

I get to the maze at 5:10 p.m., but Riley is nowhere to be seen. Perhaps the next group have been ushered inside to start. I pull out my cell again, swiftly dialing Riley. It only gives two rings before it cuts off, and I groan, glaring at the signal bar that keeps dipping in and out.

"Are you going to try to escape the maze?" A man approaches me suddenly and I jump with a squeal at his clown makeup.

Night is falling, and he holds up a flashlight and a map for me. I take it despite my anxiety growing at his widening smile. *He's just an actor. This is all part of the thrill.* Usually I'd be giddy, but I've always had Riley or someone else with me.

"Have you seen a woman with blonde hair and blue eyes go in? She was probably wearing brown and white and might have had her hair in a braid with a bow?" I ask him.

He ponders for a moment. "I think so. With two other women and one guy."

That sounds like them. I smile with new confidence, muttering my thanks before taking the map and flashlight and heading to the entrance.

Weston stops me. "I'm under very *firm* orders to make you wait here until Agent Kaiser comes."

I turn bitter at the name. "Well, he's late. Perhaps not even coming since it doesn't seem to be important to him. And I'm not missing out. My friends are inside and I'm not having a guard trailing me in there when it's supposed to be scary and fun."

"Miss Kinsley, please."

I stop at the genuine nerves in his tone.

Weston is likely more than ten years older than Rhett, yet the poor guy seems frightened by the authority Rhett imposed on him tonight.

"You won't get in trouble with him or my father, I promise. Thank you, Weston," I assure him.

He doesn't believe me, but he gives a pained smile and a reluctant wave like I've just ended his career before I turn and enter the maze.

I keep my phone out, trying Riley a couple more times, and she even tries me back, but our call never fully connects. The deeper through the tall corn maze I get, the less the damn signal bar makes an appearance. I groan, giving up and stuffing my phone into my pocket. If they haven't gotten lost yet I can catch up. So I focus on my map instead.

The picture is a giant clown holding a balloon, and I decide this year is my least favorite theme. It's beginning to freak me out. I turn on my flashlight when it becomes too eerily dark. I'm gaining some distance from the main fair—the music sounds far-off.

A rustling makes me jump with a gasp, but I find no one. I press on quicker, sure I'm following the map correctly. Every year I'm always put in charge of leading as I usually get us all out without any wrong turns. But I come to a dead end. In front of me are thick, tall rows of corn.

I take a few breaths to calm myself, knowing there are actors throughout the maze that could surge my fright any moment. I turn around and scream at the figure a few feet away. A clown holding a balloon.

"A little mouse in my little trap," they sing.

I back up slowly. They have to let me pass when I'm at the end of a path. Yet they don't move. When they take a step toward me my heart starts to thunder.

They're supposed to scare you. Just go past him and he won't harm you.

"Wanna play, Ana?"

I stop advancing. Many people know my name here, but it seems highly inappropriate for one of the actors to use it.

They jerk forward suddenly as if they'll run and grab me, and I whirl, having no other choice than to veer off the trail and escape in a run through the tight stalks. Creeping, sinister laughter follows me and my eyes prick with fear. I'm all alone. What if I never make it out?

The laughter fades away, but I can't stop running. Finally, I break through onto a path again, unaware of the cuts over my hands from shielding my face against the crops.

I can't breathe fast enough. I'm scanning around helplessly and I've dropped my map.

You're fine. You're going to get out in no time. Someone has to cross paths with me soon, and I'll join them.

Focusing on reeling back some calm, I walk carefully, my senses on high alert, jerking at any small sound. Down the next path I whimper at the figure at the end. Another clown.

"Please, I don't want to play anymore," I say pathetically.

They're supposed to stop. If you ask them for help they should take you out of the maze safely. But this person stalks toward me in slow, predatory strides, and a tear escapes me.

I turn to run again, but another clown rounds the corner.

"Please," I whisper. I've never known this kind of helpless entrapment before.

"All alone she wanders, toward the hanging tree," one sings.

My skin crawls.

"Here come the singing clowns, not one, not two, but—"

"Three."

I scream when someone grabs me from behind out of nowhere. Spun in their grip, my body seizes in stilling terror at the close glint of a blade at my face. He wears a mask, not face paint, and lets me go only to grab a fistful of my hair. The knife slices below my nape. I cry out, but he lets me go, and the laughter from all of them drums in my ears as I turn and sprint.

I don't know where to go, not on any path again, but I don't stop. I've dropped my flashlight and can hardly see in the dark with my blurry vision. I can't stop sobbing, desperate to be free, and I only want one person. Rhett. The only thing that feels like true safety right now, and he didn't come.

Breaking through the tight rows of corn again, I slam into something that grabs me tightly, but I fight harder this time. With everything I am. I sob loudly and frantically, but they're too big, too tall. Arms clamp around me to prevent my struggle, and then we're both falling.

"I'm here, baby. *Fuck*. It's me and I'm right here."

When the ringing in my ears stops and I finally recognize the voice I only cry harder. Rhett holds me straddled over his knees, smoothing his hand over my nape. I don't know how long we stay like that before my heart calms enough to let me breathe right and I stop being a silly, blubbering mess.

"Rhett."

"I've got you."

"You left me," I croak.

"I'm so sorry, Ana. I should have been here. I wanted to fucking be here."

"Where were you?"

His pause of silence slices through me. Rhett has secrets and I don't mean enough to him to know about them. Yet I can't be upset right now when his stroking along my spine and the blanket of his warmth are the only things keeping me grounded.

"What happened?" he asks tightly.

"I don't know. It was a stupid prank, I think. Someone who doesn't like my father, perhaps. I don't know, Rhett."

My tears are flowing again, and I hate being this vulnerable in front of him. He's fierce and brave, and I want to be that too. Yet one scare too far and here I am, unable to handle myself.

"This isn't a fucking prank," he snarls. "I'm going to find out who did this to you."

His heart is beating so fast against mine, his hold so tight and promising that I don't want to get up, but I can't be seen like this.

"I want to go home," I whisper.

He presses his lips to the top of my head. "Let's go home, baby."

He stands, cradling me to him, and I'm too exhausted to protest. Far too comfortable to want to let go. When we finally come near to the end of the maze that exposes the fair, he sets me down.

I sniff hard to rally composure and lift a shaky hand to the back of my head. Only a few full lengths remain from where they didn't cut right through, and I bite my lip against breaking again.

Rhett pulls my hat off gently. "You look sexy as hell with short hair," he murmurs.

I try to smile, but it feels hollow. I let him help twist what's left of the lengths up before fitting my hat back on to hide the hacked mess. He takes my face in his hands, brushing his thumbs over my wet cheeks, and gives me a slow assessment all over.

"Do I look hideous?" I huff a laugh. I can't be photographed like this.

"You're the most stunning thing I've ever seen."

My brow crumples. I'm trying not to cry, but these are tears of such gratitude from the sincerity he's holding me with.

Now there's a little carnival light flooding over to us, my gaze catches on his cheek.

"What happened to you?" I gasp. There's a bruising cut along his cheekbone.

"Doesn't matter. Nothing matters but you right now."

Rhett pulls out his phone, tapping fast before he slips it back into his pocket. "The path to the car should be clear," he says, hooking an arm around my waist and guiding me tightly by his side.

He uses his whole body as a shield from any wandering eyes, and I keep my eyes glued to my steps in shame. I don't want to feel this way, but I can't help it.

In the car I curl into myself on the seat, pulling nervously at my hat. It doesn't matter that it's just hair—it was taken from me. I feel violated and disgusted, and my tears fall silently, but I don't want Rhett to see them as I watch the passing streetlights.

I keep my hands tucked to my chest and he strokes along my leg while he drives. I'm grateful for the silence since my throat is too tight to speak. I'm so damn tired, slipping my eyes closed and feeling exhaustion lap its slow waves over me.

CHAPTER 18
Anastasia

When I look in my bathroom mirror I want to force Rhett away, but he leans with arms crossed in the door way, watching me through the reflection.

He lied. I look absolutely terrible. My eyes are red and puffy, with black smudges from my mascara. All my hair is hidden in my hat still and I'm too nervous to look at the damage.

"You don't have to stay," I say quietly.

He pushes off the frame, stopping close behind me. "I'm not going anywhere."

My chest flutters as his hand reaches up, pausing on the hat. I nod, taking a deep breath as he pulls it off. My hands shoot over my eyes immediately. *It's bad.*

"Nothing we can't fix," he assures me. "Do you have scissors?"

I peek at him through the reflection. "You want me to trust you to cut it?"

"I'm happy to wait and take you to a salon tomorrow. I still suggest we do. But if you'll let me, I'm more than capable of making it even at least."

I smile sadly, opening a drawer and fishing out some salon scissors I keep for when I just need a little trim between visits.

Rhett takes them and then my hand as he sits on the toilet and guides me to kneel on the soft mat between his legs.

"Don't give me a pixie cut," I warn.

"You could pull it off," he teases.

The asshole in the maze chopped my hair to my shoulders. I sit back, tucking my knees to my chest. It isn't the end of the world, but I'm so incredibly sad it wasn't my choice even when I've debated short hair before.

"What happened to you isn't a joke. It was assault, and if I thought the police would be any damn help I would be marching there now. But I'm going to find out who was behind it."

"It was dark. I don't have any identifiers to give anyone."

Rhett stops cutting. His hand grazes under my chin, forcing me to look back at him. "They're going to pay for what they did to you," he promises.

The knot in my stomach tightens. I don't know how he'll do it, but I believe him.

"Thank you," I whisper, turning back around when he lets go.

He cuts away a few more strands. Every comb of his fingers through the shortened lengths makes my eyes flutter, and I suppress my moans.

"Don't ever thank me. I'm yours, remember?"

"My guard."

He leaves a pause of silence. "Yes."

"I don't think you could have predicted hairdressing being part of the job," I muse.

"You do keep it interesting."

I smile to myself. When he seems finished, I look at the bundles of hair on the vanity counter sadly, but I wander over to the mirror, and with it all an even length I actually like it. Though it could do with a few layers and shaping. I'll get it fixed tomorrow.

Rhett hasn't moved, and my chest tightens at the blooming mark on his face. I take a washcloth and run it under the water, coming back to him.

I sink to my knees again, facing him, bracing a hand on his thigh. I can't decipher the emotion swirling in his blue eyes. Pained . . . perhaps vulnerable. But he lets me bring the cloth to his face and his brow pinches with the sting. I clean away the blood around the cut gently.

"Want to tell me what was worth getting into a fight over?" I ask carefully.

"Can I ask you something?"

His question is so . . . scared.

"Of course."

"If you plan to tell your father what happened, can we tie our stories together? That I got this at the same time?"

My heart begins to drum. So whatever he was up to, my father doesn't know about it and he's trusting me to keep his secret.

"What did you do?" I whisper.

He takes my hand at his face and I've never seen him look so lost.

"It's better if you don't know. Can you trust me?"

I shake my head. "You want me to lie for you. You were

supposed to be with me tonight and you left me for something that got us both hurt."

Misery fills his eyes. "I am so. Fucking. Sorry I wasn't there tonight. It was all so unexpected and sudden. Your safety is everything to me, and telling you where I was is a huge risk to that."

"My safety is your job," I snap, pushing to my feet.

I trail over the rest of him like I don't know who's been by my side all this time. If he's capable of lying now, what else has he been hiding? There's a tear in his black shirt at his bicep, and when he stands I don't see the color of his tanned skin through it.

"Ana—"

"Take off your shirt," I demand. He looks confused before I add, "You're hurt worse than just a right hook to your face, aren't you?"

Rhett's face falls. I don't think he'll do as I ask, but when he reaches back and folds out of his T-shirt I suppress my gasp at the deep slash over his bicep.

"You need stitches," I scold, angry for some reason that he didn't tell me sooner. That he was tending to my damn hair when he was sitting there with a wound from . . . a knife? A gun? *Shit, what did you get up to, Rhett Kaiser?*

I march to the sink again, soaking my towel and wringing it.

"Sit back down. You're too damned tall," I grumble, not thinking as I put a hand on his chest to guide him back. The warmth and firmness of him catches my breath.

I stay standing, silently cleaning his arm from the blood and wanting to ask again how it happened. As I do, my traitorous gaze wanders over the impressive contours of him, getting a closer look at his huge serpent tattoo. His skin is marked with more scars than any person should have. He's an uncharted map, and I become engrossed learning every marker of it. The stories behind every mark that makes up the pieces of Rhett. I don't realize I've stopped moving with the hand holding the cloth, because the other begins tracing a single horizontal line over the left side of his chest.

"What does it mean?" I ask thoughtfully.

I wonder if I'll ever know when he trains his eyes on the ground and the silence stretches.

"My heart died when hers did. Almost four years ago."

And mine . . . it shatters for him with that explanation.

"What was her name?"

"Sarah."

"She was lucky to have you." It slips out of me before I can think anything of it. But it's the wrong thing to say.

Rhett's bitter laugh turns me tense. "You know nothing, Ana."

My hurt at that comment turns to annoyance. I grip his chin, forcing him to look up at me. As we stare off, something grows between us. It's crafted of anger and pain and longing.

"Then *tell* me," I say with determination. "I'm not her. But I'm not going to break. If you want to push me away, then fucking do it, but this time you're not getting to pull me back."

Rhett grips my waist, pulling me over his lap, and my breath catches unexpectedly. "You are something else, Anastasia Kinsley," he growls. "No, you're not like her. You're all fire and passion and a determination that hasn't had the chance to be unleashed yet. You're something I can't stand to be around because it's so fucking addicting, and you don't even realize."

"You're a—"

"Don't call me a coward, little bird. I won't be able to stop if I have to prove you wrong."

Heat gathers at my core, and I'm close to doing exactly what I did in the cinema room. But I don't want to lose him. This past week was miserable with the friction of what I did, and I can be patient.

Though not with kissing him—I need *something* tonight after what we've both been through.

Rhett groans against my mouth, but this kiss isn't as urgent as the first time. It's slow and searching. Utterly igniting, and it's felt far more in my chest than anywhere else. I pull away, resting my forehead to his.

Then I climb off his lap, grabbing a few alcohol swabs and a bandage. "We need to go to the hospital," I say, doing the best I can at wrapping his arm, which has already started bleeding through.

"No hospitals," he says quietly.

There's enough pain in his tone that I don't push.

"It'll scar worse without stitches," I advise him.

"Another scar isn't going to matter."

My touch lingers after tying the bandage.

"Every one of them matters," I say. "You matter."

Rhett doesn't look up, but his frown deepens and I want to know what he's thinking.

"You must be really tired," he says softly.

I nod, pushing aside the twist in my gut that I might have said the wrong thing.

When I've washed my face, brushed my teeth, and changed into pajamas, I'm not shy anymore to wander around the room this way. "Can you stay?" I ask, erupting with nerves at his likely rejection.

"Are you sure you want that?"

"Yes."

More than anything right now when the thought of being alone in the dark is already giving me flashbacks from tonight.

Rhett says nothing as he comes over to the bed. I nestle down, facing away from him as he takes off his black jeans, and my face warms with the urge to see him in nothing but boxers.

I'm good. I resist.

When he flips the light off and lies beside me I can't close my eyes. Something isn't right.

"Ana," he whispers. The bed shifts, and I shiver at the energy growing closer to my back. "Can I hold you?"

I smile into the dark, wiggling back in answer until I feel his body encasing me from behind. My head lifts to the arm he slips under me while he tucks the other over my chest. It's so reassuring, and I've never been held this way before. Like he could protect me from the world. His breath blows across my shoulder blades before he plants one kiss there, and I sigh contentedly.

"I'll keep your secret from my father if you promise not to keep it from me forever," I murmur sleepily after a moment of peace. My hand traces over his forearm pinning me down.

"Okay," he agrees.

"And I need you to keep one for me."

"Mm-hmm?"

"After tomorrow. You'll see."

He groans, the vibrations of it against my back riling an unsated need I'm trying to ignore. "You have a penchant for wanting to get me in trouble."

"Like being in my bed?"

"Exactly. What happened to not scandalizing me?"

"You have poor resistance."

"Only for you, little bird. Only for you."

CHAPTER 19
Anastasia

I wanted to skip class this morning and head straight to the salon, but as Riley called to remind me, we have an in-seminar assessment today that I can't miss.

That aside, I *almost* missed class when I awoke tucked securely into Rhett, and I would have happily skipped my alarm to stay there longer. To my dismay, he had far better willpower than me despite my best efforts to entice him to lie in with me.

The whole day my fingers have combed my hair subconsciously, knowing they won't continue catching on strands down past my ribs.

"Have I told you how beautiful you look today?" Rhett murmurs in my ear as we sit in the cafeteria alone.

A blush creeps along my cheeks as he hooks a strand of hair. "Once or twice," I say.

"Hmm." He kisses my temple. "I need to do better."

I jump when a stack of papers and books thumps down onto the table, followed by the frustrated groan of my best friend.

"What's got you so worked up?" I ask as she throws herself down onto the seat. With the look she cuts me, I can hardly suppress my smile. "Let me guess—he's over six feet, wears glasses, and the sexual tension in the permanent scowls you wear for each other is obvious to anyone but the two of you."

"There is not— *Your hair!*" Her sudden rise of pitch when she notices makes me wince. "You didn't tell me you were serious about cutting it this time!" she goes on, beaming brightly.

Rhett takes my hand before I can even begin my nervous habit. It doesn't feel like the right place to explain what happened.

"I didn't find you yesterday," I say. "I went into the maze and I tried calling, but there was no signal, and then it got dark and there were these clowns, and I . . . I got lost."

"Oh! Sorry, I thought you got my text. Lacy and I were going to do the maze, but we took one look at the spider map and no, thank you. We never would have made it out without you."

My blood turns cold.

"The map wasn't a spider," I mutter vacantly.

"Okay, most of it was the web, but that's even worse! I can't do spiders, even those cut into corn, and I was not risking them potentially unleashing hundreds of them in there for sick fear thrills."

It was a trick from the start. I was handed a map that never would have gotten me out of there for the clown cutout that was on it.

"Nice hair, Ana." Adam's voice pricks the hairs on my arms. He comes around the table, looking at me with slow, taunting assessment. "Though it doesn't quite suit you as much."

"What makes you think you can talk to her?" Rhett says with a chilling calm.

"Is there a problem?" Adam antagonizes him.

"You won't have a problem if you don't leave—you'll have a fucking nightmare."

"I could ruin your life for threatening me like that."

I squeeze Rhett's hand, but he's beyond reaching as he stands. Adam straightens from leaning over the table.

"You can fight with money, but just remember, paper will always burn fastest."

Adam stares at Rhett with such hatred I almost tremble, but when his gaze slips to me, I'm surprised by myself as I smile sweetly. I swear a flame flickers in his eyes before he storms off.

"Want to go?" Rhett asks.

I twist back to Riley, who's flicking her gaze between Rhett and the ghost of Adam, quietly stunned.

"I'm heading to the library anyway," she says, pilling her books back into her arms. "If I don't score higher than Nolan on midterms I'll never live it down."

I chuckle. "What do you gain from this?"

"I found out today he's applying for the same internship as me at Keithlington. You know how much I've been gushing about them, and I swear he's applying just to antagonize me when they're only taking on one student next year!"

Riley wants to be a copy editor and Keithlington is the top firm in the state.

"If he gets the placement over you, I'm ready for whatever shady sabotage you need me to do," I say.

She huffs but gives a devious smile. "Catch up later?"

I nod. I still want to tell her about what happened last night, but right now I'm eager to get out of here.

"You said I'd find out a secret I had to keep for you today," Rhett says as we walk hand in hand to the car.

Butterflies erupt in my stomach. I'm sure I'll go through with it now the decision is right here.

"First," I say, gesturing to my hair, "your hairstyling job could use a bit of tweaking."

It takes three hours, and I grow increasing guilty at making Rhett wait so long because of the decision I've been toying with since last night. Sitting in the chair and chatting to the stylist, I guess I'm entering my "fuck it" era as she finishes blow-drying and I stare at the deep wine-red tone of my new hair. It looks . . . *great*. I wasn't sure how I'd feel, but the new color and added layers for volume and style almost make me question who I'm looking at.

My nerves wreak havoc inside me as I head to the front waiting room, where Rhett is frowning deeply at his phone while sipping his takeout coffee.

"I wouldn't want to be on the receiving end of that scowl," I interrupt quietly.

His head snaps up and I curse his natural ability to hide any kind of reaction or emotion. The guy has a masterful poker face.

"Please say something," I rush out as he stands, slipping his phone into his pocket while his eyes never leave me.

He breaks a smile then, approaching slowly as he takes in every detail. I take the other coffee cup he offers out, and with his hand freed, his fingers brush through the ends.

"I don't think me not telling your father is going to stop him noticing," he muses.

I huff a laugh. This isn't my secret. That's still to come if I maintain the courage.

"You've always been the most stunning thing I've ever seen no matter the length or color of your hair. But you look absolutely, devastatingly wicked like this, little bird."

"Wicked?"

"Put it this way: I wouldn't want to cross you."

The confidence he gives me feels powerful. Perhaps it's dramatic and the new hair has just given me an air of arrogance that makes me feel like I've stepped out of a Bond movie, but with Rhett I think we could fit the part in the real world.

"Rhett Kaiser, super-badass, sexy agent, would kneel for me?"

His jaw works and my core heats at the lust clouding his irises. "Absolutely, I would."

I pay before Rhett can. Seriously, this man is intent on draining his salary on me as though he often forgets I'm his job.

When we're standing inside the tattoo parlor, my stomach roils with uncertainty.

"This makes more sense," Rhett comments, surveying the space for any danger. "Your father would certainly have a hit on my head if he knew I was an accomplice to this."

I push into him playfully. "I'm twenty-four, not some underage teen gone wild."

"Your wild stage is blooming late. I can't say I'm not thrilled I get to witness it."

After speaking to the artist and pep-talking myself into it, I lie on my stomach on the tattoo bench. I specifically wore a tank top to allow access between my shoulders. Rhett sits beside me, holding my hand in his two massive hands as he leans on his thighs.

"When I called you little bird, I didn't know you'd take it so seriously. Are you sure about this?"

I scoff. "It's not for you or because of that. It just feels . . . right."

Near the top of my spine will be a very small birdcage with an open door and a little bird flying free.

The buzz of the machine starts and I grip Rhett tighter in panic. He has a huge tattoo, so I must look like a wimp to him. He kisses my hand before brushing the hair close to tipping over my eyes. When the needles meet my skin it burns more than I anticipated. My face must convey as much, because Rhett can't contain his soft chuckles.

"Don't laugh!" I scold, only because I'm at risk of joining him and I don't want a botched job for my first tattoo.

It only takes half an hour, and I'm beyond giddy to see the end result when I push up from the bench and the artist shows me with a handheld mirror. Rhett follows my gaze, and as I admire the delicate tattoo with flutters of joy, his hand meets my waist and he presses lips to my shoulder.

"Perfect, little bird," he murmurs against my skin.

I can't explain why it feels empowering. Despite the rocky confrontation this morning with Adam, I now feel ready to conquer the world. This is me taking back the control of my life that was buried under the expectations of other people for so long. Expectations that I'll act poised and proper with family name I carry. My mom will freak at the hair I can't hide, its unnatural color, but the tattoo is just between me and Rhett for now.

My phone rings and I pluck it out before we get to the car. It's Riley.

I pick up with a cheerful greeting, but she rambles right over it, and I have to stop walking to keep up. Listening to her relay her frantic message, I'm slammed by shock. Then adrenaline pounds in my chest.

"Are you sure?" I ask out of nothing more than blank shock. I can't believe what I'm hearing.

"I'm heading to the hospital now. Need a ride?"

"I—uh, no, I-I'll meet you there," I say blankly, not fully able to process.

"What's wrong?" Rhett asks the second I hang up, his face drawn together with a seriousness that lets me know he'll act on anything I ask.

"Can you take me to the hospital? My friend, she, uh . . . we thought she left five years ago, but it turns out—"

Oh god. It's starting to sink in. The details were vague, but Riley seems to have heard Nina Temsworth is back, or found, or — I don't know what to make of the story about our friend yet, only that she's in bad shape.

"Of course. Get in," Rhett says, guiding me as I'm hardly grounded with the news.

The hour-long drive to the hospital passes mostly in silence. My thoughts are reeling and my emotions tangle. Above all, guilt crushes me slowly.

I rush in, and Riley is waiting for me in the reception.

"Oh Ana," she sighs, pulling me into a hug. She's been crying.

Following her, I fall into a state of numbness as she explains vague details. I can't believe it.

Kidnapped.

Held captive.

All this time and we so easily believed she'd run off because she had before.

When we get to the right room, I don't know who I'm looking at sitting up in the hospital bed. She looks like Nina, but also not. People used to always say we looked alike, but I don't think anyone could say that anymore. Her brown hair is dull and messy, her face so pale and hollow. But it's in those eyes the full impact of this reality hits me. Her hazel eyes could once light up any room she walked into, along with her infectious smile. Now they're empty and the smile she attempts is so sad.

I come around to her bed, not realizing my eyes have filled until I blink and a tear rolls down my cheek. I take her hand gently. "I'm so sorry," I whisper, unable to find my full voice.

"You couldn't have known," she says, her voice so different from what I remember. Like it's aged decades and lost all its joy.

"I'll wait outside," Rhett says, barely able to look at Nina.

I nod, and as he leaves I take up the seat next to the bed. Nina frowns at the ghost of him.

"He's my . . . *guard*," I explain. "My father's running for president this year and is stupidly overprotective now." I try a laugh, but it's weak.

Nina looks at me, but her confusion doesn't go away. "He seems . . . familiar."

It's my turn to follow after him with a frown. Until I relax. That's impossible.

"He's fairly new. Nearly three months now, I think."

What unnerves me is that this information doesn't immediately erase her puzzled look.

"We're going to look after you," Riley says, taking her other hand. "And find out who's responsible for this."

For the next hour Nina tries to explain what she can of her ordeal. My sickness rises with what she shares, and knowing it isn't all the details of what she's endured, I don't know what lies ahead for us or her. But above all, I'm so happy she got out alive and made it back to us.

When we're forced to leave after visiting hours we promise to come see her as much as we can. I'll get her a phone so we can keep in touch while university is getting intense. Riley and I leave, leaning on each other for comfort, but we speak very little, needing to process our feelings.

The car ride home is mostly silent too, but I'm content, safe, in Rhett's company. Now more than ever, I've never been more glad to have him by my side. It's like every fear and fable just became a chilling reality, breaking apart our ignorant, oblivious peace.

CHAPTER 20

Anastasia

Surviving until fall break is the first checkpoint of accomplishment in every college student's year.

I'm up long past midnight trying to finish a damn paper due for our last day tomorrow. I've left it until the very last minute, as I always do. But this time it's been from spending many days at the hospital over the past few weeks.

After grabbing a late-night snack to push me through another hour so I can read over what I've written, I head back to my room. I'm about to go inside when a quiet mumble comes from Rhett's door. He said he was off to bed more than two hours ago.

I shouldn't be nosy, but I can't help inching closer to his door. It's silent again. Then my heart speeds up at the next disruption. Hardly coherent, but I think I hear "stop," which is enough to raise my concern.

Tapping his door quietly, I say his name. No answer, but every now and then I'm sure his voice strains some words.

Throwing all calls for privacy to the wind, I open his door a fraction, but I can hardly see in the dark.

"Rhett," I whisper again.

This time, when he doesn't answer, I enter fully. My eyes adjust to the dark as I close the door behind me and creep toward the bed. *I shouldn't be here. This is certainly stalker-type stuff.* But something presses me forward.

He's asleep, the duvet slung over his lower half and his toned chest stretched out, looking godly. One hand fists the sheets while his other arm is folded over his face.

Is he having a nightmare?

"Don't hurt . . ." he murmurs with a jerk.

My chest drums wildly. "Rhett, wake up," I say a little louder, but not wanting to scare the shit out of him.

I reach over to touch his forearm, but it's me who ends up frightened beyond belief at his sudden movement when he grabs me, and before I can process how the fuck anyone can move like that I'm pinned to the mattress, hands locked above my head in one of his hands while the other wraps around my neck. Lucky for me, he seems to register I'm not the monster of his nightmare before he crushes my throat.

He seethes down at me with such vengeance and fury I'm terrified at what he's capable of. Not that he'd do it to me. It only lasts for seconds before he comes around through long, labored breaths and his face relaxes.

"Fuck, I'm sorry," he says.

Instead of letting me go, Rhett leans his forehead to mine, shifting his weight until his body is between my legs instead. Desire runs through me as it brings our skin closer to being flush.

"It's okay," I get out, still racing with adrenaline, and this position certainly isn't helping. "I just . . . I heard you and I came in. I didn't mean to scare you."

"You didn't scare me," he says. "You saved me."

I don't want to imagine the scene he's met in his nightmares many times. His fiancée's death.

"Do you want to talk about it?" I ask carefully.

Rhett shakes his head. My pulse skips.

"I want to forget about it."

"Okay," I breathe, on a razor's edge of anticipation.

"What are you doing to me, Ana?" he whispers.

Rhett kisses the edge of my jaw, then he trails his mouth down my neck, still holding me helpless against him. The hand that was around my neck slips down the side of my body, and I curve into him with a soft moan.

"Fuck," he breathes, bringing his head back up to crash his lips to mine, and then I'm done for.

Rhett's knee hooks beneath mine, pressing his hard length to my core, and the thin fabric between us becomes torturous with his slow friction. His hand explores my ribs, stopping under the curve of my breast, and I'm so damn close to *begging* for him to touch me.

"I want to fuck you, Ana," he growls against my lips. "So badly it's been driving me insane."

"I want it too," I say, near desperate with my skin on fire against his.

It's all he needs, and when he finally squeezes my breast I moan into his mouth, pushing into him.

"You're a needy girl," he groans.

"Stop treating me like glass, Rhett. I won't break."

He gives a low noise of approval before his assault intensifies. Slipping my top higher, his tongue flicks over my nipple, and I writhe beneath him. He finally lets my hands go, and I fold out of my top before diving my hands into his silvery-blond hair as he descends. Shit, I'm so embarrassingly wet for him.

Rhett hooks my shorts down without his lips ever leaving my skin. Lower and lower. Cool air breezes across my slickness, which is practically dripping out of me. Instinctively my knees try to pull together, but Rhett forces them apart.

"Keep these legs spread for me, little bird."

Looking at him between my legs, kissing along the insides of my thighs, I'm so worked up with need it's bliss and torture.

"Rhett, please."

"Please what, baby?"

"I need to come," I beg.

Rhett's tongue slides through my folds and I cry out, grabbing fistfuls of the sheets on either side of me.

"So sweet," he says, teasing a finger at my entrance. "So damn tight."

He sinks in slowly, sucking at my clit, and I'm already rapidly chasing a climax.

"Are you always this needy for me?"

"Yes," I gasp.

After a few torturous strokes he adds a second finger, playing me like a fucking fiddle, and I lose my damn mind.

My hand threads through his hair while my hips lift, chasing more when he's already teasing me beyond sanity. He chuckles darkly against me.

"I knew you would be sinfully greedy," he says huskily.

Then he devours me.

My thighs want to clamp tight with the orgasm forming in my lower belly, but Rhett growls, pushing my thighs open in warning with one hand while the other pumps two fingers in and out of me in a faster rhythm when he feels my walls tightening.

"Come on my tongue," he orders, dipped in such sin it's my unraveling.

My back bows off the bed, head thrown back, and I have to clamp one hand over my mouth out of fear I might wake the damn household with the crash that erupts from every part of me. I start to get dizzy when he doesn't stop, continuing his assault to stretch out my climax to the point of overstimulation.

He retreats all at once and I pant hard to collect my damn mind.

I moan when he trails kisses over my stomach, climbing my body, and when his cock slides along my pussy I can think of nothing else but taking him inside me.

"You taste better than I imagined," he says, kissing my mouth hard.

My hand reaches between us, gripping his cock and pumping a couple of times until I find the right pressure that has him jerking into my palm.

"I don't have a condom," he says, ready to leave this at foreplay, but I'm not.

"I'm on birth control and I'm clear. Unless you want to confess to your string of affairs without being tested . . ."

I line him up at my entrance, and his answer comes in the slow sinking of his cock into me. My brow pulls together at the fullness that creates a pinch with the size of him.

"It's been a while, and I've certainly been tested and cleared since," he confirms in a thick, raspy voice as he stares down between us.

He stretches me until his hips meet mine and we share a ragged breath.

"It's as if you were fucking made for me," he grinds out, beginning a gentle pace so I can adjust.

"You take your job very seriously, Agent Kaiser," I breathe, so euphoric and full with him inside me.

Even in the low moonlight I can make out his wicked smirk.

"Protecting your body is my greatest damn privilege, Miss Kinsley." He pulls nearly all the way out only to slam back in, and I cry out his name. Something about the title and the sinful way he speaks it makes my body sing. Like this is wrong, forbidden, but it's unstoppable. This magnet between us we've resisted for too long.

Rhett fucks me hard, hooking my thigh around him to sink in deeper.

"Touch yourself for me, baby," he says, flicking his tongue across my nipple. It skitters sparks right down to where he wants my hand.

I circle my clit, and what was slow-building speeds up in a sprint. I feel his cock sliding in and out of me between my fingers when they pass down lower, and it's so erotic my climax is right. Fucking. There.

"Right there," I rasp when he's hitting a certain spot inside me that draws out unchecked sounds.

"Good girl," he praises, slipping his arm under my arched back to pound into me tighter. "Always tell me what feels good."

Pleasure explodes with every thrust, like small climaxes building toward something earth-shattering.

"Rhett, I'm going to—" I lose my own words under a wave of pleasure.

"I know, baby. You're squeezing the damn life out of me."

He sucks on my nipple and I come apart. My fingers dig into his forearm and then claw his chest. He growls with it, driving into me harder as he reaches his own orgasm. He pulls out right before, pumping his dick as hot cum ropes over my stomach where I lie quivering with the aftershocks.

Holy fucking shit.

I knew sex with Rhett would be incredible, but that was mind-blowing, unlike anything I've experienced before. I'm still coming down from it when he kneels between my open legs, catching his breath.

"Are you okay?" he asks carefully.

Is that a trick question?

"More than okay," I say. He gets off the bed and I watch his perfect ass head to the en suite, flipping on the light before he disappears inside.

A few seconds later the water is running. It's too heavy to be the shower. He comes back and tenderly cleans my stomach with a wet towel while the bath fills.

I don't know if he wants me to leave and bathe alone. I'll shower in my own room . . .

His hand hooks under my bent knee, and I squeal when he pulls me around before hooking his hand under the other knee and dragging me to the edge of the bed. It's the sexiest thing I've ever seen.

Rhett leans over me, kissing me firmly once before slipping his arms under my back. My legs tighten around his waist as he lifts.

"I'm not ready to let you go tonight, if that's okay with you," he says, carrying me to the bathroom.

"I don't want to be anywhere else."

His smile is so content—a kind I rarely see that makes him appear so much softer.

Rhett gets in first, then he helps me, and I settle with my back against his chest. I scoop bubbles while his fingers idly trace my arm and his lips occasionally press to my shoulder. The silence is peaceful, but I can't settle my anxiety that this is only one night and he'll put distance between us tomorrow.

"Do I get to know your secret yet?" I ask quietly.

His fingers stop moving. "Have you always been attracted to dangerous things?"

"You can stop trying to scare me away."

"I'm not. Because even if I were, I don't think I'm capable of truly letting you get away from me anymore."

Something in that is threatening. In a way that makes my stomach coil like the thrill of a chase. And the forever promise of being found. Never lost again.

My head tips back against his shoulder. "I think you opened the door to my cage," I say, reflecting.

"No, little bird. I might have shown you there was a door, but opening it was all you, and I think you're yet to fully fly free."

Perhaps I'm too afraid he'll leave me. That he'll think I don't need him anymore if I do. Needing Rhett doesn't feel like dependency; it feels like security. Like we can take on anything together.

CHAPTER 21
Rhett

Ana is exquisite, powerful, sitting in the chair across from her father. Her long legs cross over each other, shifting her tight black skirt higher, and— *Fuck me*, I have to stop blatantly staring at the senator's daughter while he's right fucking there.

I stand by the side of the room, merely observing, as she's come to them with her demand and I'm sure to be involved.

"Look at her hair, Archibald!" Ana's mother cries. I've never heard her address her husband by his full name.

Her father says, "It's lovely, darling, really. But it's . . . bold."

Ana smiles at that and my chest beats with pride. It makes my soul fucking soar to watch her come into her confidence, which could shake a room. The bastards who traumatized her in the maze didn't get to make a victim; they made a goddess.

"You should have asked us first. What is the press going to make of it?" her mother goes on, pacing.

She's beginning to grind on my nerves. Ana looks damned

incredible and she made herself. That's all that matters, not some tabloid gossip.

"I came to say I'll be going to New York next week. Liam invited me to the charity gala," Ana informs them.

"I cannot allow that," her father says immediately.

"I wasn't really asking," Ana counters, growing irritated.

She has every right to be.

Of course, Ana doesn't know the threats made against her life. The night of the maze . . . I've not felt a terror like that since Christmas Eve three years ago. The helplessness in those minutes it took to find her . . . I never want to feel close to that helpless terror again.

I crossed the final line with her last night that I swore to myself I wouldn't. But it was inevitable. Not because she's stunning. That's obvious to anyone. No—what draws me to Ana like a moth to a flame is her spirit, her kindness, and what I can't stop reaching for is something so much deeper I want to protect it with every fiber of my being. Ana deserves far more than what I could ever offer her. But for now, for the rest of this post, maybe the pretense will be worth the wound of leaving her at the end.

"I'll be accompanying her," I interject. "And she's agreed to have two plainclothes guards trailing us at all times."

Ana casts me a glare. She agreed to no such thing. It's damn adorable. New York is stunning at this time while it prepares for the holiday season. I'm excited just thinking about watching her joy in the city.

My cell rings before the senator can voice the protest lining his face. I check the ID.

"I need to take this." I excuse myself.

Ana can handle herself against her parents, and I'm sure they'll cave.

"What have you got for me, Allie?" I say, mindful of my volume while scanning the hall.

"Oh Rhetty, you are going to owe me a mansion in the Bahamas," she practically squeals.

"Doesn't your family own one of those?"

"I want my own!"

I smile, picturing her delightful face.

"We struck big—very big—with what you found in that house. We've never come this direct to Uncle Fuckface before."

One thing I love about Allie is that she never uses my uncle's name. I don't mind it—I use it myself—but I don't know what I did to deserve her love and loyalty.

Catching a glimpse of Ana through the sightly open door of the office I've strayed from, I wish pitifully that they could meet. That Ana could know all about me without it putting her in a difficult place of conflict considering who her father is. If he knew about me . . . what I did to get this position with his daughter . . . I don't think I'd even make it to my jail cell.

"I don't have a lot of time," I tell Allie. "Are you saying Rolf Sullevan has had direct contact with Lanshall? Is it just a sick, predatory ring and he's the customer?"

"That would be a plausible guess, but no. You were right. That was a stop house. But it's the *last* stop. Meaning Sullevan must be in charge of escorting them from there, likely to a new state, and selling the victims."

My fist tightens. Sick fucks, using people as currency.

Allie goes on. "But here's where you're going to be super pissed, and I need you to promise you're not around breakable things that might blow your cover."

My heart speeds up. "Ana's hit?"

"Yes. I recognized the code work from what I saw when I

hacked the server to get you the intel in the first place. It was used in the documents you found in her safe. I can't be certain—I mean, not one *hundred* percent sure—but my guesses are usually pretty accurate—"

"Allie," I plead. *Fuck*, it's both torture and a win to potentially be closer to the source that sent out a hit on my little bird.

"It might not be Rolf Sullevan, before you lose your shit and do something completely stupid. The home belongs to him, but it's been leased for more than five years. Someone called Matt Heizer."

Recognition flashes in my mind. "Did Rix send you what I found in Sullevan's hotel room in Cali?"

"No . . . Should he?"

"There was a credit card. That's the name that was on it."

"I don't know the name. I take it Rix hasn't found anyone in the databases."

"Call him, please. Check everywhere you can. This could very well be our guy."

"So not Sullevan?"

"The men at the top don't like to get their hands dirty. If Sullevan is orchestrating, this guy is our confession."

"Makes sense."

I ask her what's been nagging on my mind. "Have you ever looked into Liam and Matthew Forbes?"

"Of course. I've found no trace of anything bad in their history. All records check out, nothing suspicious."

It should be a relief, but I can't settle. Ana's clearly close with Liam, and I can't deny there's a note of ugly jealously as I wonder if there's any romantic or sexual history between them. Then there's his brother . . . who isn't subtle in his eyes for Ana, but she doesn't respond to him with the same genuine enthusiasm as when she was on the phone with Liam. It doesn't make sense.

As I stare at the flicker of Ana and imagine their potential brotherly tensions over her, I have to remind myself none of it matters. She's mine. Thoughts of last night twitch my cock. She wrapped so damn perfectly around every part of me that it took everything in me to see her walk out of her room this morning dressed in red and black and not fuck her against the hallway wall. I have no care for decency with this woman.

There might come a time when I'll have to let my little bird fly away from me, but I'll never lose track of her.

"He's harmless," Allie adds, snapping me back to the conversation.

I frown at the wall. "Do you know him?"

"Who, Liam? No. Well, I know *of* him, I guess. When we were kids."

Her nervousness piques my curiosity.

"How young?"

"Unimportant, Agent Kaiser. Focus on yourself."

"I need you to look again," I say firmly. "Into why Liam is in New York. I'm heading there with Ana next week."

"Ohh, how is the babysitting going? Has she driven you up the wall yet? It's not hard to do."

I'm going to drive her *up a wall.* Soon, if I have my way.

"She's . . . surprising."

I shouldn't have said anything. Allie gasps. "In all the years I've known you, you've never had such a tone talking about a woman."

"You read too much into things." I dismiss her.

"I wouldn't be good at my job if I didn't."

"Is that all you have right now?" I ask.

"Is that all! You have no idea how hard it was to dig into someone as guarded and prolific as Rolf Sullevan. I think there's more to find, but it'll take some time. Oh, and tell Rix I'd like my new Gucci bag in beige. I got the information first. We made it a race."

"Again, can't you just buy yourself these things?"

"Treats taste so much better when victory delivers them."

I huff a laugh. "Thank you, Allie," I say, hanging up just as Ana comes strutting out her father's office.

From the triumphant grin she bares to me I guess she's succeeded in her persuasion. It takes every effort not to draw her to me when she's close enough, but for all her parents know, any touch we share is merely in aid of our relationship ruse in public and inappropriate elsewhere.

If only they knew.

"I did my part. Your turn," she sings to me.

"I think my persuasion techniques are smoother than yours. I won't be long."

She folds her arms at my arrogance. "I've already done the majority of the work—he's just going to badger you about the security detail."

"Like I said, I won't be long." I risk slipping my hand across her face as I pass, needing to touch her so often it's concerning.

Back in the senator's office, he sits with his chin in his hand, a faraway look of concern on his face. His wife has left too, and I close the door behind myself.

"I don't like this," Senator Kinsley mutters.

"She's a grown woman—she needs to be able to live like one. If I may observe, sir, I don't doubt she's capable of handling herself and staying out of trouble, and I won't let anything happen to her."

"She speaks very highly of you," he says, assessing me. "Above that, I can't help but notice a change in her since you arrived."

I'm not afraid of his judgment, nor what he thinks of my skills. But when it comes to his scrutiny about the kind of influence I'm having on his daughter, yeah, I'll admit, I'm sweating a little.

"She hasn't made it easy, but she's a strong-willed woman and I can only admire that," I say.

He yields a tender smile of agreement. "I'd like to think I can trust you with something so highly sensitive and serious regarding my daughter. Truthfully, I'm at a loss for how to deal with it. I'm confiding in you personally—not as secret service, but as someone who can help keep Ana safe without the knowledge of this getting out to anyone."

I think I know what he's going to say, and it's about time he told me.

"Of course."

The senator unlocks a drawer and pulls out a box that must have been put in there after I searched it. "Ana has been in danger since your placement. I hired you and an extra security detail to help, but I fear it's something far out of my means and I can't keep quiet anymore."

When he removes the lid, I know exactly what it is with a flush of fury over my skin.

"I think you know what this is."

Ana's hair. There's a sick, twisted bastard on the loose making a mockery of her, and I'm itching for his throat.

"Did anything else come with it?" I ask, already trying to piece things together with what little knowledge I have. "When did it arrive, and from who?"

He hooks a brow as if he wasn't expecting my quick interest, but he's severely underestimated how seriously I'll take anything regarding my little bird.

"It came a few weeks ago," he informs me, and I have to refrain from releasing the glare twitching my eyes. "Admittedly, I confided in a particular . . . *unorthodox* private investigation company I hoped would have found them by now, but they didn't get anywhere before they dropped the case."

I know everything, but I act engrossed and attentive. I imagine Ketos got one lead toward Alistair or someone like him involved in this and backed the fuck away. Honestly, I debated slipping Xoid's card in a place he'd find it and become curious, but technically we're already all over this shit, and there's no benefit to having the senator in the know.

At least I thought we were all over it. Now I know he's been sitting on this particular lead for weeks it will be near impossible to pick up the cold trail. It's a missed opportunity, and that has me wanting to wreck this office.

I breathe and compose myself.

"It only came with this note." He slides a creased piece of paper across the table.

It reads three words. Three words that steal my vision from rage for a split second.

My little bird.

The paper is lost in my fist before I can stop it. It's at risk of becoming dust in my palm.

"Does it mean something to you?" The senator straightens at my reaction.

"I've joked about it with Ana," I say, trying to rally a response for him, when really I want to march right out of this room and get Rix on the phone. "It makes me believe someone's been following us."

But how, where, and fucking when?

I try to think of every instance where I've called her that, who could have been around to overhear me, but there are far too many names battering my mind.

"I feared as much. It's why Ana has you and her plainclothes guard. I can't put her under lockdown." Kinsley sits with a sigh of exasperation.

I pity him, understand him. The concern of a father is heavy on this expression. I don't know how to tell him on my watch Ana is as safe as she could ever be, even if the damn FBI were involved.

"On my life, sir, she's safe with me."

He doesn't know who I am or what I've done. He can't fathom the lengths I would go to for his daughter.

I don't need him to.

Whether I'm by her side or having to stalk her for the rest of her life, the only way Ana won't have my personal protection is if I'm dead. For the first time in so long it strikes me with pain and guilt—so much soul-tearing guilt—to admit . . .

I *want* to be alive for her.

CHAPTER 22
Anastasia

I sit in the chair next to Nina's hospital bed, so glad she's beginning to laugh again. It's been some weeks, but it's taken all this time for her to start believing she's truly safe, and my heart is broken for her.

"They want to discharge me soon, but I'm not sure where I'll go," Nina says, frightened.

I take her hand. "You've never accepted my help before, but this time I'm not giving you a choice. There's a safe house set up for you with surveillance, and police will be keeping watch. We need to find out who is responsible for this and if there might be others."

"There was . . . every now and then," she admits. "I don't know why he kept me."

Just then Rhett opens the door, but he doesn't come in fully.

"Just to let you know, there's a delay with the jet. We can spare another hour before we need to leave," he says gently.

I nod with a smile and he leaves again. Despite me saying he can be in here, he always waits outside no matter how many hours I visit for.

"I'm heading to New York for a few days. I've always wanted to go," I say to Nina.

When I turn back to her, she has a frown fixed on the door.

"He was there," she says.

My skin chills at that haunting statement. "Where?"

"At the house. He . . . he found me."

I shake my head. "That's not possible. He's my guard—he's always with me."

Nina remains adamant. "His voice. I'll never forget it, Ana. It was the first of any real kindness I heard in five years."

She has to be mistaken. Someone else could have a similar low, smooth tone and she's just confused. I can't imagine the adrenaline of such an ordeal. Details are bound to be hazy.

Nina holds my eyes and her face begins to drop, perhaps reading that I don't believe her. Don't *want* to believe her, because denial is easier for *me*. It's selfish, and my heart speeds up as I try to think about the possibility.

He's always been with me . . . except the night of the fair.

Oh god. He was in some kind of fight. His arm . . . was it from a bullet? An altercation trying to get Nina out of that house and it went wrong. Almost so horribly wrong.

I stand suddenly, trembling, as the conclusion won't erase itself from my mind. It's too much of a coincidence, but Nina won't be able to confirm the date.

"I have to go," I say vacantly. "I'll visit you when I'm back. Riley will be here to take you to the safe house."

Halfway to the door, Nina calls. "Can you tell him thank-you? I guess he doesn't want anyone to know, but I wouldn't be here if it weren't for him."

I nod, pushing back the nausea rolling in my stomach. Because *why* would Rhett have been there in the first place? And what else could he be hiding? Information starts to batter the forefront of my mind. Everything about him since the day he became my guard.

My heart is speeding too fast and I'm shaking. I can't face him here. Not right now.

I take a different route that will evade the waiting room he's sitting in.

When I find another exit, the wintry air spears my throat with the panic rising in me. I don't have a spare key to the jeep this time, so I take off in a fast walk, nearly jogging, down the street. I can't escape him—I know this. Somehow he'll find me, and my eyes begin to prick with the fear that it isn't safety I should feel but terror. I've been stalked by some sinister person and become content in their presence all this time like a lamb up for slaughter.

I find a park that's deserted with evening starting to fall. Through it is some woodland, and maybe I can hide in there. I don't know for how long. I could call my father or the police. But my chest aches, so damn tight, at the thought of turning Rhett in even if I don't know what for yet.

When I turn around my scream doesn't escape because a hand immediately clamps over my mouth and a strong arm encircles my waist. Rhett's icy eyes are furious, bearing down on me. I do the only thing I can think of and bite his hand. It doesn't achieve anything except bringing a mild wince to his face.

"Get the fuck off of me," I hiss when he uncovers my mouth.

Rhett lets me go and I stumble back.

"No matter what's going on, don't *ever* leave without me," he says seriously.

He has to be fucking joking.

"Where were you the night of the fair?" I demand. I back up slowly, my adrenaline sharp and ready to run. "Nina recognizes you. You were at that house, weren't you?"

His eyes narrow a fraction, and while I'm prepared to fight with him if he denies it, he doesn't bother.

Now my chest is racing. I can hardly breathe right.

"You've always been able to find me so fast. Every time there's a security camera you notice it, like you already know exactly where they are in every new place, and you know who's watching. Your watch costs far more than someone on your supposed salary would spend. You're always on your phone, always in contact with people you don't want anyone to notice with the earpiece you wear. You were never supposed to be my guard, and something happened to Victor conveniently right before he was due to start, giving you the perfect opening, and you were right there . . . waiting." I tie everything together with one final missing piece, though I'm terrified to know his answer. "Did you kill him to take his place?"

My breath clouds the air and I can't draw it fast enough.

"Yes."

I don't expect his honesty. So I don't know what to do with it when it slams into me so hard.

"Stay back," I warn as his steps keep advancing, ready to chase me the moment I run.

"Ana, there are things you don't know."

"I know enough," I snap. "You're a murderer."

"Yes, I am. Because sometimes to fight a monster you have to become one."

"Please let me go," I whimper, almost at the tree line of the woods.

"Not going to happen, little bird."

With nothing left to lose, I spin on my heel and break into the fastest run of my life. I'm quite a good runner—the treadmill is a favorite of mine to train with in the gym—and I push harder than I ever have before. But this isn't a stationary piece of equipment. This is real, and it comes with the obstacles of snapping branches and loose forest debris. It comes with the threat of a beast on my heels, the weight of unsuitable clothing, and the freezing night cutting my cheeks.

It's practically over before it has begun. Rhett's powerful arm hooks around my waist as I manage to get deep into the woods, and perhaps that's my biggest mistake since no one will hear me now.

I become caged between a thick tree and his unmoving, tall body no matter how much I thrash and cry. When I don't give up he restrains my hands above my head.

"Please stop," he begs softly, such a contrast to my frantic struggle.

Exhaustion sweeps in when I accept my attempts are futile. He's caught me. He will always catch me, and I was doomed from the moment I stepped into the spider's web the day we met.

"What do you want from me?" I whisper in scared defeat.

"Everything. I want absolutely everything you are and all that you're willing to give me. I tried not to want you. So fucking hard, and still I wish I could stop. You weren't supposed to find out about me, certainly not like this—at least not until I'd found the threat against your life and the evil I've been hunting for all these years."

I start to calm, only so I can process what he's saying. "You're the threat to my life," I say, though it cracks in my chest.

"I am. But there is something worse after you. Worse because they're still anonymous, but not for long. I promise you'll be safe. You're safe with me."

I want to believe him, and it's so fucking wrong and ironic. My naïve side is too soft to his words. His touch.

"How can I believe that?" I ask.

"I'll tell you everything. Then you can decide what you want to do with the information."

What I want . . . Maybe I'm the fucked-up one, because all I start to think of is his firm body pinning me to this tree. How he's looking at me with pained blue eyes, both of us straining with the need to unleash something raw and furious. It's like he can he read my thoughts. I'm in so much shit I can practically feel a tether forming from me to his anchor heading straight to hell.

Rhett kisses me. Hard.

He releases me and my hands fall around his neck when he pulls my waist to crush us together. I come alive. So sinfully for this man I should be fighting. Running from. Yet the space between my thighs only grows hotter with the fact.

Rhett's hand climbs the inside of my thigh and I moan, hooking my leg around his waist to give him better access.

He groans, passing his fingers over my tights and panties. "You're fucking soaked through for me. Did that turn you on, little bird? Running from me, knowing there's nowhere you can go I wouldn't find you."

"Yes," I pant. It's the truth. And I need him so badly it's shameful.

"Such a bad girl." He tuts. "But now you're going to take my cock like a good fucking girl, aren't you?"

He rips my tights between my legs, and it's so damn sexy I

surge toward a climax the moment he pushes my panties to the side and slides a finger into me.

"Rhett, please."

"This is going to be quick, baby. We have a flight to catch," he growls. "Take out my cock."

I fumble with his belt until it comes undone, pulling his zipper and dragging the heel of my palm down the silken length of him.

My breath catches when he bends enough to hook my other thigh and his dick lines up with my entrance. I can't help myself, using the tip to rub my folds a few times, moaning at the sparks shooting through me with every knock of it against my clit.

"You're such a fucking tease," he growls into my neck. "Let me sink into that pretty little cunt before I drop you, spin you around, and I won't be nice."

His words are so daring and promising that they make me so wet it's unreal. As soon as his tip passes down to where he wants Rhett plunges into me all at once, and I cry out with the sudden fullness, pulling his hair so tight he makes a sound of pain, but it only encourages him.

Rhett slams into me mercilessly, like he's punishing me for running. Hating himself for chasing. Both of us are angry for being unable to resist this thing between us.

"Come for me, baby," Rhett says between thrusts, kissing and sucking along my neck, which only amplifies my pleasure.

I reach between us, circling my clit, and it doesn't take much when I'm already sprinting toward my orgasm that crashes over me in waves. I cry out his name, clawing the back of his neck, and his grip on my thighs tightens with pleasurable pain as he slams in once more with his climax, jerking as he spends himself inside me.

He lets me go and my knees almost buckle trying to take my own weight as he pulls my skirt back down and tucks himself away.

"We don't want to be late," he says, voice raspy from sex, and my mind is still clouded with it as he takes my hand and leads us out of the woods. "Your punishment for running is dealing with the mess of us between your legs until we get on the jet."

CHAPTER 23
Anastasia

I'm curled up with a blanket on the wide beige seat of my father's private jet having the most intense stare-off with Rhett across from me.

"Tired, little bird?" he taunts with knowing.

My eyes narrow. I'm exhausted from the running, the emotions, then the wild sex in the woods that I can't stop replaying, and it's getting damn frustrating. I changed into leggings and a sweater the moment we were in the air, making do with what I could to clean myself off in the small toilet.

"No," I lie. "I want you to start talking."

Rhett eyes the front of the cabin where the crew are out of earshot, then behind me to be sure there isn't anyone lingering.

"Victor Ross was a vile man. He paid to rape unwilling victims in the type of network your friend was saved from," he begins.

Suddenly I'm wide-awake, shifting to sit straighter.

"How do you know?"

"Because it's my job to know. Long before you. I'm not a good man, Ana, and I hope you never try to see me as one. To take down these types of people I need to fight fire with fire. I've killed a lot of people in my work trying to stop them trafficking women, children. Selling drugs that are ruining lives and taking children from their parents. There is no limit to what these kinds of people will deal in. The worst that you can think of, I assure you, is not the worst that is happening in our sick, cruel world."

I don't know what to say, how to process this.

"You're not secret service," I whisper.

"No."

"Then how did you get hired?"

How the fuck could someone bypass some of the highest security systems to give him what he needed for the riskiest façade?

"I have a connection in the FBI. He was able to pull some strings and forge the credentials I needed with the help of those in my network. It's no small or easy feat. No one would be able to if it wasn't for my guy on the inside, close to the secret service already."

"Why . . .?" I breathe, overwhelmed with the information. "Why this position? Why me?"

So many questions rush to be answered, and it's going to be a long and heavy night getting to them all.

"I need you to know and believe you're safe. With me, on my life."

I believe him. Those icy blue eyes hold me with such promise that I nod. Rhett takes a long breath and I brace for what's to come.

"One of my team found out there was a hit on you on the dark web. For your kidnap. We think it's to lure your father out for assassination. I wish I could say at the time I cared, but I didn't. I knew I needed to get this position because the hit against your family was traced to someone in mine. My uncle, who I've been hunting for three years. He's at the top of it all. The ringleader of the most vile and evil roots of poison through many states. I took this role with the intention of tracing him if I could figure out who was in on the hit, and being here, close to you and within your father's home, it was a ticket I couldn't pass up."

"I'm a ticket," I snap suddenly. My nose stings as I find out all this time he was using me. My family. "You don't care what happens to me or my father so long as you find your uncle."

"At first . . . yes."

He may as well have aimed a gun at my heart and pulled the trigger. "And you thought to gain a good quick fuck while you were at it?" I hiss.

"No. In truth I wanted you to be the stuck-up, difficult princess I anticipated. An insufferable, selfish heiress who would make not caring pretty damn easy. You're anything but easy, Anastasia Kinsley. You're a flame that can burn against ice, because I'm a cold bastard. I haven't truly felt anything real since I lost everything, and now . . ."

My pulse skips. His jaw locks as if he's fighting against spilling his next words, but I *need* them to soothe the insecurity taking over me that I mean nothing to him.

"Now . . . ?" I repeat.

"I'm terrified," he confesses. "I've been wounded to near death, seen unimaginable horrors, and been numb to it all. When I found you in that maze I realized how fucked I was. Because for so long I've only known vengeance to catch my uncle, and for the first time I felt something stronger. Still rage and revenge, but I feel it all for you with the thought of someone harming you."

He sits there like steel, yielding none of the emotions I try to decipher.

"How did you get that scar?" I ask, wanting to trace the jagged line down the side of his face.

"The night Sarah died. We were ambushed. My uncle had finally found me after I managed to escape him at sixteen. I'd lived nine peaceful years thinking he'd given up. I wasn't really worth it to him, but it was the fact I'd escaped him at all that meant he would never let me go. He sent them and they killed Sarah right in front of me, shot her, because he knew living with that was a far worse punishment than death."

"Are you closer to finding him now?"

"I think so."

"I want in."

He breaks his firm expression to show shock, which quickly turns to a frown of protest. "I don't know what you mean by *in*," he hedges, "but you even knowing this is dangerous. I'm not putting you in harm's way."

"There's a hit out on me—it's too late for that," I counter.

"It means nothing when you're not going to leave my side. You noticed my attention on the cameras. It's because I have a guy who can tap into any feed I ask, and he's been tracking us. I have two other guys who have been trailing us at all times. You haven't noticed them. No one is getting within a few feet of you before I shoot them down."

My lips part at hearing of the extra guys who've been stalking us this whole time.

"They weren't much help in the maze. Someone could have killed me there. They almost did."

His grip flexes on the arm of his seat. "I got a call from one of them that you'd entered by yourself, and he did go after you, but he lost you pretty fast."

"You didn't . . . kill him for that, did you?"

"Fuck, of course not. It was his last day on that particular assignment though. He's still a great asset. I don't kill those who displease me."

That's a relief at least.

I observe his wrists. "Your cufflinks." Two small black serpents. "You never change them."

"Everyone in my organization wears a serpent in one form or another so we know we're on the same side in raids. The network is vast with those who are willing to get their hands dirty for it and those who are hacking behind the scenes. Some have it as a tattoo, some have jewelry."

He reaches into his coat pocket, pulling out a business card and handing it to me. The logo is an open-mouthed serpent crossing over itself to create the infinity symbol. Its body is dark in the center to create an "X," and there are three other letters to the right.

"Xoid?"

"It's the name of my organization."

"'Welcome the lost, pity the found.'" I read the phrase striked out underneath.

When I flash my eyes up to him his mouth quirks as if he's reflecting on a memory.

"An inside joke, really. Xoid is made up of a lot of people from very shitty backgrounds, those without a place. They tend to wander into our path and we offer them a place and a purpose."

"The lost," I say.

He nods. "But if Xoid finds you, it's most likely your worst nightmare come for you."

The found.

I shiver at the notion. The ominous power behind what Rhett has founded. I flip over the card to find only a code and two initials: R.K.

"When do I get my serpent?"

"Ana," he warns. "That's not happening."

"I'm in this whether you like it or not," I argue.

"You're a victim of it, and you will not become a martyr."

"I'll always be the victim if you shield me from everything. My friend was held captive for five years by something your uncle is at the top of. My father is threatened and they want to use *me* for it. This is my fight now too, and I don't need a damned serpent to tell me what I can or can't do."

He falls silent, but he never takes his eyes off me. Then he says, "You think a little bird can survive in a pit of serpents?"

A thrill awakens in me. It's dark and it screams all kinds of alarms, but I'm so alive with it.

"Yes."

"I can protect your body, but I can't protect you from what you might see."

"I can handle it."

Boldly I get up, crossing the short space and bracing my hands on the arms of his chair. "I can handle *you*, Rhett Kaiser. Or is that name a lie too?" I cant my head and watch desire spark in his cool irises.

"Not a lie. It's a name I chose. My birth name is Everett Lanshall."

"Your choice is sexier."

I lean in and kiss him.

He pulls me down gently, until I'm sitting sideways across his lap. When we break apart he tucks my wine-red hair behind my ear, saying nothing with his mouth, but his eyes say enough, searching over me.

"I'm not as fragile as you think I am," I say at his concern.

"All things are fragile to the right impact."

"Even you?"

"Even me."

I sigh, resting my head on his shoulder and breathing in his musky scent of teakwood and a hint of mint.

"Just as well I have my big, bad bodyguard to protect me."

Rhett unfolds the blanket he hasn't touched, fitting it over me against him. The flight is less than an hour and a half, but my eyes slip shut with the amazing comfort of this position.

"Always."

My heart skips a beat. Will he stay even after the assignment is over? Uncertainty coils in my stomach. He's made no such promise and could decide there's no time for someone like me in his line of work. That I'm more of a liability than I'm worth.

I press into him a little tighter with the thought. I *can* handle myself, and I will show him. If that makes me a monster too, then maybe all this time I was just waiting to come out from under the bed.

CHAPTER 24
Anastasia

"For a woman who wants a secluded home, you sure get excited by flashing lights," Rhett says.

We're standing in Times Square, and I can't help my gawking at how many screens and lights flood the space.

"I wouldn't like to live here, but you have to admit, it's an impressive spectacle," I reply.

"Of a hundred advertisements killing our eyes through too-bright artificial light, yes."

I roll my eyes, pulling him along to see more.

We're seated in a fast-food restaurant half an hour later. Despite Rhett's ranting about how bad the food is for me, it's what I'm craving. The salty fries and over-greasy burger are delicious.

"So how do you always find me? Tracker on my phone or something?" I joke, taking a sip of my Pepsi.

Rhett eases a guilty smile and my eyes widen. I toss a fry at him and he chuckles.

"When?" I demand.

"When you gave me your phone that first day."

This son of a bitch.

"Stalker," I grumble.

Truthfully, there's something twistedly wrong with me to be glad he always knows where I am. Especially now I know of the threat against me when I've been cluelessly wandering around as if I'm still nobody.

"Does my father know about the threat?" I ask.

"To you, yes. It's why he's been overprotective about your safety, but he never disclosed that to me, and I doubt any other guard would have known about it. Though I don't think he's figured out he's the real target."

"We should tell him."

"Easy, little bird. We don't make such decisions so abruptly."

I tingle at the use of the word "we."

"It's his life at risk really. I'm just leverage. Plus, wouldn't the secret service be a great help to ramp up the security at the tip-off of a live threat?"

I feel sick to my stomach at the thought of my father in danger. If anything happens to him . . .

"They would, but how long will they keep it up before they decide to give the all-clear and relax the high protection detail? Whoever this is will wait it out. They won't give this up so easily if they've tied themselves to Alistair Lanshall for it now. I think your father knows that."

I hold in my wince at his uncle's name. My anger shakes at the thought of him though I have no face. He hurt Rhett, made him suffer more than one person ever should in one lifetime, from when he was a child to killing his fiancée.

"What happened to your parents?" I ask quietly.

Rhett regards me with a sad smile. "They died when I was ten. Car accident. My uncle became my legal guardian."

"I'm so sorry."

Condolences will never be enough for what he's been through. I have to show him he's worth far more than what life has dealt him. That his purpose doesn't begin and end under the judgment of Alistair Lanshall. And that will take time. For now, all I can do is attempt to fill his life with some *hopefully* happy memories.

So I smile like a child as I ask, "Have you ever been ice-skating?"

Rhett is sour at my giddy mood while we equip our ice skates at the Rockefeller Center. I don't let it dampen my excitement, because I'm determined to bring it out of him too. He just needs a little . . . *encouragement*.

"Have you ever skated before?" Rhett asks, bending in front of me. He starts tying my other boot since he's finished his.

"Just a little," I say, a small lie. Riley and I go skating a few times every year. "For someone who never has, you're swift at the equipment."

"They're merely boots with lethal weapons for balance."

"Always looking for the danger."

He squeezes my calf when he's finished. "With you, always."

I pat his shoulder before I stand. "At least try to look like you're having fun."

We waddle over to the ice, which is fairly quiet with only an hour until it closes. I skate on first, turning to find him watching me with a quirked brow, still off the ice.

"What?" I ask innocently. "It's not as hard as it looks. Promise."

"I don't know how anyone thought standing on knives to

glide across ice was a good idea," he says.

"I imagine it has a history of something practical. For those of us who don't live in arctic countries it's called *fun*, Rhett. You need to try it sometime."

I skate back to him, taking his hand, but he remains reluctant, eyeing the white floor with such wariness it's highly amusing.

Rhett grips the ledge, taking his first step on, and when both his feet meet the ice I take his other hand to force him away from it. He pins me with a look that says, "This is not a good idea." I giggle at the sight of him, so stiff and gripping my hands so tightly as if it will prevent us from falling.

"Don't worry, Agent, I'll be your protector on the ice. Just copy my feet."

"You're going backward and I'm in awe of how you're doing it."

"Oh, right. Okay, let's try this."

Letting go of one of his hands, I skate forward a little, pushing one foot and then the other. To his credit, he's a quick learner.

"Not so bad now, is it?" I beam as we begin making our way around.

"What do we do now?"

"We skate around the ring."

"Then what?"

"We go around again."

"Is that all?"

"Have you really never even seen people ice-skate before?"

Rhett shakes his head. "If I wasn't indoors a lot as a kid, I was usually being used to smuggle something or create a diversion. Then my life with Sarah . . . I met her when I was twenty and we were both pretty busy. She was in medical school and I was training a lot in my first year of SWAT with the intention of progressing to FBI."

I watch his face thoughtfully. "So you were always destined to be a super-sexy, badass agent then. Too bad I miss out on the uniform."

He gives a light chuckle. "I suppose. I would have lived a life of stopping bad things legally, but my uncle made me realize there's a world of abominable people like him that will always exist, and they can never be stopped the righteous way."

I let go of his hand and skate in front of him, turning to go backward again.

"Righteous is overrated," I say.

"Why do I get the feeling I'm corrupting you?"

"Perhaps I always have been like this." I smile wickedly.

"I guess no one would expect an angel to buy a ticket to hell."

I stop and panic crosses Rhett's face, but I grab his black scarf, forcing the collision, and he wraps his arms around me tightly.

"When the devil came I couldn't resist," I purr up at him.

Rhett cups my cheek. "I'm a bad influence on you, Miss Kinsley."

"Probably."

I push onto the tips of my skates to kiss him. Only once before I push off him, giggling at his rocky balance as he catches himself.

"Bet you can't catch me this time, Agent Kaiser."

I'm truly exhausted by the time we pull our rental car into the hotel. I don't fail to notice the plainclothes guard in the car behind us, and he certainly stands out as one with the way he acts and dresses, movie-style earpiece giving him away.

Rhett carries his bag and rolls my suitcase before handing the keys to the valet and taking my hand. At the reception, the woman behind the desk does a poor job of hiding her attraction, her gaze roving over Rhett, not even sparing me a glance. She hands him two key cards, and I realize then why she's looking at him with such suggestion. We have separate rooms.

My stomach sinks the whole way up the twenty floors in the elevator. At the first room he comes inside with me. My breath catches as we wander to the far wall made up entirely of glass. The city lights look like a kaleidoscope from up here. The room is very tasteful, with neutral colors and a large bed, and a separate dining area and bathroom.

Rhett sets the bags down, and as I finish admiring the view I watch him pace the room, checking in every cupboard and even under the bed.

"Safe from monsters?" I quip when he seems satisfied with his checks.

"All but one," he says.

I throw myself onto the bed and moan into the sinking embrace. Fatigue weighs on my eyelids.

"Your father booked the accommodation," he says. "If you want me to use the other room—"

"I don't," I cut in a little too quickly. It's kind of pathetic how much I want him to stay.

His shoulders seem to relax at that. "Then I'm taking responsibility of making sure you get into pajamas before you fall asleep."

Rhett pulls my suitcase over to me, but I groan with reluctance, rolling onto my side. I'm too damn comfortable.

I don't expect Rhett to hook my knee and yank me down the bed. As I squeal with surprise he leans down to me.

"I'm not opposed to undressing you myself, of course, but it would take a different turn than you have the stamina for right now," he says huskily.

Though my core heats at that, I really do want to sleep.

"I don't think you know enough about my stamina to judge," I say anyway.

"Don't tempt me, Ana. I'm more than willing to exhaust you to your very limits to find out."

I know if I pushed a fraction more he would hold true to that and there would be no stopping him. Because I'll lose the will no matter how tired I am.

So I smile coyly and say nothing, pushing his chest to maneuver around him to my case.

After changing and slipping into bed, I'm reconsidering pushing out of my tiredness when Rhett comes strolling out the bathroom in nothing more than loose pajama pants sitting low on his hips. He's an impeccable sight to behold no matter how many times I've witnessed him like this.

Tomorrow we'll be meeting up with Liam, who said there's a gathering happening at some highflier's casino. Then it's the gala the following night.

Rhett slips into bed beside me, and I erupt with the arm he extends in a silent invitation to tuck myself into him. It feels so right, frighteningly natural. With my head on his shoulder I begin idly tracing the scars on his chest.

"Were these during or after him?" I ask quietly.

"They were my rewards," he says.

I angle my head back with a frown. Rhett's expression doesn't shift at all. He speaks of it like it's nothing.

"Every time I completed a mission—usually smuggling—he would take a knife to my skin. He didn't want me to be afraid of pain. He would say it's the only true measure of success—that if I was prepared to take the pain for it, it was worth it."

I become so angry I can hardly contain it. "What happened if you didn't complete the mission?"

"There was a closet under his stairs he would lock me in for a week. So I would feel nothing at all, deprived of interaction and stimulation. You'd think that might be easier than a deep cut. It wasn't."

I kiss over his scars, along his neck. He sighs contentedly, hooking my leg over his abdomen.

"We're going to find him," I promise. He isn't getting rid of me now.

"I would never wish for you to cross paths with him," he says with a hint of fear. "I will do whatever it takes to prevent that."

"I'm not afraid."

"You should be. You should be afraid of *me*, little bird. But more so of him, and the things you've only heard from me would traumatize you to see in person. Promise me that if I let you in you won't do anything reckless. You won't push when I tell you to stop. This is dangerous and fucked-up shit, and I'm only sorry you found out about it when I hoped you wouldn't until I'm long gone out of your life."

I push up, angry with him. "You don't get to run from me either."

He cups my nape to pull me down for a kiss. "Sleep, Ana," he murmurs against my lips.

Though my chest tightens with the lack of assurance he won't leave me, I rest my head again, enjoying the comfort of him now.

CHAPTER 25
Rhett

My phone rings while Ana is finishing getting ready in the bathroom. I take a deep breath, anxious to see Allie's name.

"What have you got for me, Allie?" I ask, slipping a hand into my pants pocket and pacing to the window.

"Not even a hello for your favorite hacker?" she quips. "I am your favorite, right?"

"You're my absolute darling," I compliment.

She gives a satisfied sigh. "Well, I'm calling because I think we could have it all wrong."

"I'm listening."

"So we ran a trace for Matt Heizer that didn't turn up any names."

"You wouldn't call to disappoint me."

"Of course not." I can practically feel her smile.

"Have you ever heard of the name Balenheizer?"

Shit. "As in Damien Balenheizer?"

"The one and only."

He's a notorious mafia leader with not a single moral to his being. We've been tracking him for a while, but he's a real slippery one.

"You think Matt Heizer is an alias?" I ask. This could be really fucking bad if he's involved.

There's money and elegance involved in the way the likes of Alistair Lanshall works. He likes things done clean and smooth; he takes pride in what he creates. With someone like Balenheizer, even the government wouldn't attempt to take him down if he were standing right in front of them.

"It has to be. Perhaps he's taken on the hit."

My blood goes cold. There are many things I'm confident I can keep Ana protected from, but this is the worst of all the targets that could have set their sights on her.

"To what gain?" I snap, only out of my fury as it boils over the edge. I want to take Ana away, hide her somewhere far and use every resource I have.

"That's what's puzzling me. It doesn't seem like his type of interest. He's married, and they say his wife is everything to him. He kills people for merely looking at her wrong."

"Children?" I ask.

"Rix is looking into him still. He doesn't hide much, but his family line is somewhat . . . *rocky*. His current wife isn't his first. He has three kids with her, but we're yet to find out if he has any from his past wife."

I'm shaking with anger and fear. So much fear I haven't felt in so long I hardly know what to do with it.

"Just stay calm," Allie tries to reason as if she can feel me vibrating through my silence.

"Too fucking late."

"Balenheizer would have no reason to use an alias. If he wanted Ana, you know he would have come for her already and proudly let everyone know it was him."

It's a small consolation because she's right. I try to breathe steady and believe this is just a coincidence. That whoever Matt Heizer is, he has some damn nerve linking himself to someone so prolific.

"I want everyone on Matt fucking Heizer to find out who he is. This could be our guy who has it out for the Kinsleys, and he could lead us right to Lanshall."

"We'll get him," Allie says with more confidence than I can muster right now. "There's something else. You've been wanting to pin Adam Sullevan for the attack on Ana, and I think we might have him. Surveillance around the carnival car park shows one of those clowns getting out of a car. I can't see the driver to confirm it's Adam, but the registration comes back to the Sullevans."

That very name scorches inside me with such hatred I'm proud of my own resistance to beating the shit out of him with his every appearance at the university.

"You're sure?" I ask tightly.

"Are you really asking me that?"

"So that was just a sick way to torment his ex?" I question, lowering my tone to be sure Ana can't hear me. I don't want her to know yet as it will only upset her.

"Spook her and get a rise out of you. Are petty reasons really that far-fetched?"

"So the Forbes are off the hook?"

Not my hook. I can't shake them from my mind.

"From our end, they're clean. You should see if there's

anything you can find out while you have the chance to be close to them all, but they might be just as harmless as Kinsley. But we're close, Rhett. I can feel it."

Riddled with anxiety at that fact, I can only think of my little bird. I'm so close to catching the uncle I've hunted for three years, and now all I want is to run far and fast with her.

But that didn't work before. And I will not lose Ana.

"One more thing," she adds. "The gathering at the casino you're going to tonight—turns out it's more of a big deal than some meetup for the elite to drink and gamble away their fortunes. It's set up by a man named Jacob Forthson. The gala tomorrow . . . it's his event. I can't quite place what the connection is yet, but I think it's worth keeping in mind."

I should have known the devil's work would always be calling.

"Can you contact Rix for me, tell him the setup we might need around that venue tomorrow in case I discover anything?"

"Will do," she sings.

"Thanks, Allie," I say and hang up.

Ana might have been waiting until I finished the call. I catch her reflection in the glass. Turning, I can hardly organize my thoughts as they explode into a hundred desires and admiration of her in a little black dress. Simple, yet so damn elegant and sexy, with heels that make her legs appear endless.

"Do I have competition?" she asks with a low edge of seductive challenge.

I stalk to her with eyes that rove over every inch of her. She's a fucking goddess and I'm prepared to fall to my damn knees to pray to her.

"You're going to make my job *very* hard tonight."

"You've never called *me* your darling," she says, tipping her chin back as I come close enough to touch.

"You're far more than that, Anastasia. You're my damnation and my redemption."

"That's a contradiction, Agent."

"Can something not mend what it breaks? It's rare, valuable, but the possibility exists."

I tug her waist until she's pressed against me, wanting to claim her mouth, but I figure she might scold me for ruining her perfect red lipstick. *Fuck*, the thought of those lips wrapped around my dick strains every tether of control in me not to force her to her knees right now. And she would do it. Her eyes are dancing with desire, and we have to leave now before we decide to abandon the night at the casino.

I have to meet Liam Forbes and see if there's anything I can discover about him that will give us any leads. Like why he's here in New York.

"My call was with someone on my team called Allie. I would say you two get along, but truthfully, I'd be scared of you both in a room together."

"How so?"

"Too much intelligence and beauty. Every man would be compelled to sit while you two walked your power into a room."

"Your flattery is impressive."

"Just honest."

Her smile is a light to the darkness I'm shrouded in. In all I wear and all I am within.

"I promised I wouldn't keep you in the dark about what I know. But this concerns your friend, Liam, and I need you to swear to me you'll stick to *my* plan and not say anything you shouldn't to him."

Her face turns serious and I adore her fierce will.

"What could he possibly have to do with any of it?"

"I'll explain on the way," I say, taking her hand and kissing her knuckles.

CHAPTER 26
Anastasia

Rhett pulls us up to the casino, which is *expensive*-looking even compared to some of the elite places I've been invited to before with my father. I go to the entrance while he hands over the keys to the valet, talking privately to him—his first marker to try to gain any small intel he can about those here tonight. The blatant stares of the men lingering outside doesn't riddle me with anxiety like they normally would. I almost dare them to approach me with a look back, only able to revel in their quickly wiped confidence because I know Rhett will come for me. Claim me.

My stomach erupts with a giddy thrill at the thought.

"Ready, baby?" he says, slipping an arm around my waist.

The men's lingering looks quickly avert.

I smile sweetly up at him. He's a breathtaking sight in his suit. No tie, all black. My mouth is practically watering. I don't know how I'm going to cope with him in a tux tomorrow for the charity gala.

Inside Rhett's hand squeezes my waist as if he anticipates the liveliness of the night will make me shrink within myself. Surprisingly, I'm fine. More than that, I'm excited to be here, even more so with the mission we're on being unknown to everyone here. I don't know what that makes me. Twisted, dangerous, naïve. I don't care. Some of the people here are innocent, others are wicked disguised in their finery, and I want to be party to snuffing them out.

We head to the bar, and I order a dry martini while Rhett requests a water.

"Still not just one drink?" I lean in to say.

"If I'm out with you, it will always be a no."

I don't quip back about how he takes his job too seriously and that I can handle myself. Because there's a different kind of pain when he answers, and it strikes me that his soberness is something personal he hasn't told me yet. I'll wait for as long as he needs to tell me everything.

I take his chin while he leans sexily on the bar watching me sip my martini.

"Fine," I say. "But you have to at least try to appear happy to be here."

He takes my hand as it drops. "You're saying I don't? I've been putting in tremendous effort."

"Baby, if you want to put that scowl to use, we're in the perfect place to win big tonight."

Something wild flares in his eyes. He brings my hand to his lips, taking a deep breath as if devouring my scent. "You haven't done this in a while," he says, kissing my thumb.

I didn't realize. The skin is healed, and my manicure has lasted far longer than usual given my incessant nerves that cause me to pick and bite. It warms my chest more so that *he* noticed.

I don't get to respond as he drops my hand and straightens with a hardening look behind me. Hands touch my waist and I jump, but my fright chokes to a squeal at the sight of Liam. He vibrates with chuckles when I throw my arms around his neck.

"So glad you made it, Ana," he says, pulling back with a bright grin. He examines my hair. "I almost didn't recognize you."

"You know I've been wanting to try short hair," I say. He doesn't need to know of the attack behind it; I've already decided they don't get to own this change in me. "You scrub up well," I tease, plucking at his white shirt collar.

"Speak for yourself. The red hair really suits you. I have a feeling you'll be giving your bodyguard plenty of work tonight," he says, eyeing Rhett over my shoulder.

He has no idea. My stomach hollows with what I know. The danger Liam and his family could be in, or involved in. I don't want to believe that Liam, the charming, selfless man I know, could play any part in the kind of crimes Rhett takes down for a living.

I step aside. Rhett hasn't eased his scary expression, tracking Liam's every move like a hawk.

"Rhett Kaiser, isn't it?" Liam greets him with an extended hand.

Mercifully, Rhett accepts the handshake.

"Yes. And you're the famous Liam Forbes."

Liam casts me a side-smirk, drawing me into his side with playful flirtation. "What have you been saying about me, sweetheart?"

"How much have you had to drink?" I giggle.

"You'd need at least two more of those to catch up," he says, indicating my half-finished martini, and he takes a drink of his whiskey. "I saw your picture together in the tabloid, albeit a lot later than everyone else, and my father had to catch me up on when you told me about your replacement guard. Man, are they quick fuckers to paint a story that sells. The boyfriend ruse is genius press, really. America's sweetheart is a hopeless romantic. Don't worry, your secret is safe with me."

Liam gives me a wink and my chest unsettles with the enlightenment our relationship is just that—pretend. My eyes skim Rhett, but he's looking off over the venue as if he's giving us privacy in our conversation. Like a bodyguard.

I don't know why it frustrates me. It's not like he'd say otherwise. Not even to me. Rhett is noncommittal. Dangerous. I know this and I won't let my heart truly fall for him. We're merely two adults in a situation that forces our proximity, and sexual chemistry is natural.

"We have a table—come," Liam says, guiding me by the waist.

I'm never normally uncomfortable with Liam's touches, but with Rhett here I can't shake the want to be in his arms instead while he walks on my other side.

As we get deeper into the casino, Liam leads us through black curtains that are pulled back without hesitation for him. I thought the main room was lavish, but this VIP lounge takes a further step up in wealth.

"What do you say, Rhett Kaiser, a game of poker?" Liam says to him as we approach a table setting up for a new game.

"I don't think I'm in the league to play." He brushes him off.

Something tells me that's a lie.

"You have the perfect face for it," I say, giving him flirtatious eyes. It's part of our ruse after all.

Liam chuckles. "She's got a point. Only five minutes with

you and I'm intimidated by how little you give away. I can see why they chose you to guard our little Ana," he muses.

I push him away, actually relieved when his hand drops from me. Rhett's doesn't replace it, and I grow irrationally frustrated.

"Gentlemen, allow me the pleasure of introducing the remarkable up-and-coming America's sweetheart," Liam says, drawing the attention of all the men and women around the table.

Resisting the instinct to cower into myself, I smile at the attention raking over me. Several women linger around the backs of chairs and one perches on a man's lap, but he taps her thigh to get her to stand as his gaze feeds on me. That's all I can think of in their eyes. Hunger.

"Anastasia Kinsley," that man drawls, standing slowly. "It's an honor to have you join us. We weren't aware you were in the city. I'm Darren Rutherforth."

Somehow I detect that to be a lie. Perhaps he wasn't informed I'd be *here* tonight, which doesn't settle well paired with the subtle glances he spares the others as if one of them messed up.

Rhett's arm finally snakes its way around me. I don't take my eyes off Darren as I lean into him.

"Rhett Kaiser," he introduces himself. "Do you have space for one more player?"

"It would be our pleasure," Darren says brightly, his gaze lingering a little apprehensively on Rhett.

A chair is pulled out and his hand gives my waist a squeeze. I take the seat while surprise spreads across the faces of the six men around the table. As Darren sits again, his eyes twinkle on me. He has to be in his mid-thirties at least, and the rest range around the same age or a bit older.

"What are the stakes?" I ask as the cards are dealt.

"A dinner with you would be the highest prize on offer tonight," he suggests.

I keep my composure and play along though the thought makes my skin crawl. "I'm afraid I'm spoken for," I say.

"A darling like you shouldn't be tied down."

"Do I look tied, Darren? Loyalty isn't shackles—it's respect."

His eyes flick up to where I imagine Rhett is behind me. Darren's throat bobs, but he shifts to hide his intimidation at the sight of my guard and I'm internally giddy.

Liam sits beside me to be dealt in. "Stakes are a hundred, princess," he says.

One hundred thousand dollars. If I lose, which is highly probable, I'll have some explaining to do to my father. But I've placed myself in the game not out of arrogance or as some power play, but because Rhett needs to go looking for information since no one will trust speaking to a hopeful president's daughter. As much as I don't want him to leave me, this gives Rhett an excuse to mingle among the others and not look like a stupidly overprotective boyfriend.

My back curves at the slow trail of Rhett's hand cupping my nape. Turning my head brings our faces intimately close before he leans his mouth to my ear.

"I'll get you another drink. Are you sure you'll be okay here?" he asks with genuine concern and reluctance.

"I'll be fine. Do what you have to do. I have Liam," I say so only he can hear.

Rhett's fierce blue eyes hold me, pulling at a deeper part of me.

"If I kiss you, am I going to regret it?" he murmurs.

I fight a smile. "You think I'd wear a lipstick you could ruin?"

"Thank fuck."

Rhett kisses me hard, deepening it only for a few seconds as he takes the opportunity to lay his claim over me and warn the others. I erupt inside, wanting it to be real, and so I force away the nagging voice that taunts it's all a show.

When he pulls away, he says, "Call for me, I'll drop everything and come back in a heartbeat."

I nod, breathless from him. When he leaves I take a deep breath to compose myself, not meeting anyone's blatant stare as I pick up my cards, and then the game begins.

Players take their turns around the table and I drop my voice to talk to Liam while we wait and observe.

"So where are your bodyguards? You claimed your father was appointing two," I say.

Liam groans low. "Five o'clock and eight o'clock. They blend in with the casino security at least." Then he says, "Seems yours worked out pretty well."

I don't miss his hint of suggestion. "He's not the worst, I suppose."

"Lucky Kaiser was available so quick with such a sudden accident regarding the first appointed."

It's my turn, and it doesn't take me long to decide on my card. The croupier turns over another card from the deck.

I can't have detected suspicion in Liam's tone . . . he would have no reason to speculate.

"Not so lucky that barely a day in and suddenly we're America's front-page new couple."

"You seem to be making that work just fine."

I fight the urge to wipe the teasing smirk off his face.

"All I'm saying is, the guy is one lucky son of a bitch. Bet he didn't anticipate the work with benefits."

"If you're suggesting I'd sleep with my guard, that's highly inappropriate."

He slices me a look that says he doesn't believe a word. I merely feign innocence.

"My brother's here," Liam says, and I hate his drop of enthusiasm at him being in the same venue.

"What's he doing in New York?"

"Same as you—here for the gala."

It must be more of an important event than I originally thought. Still, I grow as uneasy as Liam at the coincidence Matthew is here too when he was at the debate in Cali.

"Didn't take him for one to be so eager for a gala."

"He's been around more lately."

"You don't sound pleased."

Liam huffs a bitter sound. "I think my brother has far more fondness for you than he's ever had me."

That stings inside. I need to make more of an effort to be present with Liam when sometimes I feel like I'm missing so much of his life despite our years of friendship. He's so closely guarded about his past and current affairs that I've never pried, but maybe that's what he needs.

I watch a woman approach the table toward Darren as he takes his turn. She smiles, but there's something sad in it. My eyes are drawn to the glint of her large emerald earrings, which are a flashing marker of her wealth.

"A beauty indeed." Darren admires her, leaning back in invitation for her to perch on his lap.

It doesn't sit right with me. She doesn't hesitate, but she isn't all that willing either.

Liam keeps his eyes on his cards and his jaw tightens. All the other men are admiring this woman now and chatting quietly among themselves.

"Am I missing something?" I ask Liam in a whisper.

"No."

His short reply makes me lean away from him. I don't ask again. She isn't the only woman floating around the place checking in on patrons. They could be hired for the gathering as merely beautiful company. My skin is beginning to prickle with the attention of the eyes that keep slipping between me and this new girl who hasn't looked at me once.

I cast my sights to the curtain, not wanting to pine for Rhett's return, but he can't get back fast enough.

CHAPTER 27
Rhett

I know I'm fucked when having Ana out of my sight for even a moment sharpens my irritation to a dangerous edge. She's safe with her friend, even if the thought of how close they are and his flirtations toward her isn't helping my sour mood.

When did I become such a fucking possessive asshole about this woman? She isn't mine in that way, she'll never be mine, and I should hope she wants to pursue a real relationship.

Fuck that. I've become a complete selfish bastard over her too, not wanting to give up what we have even if it is just a sexual release. At least, that's all she can believe it is. I care about her more than I intended to. She's wrapped herself around me without even trying, and I'll gladly suffocate to stay near her.

I order Ana a drink and scan surreptitiously around the venue. It's a typical high-end casino, nothing more than what I've infiltrated before for certain jobs. They're breeding grounds for corruption and an excellent setup for laundering cash.

"We meet again, Rhett Kaiser."

I recognize the voice immediately with no small amount of distaste. Matthew Forbes takes up one of the bar seats.

"You get around, Forbes," I say in a friendly, casual manner. An effort when I'm itching for violence. Maybe it's an overreaction. I think of how bold he can be toward Ana even when I'm right fucking there. I don't trust him.

He merely gives a cocky smile. "Where's Ana?"

"Playing poker with Liam."

"She's a fine woman."

Now I can't refrain from the warning look I cut him.

He chuckles—a sound I want to take a knife to. "I'm just curious how you met and managed to capture the heart of America's sweetheart."

I want her heart. I want every damned piece of her, and the realization it isn't mine to claim flexes my fists.

"We met on campus last year. She rejected me at first, had a fling with the asshole Adam Sullevan, then came to her senses."

He hums. "Convincing story. And you two certainly play your roles well. Of course, I know it's all a ruse. Perks of being a family friend."

I don't like the way his mouth eases a partial smirk and his brown eyes glint as if he's won something. I don't like him. I can't pin why, other than he has the sly type of arrogance I have no patience to entertain.

Just then a woman comes over. She's beautiful—blonde-haired and blue-eyed, dressed in a short blue gown. My eyes are drawn to her chest, where a waterfall of diamonds adorns her neck with a ruby centerpiece. If they're real, it's worth the kind of money men abandon all morals to gain. I'm fixated on it like it's a key, but Matthew's sigh breaks my attention. He lifts a finger to her necklace and lazily brushes under the diamonds.

I can't take my eyes off the woman. They always have tells. A stiff posture, a hollow smile, dead eyes. To the room she's an elegant prize of beauty; to anyone who *sees* her, she's a woman here against her will. I train my sight on the diamonds dropping from Matthew's finger back to her chest.

"A beautiful piece. It will look magnificent on the one it truly belongs to."

I don't like how this man fantasizes something in that moment. I have pretty damn good intuition, and right now it's telling me Matthew Forbes isn't a good man. Perhaps his father helps him keep his unsavory transactions untraceable, but I don't care what it takes to deep-dive into the depths of his black soul and expose him.

"I assume you'll be at the gala with Ana tomorrow," Matthew asks.

"Of course," I answer. Calm. Neutral. "Ana has been very excited. She's even adding her own charity to fundraise for." I give nothing away of the anger coursing through me at being among the worst kinds of humanity. Men who cheer and gamble and touch what isn't theirs. Dirty money. Filthy trading.

"She always did have a kind heart. Too gentle sometimes. She's a fragile, breakable little thing."

Despite near trembling with rage, I have a feeling Matthew is important. He looks up at the blonde woman as if thinking of Ana—*my* Ana—and when he doesn't find her standing there his expression turns bored.

"She's a very capable, independent woman," I say with *just* enough possessiveness to warn him she's off-limits.

This bastard only seems to take it as thrilling insight into something he hasn't given up pursuing. He might have friends in high places, but I have friends in very fucking scary places and I don't appreciate the way he speaks or even *thinks* about Ana. It's an extreme internal response, perhaps. But what can I say? This woman is shaping me in ways she doesn't even know.

"If you'll excuse me, I have to take this to my girl," I say, picking up her martini and this time making it so damn clear Ana will never be his to even so much as glance at suggestively.

I scope the area, noticing a few more women who don't look pleased to be here. Others are. I don't have Rix in my ear here, but the fact my phone hasn't gone off once meant he isn't seeing anything else of suspicion through the cameras either.

Eager to get back to Ana, I don't waste a moment more.

She's a spectacle. A whole table of rich men and she sits as the most powerful, stunning thing. It isn't just her appearance; Ana has grown into a confidence I find breathtaking, and she isn't finished coming into herself.

Placing her martini down, I can't stop myself gliding a hand around her nape as I kiss the crown of her head.

"I'm reminded why I never participate in these games," she says, standing.

Her eyes are all fiery challenge, and I oblige her silent words to sit in her place. She doesn't disappoint, slipping over my lap, and my dick twitches with her bold confidence. I hold her cards while she leans against me, still very much the player.

"How was your walk?" she whispers seductively in my ear.

"Torturous," I say, relaxing at the feel of her on me, around me. Her scent calms my senses like nothing else.

Ana plucks a card, placing it down. She has a damned good hand and great odds of winning.

"I'm not familiar with your family name, Rhett Kaiser." Darren addresses me.

"I don't suppose you would be. My family is from far more . . . *humble* roots."

He nods as if he understands, but these types of people would never know humble even if they lost all their fortune. "You must have made quite the impression on our hopeful president to have the blessing of dating his daughter," he observes.

Meaning: she's too good for me. I beat him to revelation that long ago. Though it isn't her father that makes her out of the league of every man in this room.

"My father may run the country someday, but he doesn't dictate my life," Ana says, sipping her drink. "Besides, no wallet or family name can compensate for a bland personality or a small cock."

Fuck, she's incredible. I squeeze her thigh, certain she can feel beneath her perfect ass just how desperate I am to bend her over this table and bury myself inside her while they all watch me claim what's mine.

Just then a man walks in flanked by two security guards. I can tell by the stiffening demeanor, so subtle, of those around the table that this guy has to be important, and my mind rings with a name before Darren greets him.

"Jacob Forthson."

Everything about him speaks sickening kinds of wealth, and my suspicions about how he gains it make every sleek inch of him, from the tips of his dirty-blond hair to the polish of his shoes, look like filth to me. He's younger than I anticipated, around my age of twenty-eight, but unlike Liam Forbes, I don't get the impression he runs by anyone else's rules. Only his own.

"Gentlemen." Jacob greets them with enough arrogance to place him above everyone else. "I hope you don't gamble too much away with the prizes on offer tomorrow."

That earns a round of light chuckles out of nothing more than feeding this guy's ego. When his eyes land on Ana and hold for longer than I can tolerate I place down her fan of cards, leaning forward to press her to me.

"Anastasia Kinsley," Jacob marvels like he didn't expect a diamond in his trove tonight. "An honor to have you in my venue. I wasn't aware you were stopping by tonight."

"It was a last-minute decision. My boyfriend and I came for the gala you're hosting tomorrow."

Her fingers playing absentmindedly with the short lengths of hair at my nape is the only thing grounding the beast inside me right now. Pride and relief swell in my chest that she's asserted who I am, taking herself off the table as a prospect immediately.

Jacob says, "It's a great opportunity for press. I was thrilled to hear you accepted my invitation."

This confuses us both. I was under the impression it was Liam's idea. He keeps his eyes mostly on his cards, the only person to give a nonchalant response to Jacob, who pays him little notice in return.

"Thank you for inviting us. It's been an ambition of mine to visit New York," Ana replies kindly.

"I invited *you*, darling," he corrects. "I hoped it would be just you, but it's no matter." He doesn't even look at me.

My rage must be tangible from the way he practically declares Ana available even while she's sitting on the lap of someone else.

"Rhett Kaiser," I say tightly. "I wasn't going to let my girl come alone."

"She wouldn't have been alone," is all he says.

This guy has some fucking nerve.

"I would have been bored," Ana says. "Like right now. Take me home, baby?"

I don't want to concede to Jacob, but he's a powerful man, and right now I'm in his territory. I'm a public spectacle by Ana's side, and I can't do something reckless like my boiling anger wants me to. I could kill Jacob Forthson and sleep like a fucking babe. For the activity I'm close to being certain he was involved in, sure, but more so now, for the eyes of lust and pursuit he's set on what's mine.

Folding out of the poker game loses me a shitload of money, but something about the men in play tells me they wouldn't be graceful losers. It's safer for Ana if I don't continue.

We leave, and the drive back to our hotel builds tension between us. We didn't make much immediate progress in figuring out what was at play, and I explain this to Ana. Some things take time and sensitivity, especially when dealing with such high-profile individuals.

In the elevator, the moment the doors close, Ana presses her body to me. Unexpectedly, as I've cast myself off in my own mind, going over every small interaction I had tonight.

"You are incredibly sexy when you're focused and possessive," she purrs in that sexy tone of hers.

I grab her ass, groaning at the incredible plump feel of her. "You're turning me into a madman."

"You were already there when I met you, Agent. You're just letting the world see it now." Her hand slips between us and she drags the heel of her palm down my aching cock.

"Fucking Christ, Ana," I say through gritted teeth.

She smiles coyly, doing it again, and we're only eight floors away from our room, but it's too fucking long. I pull out my phone, tapping only for a few seconds.

"If you're going to be a tease, you're going to do something about it," I growl, slipping my phone away and slamming the elevator stop behind her. "On your knees, little bird."

Her eyes flick up just as the red light under the glass elevator roof panel goes out. Then she obliges with a wicked smile, working on my belt, and it's the single most erotic thing I've witnessed as I brace my hands on the wall behind her to watch her on her knees.

Ana frees my dick, looking up at me through long, alluring lashes as her small hand grips me and her tongue traces from my tip to my base. I won't take long—not when I've fantasized those perfect red lips around me too damn often.

"Take me all in, baby."

She laps over my tip before she sucks, cheeks hollowing as I sink deeper into her tight throat. I don't think she can fit all of me, but she's clearly fucking made for me as she keeps going, taking every inch.

I hiss, one hand slipping into her hair, and it takes all my restraint not to pump my hips and fuck her throat. I want this time to be all her before I test her limits.

Ana works her hand at my base and sucks me off with the right amount of pressure, driving me to the brink.

"So fucking exquisite sucking my cock," I praise.

She hums around me and the vibration tips me over the edge.

"Good girl—*fuuuck.*"

I can't stop the few shallow thrusts into her mouth as I come. My forehead leans against my arm on the wall as she swallows all I give her, and the orgasm feels endless, fucking euphoric.

She keeps sucking, slowing her pace and wringing me dry, until my fingers tighten in her hair in a warning that I can't take any more. Her soft giggle of pure triumph sings to my senses as she lets go.

Ana stands, trapped between me and the wall I can't peel back myself from as I catch my damn breath.

"What have you done to me, Anastasia Kinsley?" I kiss her neck, losing myself piece by piece to this woman.

"Given you a world-rocking orgasm, I think," she says with satisfaction.

I chuckle, tucking myself away before I hit the elevator button and let Rix know he can release the surveillance feed—at which I receive no small amount of jesting.

"I won't forget I owe you two in return."

CHAPTER 28
Anastasia

To my surprise, Rhett is a very compliant shopping assistant. Even if he occupies himself on his phone with work, he follows me around many shops without complaint, and he's even great at giving opinions. I need a gown for the gala tonight and I've acquired every possible accessory except the main item.

"What color?" I think out loud, glancing over the racks.

"Red," Rhett says without looking up from his phone.

"What's got you so invested today?" I wonder.

He smiles up from his phone, finally tucking it away with the hand that isn't carrying my shopping. "Plans for the gala tonight," he says.

I frown. "Are you expecting trouble?"

Rhett comes forward, placing a hand on my lower back. "With you I'm always expecting trouble."

Rolling my eyes at the twinkle of thrill in his eyes, I continue my search for a gown.

"There's someone I'd like you to meet," Rhett says. "Allie, from my phone call last night. She's driving up to New York and asked if we could meet for dinner before the gala."

I beam at that, erupting with joy at getting to meet someone he's close with. It feels like a step closer to him and a token of his faith in me.

"She could come to the gala with us too," I suggest.

Rhett shakes his head. "She can't be seen with me. Allie is from a very wealthy and well-known family."

That grabs my interest. "Would I know of her?"

"Perhaps, if she told you her real name. It's not mine to give."

I nod in understanding. Rhett is good. He doesn't want to see it, but despite everything, no matter what he does to fight back, he guards a kind heart.

In the changing room I try on three gowns, but I hate all of them on me.

"I've been good all shopping trip for this moment and I'm not even getting a show," Rhett complains from outside the curtain.

I poke my head out since I'm standing only in my flimsy nude underwear. "I think you were right about the color. None of these feel right. I think my hair is throwing it off," I say sheepishly.

I looked at style over color and ended up plucking two navy dresses and a lighter blue.

"Can I bring you one I saw?" he asks.

"How did you see any of them when you hardly looked up?"

Rhett only smirks, standing from the sofa and heading out without a word. He returns, asking permission to enter, and though I look naked, it's not like he hasn't seen every inch of me already. We're the only two people in the dressing room.

My stomach flutters when he draws the curtain half-back, standing there looking like a freaking masterpiece presenting a deep red gown on a hanger. It's stunning. Rhett is so damn observant to have spotted it, and clearly a man who knows what he likes.

He doesn't bother to close the curtain. Instead he leans sideways and crosses his arms in the frame of my dressing-room mirror, watching my every movement like he's refraining from devouring me right here. It's utterly inappropriate to want him to pounce on me and do very bad things to me in this public space. Rhett steps wordlessly in to zip up the back when I slip into the dress.

"You have the most perfect ass, little bird. It's taking everything in me not to bend you over and sink my teeth into it."

I shiver.

Not. Helping.

When he finishes, I admire the ruby gown like sheets of satin hugging my body, making my breasts look incredible with the strapless plunge neck. The high slit bundling at my hip gives my leg free movement.

"Incredible," he murmurs, kissing my bare shoulder.

"So you have great fashion sense too. Is there anything you're not good at?" I muse, needing a distraction from the flutters in my stomach.

I don't know what's happening between us. It's sexy and warm and safe. But I also know he might never open his heart to give anything more, and maybe I can live with that.

"Music, actually," he answers. "I've never been good at instruments, though they fascinate me."

I haven't played my violin for anyone in a long time. So it

frightens me then, how much I want to promise I'll play for him one day. It never leaves my lips.

After our shopping trip, Rhett drives us to the restaurant we're to meet Allie at. He leads us inside the low-lit venue with its giant crystal chandeliers and a pianist at the far end of the room playing beautifully soft music. My gaze lingers on him enviously—how he seems oblivious to the room full of people, lost only to his music. Rhett lets go of my hand only to circle my waist and draw me into him, fanning his breath across my ear.

"How exquisite you would look up there," he says in admiration.

I don't know why it awakens the desire to show him my playing when my parents have asked many times if I'll perform at various parties and I've always declined out of the horrible stage fright I'm cursed with.

When a stunning dark-haired woman stands, beaming at us brightly, a knot of insecurity blooms in my stomach. *This is Allie? Mastermind, hacker, and insanely attractive.*

"When I heard you were both coming to New York I couldn't wait to meet you!" she gushes, pulling me into an embrace as the first greeting, and all I can do is accept it in my shock.

"Allie," Rhett warns playfully.

"Oh! Right." She pulls away sheepishly. "I've just heard so much about you it's like we're already friends. But I bet Rhetty neglects to talk about me." She pouts at him, but he smiles—the kind with rare warmth that he hardly ever shows—before embracing her.

"You were my hardest-kept secret," he says, which seems to appease her.

Our table is round with four place settings, and Rhett sits closest to me.

"I only recently learned of Rhett's . . . alter ego," I say, slipping my gaze to him.

He reclines in his chair, looking so relaxed in our company and setting that it warms something inside me.

"That's one way to put it," Allie says, sipping her red wine.

I order the same while Rhett sticks with water as always.

"Your work is incredible," I say with genuine admiration. "I don't know much about it, but what you risk to save people, and the skill it must take . . ."

I trail off, suddenly realizing my insecurity around Allie isn't from how beautiful she is, even if it crosses my mind how perfect she seems for Rhett. I'm more unsure of how I possibly thought I could be of help to him—part of his network, Xoid—when I know nothing and have nothing to offer like Allie's intelligence.

She waves me off. "My actual job as a lawyer gets *seriously* dull. Rhett practically saved my sanity taking my help. Is it weird to say he tends to my daddy issues? In a completely platonic, nonsexual way, of course. I crave the praise when all my father gives is disappointment." Allie sighs like it isn't really a big deal.

We order food, and I find Allie such a contagious presence I don't think I speak much, but listening to her makes me laugh, fills me with awe, and surprises me so much. She's a powerhouse, and admittedly, if she wasn't so bubbly I'd be intimidated in her presence. I find her serpent, the token of Xoid, around her neck as a delicate black diamond-encrusted pendant.

I cast my attention to Rhett, who hardly speaks at all. His face is so relaxed and bright and I've never seen this side to him. Close, but. . . there's something completely burdenless about his whole demeanor. Like he's home.

"You'll have to move over—she's my darling now," I say.

Allie winks at me.

My hand meets Rhett's thigh and a sparkle enters his eyes as he leans closer to me.

"Like I said, too much power in one room."

If I leaned a little closer I could kiss him, but a flicker of familiarity catches my attention and makes me straighten up.

"Liam!" I say brightly.

His dark head of hair turns and spots me. He's by the door about to leave. He begins to make his way over and Allie swears. It's the first wavering of her composure I've seen. She turns flustered as if hoping an escape route will present itself. As Liam gets closer, his gaze slips from me to Allie and shock overcomes him. Even falters his pace for a beat as if he's an inch from walking into stone.

"Alyra?" he asks, stunned. His green eyes widen and fix on Allie.

Rhett stands then, and even if I hadn't gleaned his threatening expression, it's practically radiating off him.

"I, uh— *Shit*. I need to go," Allie says. She doesn't get a step away before Liam intercepts.

My hand instinctively wraps around Rhett's bicep. He's about to intervene and I can't figure out what the fuck is going on.

"I thought you moved from New York years ago," Liam says to Allie. The way his tone softens . . . he's hurting. Clearly he knows Allie as far more than just an acquaintance.

"Yes. I did. I'm just here for a visit," she says coldly.

Liam's eyes slip to Rhett and then me with new confusion. "How do you know each other?"

"Rhett is a client of mine," she lies smoothly. "He was in the city. We met up. Now, if you'll get out of my way—"

"Can we talk?" Liam asks quietly, hoping we won't hear.

"We could have. Years ago, if you'd ever bothered to return my calls. I'm long over it now and completely uninterested in your reasons."

My body tenses with the awkwardness of being a bystander, but when misery falls on my friend's face my heart aches for him despite not knowing a thing. His mouth opens and closes a few times as if he keeps reevaluating what he wants to say, and ultimately he chooses silence.

Despite her words, Allie's eyes drop in disappointment like she expected him to try. To fight her. It's the kind of pain that tears at an old wound.

Gregory Forbes appears in the foyer, spotting us as he looks for Liam.

"Shit." Rhett swears under his breath.

Gregory makes his way over, and that's when Liam turns regretful.

"You shouldn't be here," he says to Allie, just before his father claps a hand on his son's shoulder.

"Alyra DeVerre, what a delight it is to see you again," Gregory says in surprise.

DeVerre . . . The name strikes with familiarity. Then it comes to me. Her family owns one of the most renowned law firms in the United States.

I think about a scandal I heard once about them; the eldest DeVerre son, set to inherit the empire his father had built, disappeared years ago. He was confirmed alive and I somewhat relate to his simple want for a quieter life instead. Their family is famous, and of course one of New York's hottest and wealthiest bachelors going incognito somewhere in the world was cause for a social media breakdown.

Was he Allie's brother? Cousin? *Unimportant right now.*

"I was just leaving," Allie says tightly.

"As were we. Let us escort you out," Gregory offers.

She nods but isn't fully comfortable with the idea.

"We were all just leaving," Rhett says, dropping an amount of money that's likely far too much onto the table before slipping his arm around my waist.

"Can we drop you off somewhere? I'd love to catch up and hear about your father," Gregory says when we're standing outside.

"Rhett is heading my way, actually, but thank you. It was lovely to see you after so long," Allie says politely.

Gregory only nods and Liam barely looks at her, standing with his hands in his pockets and a faraway look of detachment. I long to talk to him, just the two of us. Even if he hasn't told me all of what's between him and Allie, I've never seen someone so in need of a friend as Liam looks right now.

"I'll see you at the gala tonight?" I ask Liam.

He forces his head to me, wearing a hollow smile as he nods.

When the valet comes around with the car, Rhett doesn't miss a beat, opening the back door for Allie and then the passenger door for me. He speeds off, and the tension in the car could be cut with a knife.

"That was . . ."

"A fucking nightmare." Allie cuts me off.

I wince, glancing in the rearview at her troubled look as she stares out the tinted window. "How do you two know each other?" I try carefully.

Allie's head slumps back against the seat. "He's an old . . . acquaintance."

"Acquaintance," I repeat, knowing the hidden meaning behind that.

She groans. "He was the first boy I ever fucked. Better?"

My eyebrows shoot up. I expected a past relationship, but this is . . . unexpected.

"Boy?" I hedge.

"We were sixteen."

"Ahh."

"We dated, but it was short. He left New York one day and didn't tell me. Zero contact. He's a fucking asshole and my first and only broken heart. I was a young, fragile teen." She sighs.

Allie tries to play it off now, but she can't hide the look in her eyes. She's still hurting even after all these years.

"Oh shit," I mutter suddenly. Is this who Liam has been hung up on in all the years I've known him?

"What's wrong?" Rhett asks—the only time he's broken from his deep concentration.

No, it has to be a coincidence. There is no way in hell. What are the damned odds?

"Nothing," I mutter quickly. "What's got you so worked up?"

Rhett lets go of some of his distress that was starting to choke the air. "I've never been seen with Allie before. Should anyone discover things about me, I never want any of my team to be linked to me. Not even believing this is a client relationship. I've been *very* careful, Ana. I can't have anyone my uncle could use to get to me, and tonight fucking ruined that."

I turn so stiff in my seat, feeling like I caused this. Liam would have otherwise walked past if he hadn't seen me and I hadn't beckoned him over. Then there's something more . . .

Rhett's words aren't only about Allie, but about how I've become tied to him. The first person he can't hide his connection to—not anymore.

"It will be okay," Allie says when I can't. "Liam is . . . harmless. Except to teenage me."

"We don't know if Gregory is in the clear yet," Rhett argues.

They keep chatting while a lump forms in my throat. It's pathetic, selfish even, to cling to his words like they're regret for knowing me. Getting close to me. I will always be a weapon that can be used against him, and any moment he could leave me. Cut all attachment and then he'll be free from that burden of vulnerability.

We drop off Allie at her hotel, lingering for more than ten minutes as Rhett wants to be sure no one follows her in or looks suspicious outside. I don't look at him, watching the people out the window absentmindedly instead. Part of me wishes he'd touch me, talk to me. He doesn't.

He drives us back to our hotel, and we make it to our room with all our shopping in complete silence. I'm about to take a shower to get ready for tonight, wrapped only in a cotton robe, but when I see Rhett sitting on the bed leaning his forearms over his knees in an intense stare-off with the carpet, my frustration snaps.

"Did I do something wrong?"

He doesn't even look up. "You could never do anything wrong," he says, but it's as if he's not even present.

"Sure, I could," I say, wandering across the room. "I could walk out of here and flash the next guy to walk past. I could sneak behind the lobby bar and steal a bottle of tequila. Or, apparently, I could fuck up dinner."

He runs a hand through his silvery-blond hair, which is already disheveled from many times previous.

"Dinner was not your wrong," he says with an edge of bitterness that actually stings.

"Then tell me."

"I'm you're wrong, Ana. Jesus, *shit*." He stands abruptly, turning away as if he can barely stand to look at me.

I'm hurting. I don't know when I gave Rhett Kaiser the ability to hurt me. But there it is, in every second he's displeased because of me, and my defense only breaks out its claws.

"You're just a good fuck, Agent. There's nothing more to this, so you can damn well relax." I storm to the bathroom, until I decide I'm not finished. "You can try all you want not to let people in, but we're all dodging a thousand dangers every day. You're no different. No more frightening. You say you're dangerous, but all I see is a coward."

That snaps something in him, but it breaks a wild thrill in me that with his first step toward me I run into the bathroom, locking myself in. Rhett's fist bangs against the door seconds later and I'm sick to find pleasure in provoking him.

"Open the door, Ana," he says, so low and daring my eyes *flutter* at it. Heat gathers between my legs and I come alive with daring sin.

"So much of a coward that I have do to this myself," I taunt. My hand slips under my robe, needing some relief from the slickness pooling out of me. My head tips back against the door with a soft moan as I circle my clit.

"You'd better not be touching yourself," he growls.

"Why not?" I say, a little breathy, giving away that's exactly what I'm doing.

"If you're going to do so while I'm in the room, you're going to do it as I watch."

My brow pinches, and while I want to open the door and do exactly that, the thought of how riled he'll be if I don't turns me on even more. I moan again, slipping two fingers inside myself.

"Ana, open this fucking door."

"You want to be alone," I say, panting between the orgasm I'm chasing. "This is what it feels like."

"If you come right now I'm going to make sure the next time you do you're begging for it, and let me tell you, I won't give in to you. Not until you're starved for it to the brink of insanity."

Holy fucking shit, that shouldn't be as much of a turn-on as my body takes it to be. Stripping my robe, I sink down, spreading my legs and fucking myself harder, thinking of him watching. Of his inability to reach me right now and what he would unleash on me if I caved and let him in.

He gives a low groan of pain, knowing I'm too stubborn to go back on it now.

My climax crashes over me and there's no hiding it as I cry out with the force. I've masturbated plenty, but this has to be the hardest orgasm I've ever reached on my own.

"Oh, little bird," he says right by my ear as if he's crouched down with me. "You're in so much trouble."

CHAPTER 29
Anastasia

I can hardly suppress my triumph. We don't speak after I prove my little *point* alone in the bathroom, but the room weighs with delicious tension, waiting for one of us to break, and it will not be me. So we get ready in silence, but our glances at each other speak far more than words, making the air static and my skin vibrate with his subtle attention on me at all times.

In my dress with my hair and makeup done, I slip into my heels near where Rhett sits adjusting the serpent cufflinks on his all-black tux. My leg lifts, planting my sole on his shoulder. I don't think twice about it since the heels are brand-new. Rhett's blue eyes flick up to me, all sinful dark challenge.

"You're playing with fire, Miss Kinsley," he warns, but he doesn't hesitate to cross the straps up my calf before fastening them halfway up.

"You came with matches, Agent—what did you expect?"

He squeezes my calf as if he's restraining himself from reaching higher.

Calmly lifting my foot from his shoulder, I raise the other, not breaking eye contact.

"You're a wicked little creature," he murmurs, this time kissing the inside of my thigh as he finishes fastening the tie. "Don't think I've forgotten for a second what you did. And I can't wait to deliver your punishment."

My pussy near aches at the taunt, having not forgotten his threat for a second either. I merely smile in a way that dares him to try. A low groan leaves his throat as I straighten and he stands.

Rhett Kaiser looks absolutely devastating in his tux. Most would at least wear a white shirt, but he never does, always shrouded wholly in black. His silvery hair is sleekly styled, impeccable, though a few loose stands still fall over his forehead.

I pluck another final detail for him, which I bought today. When I stand before him he eyes my hands with a tight jaw, but he allows me to reach up his chest.

"I've never seen you wear any color," I muse, fitting the red handkerchief in his tux pocket.

"I've been in mourning," he says quietly.

My fingers stop moving on his chest. My heart cracks for him in silent agony, like the slow drag of a knife splitting deep inside me. I can't fathom his pain, his loss. All this time.

"I'm sure I have black—"

"No." He catches my wrist as I try to turn. Rhett swallows, at war with what he wants to say. "You make me want to heal, Ana. It's something I've never wanted. Many have tried to persuade me, but you didn't have to."

"Rhett, I—"

"I loved her, Ana. I owe it to her to always love her. But I'm so fucking obsessed with you it's killing me. Because I don't deserve it—I never will—but I'm so selfish I can't let you go."

"Don't," I say, closing my eyes and leaning my head on his chest. "Don't ever leave me, Rhett Kaiser. We're stronger together. I may not be able to fight like you or hack like Allie, or really offer much, but . . . I can be yours. There has to be something in that. Tell me you want to live for that."

He sighs, and for a second I think it's with disappointment and he's about to push me away.

Rhett takes my face in his hands. "I want to live for *you*."

Relief washes over me. He dips a hand into his pocket and I blanch, then turn hot, then—

Holy fuck, is that . . . ?

His chuckle of amusement vibrates against me.

"Not quite the proposal you're thinking of, little bird."

Opening the small black velvet box, I gasp at the contents, snapping wide eyes to him.

"The name stays. But if you're adamant, then let's make your condemnation official."

I examine the jewelry closer: two small red serpent earrings. "Red?" I question, taking out the diamonds I have in.

"I'll get you whatever color you want."

"No, they're perfect. But doesn't everyone have black?"

He smiles at that, lifting one earring from the box and fitting it through my ear. "You are not everyone. You're mine."

I admire them in the mirror. They're perfect. Empowering. *I belong*. It may be a mark of my space carved in hell, but I've already taken the hand of the devil creeping up behind me.

"Beautiful," he murmurs, pressing his lips to my bare shoulder. Then over my neck, shooting sparks straight to my core, and I start to contemplate ruining my hair and makeup and pushing him onto the bed.

"We should go," I say, a little breathless as his hands roam my waist until his fingers brush my thigh at the high slit, tempting my lust, while his mouth explores my neck.

"I'm going to be in contact with Rix the whole time. If we find anything, or if something goes awry, you mark every word I say and you do as I command. This isn't the kind of shit you defy me in. Tell me you understand."

I find his tone, thick with firm authority, insanely sexy.

"I understand." I'm ready, though admittedly kind of frightened.

I hope it's all precautionary and the gala will be as simple to be over with as any other. But Rhett has turned into someone I've only glimpsed before. A man who won't take or give a second chance. Willing to do whatever it takes to keep me safe and stop any villain in his path, even if he has to become one himself.

I spin in his arms, resting my hand on his chest. "Whatever you say, Agent. I trust you."

The venue is just like any other fancy gathering I've been to. A red carpet has been laid out front and photographers are kept behind rope as they snap their shots of each new arrival. My nerves begin to jitter as we pull up. Rhett's thumb idly strokes mine.

"You ready?" he asks.

I nod and he cuts the engine, heading around to my side, and as soon as he opens my door the flashes begin. I've become more used to the attention recently, but this is the most I've experienced so far. Rhett is right here with me, circling my waist to keep me close to his side while we walk.

"Anastasia, over here!"
"Is there a proposal on the cards?"
"How long have you been dating?"
"We love the new look, Anastasia!"

They're all interested in us. Our relationship. Nothing about my father. We're requested to stop and pose for the photo op, and I've done this plenty of times with my parents, but with Rhett, there's an element of tension as I consider how he must be feeling. He didn't ask for this, and if we'd never been caught that first instance when he was forced to pose as my boyfriend, he'd be on the sidelines now, free from the spotlight.

Yet he plays the part so well. Keeping adoring eyes on me, the people gush over us and my stomach flips. Then it clenches and I wish it were real. It's selfish to want this when he'd been forced into this position. While this is my life now, it's temporary for him. All I can think of then is how tomorrow the headlines will be doting on this facade of a relationship, but in another few months they'll be spilling the heartache of a breakup.

"You are magnificent," he whispers in my ear.

I smile at that, my stomach fluttering as he pulls back. His mouth curls too, thumb brushing my lips.

"That's better," he says, and then he kisses me.

The snapping amplifies and I don't care for the attention, lost in the taste of him, which is over far too soon. He takes my hand, leading us inside, and I relax.

"Will you be participating tonight?" the concierge asks.

"Yes," I reply. "And I believe my father has made a few donations for auction that will go toward my charity?"

I feel Rhett's eyes on me as the man checks his records and smiles broadly.

"It's all right here, Miss Kinsley," he confirms.

We're given a paddle with the number eleven on it and my hand circles Rhett's arm as we enter the ballroom laid out with many large round tables. Checking the seating chart, Rhett surveys the venue over my head.

"You still haven't told me about this charity," he finally says.

"I think I decided what I want to do," I explain. "I'm going to open a school for underprivileged kids. Homeschooling isn't an option for a lot of parents, and public schools are lacking in resources."

When we find our seats our table is half-full. Rhett takes my hand over the table.

"That is an absolutely selfless and incredible idea, baby," he says with such pride I don't expect it. He leans in to kiss me briefly before our table begins to fill up.

"Hey, princess," Liam says, startling me as he creeps up behind us.

I giggle at the kiss he pecks on my cheek before sitting beside me.

"Good to see you again, Kaiser," Liam greets, leaning around me.

Rhett forces a smile, but Liam doesn't seem to notice the chill to it. After hearing Allie was hurt by him, even so long ago, I can't blame him for it.

I inch closer to Liam, talking quieter between the two of us. "When were you going to tell me sixteen-year-old Liam was a player?"

Guilt washes over his expression as he reaches for his wine. "Is that what she told you?"

"She didn't use that word, but it seems fitting."

Liam leans back in his seat. "It's . . . complicated."

"She's not the woman you've been hung up on since I've known you, right?"

He merely takes a drink for too long for it to be casual.

I gasp. "Now you really need to explain."

Matthew Forbes takes up a chair across the table from me, catching my attention. He gives me a smile that breaks a shiver, but I brush off the attention when Rhett's hand slides over my thigh.

Liam is off the hook about Allie for now since the lights dim and the host calls everyone's attention to the stage. The gala goes on. We listen to a breathtaking performance by a pianist and a singer. Small foods are offered to us, and I fill up on a few while Rhett finishes off what I don't.

Then the auction starts. Paintings and sculptures are sold, increasing in value. I'm not sure if I'll bid on anything, but I took a number just in case, as Rhett advised. They start on the jewelry.

I watch in fascination, noting how the bidding activity picks up for this the most. At some point Rhett's chair ends up near flush to mine, his arm draped over the back of mine while his hand strokes idly over my thigh, exposed by my crossed legs. Every now and then he climbs daringly high, riling me to no end.

"Would I find you bare?" he whispers sinfully in my ear as the next piece of jewelry is auctioned.

"A woman never tells."

"A gentleman would never reach to find out," he says. "But I'm no gentleman."

My breath catches with the bold slip of his fingers at the top of my hip. My heart pounds and my pussy heats so inappropriately for the fact we're in public.

"Just as I thought." He hums in satisfaction. "My girl is ready to take her punishment at any moment."

I'm melting in my seat, and this is just the beginning of his torture.

The next box onstage contains a breathtaking set of emerald earrings that spark with a familiarity. My chest beats at the image that flashes to mind, and I don't even realize what I'm doing until the paddle in my hand rises.

"Switching colors?" Rhett questions in my ear. "Emerald would look exquisite on you."

I don't want the jewelry.

"I don't have the money," I say.

Yet my paddle keeps rising against two other bidders.

"High theft isn't exactly what I planned to exhaust my resources on tonight, but for what you want . . ."

Finally, I win. For a million dollars.

The next item is brought onstage, and the box is opened to show a diamond necklace with a ruby center.

"Shit." Rhett swears quietly in my ear.

"Some were wearing these pieces last night. It means something, doesn't it?" I conclude. I don't want to be right. Not with the insidious feeling that starts to overtake me.

It's a masked event to keep buyers anonymous. Because what they're truly buying isn't jewels, but flesh.

"Do they . . . Are they selling the woman from last night?" I breathe. "The jewelry correlates to each one."

"You figured it out, little bird," he says, kissing the hollow spot below my ear. "Well done."

"And finally, our main prize of the night," the host announces about the ruby necklace.

Rhett is so subtle in reaching into his pocket for his phone, barely glancing down as my body covers his quick typing. To further keep us looking completely enamored, I lean back with a smile, cupping his cheek, but I can see his calculations over whatever splits his attention.

Fury simmers over his features and my body turns taut. His hand brushes my nape as his breath caresses my ear.

"Go to the restroom, baby. Don't leave until I come for you."

I smile, playing along though my heart is racing. Liam casts me a look as I reach for my purse. Something is off, missing, about the cheerful demeanor I greeted him with earlier tonight. I give his shoulder a squeeze as I stand and head toward the restrooms.

The bidding begins, and even as the voices fade it's the most activity of the night, very quickly surpassing one million dollars. Then two. Jumping to five.

In the restroom I'm alone. Slumped against the counter, I take steady breaths, mind reeling with the very real and very active heinous crime happening right outside. A room full of despicable people here to buy women while the others around them remain oblivious to the sickening scheme right in front of their eyes.

I want to help with whatever Rhett is up to, but I promised I'd act by his command as it could be dangerous.

A woman enters and I straighten, pretending to fix my hair and lipstick. She washes her hands behind me, but her gaze flicks up to meet mine a few times through the mirror, and I smile kindly at her.

Then I double-take.

I spin around and she straightens with a flicker of hope in her eyes.

"I saw you last night . . ." I trail off.

The emerald earrings. I bought them tonight. She was wearing them last.

Whatever composure she's trying to hold onto crumbles, It's as if this is the first time anyone has ever noticed her at all.

"Please," she whispers.

My adrenaline spikes. I cross over to her and survey the area to be sure we're alone. I can't be certain there aren't hidden cameras. I hold out my lipstick to her, hoping she'll play along. Taking it, we turn to the mirrors, fixing ourselves.

"Is it just you?" I ask carefully.

"No," she says, applying my lipstick, which is a darker shade of red, but no one will notice.

"All the jewelry . . ." I trail off then shake my head to rally composure. It was one thing to hear about it, but to be around the activity is making me boil with a dark desire to storm out there and confront whoever is responsible.

Of course, that would be reckless. Irresponsible. And Rhett would be furious.

"What's your name?" I ask her.

"Dalia," she whispers, like it's condemning information to share.

"You're going to be safe," I promise. "Hide this."

Giving her my phone, I help her arrange it under her bra strap since she has no purse.

"You're missing the event," a sharp voice cuts in just as I step away to make sure the phone is concealed. A woman with a disdainful expression stands expectantly in the entrance.

"Sorry," I slur, blinking as if I've had too much to drink. "My fault. She kept trying to leave, but did you knowww people used to believe 'fuck' was an acronym for 'Fornicating Under Consent of King,'" I laugh, balancing against the counter. Hey, the weird facts you learn among peers in a literature degree, right? "Turns out fuck really just means sex, pretty much. All original speculation derives from the Indo-European root word 'peuk': to prick."

The woman in the doorway looks at me like I've lost my damn mind, but it does the job of erasing any suspicions about what we were talking about in here.

Dalia gives me a timid smile before she leaves.

"See you later, Delilah," I call lazily. For extra measure.

Sobering up the second they've left, my adrenaline is racing. Rhett said he'd come for me, but without my phone, and being in the ladies' restroom, I wonder how he plans to do that. So I leave, remaining casual as I scan back to my table, which is too empty. Rhett, Liam, and Matthew are gone. Deciding to head for the exit, thinking that's where Rhett will be, I'm intercepted in the lobby by Jacob Forthson.

"Leaving so soon, darling?"

My mind screams to get away from this man. This is his event. Is he behind the trafficking too, or is he just the accomplice? The distinction doesn't really matter to me.

Jacob is beautiful, from his dirty-blond hair and green eyes to his conventionally attractive features, with a tall, slim build and a posture that screams arrogance. But he's got nothing on Rhett. The fact Rhett even comes to mind only further sheds a light on the contrast I feel right now, just as I did last night. Danger instead of the safety I've always been encompassed in in Rhett's presence.

"The main event is over. It was a wonderful show and auction, but I'm ready to retire," I say politely, trying to sidestep him, but he mirrors my movement.

My heart skips a beat.

"It's not over yet. People are yet to claim their biddings, and there will be a violinist. Am I not correct in saying you have a particular talent for the instrument yourself?"

That isn't common knowledge. Sure, the one performance I gave years ago was public, but I've never played again, certainly not enough for it to be a well-known fact about me. My reservations about this man are all sinister beauty.

"I used to. It's an old hobby. If you'll please excuse me—"

"Ana." Matthew says my name, appearing as my savior out of nowhere.

I think Jacob will show a hint of ire, but his pleasant reception toward Matthew seems genuine.

"I was looking for you," Matthew adds.

"Me? Why? Where's Liam?"

"He left shortly after you. When Kaiser slipped out I thought you'd maybe fallen out with him, and I came to see if I could assist."

"I assure you that's not the case," I say quickly. "I'm actually looking for him now. I'm not feeling so well and would like to go back to our hotel."

"Was it the large purchase you made? I can take you to collect," Matthew offers.

"No," I say a little too quickly, and I swear his eyes flex with impatience. "Rhett is looking for me."

Part of me wants to go to see if they'll take me to Dalia, but instinct screams that wouldn't be the case. They wouldn't expose the real auction to me, so what might they do with me instead? Rhett would tell me to stay here, somewhere public and open. He'll come for me.

"You're too good for him," Jacob chimes in casually. One hand slips into his pocket and I want to punch his stupid face.

"Then you don't know him," I grind out.

"He's not like us, Ana. He'll never *truly* understand you," Matthew says, trying to be *gentle*, and I decide I'd like to swing at him too.

Fucking pretentious, arrogant assholes.

"He's the only person who's ever understood me," I snap when Matthew tries to lay a hand on my back. "Now I'm leaving to find my boyfriend."

"Hey, princess." I've never been more relieved to hear Liam's voice. "Kaiser sent me for you. He's getting the car."

His brother doesn't appreciate the interruption. Relief drops my tense shoulders.

"Thank you," I say to Liam. Then I reluctantly force a smile at Jacob and Matthew. "It was good to see you both."

It certainly wasn't.

As I step around them Jacob's grip on my arm makes me jump.

"Do we have a problem, Forthson?" Rhett's chilling tone from behind me breaks a shiver. His hand curls around my waist.

"No problem. Ana and I were just talking," he says smoothly.

"Then we're about to have one since your hand is still on my girl."

It's a power play. Jacob knows he has all the authority in the room. Despite Rhett's dominating height over him, his build, the fact he practically radiates his threat, Jacob's small smile shows he takes sadistic pleasure in provoking him.

"No harm, no foul," Jacob says, releasing me. "I'm sure I'll be seeing you soon, Anastasia."

Rhett's fingers flex on me at that. I can't even smile. My feet press forward by Rhett's gentle coaxing, and I've never wanted to be so far from a venue so fast.

Outside, the valet is just bringing our car around when Rhett spins me suddenly into him. His hand slips over my jaw as he leans in close.

"I asked you to wait for me," he growls. Then he kisses me hard. Possessive. Crushing my body to his as if Jacob could grab me again at any moment.

"I gave the woman with the emerald earrings, Dalia, my phone in the restroom. Can we track it? Maybe find the others with her?"

Rhett's eyes search me, blazing with something I can't decipher. Until his lips crash to mine again and passion consumes us both until we're breathless.

His forehead is on mine as he says, "You're brilliant. I hope you know it's because of you we'll find them easily tonight."

Relief bursts in me. An ache like nothing I've felt before escapes in euphoric laughter from my lips.

Fuck you, Jacob. I win.

Those women will be saved by Xoid, and I'm so damn proud to be a small part of it.

"We should go. Track it now."

"Rix will track it. My team will intercept the transport of the women tonight." He kisses me again and I moan in the back of my throat. "You and I are getting the fuck out of here."

Rhett is about to open the car door for me when something catches his attention over my head. I've never seen such a look widen his eyes—like he's seen a ghost, but it quickly falls to something so glacial and murderous that I shiver as I turn my head.

A man is taking off his mask as he chats to a friend. He's in his late thirties with several scars over his face.

"Get in the car," Rhett says with a distant but firm command.

"Who is that?"

"Get in the damn car, Ana."

That makes my head snap around. Rhett tears his gaze from the man only for a second, and I don't recognize him behind those familiar blue eyes right now. I do as he says, and Rhett leans into my side for a brief moment.

"Don't leave until I come back," he says, and then he slams the door shut.

My heart races from the echoes of his rage. I watch as the man leaves his friend and starts heading down the street. Rhett follows him.

I should not get out of the car.

I promised I'd do as he said.

But this is different. Whatever's sparked Rhett's rage right now isn't to do with the gala. I can't place it.

Shit.

I chastise myself as I get out the car and follow him. Rhett will be pissed I've defied him, but I can't explain the need to see what's wrong.

Around the next corner I don't see either of them. I keep walking until some commotion down the next alleyway makes me stumble to a stop.

They're only dark silhouettes, but I'd never mistake Rhett's towering form. What chills my blood is the vicious attack he inflicts upon this man. Rhett punches him again and again, and there's no way he stands a chance at fighting back against him.

I knew this side of Rhett existed, but it's a whole new heart-stopping awakening to see it. It's terrifying. Yet my steps don't stop advancing.

"Rhett," I say. It's barely audible, but somehow he hears me.

Landing one last punch, the sickening crack before his body slumps turns my stomach, and Rhett heaves his breaths.

"I told you to stay in the fucking car," he snaps, so angry and sharp it pinches my chest.

"Who is he?" I ask.

Rhett's expression twitches as if he's acknowledging the man all over again with new wrath. Faster than I can blink, Rhett pulls a gun I didn't know he was carrying from inside his tux jacket.

"He's the man who killed Sarah."

Then it all makes sense. I don't know what it makes me to look at the man on the ground who was brutally beaten and feel nothing at all.

Rhett crouches suddenly, grabbing the man by his jacket and shoving him against the wall, bearing his full weight against it since the man can't stand. My mouth dries out at the bloodied mess of his face. I understand Rhett's violence, but it's still difficult to witness.

"Where is Alistair Lanshall?" Rhett asks with a chillingly deceptive calm.

"I-I don't w-work for him any-anymore."

"Bullshit. Once you sign your soul to Lanshall you're his for life or dead." One of Rhett's hands holds the man up by his throat. He chokes, clawing at his fingers weakly. "You have five seconds or you're no use to me."

"P-please."

Rhett ignores him.

"Four."

"Are you sure you want to do this?" I whisper, scared to intervene, and it seems ludicrous to ask him that. But I don't know what else to do.

"Go away, Ana."

I know he doesn't want me to see this side of him, but I can't leave.

His jaw shifts with impatience at my silence, but he doesn't take his eyes off his target. "Leave!" he shouts, finally shifting those blazing eyes at me, and I wince then.

He's just hurting. Being confronted with the man who killed his fiancée . . . I can weather his pain.

"No."

His eyes flex at my defiance. This is Rhett Kaiser, the notorious leader of Xoid. This is where our worlds split clear and far.

One from the underworld, and one from the shiny and oblivious topside.

One exposed to every wicked truth of the world, and one who remains ignorant to it.

Rhett lets go of the man's throat, but the point of his gun follows him to the ground.

I'm trembling from the cold, from fear. Though not fear of him as I gravitate closer. Rhett's breathing is hard and calculated, like he wants to tell me to stop, but he doesn't.

When I'm close enough my arms slip around him. He doesn't break eye contact with me. Those blue eyes are so torn, as though he wants to reel himself back in, to walk away from killing this man, but he can't.

And I don't want him to.

"I don't want you to see this," he says—a quiet plea as if I'll run.

"I'm not going anywhere," I say, resting my cheek to his chest, staring away from the man who's trying to peel himself off the ground. "He doesn't get to take someone else from you. I'm staying."

Rhett's hand smoothes over my hair before cupping my face over my ear. I tense though I know what's coming. I don't close my eyes from staring at the dark brick wall.

Then the gunshot rings out. I hug him tighter with the sound that pierces through me despite my ears being covered by his chest and his hand. I've watched plenty of movies with that sound, but there is something condemning, like a fraction of lost innocence, in hearing it for real knowing the bullet took a life. An evil, lawless life, but still a final breath all the same.

Rhett peels me from him and scans every inch of my face. I can't decipher his as it's still so firm and calculating.

"Don't look," he says, then he takes my hand after fitting his gun back in his holster.

I have no desire to look at death, so I let Rhett lead me back to the car. I don't know how to feel. I look back to the hotel, which is a mistake when I find Jacob Forthson in the window. Staring right at me with a whiskey glass in hand.

Rhett speeds off seconds later and I try to arrange my thoughts from tonight's events. He doesn't speak. I wish he would, but what is there to say? His grip is tight on the wheel and I notice his split knuckles.

After a few minutes I spy a gas station.

"Pull over," I say.

"We're almost back—"

"Pull the fuck over, Rhett."

His eyes slide to mine at the demand, and for a few seconds we're at war with our stares. Until he concedes and we pull into the empty gas station.

I get out the moment he stops, and of course he's out a beat later, but I don't head inside. Instead I cross the street to the small liquor store first. Ignoring his silent, looming presence, I grab a bottle of vodka and head to the counter. I go into the gas station next for one more item.

Back at the car, I open the driver's side door and Rhett simply watches me.

"Sit," I order him.

"We should go to—"

"Do you ever do as you're told?"

"Not any more than you do."

That's a fair point.

"Will you please sit in the car?" I try soft pleading instead. It works. Though not without an eye roll and a grumble of reluctance.

Rhett sits sideways in the car and I kneel, uncaring of the dress I'm ruining against the asphalt. I take out the vodka.

"You don't have to do this," he sighs.

"Just let me," I say.

He gives me his hand and I pour the alcohol over his wounds. Rhett doesn't utter a sound, but his fingers flex around mine with the sting.

"How did he get away . . . the last time?" I can't help my need to understand what happened that night as if it will bring me closer to Rhett.

He doesn't answer while I tend to his other hand.

"You don't have to tell me," I say. "I'm just trying to figure you out."

"I didn't want you to see that. What I'm capable of. And that's not even close to the worst of what I've done in my past."

"I wanted to be with you. I want to see all of you, Rhett Kaiser."

He doesn't look up from watching me tend to his hands by wrapping bandages around them now.

"I killed a man tonight, Ana. After beating the bloody shit of him. You should never have to be comfortable with that—witnessing it or defending it. I let him go three years ago to tell my uncle I was coming for him. Seems fucking pointless now. I should have killed him all that time ago. Who knows what corruption he spread all these years? In my rage and delusion I thought I would have found and killed my uncle long before now and collapsed his precious, twisted empire. I feel nothing for it. I didn't expect to after all this time, but I knew when I saw him again I'd kill him. Honestly, if you weren't there, I can't say I would have done it so fast. I might have taken him somewhere and strung it out for days, weeks, put him through unimaginable torture. Had you not been there—" He looks up as if he expects me to be staring at a monster with his confession. Rhett shakes his head and I don't know what it means. "You wouldn't be so forgiving of me as you are now. I don't think you'd even be able to look at me the same again."

I finish tying one hand. "I'm not afraid of you," I say, pouring alcohol on his other hand. "I'm not comfortable, Rhett. Neither are you. None of this is fucking *comfortable*. That's what keeps us human. Next time, don't let it end so quickly on my count."

"Ana." He says my name in disbelief. "There will not be a next time."

"You're done eradicating bad guys?"

His jaw shifts and his eyes fill with warning. "Around you, yes."

"You're always around me. Monsters are always around us. Seems inevitable, Agent."

"Stop," he says sharply.

I finish tying his second bandage. "We're going to find your uncle," I say fiercely. "Unless you hide from me, I'm not going anywhere."

"You don't belong in my world, little bird."

"I belong with you."

It slips out of me before I can think about those words. They're terrifying as I kneel here in the vulnerability of them, waiting for him to reject me.

"You shouldn't be kneeling in some rundown gas station car park for me. *Fuck.*" Rhett pinches the bridge of his nose as if he can hardly stand to look at me.

"I'm not some precious princess, Rhett," I snap. I'm actually insulted. "I can handle it. I can handle *you.*"

He drops his hand, taking mine on his lap.

"You shouldn't have to."

I stand, boldly slipping into the car onto his lap.

"I'm sorry I didn't listen to you tonight, but I think sometimes your instructions are bullshit. Say we're in this together."

When he shakes his head I grip his chin. It flares a spark in his eyes that I almost smile at.

"You're something else, Miss Kinsley," he says as his fingers trace up my bare thigh, exposed with the cut of my gown.

"Shut up and kiss me."

He doesn't miss a beat. There's something loose and unhinged about this kiss. Rhett grips my bare ass unashamedly and groans into my mouth like he's finally starting to see I'm not breakable—at least I can't be broken by anything I see or learn about him.

When we part I brush a soft lock of fallen hair over his forehead.

"There would have been a first aid kit at the hotel," he says.

"If you're going to participate in street fights, I'm going to patch you up like it."

He chuckles softly, absentmindedly running his fingers along my thigh. Neither of us is in a hurry to move. "That's fair."

"Did you find out any more about Jacob?" I dare to ask. It breaks our small moment of peace, but I can't stop thinking about it. "Is he the leader of this?"

"He's not a man you should have ever been in the sights of," Rhett says.

"Me? What do I have to do with it?"

Rhett sighs, tipping his head back. "I don't have proof or any leads yet, but just from his interest in you, I have a bad fucking feeling, and it's taking everything in me right now not to turn around and do something *very* stupid and reckless."

"He's just another arrogant, too-rich asshole."

"No. He wants you. And someone like Forthson has never not gotten what he wants, and that makes him a threat."

"He can have any woman he wants. I'm not worth his efforts."

Rhett cups my cheek, brushing his thumb across my skin so tenderly.

"You are worth war, little bird."

CHAPTER 30
Rhett

The week after we return from New York, a wedge of tension I can't shake starts to grow. I know Ana feels it too. She asks about the women at the gala a lot, and while we successfully saved those in the car being taken from the venue, we didn't find them all.

Two of the jewelry items sold that night were unaccounted for. A set of sapphire earrings and the ruby necklace that sold for far higher than anything else. It keeps me on a sharp edge. I don't like loose ends, unfinished business. It leaves me itching and volatile with a want to hunt down Jacob Forthson as the event organizer. Personally, my way. I want to kill that son of a bitch with the eyes he set on Ana, and when he grabbed her . . . I almost lost my whole fucking composure right there.

I can't stop replaying the moment of torment at seeing the monster from my past and slaying him. He got off too fucking easily, and I don't know what I would have done with him if Ana hadn't been there. She's only caught a glimpse of what I am, and the fear won't leave me that she'll run if she keeps pushing to see more. Maybe I want her to. I'm too much of a sick, selfish bastard to want to keep her, and the only way for her to be spared from the clutches of sin is to save herself.

I swipe my phone, picking up before Rix's second ring.

"Tell me you have something," I snap.

"Does Allie get this kind of aggressive reception?"

I don't deign to answer.

"Didn't think so. Listen, man, I don't have anything good. Like, it's never *good* with the shit we do, but there's nothing on where those two items went. They definitely got sold—anonymous buyers, of course. But then it's like they vanished. Not even Allie can find a trace through her rich-people connections, and this is some high-value shit."

I remember the ruby necklace. The woman's face. We've scanned every missing-persons database and we can't find her. Someone who sold for millions, I would guess, to someone of high profile. The sapphire earrings I don't recall seeing at all at the casino, nor at the gala. The women were each wearing replicas of what was sold on stage. At the casino, those women walked around with them like fucking price tags that only those browsing for the gala auction knew about.

"Keep searching," I grumble.

"Yes, boss."

I hang up, trying to convince myself my bad feelings are irrational. That they're only because I'm terrified since Ana is now in the sights of someone as powerful and dangerous as Jacob Forthson. I should have sniffed him out sooner, done better due diligence for that trip to New York, and made sure Ana never fucking set foot there. I take deep breaths. I know better than anyone that when the damage is done there's no gain in fixating on all that could have been prevented. All I can do is make sure Ana stays safe, and that's all that matters to me now.

I find Ana in the gym. She's so damn sexy when she does her cool-down stretches. Her face brightens when she sees me, and my chest fucking aches. I never should have allowed her to worm her way into it, but now the beaten, cold, and broken thing that beats in me belongs to her. There's no getting it back, and I don't care if she's the one to end me once and for all.

"Hey, you," she says as she jumps up. So preciously happy, but I know she hasn't forgotten a thing about New York and it burdens her too. She tries to be our balance when I don't have it in me to shed any light. Here she is, making sure the darkness can't smother me.

"Here to get your ass kicked? I swear I'm getting there."

I chuckle at that. She's certainly advanced her combat skills since she started training with me. Ana absorbs everything like a sponge, and her determination to succeed in anything she puts her mind to is like fanning a fire I want to always burn in the heat of.

"I want to take you somewhere," I say. "Can you be ready in an hour?"

She eyes me with teasing suspicion as she finishes a long drink of water. "Do I get a clue?"

"We're going to see a friend of mine, but that's not the best part."

Her brow hooks, excitement skipping her step. "Intriguing. I'll be ready in forty-five minutes then."

When I spot the shoulder-length, wavy brown hair of my old friend, Xavier Laith, his bright grin breaks on me too. I'm not a very sentimental man—not anymore—but Xavier is the only fragment of my past life that remains, and it'll always bring pain and gratitude to see him.

"It's good to see you, man," Xavier says as our hands meet and we pull in for an embrace. "Was beginning to think you'd forgotten eight years of bonding in the police and SWAT trenches together."

"Never," I say. My arm naturally curves around Ana. "This is Anastasia Kinsley."

"Our future first daughter," he muses.

I don't respond to the suggestive side-eye he gives me.

Ana's father won the presidency election last month. The night filled their estate with so much press and so many politicians high with stress and anticipation. She could hardly contain her own nerves with the suspense, and I distracted her most of the night, both of us curled up watching movies in the cinema room until the results came in. I didn't expect to be proud of President Kinsley, but Ana's joy and his humble win that night made me see why she looked up to him so dearly.

"I was beginning to wonder if he'd made you up so he wouldn't seem like such a loner," Ana says.

Xavier chuckles. "He's still a loner when he's forgotten how to pick up the phone every once in a while. *Not* for illegal favors," he mock-scolds.

"Ahh, so you're to blame for the security breech," Ana concludes.

For a second Xavier shifts nervously on his feet. "That bastard better get more years behind bars than me if he pisses you off enough to spill."

"Your illicit activities are safe with me, Agent," she teases.

Something possessive in me stirs with the way she addresses him. Technically, Xavier is the only real agent here, but I've grown to like the way she uses the title on me.

Ana surveys our surroundings. The compound out the back is where we head to, and she keeps patient, surprisingly. Christmas is only a few short weeks away, and I figure now is the best time to present her with the idea that's been probing my mind. Xavier unlocks the back compound and then there's no hiding where we are. Slipping away from me with a small gasp, Ana skims her hand along the fences of the kennels as some of the dogs bark at the intrusion. The awe on her face is priceless.

"Shadow may be at the end of his working life, but he still has a lot of years left to give. I'm glad you called for this, even if not just to see me," Xavier says, heading deeper through the kennels. "He's a champ and he deserves a good, spoiled retirement."

Ana follows after him, confusion furrowing her brow. When he stops at the end kennel, they stare at a stunning all-black German shepherd lying peacefully at the back of his stall. I watch Ana as she crouches and coaxes the dog to come over.

"He's being retired? What happens to him now?" she says with a hint of sadness, poking her fingers through the fence.

Xavier finds the key he's looking for and jams it into the kennel.

"He's yours," I say.

Her head whips up to me. "Mine? There's no way my father will agree."

"He already has."

Her lips part in shock and she stands as the stall swings open, but the dog stays put.

"Come," Xavier commands.

Shadow doesn't miss a beat.

"Heel."

The dog sits, peering up at him and waiting for the next instruction.

"I'm going to miss him. I'm not his handler, but he was one of our top dogs for many great years."

Ana falls to her knees fully, calling the dog's name, and with Xavier's permission the dog relaxes, nuzzling into Ana like a bear. She giggles, the most joyous sound in the world, hugging the beast. I don't realize I'm smiling like an idiot watching their interaction until my gaze wanders up to find Xavier smirking at me.

"He'll learn quickly who his new owner is," Xavier explains. "If you guys have time, I'd like to run over some training with you for him so you know his commands and traits."

Ana sniffs and I move like clockwork to her, crouching and scanning her face, not expecting the watery eyes.

"If you don't want—"

"Of course I do." She cuts me off. "He's perfect. I just didn't expect it. And I have no idea how you convinced my father when I've been trying for years to even get a tiny thing."

My fingers trail her spine over her jacket. "Shadow comes with the perk of being a big, scary police dog pretty much capable of replacing me for your protection."

She leans into me with a laugh that's a partial sigh of emotion.

"Plus, you said you wanted to get your own apartment when your father takes office. He'll help your case with the added protection detail too."

Ana sniffs again, looking at me like I've given her the world when I'm not even close to that yet. A part of me wants to recoil at the thoughts slamming into me that come with so much terror and taunts that I'll repeat the past. I want to swear to her, to myself, that we'll have the time for me to give her everything she deserves and more, but that feels too fragile of a promise. One I've broken with someone before. With Ana . . . I won't survive losing her even to seek vengeance.

I kiss the crown of her head. "Merry Christmas, Ana."

"All right, you two, let's get to work so we can grab dinner too. I'm starved," Xavier says, clapping his gloved hands together.

We spend nearly two hours going over Shadow's commands and routine. Watching Ana's joy and enthusiasm is my favorite fucking thing in the world. I laugh, a sound and feeling I'd long given up believing could be pulled from me again in such long, genuine bursts, yet Ana's antics with the dog are so endearing and entertaining, and— *Fuck.* I'm in such deep shit.

Leaving Shadow for an hour, we come to a nearby restaurant, and I don't realize how much I've missed my friend. Even as I think of the term, it doesn't seem enough for someone who's never given up on me no matter how deeply I spiraled, nor how dark the path I strayed onto.

"How's the job been going?" I ask him after our meal is finished.

Exasperation weighs on Xavier's face, which makes me hook my brow in amusement. "It took a lot of persuasion, but they allowed me to take on a case I picked up myself out of curiosity, actually. There's been a string of homicides they think are all connected."

"A serial killer?"

"Kind of. But they don't always kill."

"What's the common trace that leads to one person?"

Xavier winces. "Castration."

I never would have expected that.

"Right?" he says to my strained reaction. My balls shrink as if to protect themselves at the mere thought. "It's like their calling card."

"Isn't that a case for the FBI?" Ana asks.

He looks at me accusingly. "I see you forgot to tell your girlfriend about my existence altogether, not to mention my progression from SWAT to FBI last year. I'm hurt."

"I'm not his girlfriend," Ana says with a nervous chuckle. "Didn't he tell you it's all a ruse because of some tabloid on his first day that made us out to be America's hot new couple?"

"Ohh," he says, and then he leans back in his seat as he looks between us, puzzled. "Are you sure?"

Ana only spoke the truth, but it disturbs inside me. I don't care about labels, but one thing is for sure: Ana is mine even if I'll never be hers.

"It's been a very busy few months." I brush him off. It's a poor excuse, and they both pin me with accusation.

"Well, anyway, everyone is at their wit's end. It's been going on for years, and when I stepped up to FBI it was practically cold."

"But you warmed it up?" I muse.

He smiles deviously. "You know I can't put down a challenge once it's in my hands. But even I'm beginning to lose my shit over it. This person is like a ballerina around us. We get so close, but it's like they want us to—like they get joy out of watching us."

"Sounds like a typical serial killer characteristic," I say.

Xavier hums, and I see his work start to fill his mind. "This person is *not* typical. I can't place it."

I've always admired his focus and determination. Once he puts his mind to something, he won't stop until he achieves his goal, and it's probably why we understand each other so well.

"Are you heading back to Philly for Christmas?" Xavier asks carefully.

I tense, having not brought it up to Ana yet. She mentioned a party her father was throwing on Christmas Eve and he'd asked if Ana would perform at it, to which she replied she'd think about it. Every other year they ask, she immediately refuses, and I can't bring myself to tell her yet that I won't be there but I want her to play regardless, knowing she'll love herself for it, if only she'd push through the nerves.

"I don't know," I say tightly, feeling Ana's eyes on me and being too much of a coward to meet them.

I've been warring with myself, wanting to be there for Ana to watch her play her violin, but I don't know if I have the strength to do anything except give over to one night of drinking alone, visiting Sarah's grave on the anniversary of my failing her, as I have done every year for the past three. How can I bask in anything warm that day when she's lying cold because of me?

"We should get going," I say, slipping away into a detachment I know all too well.

Xavier gives me pitying eyes and I don't want to unleash my resentment for it. I've enjoyed seeing him, but now I remember why I don't deserve a consistent friendship. Or love. Or joy.

My goodbye to him is shitty, but it's better this way. Guiding Ana to the car with Shadow, I'm distant and she knows it.

"You could have told me," she says quietly, breaking our

twenty minutes of silence. "I don't need you by my side at all times."

"I requested the leave from your father the day I took the job. Just for two days. Christmas Eve and the day. I kept it from you because you've been psyching yourself up to perform, and I worried my not being there would discourage you."

"I wasn't going to do it for you," she snaps.

It comes from a place of hurt that lodges a knife in my chest. She thinks I don't care enough, that she means so little to me that I'd abandon her on that important day. What she doesn't know is that she's everything to me, and I'm just a pitiful, scared coward.

"Good," I say, forcing down my pain and hoping her spite toward me will see her through that performance if that's what it takes.

Ana doesn't talk to me again and I can hardly breathe with her anger toward me. It feels so wrong. I want to be angry with her—toward the world and all its wrongdoings—but I never want us to be angry at each other.

CHAPTER 31
Anastasia

I don't want to leave my room with the large gathering downstairs for our annual Christmas Eve party.

My mom bought me a beautiful short red silk dress with a flowing skirt, tight bodice, and a low-cut neckline. I pair it with white tights and matching red heels. I don't care much for how I look when there's only one person whose eyes I want to watch light up at seeing me. It never fails to make me giddy. Rhett left early this morning, knocking on my door only to wish me a happy Christmas and to leave a red rose on my dresser, which I haven't touched.

Shadow's fur grazes my hand and I crouch to him, giving his goofy face a good scratching to help boost my mood. He's the most treasured gift, and even though I'm sad Rhett isn't here and angry he'd kept his inevitable absence today from me, I can't truly stay mad. He isn't mine, and this is his job, nothing more, which he is long overdue a break from. Above all, my heart is cleaved by the knowledge Christmas Eve was the day Sarah was killed.

"Ana, they're expecting you, dear," my mom says after a shallow knock. She enters—not fully, as she's somewhat frightened of Shadow—but her face gushes, eyes trailing over me. "You look beautiful."

I force a smile and take a long breath. I can do this. I *want* to do this.

"I'll be right down."

Mom nods and leaves me. My eyes fall again to the rose on the dresser by the door. I pick it up, bringing it to my nose, and only then do I notice the small tag dangling from the thornless stem.

Your gift is in my room.

My stomach coils with a tight thrill and I leave immediately, crossing the hall. On his made bed there's a long black box with a red bow on it. The closer I get, there's no mistaking what it is from the shape.

Unclipping the case, my breath catches at the stunning deep red violin. It must have cost a small fortune. My fingers graze along the polish until I see a small engraving, and I lift it out to read it closer. My nose stings and my eyes prick with tears at the two words: *Little Bird.*

Fuck. I miss him. Not for the length of time he's been gone, but in my damn chest he's carved a place and I need him, want him, tonight.

Shadow whines like he can sense my drop in mood as I sit on Rhett's bed. He jumps up, lying his huge head beside me. I take a moment to collect myself, finding comfort in running my hand over his soft black fur.

I spend ten minutes tuning the new violin with a short practice before I head downstairs. The foyer is littered with bodies, and as I make my way to the main room of the house I greet so many people. I'm already getting lightheaded. In the center of the room a pianist is playing softly, and it helps to soothe my senses.

"Oh Anastasia," my father says warmly when he spots me. "We are most looking forward to seeing you play."

So are the press, I think, noticing the cameras ready to take their shots.

I step up onto the round platform with the pianist, who acknowledges me kindly, and take out my new violin. There's a certain comfort that settles in my chest with it.

My palms clam up and my heart speeds even though I'm excited to play. I want to block it all out, but this is always the hardest part. Beginning. Lifting my violin and settling in the chinrest, I hate that my eyes prick, only because I realize I'm searching the eager crowd for one face I won't find.

How am I going to go on if he leaves me after his post? After he gets what he wants from it in taking down his uncle.

Meeting eyes with the awaiting pianist, I give a nod, and I play.

I don't have Rhett's eyes to anchor me, but his presence has wormed its way inside me, and that's all I think of as notes sing from my strings. It awakens me from within like dormant joy, flooding me with so many emotions all at once. When I play, it's just me and the instrument in my hands. The nerves dissipate on high and low notes, and I spill the sound of my soul to a crowd that doesn't even exist to me anymore.

When I finish, my first breath after the echo of the final note crashes me back to reality. Clapping erupts, cameras flash, but I'm slammed by only one thing.

How could I have been so selfish?

I'm not where I'm supposed to be. Rhett hasn't abandoned me—I've abandoned him.

I hurriedly pack away my violin before grabbing the case and rushing off the platform. I find my white coat and scarf and change into red flats.

"What's the matter, honey? Is it your nerves again? You played so beautifully," my mom fusses.

"I loved it," I say hurriedly. "Every second, and I'm glad you got to hear it. But I have somewhere I need to be, and I won't be back for dinner tomorrow."

I know I'll be met with protest, but I have to make her understand.

"I can't explain, but I need to do this. I love you and I'll call!"

"Ana!"

I spin around before reaching the door. Dad strides to me with a firm expression, and I'll admit, I'm nervous to defy him.

"I can't let you go alone without your guard."

"I'm going to him."

"It doesn't matter."

"Then send whoever you need with me, but I'm going."

His lips firm. He can't hold me here unless he puts me under lockdown, and I would never forgive that. He seems to war with that conclusion as well.

"Two security guards will be taking you there."

"Thank you."

I know it's hard for him. He's been so worried about the safety of our family with his running. With a deep sigh of reluctance, his large arms open and I step into them.

"Merry Christmas, my darling girl."

"Merry Christmas, Dad."

"The jet will be ready for you when you get to the airport."

I smile before heading out as a driver pulls up to take me there. The flight is only around an hour, and I just hope Rhett won't want to cast me away the moment he sees me tonight. On the anniversary of his fiancée's death.

I called Allie before I boarded, and by some means beyond my comprehension, she's managed to share Rhett's location with me through this protected app he installed on my new phone again. He isn't at the cemetery she said he was likely to be at. When I get close enough to his pin, I hop out of the car and walk.

Until I find him.

He's leaning his forearms on his thighs, sitting on a bench down a quiet market street with twinkling fairy lights all around. The snowfall gathered on his silver hair and black jacket indicates he hasn't moved in some time, and my heart breaks at the lonely, lost sight of him.

I approach slowly, suddenly awash with nerves that maybe he doesn't want me here. Maybe this is crossing a line. But I can't leave him like this, and I never should have let him come here alone at all.

Finally, his head turns enough, and he straightens in shock when he sees me, bracing a hand on his thigh and scanning me once. Twice. As if he expects me to turn into a ghost if he dares blink.

"Ana?"

I nod, fighting back my tears, because I've missed him. And I mourn for his pain, wanting to take it all when in this moment he's showing more vulnerability than ever before. This day will always break him, and he doesn't pretend otherwise. Instead all my tears flood to the surface when his do, like a straining dam finally caving in, and his fingers pinch between his eyes as he drowns.

I sit beside him and Rhett leans into the arms I wrap around him as he releases the barrel of emotions he's bottled up for far too long in his silence.

"I'm here," I choke. "I'll always be right here."

He shakes under me and I just hold him, not knowing what else to do, but at least he doesn't push me away. I cry for him. With him. If he's going to suffer this day then I will too. I peel off my gloves and take his hands, which are ice-cold.

"You shouldn't have come," he barely whispers.

"Do you not want me here?" I ask. I won't be offended if he doesn't.

"That's not what I mean," he says, finally looking at me with ocean eyes split with misery. "I'll always be a danger to you. And you're going to say you want to take that risk, but you shouldn't. I'm not *good*, and I never will be."

"I know who you are, Rhett Kaiser. I know *what* you are and I haven't wanted to leave. I don't want *you* to leave. If you do, that is not my choice and you do it for yourself." My hand cups his cold, flushed cheek, brushing away the tears he let fall, and I'm so glad to see them when they'd otherwise keep turning into glass within him, cutting him instead.

"You're so damn stubborn," he mutters. Then he holds my face and brings his mouth to mine.

His lips are freezing, but I kiss him back, pulling him closer when he tries to break away. I straddle him on the bench, uncaring of passersby and the snow seeping through my tights at my knees. I kiss him like I can warm him with my body alone, but I know it's not enough. I want to be in a hotel, stripped bare and slick with sweat in contrast, because he'll fuck me again and again and we'll wake up tomorrow together and he'll never be alone with his pain for Christmas Day ever again.

"I'm a broken man, Ana, but I'm yours."

Rhett Kaiser is sharp and no doubt deadly. But there's so much to be found behind the broken, so much to be loved, and I'm committed to seeing it all.

"We're all different kinds of broken, Rhett. Your pieces are just a little sharper than most."

He smiles and I melt at the soft gratitude in his blue eyes. "We should get somewhere warm."

I giggle, brushing the fresh snowfall off his wet hair and thinking how gentle and beautiful he looks with the cold turning his nose and cheeks pink.

Hand in hand we walk, in no hurry, through the streets awake with Christmas lights. When I pick up on the soft playing of a piano I gravitate to find it, until we stumble upon a breathtaking pavilion lit up beautifully with a single pianist. A few families and couples have stopped around to admire the show.

My fingers flex on the handle of my violin case. An idea sparks to mind as I recognize the chords of the next song the pianist is easing into. Pulling Rhett closer to the pavilion, my heart thunders. Am I really about to do this?

Fuck it.

"What are you doing?"

I drop down, opening the case and pulling out my violin.

"I played for an audience for the first time in years tonight," I say, "and the person I have to thank for helping me realize me I could conquer my fears never got to hear it."

Rhett looks me over with surprise, then the brightness that filled his eyes is all the confidence I need. So I join the pianist, and I play for him.

CHAPTER 32
Rhett

I resist the demand to fall to my knees when notes begin playing from Ana. She is magnificent. The most exquisite and perfect thing I've ever seen. Or heard. Or felt. She weaves the sort of magic in the air that makes the world feel less cruel and gravity less heavy.

Ana moves as if she's one with the song that touches soul-deep. Her body's so graceful, answering to the push and pull of her bow against the strings as if the world is lost to her. Except me. Every now and then her eyes flick to me and such raw emotion spills over her face, like she's communicating all she can't in our language with music instead. And I hear her. I fucking hear and see every piece of her that she bares to me and my chest pounds to give her all of me right back. No more hiding.

I became fiercely protective of Ana the moment I met her. When I got to know her, I decided she was mine no matter what happened, even if I couldn't keep contact with her after my post.

But it's in this moment I fall in love with her. Since I first laid eyes on her I've been climbing toward this inevitability. The plummet there's no coming back from. I am wholly, irrevocably in love with this woman. It's the kind of love I didn't know truly existed. A love that believes in immortality, because no amount of time on this damned earth is enough with her.

My heart belongs to her; my soul belongs with her.

I'm absolutely terrified to condemn her to me. It's selfish. Cruel. She deserves far more than I can ever be for her. Yet as her song finishes and the crowd erupts with applause, I barely hear any of it. I move to the gravity always pulling me toward her, and as she lowers her violin and searches for me with the brightest grin that banishes all the darkness around me for just that moment, I take her face in my hands and claim her mouth—her body—her soul—uncaring of the crowd around us when nothing matters but her. I need Ana to feel even a fraction of what's taking over me. Fear, passion, desperation. It floods out of me and onto her in a kiss that is transcendent.

We break apart, sharing breath as I lean my forehead to hers.

"What was that for?" she asks, so oblivious to my reforming world around her.

I kiss her again. Just once.

"I need to have you," I say. "Now."

We find the closest hotel, not caring about lavish or anything when I'm aching to get her to bed. I can hardly keep my hands off her, my lips off hers, still reeling from the fact she's here in Philadelphia at all and drunk on the high of the performance I didn't anticipate could strike such euphoria in me.

Every now and then my wicked demons surface. They want to banish this comfort on today of all days. Sarah died four years ago today, and I battle with the notion that engaging with Ana like this means defiling Sarah's memory.

"Hey," Ana says softly, wrapping her arms around me as we head up to our room in the elevator. "Stay with me."

I know what she means. She can read me like a fucking book, and that is both daunting and liberating.

"I'm right here, baby," I say, kissing her and drinking in every little breathy moan of hers that makes my dick twitch.

My arm tightens around her waist, and the way she lifts herself into my arms so easily, legs circling my waist, further proves to my demons this is right. Something sure and promising I didn't think I'd ever find again.

Our mouths barely part as I carry her to our room and swipe the key card. Our jackets and scarves are on the floor in seconds and she's pressed under me on the bed.

I can't stop touching her with a new wild hunger and raw passion now the confession is free in my mind. *I love her.* I will love her, protect her, and worship her until the day I die.

Yet as I finally pull back to look at her beautiful flushed face, I won't say it.

It will be my salvation at the end of this nightmare. One that began not just four years ago, but the day my parents died and I became the meticulously crafted weapon of a monster. Alistair Lanshall has to die. Then Anastasia Kinsley will have the power to save me from the wreckage of all I've become, or she'll shatter me once and for all.

"Are you okay?" she asks gently, tracing delicate fingers over my nose and cheek.

"Far more than okay, little bird," I say, kissing her chest and down the dip of her little red dress, which is driving me to madness. "You didn't have to come all this way. I didn't expect you to."

"I know, it just . . . feels right."

Yes, it fucking does.

"I can't tell you what it means to me," I say, barely a whisper when this woman is making me feel more in one night than I have in a lifetime.

Ana pushes up on her elbows. "You can show me."

I groan, kissing her again. Deeply—but nothing ever feels enough. That's what I discover love is: being forever greedy and yearning for one person about whom there are infinite things to discover. I'll never stop wanting. Craving. Demanding. Everything I can get from her. I'm completely undone.

"We should get you warmed up," I mutter against her lips.

"I'm sure you'll figure that out."

Before she can pull me down I slip off the bed, hardly able to suppress my amusement at her adorable bewilderment. I go into the bathroom, turning on the shower, not wanting to risk her catching an illness from the cold. I find her standing with her back to me. Ana rubs the goose bumps on her arms and then reaches behind herself for her dress zipper. I catch it before her fingers can pull.

Undressing Ana is like unwrapping the best fucking Christmas present. Her dress pools to the floor and I have to take a moment to close my eyes, press my lips to her shoulder, and collect all my damn sanity while my cock juts at the sight of her lacy red underwear and high white stockings clipped to a suspender belt.

She turns in my arms, circling hers around my neck with a

seductive twinkle in her eye. "Merry Christmas, Agent Kaiser," she whispers.

She's going to be the death of me, and at the same time I've never felt more alive.

Tucking the loose strands of her deep red hair behind her ear, I say for the first time in years, with nothing on my mind but Ana, "Merry Christmas, baby."

I bend, lightly biting her peaked nipple through the thin lace of her bra. She gives a delighted moan of surprise.

"You look so fucking exquisite I can't decide if I want to fuck you right now with it on or take you in the shower."

"Both," she pants, tightening her fist in my hair as I give her other nipple the same attention.

"Greedy girl."

I plant hands on her waist, and Ana squeals as I lift and throw her on the bed beside us. I'm upon her like a starved, insatiable man, pushing her thighs apart and kissing along the inside of her soft flesh. She's a damn goddess in her red lace against the white sheets. Mine. All fucking mine.

I waste no time in hooking her panties to the side and running my tongue through her slick pussy. It practically melts for me. Humming in satisfaction with her cry, I suck hard on her clit and then spear into her like I can't get deep enough. Her hips undulate against me, and I love that about her, how she takes what she needs.

Stopping my assault, I climb up her body before hooking her waist. She gasps as I flip us, hands planting on my chest.

"You're going to get up here and ride my face like you've been begging to," I say. My dick is rock-hard restrained in my pants and it's torture, but I need this to be about her for now. Need her to know how treasured she is.

She looks unsure for a moment. "I-I've never done that before."

That arouses the fuck out of me and also annoys the hell out of me. How has no one else ever given this woman every single thing she desires without her needing to ask for it?

"Good," I growl, coaxing her by her thighs as she shuffles up my chest and over my shoulders. "Hold onto the headboard and lower those hips for me."

Like a good fucking girl she obliges, and the moment her pussy is back on my face I devour her like my favorite fucking meal. She tries to push up in her uncertainty at first, but my hands around her thighs pull her right back down. It takes a short moment, but she begins to find her rhythm, moving her hips and knowing exactly where she wants me to fuck her with my tongue and mouth.

Slipping a finger inside her draws out the most beautiful sound, and I add another one right away, greedy for her noises and the way she rocks harder against my face. My tongue flicks over her clit while I slide in and out of her tight heat. She's close. I can tell from her short pants and the quickening pace as she chases her orgasm. While I want to feel her explode over me, I don't forget her little stunt in the last hotel we stayed in. When her pussy clamps tighter on my fingers I pull them out, stopping my assault, and she quivers with a precious cry from the denial of finishing.

I chuckle darkly, kissing each of her thighs. "Oh, little bird, you followed through on your threat. I'm holding to mine." Unhooking her thigh, I reach up her back and unclip her bra.

"Please," she says, so needy for the orgasm she was on the cusp of.

"We have a few more of those pleas to go before I let you come."

Reaching lower, I unclip her belt before peeling her long, stunning legs from each of the white stockings. Then, finally, I hook her panties and slide them off. Her full nakedness will never fail to make a deranged man out of me.

I begin to unbutton my shirt, and Ana finally comes around enough to tilt her eyes in a sultry challenge as she pushes up. She doesn't take those stunning hazel irises off mine as she swiftly undoes my belt, not hesitating to pull out my cock and shifting to her knees as I rise on mine.

Combing fingers through her hair, I don't want to miss a flicker of her face as I hold it back in a tight fist, hissing at the warmth as she licks across my head.

"I'm going to fuck your throat and you're going to take it," I say tightly, but I wait for her hum of permission and let her suck me on her own for a minute. It's damn erotic to watch.

Then she rests her hands on her thighs, mouth wide and eyes flicked up to me as if she's fucking praying for my cock.

"Good girl."

Both my hands are in her hair now, holding her head in place as I test her slowly at first, loving the sight of my tip on her tongue before it disappears down her throat. My teeth clench so tight at the glorious wrap of heat. Then I can't hold myself back anymore. I use her mouth like she used mine, and she weathers it beautifully, bracing on my thighs as I hit the back of her throat over and over. I'm not gentle, but Ana hums, occasionally gags, and her nails dig into my flesh as if she can pull me closer. *Fuck, she's incredible.* I want to spill myself down her throat so badly, but I can resist. This night is so far from over. I pull out of her with a loud groan of restraint, wrapping a hand around the neck that buried my dick in it perfectly seconds ago.

"Shower—now."

Ana's eyes flare at the command. She scoots off the bed, giving me the most impeccable sight of her plump, round ass. I shed my pants as I follow her, stepping under the spray behind her as she slicks back her wet hair. When I grope her breast she sighs contentedly, leaning back against me. My other hand snakes its way around her, dipping between her legs, and she tenses with a pained moan, sensitive from her near orgasm. My dick jerks against her ass.

"Rhett, please," she begs again.

I ignore her, nipping her ear and running my tongue along her little serpent earring.

The fangs of a serpent, but the wings of my little bird.

I curve two fingers inside her and she strains on her toes. It isn't enough for her, and I'll enjoy molding her to my every touch for stealing an orgasm from me. When I press my thumb to her swollen clit her hand strains to hook back around my nape for purchase because of my height.

"I'm going to—"

"Don't you dare come."

"I can't . . ."

"Ana," I warn.

I know she can't stop herself from the tight clamp around my fingers and the fact she was teetering right there on the edge already. I smile to myself, circling an arm around her waist as she trembles violently, and my fingers slip out of her only to rub her clit harder and ride out her orgasm. As she reels back, near boneless in my arms, I kiss her shoulder and tsk.

"You have a penchant for punishment, little bird."

"That wasn't fair," she pants.

"No one said I play fair."

Ana turns in my arms, gripping my cock unexpectedly and with a pressure that juts the veins in my neck. "Then how do you play at your own game?" she asks with cruel seduction, pumping my shaft with the right amount of tightness. I have to brace hands on the wall behind her and refrain from fucking her fist.

Those red-painted nails on her perfect, slender fingers around my dick are one of my favorite things. The water cascades down my back and I have to take back control.

Slapping her ass, I grip it tightly before lifting her into my arms with a primal growl. I step out with her, dropping and spinning her around before forcing her to bend over the counter. I've never felt this kind of carnal desire before. Ana makes me want to claim every part of her and wreck any innocence.

My hand slides down the length of her spine as she watches me in the clouded mirror. Reaching the curve of her ass, I lock eyes with her as my palm comes down on it, and she whimpers in pleasure.

"Would you let me fuck your ass?" I ask, soothing the reddening skin.

Her lips part and a spark of unsure desire twinkles in her eyes. "Yes."

I groan, leaning over her and kissing the small tattoo between her shoulders. "Has anyone fucked you there before?"

"No."

My little bird is so willing and eager for me. Such a good fucking girl.

"I will claim every part of you, Anastasia. Just not today. I'm never letting you go, and we have forever to make you needy for my cock in every way."

My tip lines up at her entrance and I give no warning as I drive into her fully. She cries out beautifully, clutching the counter tighter. The moment I'm deep in her heat I'm lost, gripping her hips and slamming into her over and over. It's hard to last with how perfectly she squeezes my dick, but I'm not done with her—not even close.

"You want to come so badly? You're going to give me another. Then another," I growl, reaching to circle her clit, and Ana starts pushing back, meeting me thrust for thrust and chasing her pleasure with me. "That's my girl."

Her pussy clenches me like a vise and I have to scramble my mind to think of *something* else or I'm going to explode with her, and that won't do. So I pull out, dropping to my knees and tonguing her cunt until her knees almost buckle, her orgasm unraveling with such a scream of pleasure I'm certain it's heard through the walls.

"I can't do that again," she rasps as I stand. She's still shaking, so beautifully fucked.

"You can and you will."

Taking her hand, I lead her into the room, over to the window. Lifting her onto the dresser, I part her thighs, running my fingers through her folds, and her nails scratch the wood from the sensitivity.

"One more, baby," I whisper, kissing her hard. "For the city to watch me claim you."

We aren't that high up—eight floors. Anyone walking by could look up to a clear silhouette of me fucking my girl. I hope they do.

I slip inside her, pausing to marvel at the sight of us joined together. Every piece of her fits me perfectly. Watching my cock slide in and out of her is the single most erotic sight in the world.

"So beautiful," I say.

Ana's face is painted with lust, but she struggles to hold on from the weight of fatigue that flutters her eyes. I grip her hips before fucking her with abandon. She moans through the sound of our slapping skin and the dresser rocking violently. Ana takes everything I give her. The rough pace has her clawing my back, scoring my flesh.

"Rhett, I can't," she pants, but she's close, fearing another orgasm.

"Give it to me, Ana. You owe it to me. And you want it, don't you?"

She nods weakly, too focused on the race she's building. I reach between us to help her along.

"Shit," she curses, sinking her teeth into my shoulder, and *holy fucking shit*, I erupt at that marking like some primal animal. "Right there— *Rhett!*"

"Ana— *Fuuuck!*"

We clamp around each other as if we're one fucking person. My hand fists tightly in her hair while my other arm holds her trembling form around her waist. I come so hard I see stars in my black hell for the first time. It's the longest orgasm of my damn life as I spill endlessly inside her. When the shocks subside and our hearts pound against each other I don't think I'm capable of disentangling us.

I don't know how long I hold her like that, still buried inside her, but our breathing calms and her head rests on my shoulder while her body begins to weaken. Hooking her thighs, I carry her carefully to the bed, laying her down, and she can hardly keep her eyes open.

"How are you feeling, little bird?" I whisper, pushing the wet, tangled red hair from her face.

She manages a small smile. "Thoroughly fucked."

I chuckle, kissing her forehead before pushing off the bed.

Walking into the still spraying jets, I clean myself off quickly before grabbing a hand towel, wetting it, and heading back into the room knowing Ana won't have the strength to shower. She's half-asleep as I clean between her legs—which makes her moan in protest with the sensitivity, but she can't sleep until I've finished.

When I slip into bed, she crawls up to me and I flick off the side lamp. With her nestled so contentedly in my arms it's utter bliss.

"Have you learned not to provoke me again?" I mumble, not sure if she's still awake.

Until she inhales, slipping her hand up my chest.

"I think you might have just given me more motivation."

CHAPTER 33
Anastasia

When I wake I'm cold.
Alone.

Panic surges me upright in the darkness as I clutch the duvet to my naked chest.

"Rhett?" I call out into the silence.

No lights are on and he doesn't answer.

I flick the side lamp on and swing out of bed. When I don't find him in the room or the bathroom my chest begins to tighten.

Did he leave me?

Oh god, does he regret what happened between us because of the day?

Guilt swims in my stomach as I get dressed. Maybe he doesn't want to see me, but my eyes fill with the determination to find him. Whether to apologize or just console him or— *Fuck*, I don't know what I'm doing, but I can't stay here.

I track Rhett through the location app and he's not far. It brings me to an expensive hotel, and I'm puzzled, my mind racing. At first I try searching down the streets beside it, but they turn up empty at this hour. So I head inside.

I'm greeted by staff who ask if I have a room or need one. I barely take in their words as the location app tells me Rhett should be right here.

"Did you see a man? He has light blond hair, very tall, blue eyes?"

The concierge remains confused. "Sorry, ma'am, I don't think so. Is there anything I can do for you?"

"No," I say, backing away.

Where is he?

My eyes scan through the bar that's closing up, and then to the empty fancy restaurant. Then my gaze drifts up.

For a second my thought seems too desperate to be true, but now I can't rule it out.

In the elevator I hit the rooftop floor.

My heart thumps hard, picking up speed with every number that ticks by, until I'm nauseous after the thirty fifth ding signals I've arrived on the roof.

Then my chest hollows at the brick keeping the escape door from shutting, because I know I've found him. And I become terrified to discover why he's here.

I'm freezing before I even slip through the open gap. I walk around looking for him until I spy a silhouette.

He sits precariously on the ledge, and my breath catches with a skip of fright.

I approach carefully, too afraid to even blink, as that's all it would take for him to disappear.

"Rhett," I whisper, stopping a few paces away.

His shoulders straighten from their slump, but he doesn't turn around. So I take another step. Then another.

"I proposed to her here. In the restaurant," he says. I hear the cracks in his voice even though it's barely a whisper against the wind, which is stronger up here. "I've come here every Christmas Eve night, and I tried not to this time. I didn't want to leave you, but I had to."

"It's okay," I say. Another slow, fearful step. "I understand."

His head shakes. "For three years I've looked at this view and made peace with the fact it will eventually be my last."

My eyes flood with heartbreak as I look out at the cityscape. I don't touch him when I finally get close enough. Instead I flatten my palms against the icy stone and hoist myself up.

"Ana, it's not safe."

I don't listen, partly because I catch a glimpse of the very *long* way down and I have to focus on swinging my legs around and taking breaths of courage. I've never been great with heights. My legs dangle over the ledge and my fingers bite into the stone.

"I'm safe with you," I say, looking over the sleeping city as if I can place myself in his mind, try to understand a fraction of what he's feeling.

Rhett erases the small space between us and my muscles loosen when his arm wraps around me. "I hoped you wouldn't wake. I never would have left if I'd thought you'd come looking again."

"I'll always come."

"Why?"

For the first time, I turn my head and I don't expect the impact of meeting those blue eyes. It feels like it's the first time, but also like I've held them for a lifetime. He's so beautiful it pains me.

Erupts in me.

I'm overwhelmed all at once.

Because I love him.

I'm *in* love with Rhett Kaiser, and it's the most vulnerable and peaceful realization that consumes me. I take in every detail of his perfect face as if it belongs to me—every part of him. Suddenly there's no seeing a day beyond now without him in it, and there's no day from the past as treasured as those since the moment he walked into my life.

"I don't want to lose you," I say quietly. That's all I can admit right now.

It's not fair to throw that kind of declaration at him when this time of year is so sensitive to the true love he lost. I fear his rejection more than anything. That he'll distance himself from me and I won't be able to bear it.

Rhett's dark brows pull together as his hand slips over my face.

"I came here tonight because I had to know . . ." he says, but he takes a pause and it's like I can feel his agony. I take his hand and circle his arm instead, leaning my head to his shoulder. He continues. "I looked out at this view tonight only to know for certain I don't want it to be my last anymore. I don't want to come back here again."

My lip wobbles and a tear escapes. I'm so relieved I can't hold back my flood of emotion.

"Thank you," I whisper. To him. To whoever or whatever is out there that gave me him.

"Look at me," he says. I do, and his thumb brushes the wet trail of my tears.

Rhett's eyes search every inch of my face, but he abandons his words to kiss me instead. Then it's like we're flying. With the wind tangling between us, around a view that I will make sure isn't his last. Whatever it takes. I'm his.

CHAPTER 34

Anastasia

This is the first Christmas Day I haven't spent with my parents, but being with Rhett, the day has never felt more complete. There's a weight of sorrow as we pause outside a tall block of apartments—the one he shared with Sarah that he's never sold.

I squeeze his hand laced through mine, pulling him gently toward the entrance.

"Which floor?" I ask, slipping a hand into the pocket I saw him tuck his keys into.

His eyes speak the gratitude he can't voice. "Six," he says quietly. "Apartment 6F."

I smile, trying to assure him in every way that I want to be here, and he will never be alone again even if we come here every year for this.

Unlocking the apartment door, I wait for him to guide us in the rest of the way. It takes him a moment, and I'm about to offer to stay outside, but he moves and I go with him, flicking on lights as we make our way down the narrow hall. I stay silent, observing the humble space that I imagine was once bright and cozy but is now neglected and cold.

Rhett told me how he stays here over Christmas every year. Alone. Last night was the first year since Sarah's death he didn't, and part of me feels guilty for taking that away from him if he only slept at the hotel for my safety. I told him I wanted to come here if he was willing, not knowing why it felt so important until now. Being here is part of him, and I need to see it. His past, his present, but I hope it isn't his future now I've painted myself in it without knowing if he'll reject that notion.

At some point he lets me go, and I gravitate around the space as if I'm a ghost here only to capture everything I can about Rhett, even Sarah, as she was once everything to him.

Picking up a photo frame, I don't know how to place my feeling at the sight of them together.

"You're into blondes," I comment lightheartedly. "I never stood a chance."

She's absolutely stunning, and I grieve the life of an innocent, selfless stranger who deserved far more time than she got.

Rhett is across the space in the open plan kitchen like he doesn't know where to place himself in his own former home anymore. He smiles sadly. "I think what drew me to Sarah is that she was everything I'm not. So kind and gentle. Maybe I thought she would make me forget the world I'm from. Change me into a better man."

"You don't have to change." I want to say more. To tell him no one is perfect to everyone, but everyone is perfect to someone. And he's mine. Every sharp edge and dangerous curve. He's my kind of perfect and I want every piece of him, just the way he is or not at all.

I find a broken wall mirror in the bedroom. As I draw closer I discover three impact points. They could be from something being thrown at it, except each break has lines of dark crimson, and I realize something. Rhett comes up behind me and I take his hand before it meets my waist, glancing down at his scarred knuckles. Now I have the story to them.

Three years. Three breaks. Too many scars to count.

I kiss his knuckles with a silent promise there won't come another. Not this way.

"I think I'm ready to sell this place," he says.

Turning from our broken reflection, I scan his face, and while it's filled with sorrow, I want to believe there's freedom lifting in him with the decision.

"We can arrange for it to be emptied once you've taken anything of value out and I'll organize the sale. You don't have to come back here."

Rhett's eyes close as he cups my jaw and kisses my forehead. "I have everything of value to me."

My eyes prick with the sincerity in his voice. "Thank you for showing me this part of you."

"I only wanted to come one last time. Truthfully, when I flew here, I didn't know this would be the last. Then I saw you and I broke. I realized right then I can't keep revisiting the past. Not if I want to see the future."

I push up on my tiptoes to kiss him. "What's in this future?" I whisper against his lips.

His arms circle me, pressing our bodies together. "A house with a wraparound porch."

My smile breaks to a grin. "Mm-hmm," I coax.

"And a labradoodle as a friend for a black German shepherd."

"Maybe a pond with ducks."

"Is that safe with the dogs?"

"They'll learn 'friends not food.'"

"Speaking of food—I know it's not traditional, but our only option might be Chinese takeout with every restaurant fully booked for Christmas dinner."

I pull at the folds of his coat. "Luckily for us, my father was able to pull strings, and there's a table waiting for us at a nearby rooftop hotel restaurant. We have a room there too before we fly back tomorrow."

I turn giddy at his look of shock.

"I don't deserve you."

"Yes, you do. Don't make me show you. You're not ready for what I would do."

"I'm ready for anything you can throw at me, Anastasia."

We lock the front door and Rhett doesn't even look back as we exit the building.

There's only forward now, and I squeeze his hand.

"Thank you, by the way, for the violin," I say. "It's the most thoughtful gift anyone's ever given me."

The streets are deserted and light snow starts to fall. It's a peaceful cloudy day.

"I just wanted you to know I was there with you. Even miles away."

I'm overcome with love for this man. It's like nothing I've felt before, and I can't stop thinking about it. I realize now it's always been there, but it needed time to grow before I could accept it as a promise and not a fleeting thing.

"You said you're ready for anything I can throw at you," I say, letting go of his hand and bending down.

My gloved hands gather snow. As I flick a devious look up, I gasp when Rhett clocks onto my meaning before I can form a proper snowball. He makes one from the hood of a car, and I squeal, ducking behind the feeble protection of a lamppost before he throws it at me.

Giggles burst from me as I toss my pathetic, misshapen lump that doesn't come close to hitting him. Then our battle erupts and the last of the daylight infuses with our carefree laughter and antics. Darting across roads, ducking behind cars. Rhett has never looked so young and burdenless. It swells in my chest and I never want it to end.

This. Us. And the *many* beautiful days we'll have just like this one.

CHAPTER 35
Anastasia

I never thought I'd see myself in a newspaper actually smiling. My parents hand it to me over the breakfast table. The picture is of me playing my violin, but not in this house. They've chosen to show me in Philadelphia, playing for *me* and Rhett. It's a beautiful shot, and below it, the moment Rhett kissed me and made us feel like the only two people in the world.

"The media is going crazy for you selflessly charming the people with your talents on Christmas Eve," a spokesperson from my father's press team, Sheila, says from the side. "And as a couple, you two are making headlines everywhere and blowing up on social media."

None of it is real. At least . . . their version of what they saw. The media will always have pictures, but they can tell a hundred stories. They don't know mine. They never will. But still I smile, because *I* know the real story of a broken man and a lost woman who found each other through the most unlikely of means. I know she abandoned everything that night to go to him, and that though he didn't know it, he was waiting for her to come. I know she fell in love on Christmas Day, a gift that arrived, as all do . . . inevitably, and then suddenly.

"Thank you, Sheila," my father says kindly, dismissing her after she's updated him.

Rhett has headed to the gym as I was requested to breakfast with my parents. We've been back from Philly for three days.

"My dear, I have to ask," my father begins. From his tone of caution I know what's about to be addressed. "I know this all started as a ruse you were forced into with your personal guard, but is there something real going on now?"

I set the paper down, not liking how he makes it sound like it would be a bad thing. "Of course not," I say.

Rhett and I discussed this on our way home. While I'm not sure what exactly is between us yet, at least for him, what we both agreed was that we couldn't stop the physical attraction. Didn't *want* to stop that. But my parents can't know, and this confrontation is proof we were right. My father wouldn't keep Rhett as my bodyguard. It would be a conflict of interest. He can't stop us from seeing each other, but Rhett won't risk losing his position at my side, and worse, it would open up the possibility of someone noticing when he doesn't return to any secret service unit. I wouldn't be able to keep seeing him.

"I've seen you two together. And leaving the Christmas party for him and this—"

"You were largely in favor of this charade," I snap.

My anxiety makes me sharp, suddenly daunted by my future. I can't see one without Rhett, but what if he needs to see it without me? If not because of his lost love, then because being near me after this post will always be a danger to him because of who my father is. With Rhett's real work, being close to the president's daughter comes with the big risk of exposing everything he's built.

Rhett Kaiser is a hero, but our society will always paint him as a villain.

"Yes, and I trusted him to remain professional."

"He has been nothing but," I defend. "There's no one who would take my safety more seriously than him."

My father's face softens as if he agrees but also won't let go of his suspicions. "I wouldn't object to your feelings, Anastasia. But in your best interests, his position could not stay."

"He's done nothing. We've done nothing," I say, hating how it stings that I can't be open about him and I have to lie to my parents. I push the newspaper away. "That was nothing more than a press move when we noticed the cameras, so you're welcome. *'Newly elected president's daughter and swoon-worthy boyfriend sway voters' hearts,'*" I make up sarcastically. "Rhett lost someone dear to him years ago and needed a friend that night, or is that not allowed either?"

"Of course it is." My mom finally speaks. She tries to smile, but her expression is a near wince too, as if the lie of what Rhett and I have done is all over me.

"I have a few things to do before semester starts back." I excuse myself, and while they look inclined to protest, they let me go.

The moment I'm alone I don't know how I feel. Sad that I have to hide how much Rhett means to me. Scared that the person I've fallen for could leave me for his own safety.

Shadow follows at my heel as usual. I don't go to the gym to find him like I planned to do after breakfast. I head to the cinema room, turning on some thriller movie in an attempt to distract myself and calm my reeling thoughts. Pitifully, I lie in the deep two-seater seat where Rhett kissed me for real for the first time.

I must have dozed off, because the thing to jerk me awake is the silence. The projector has auto powered off. A blanket is draped over me that I didn't take out myself, but I'm alone aside from being comfortably curled into Shadow. Was Rhett in here? I can't understand the tightening in my stomach and the sudden wave of fear that overcomes me. Shadow becomes alert to my urgent pace as I storm from the cinema room. I have to find him. This unexplainable need to see him speeds my pulse.

It's irrational, and I'll slap myself for becoming this desperate, pining idiot for him the moment he's in front of me.

I knock on his door, waiting only a few seconds before I enter. He isn't here. Shadow paces the room as if checking for him too, but he whines at Rhett's absence. We check the gym next, then the kitchen, then the pool. By the time I arrive at my father's office something terrible is growing within me. I don't knock, unaware and uncaring that he isn't alone, and for a second hope blooms that it's Rhett he's talking to.

It isn't him. The flicker of hope snuffs out like a candle when I find Gregory Forbes in the chair opposite my father, and both of them snap their attention to me with my intrusion.

"Have you seen Rhett?" I ask through my drying throat.

My stomach clenches worse at the falling look on his face.

"I thought he'd have the chance to tell you before he took off. He said there was a family emergency and I granted him the leave," my father says sorrowfully.

"When?"

Oh god, what's happened?

"A couple of hours ago."

"Did he say who? Where?"

The shake of my father's head sends the world spinning as I scramble to think for myself.

"Don't fret, Ana," Gregory says, standing and buttoning his suit jacket. "We have already replaced your personal guard in the meantime in case Agent Kaiser requires more time to deal with his family issues."

Family issues. The only blood family he has is a cruel and vile monster. Did he finally get to Rhett? My expression must give away my terror, because my father stands, concern pinching his aging face.

"I'm sure all will be well soon with him. He'll return," he assures me.

"Okay," I whisper.

I don't like the way Gregory smiles. Knowing. I leave without another word and practically run to my room. Finding my phone on the nightstand, I tap it desperately. My heart withers at the blank screen. No message from Rhett. I don't hesitate to call him. No answer. Not even a ring. Dread slicks my skin as I pace my room and try again and again. *Beep beep beep.* Near frantic, I try Allie. Same with her.

What the fuck is happening?

Remembering I should still have Rhett's location app, I try clicking onto it, but nothing loads before it crashes and kicks me back to my home screen. I grip my phone tightly, resisting the urge to throw it, because I need it in case he calls or texts.

Shadow grows as restless as me, and all I can do is bend and assure him with pats, but he isn't so easily soothed either. I cross the hall to Rhett's room, at a complete helpless loss for what to do. I climb into his bed and Shadow joins me. My brow scrunches at his teakwood scent with a hint of mint that envelops me from his pillow as I curl into it.

He'll be okay. He has to be. Something urgent pulled him away, and it must be serious for him not to have told me before he left. But he'll come back to me and explain it all, and it will all be okay.

CHAPTER 36
Rhett

After the gym I find Ana in the cinema room fast asleep while a movie plays. It invokes such peace in me to watch her delicate face as she's curled into Shadow. I grab a blanket and fit it over her, leaning in to kiss her head. She doesn't stir, so I leave her and head up to shower.

I've just come out and changed into black jeans and a plain black T-shirt when my phone rings with a particular tone.

"Hey, Allie." I pick up on the second ring.

"Rhett." Her quiet voice slams my steps still.

"What's wrong?" I say, immediately recoiling as dread sharpens my senses.

"I-I found the missing sapphire earrings." My adrenaline beats my pulse, quieting my world as she says, "I'm looking at them."

"Fuck." I'm throwing on my leather jacket in the same breath and out of my room in seconds. "Just a minute," I say, switching to my earpiece and pocketing my phone.

The dining room is empty, so I head to the senator's office. He's typing away as I knock and enter brazenly.

"Agent, is everything okay?"

"I have a family emergency," I rush out. "I wouldn't dare ask if it wasn't urgent. I wouldn't ask for time away from protecting Ana if I had another choice."

My chest, my mind, my fucking soul aches at the thought. But Allie is a target in real danger right now.

"Of course, son. Do what you have to and take a car if you need to. I'll have your placement covered in the meantime."

"Thank you, sir," I say, and I don't have a second to spare before I'm sprinting to the garage and slipping into the black SUV.

I checked Allie's location on the way, cursing that she was in Boston eight fucking hours away.

She's still on the line as I say, "Lock yourself somewhere. I'm coming for you."

Her small gasp slams in my fucking chest. I speed the car out the garage.

"There's no time. I think someone's here," she whispers.

"Allie, can you hide? Can you get out of that house and find somewhere safe, please?"

"There's no time. Listen to me, Rhett. There's something else you need to know, and you can't leave Ana right now. Adam Sullevan wasn't the one who attacked her at the fair. He was at least an hour away. Traffic across the city was terrible and he wasn't going to make it in time. I've confirmed his location at a club that whole night."

There's a crash in the background and my fists tighten on the wheel painfully.

"I don't care right now. Where are you?"

"I-I'm hiding," she whispers carefully. "But they're going to find me."

A violent scream is building inside me. I can't lose Allie. She can't be in this fucking mess because of me.

"Don't come, Rhett," she pleads softly. "I might have the missing sapphire earrings someone has paid for, but Ana . . . she's the ruby. She has been all this time, and you know these debts won't go unfulfilled no matter what it takes."

My insides are tearing apart, my mind strains toward insanity with two opposite directions to follow. *How could I not have seen it sooner?* The price tag stamped "SOLD" that's been on my little bird all this time. I want to burn the gala venue and all those inside it to the ground.

"They're coming for me to separate you. They know you'll try to save me."

I won't be forced to choose. I won't be forced to choose.

FUCK.

My rage is so hot and tangible I don't know what to do. How to possibly fucking live with either decision.

"Hang tight, Allie," I say as softly as I can for her terror. "You're going to be okay."

Taking out another phone, I dial Rix.

"Dude! I've been trying to reach you! We're in deep fucking shit, man—"

"Allie's in imminent danger. As in I need whoever is in the area to get there right. Fucking. Now."

"Shit, on it."

"They're here," Allie whispers in pure terror.

"We're coming, Allie. Be brave, love. If they harm a hair on your head they're going to pay for it in ways that'll make them beg for death."

I'm helpless. Completely fucking wrecked to be on the line when she cries, finally found. All I hear is a struggle and the taunting voices of two wicked men. I'm right back to the night of Christmas Eve four years ago. An utterly defeated, lost, and weak man.

"We're coming for you," I whisper. Then the line cuts off and I yell anguish into the car. Pure raw fury that pumps the accelerator.

"I'm sorry man," Rix says, as broken as I feel.

"Tell me we can track her."

"She's smart. I'm just waiting for her damn clever sign and I'll be on her faster than a knife fight in a phone booth."

"Good," I grind out.

"You should go back to Ana. Did Allie tell you—?"

"Yes."

"She sold for over twenty million, Rhett. It's record-breaking. I'm surprised they haven't come for her yet."

My little bird is no one's to sell. No one's to own but *mine*. I will find whoever thought they had a chance of having her and make sure they know Anastasia Kinsley is fucking priceless. Then I'll find Jacob Forthson for orchestrating the sale and let him watch his empire burn before I throw him to the flames without his flesh.

I'm driving on autopilot, about to turn around as I'm better served here, closer to the most important thing to me, and Xoid will find Allie within the day or I'll raise hell personally.

But I've learned by a cruel and merciless deliverance before how fast fate can switch.

That no hour is granted . . .

No minute is gifted . . .

It takes less than one minute for the speeding car to my right to slam into the back side of the SUV and obliterate the world around me. All I feel is pain, but it quickly turns too consistent and I can't pinpoint where on my body is broken or sliced. All I can hear is crash after crash, and it becomes too constant to track what's happening. All I can see is an endless, torturous black.

Then nothing.

For a few seconds it's as stilling as death.

Until I fight for consciousness.

For a flash of red hair and the brightest smile.

For a laugh that is my song.

A touch that is my heaven.

For Ana, I want the pain that returns punishingly as if my flesh has been cut a thousand times. I manage to unclip my belt with a violently trembling hand. Blood rushes to my head and I brace for the fall when I'm no longer strapped in. I grit my teeth through the explosion happening inside my head and lancing across my ribs. Glass cuts deep, but I have to make it out.

For my little bird I have to make it.

I'm coming back, baby. I chant to myself.

She'll understand. She'll say it's not my fault when that isn't the truth. Everything is my fault, and once again I've put everything I love in the line of fire by letting her get close to me.

I'm going to marry Anastasia Kinsley.

I'm going to buy my wife that damned house with the porch. Or build it from the fucking ground so it faces the view she wants.

She's going to have my children someday and grow old with my hand in hers.

I paint that future in the blood that spills from me now. I promise that to her with all that I am as I crawl from the wreckage. And I'll crawl all the way back to her like this if that's what it takes.

"It's been far too long," a voice says.

One so deep and haunting. One that will never erase itself from my mind, just like it's never left my nightmares no matter how much time has passed.

"I apologize for the methods, but you'll fix right back up, nephew. You always do."

CHAPTER 37
Anastasia

When I wake up I know something isn't right. Call it intuition or my sixth sense that manifested Rhett Kaiser. I lie in his bed like I know something I'm about to face outside his door will end me.

He didn't come back yesterday. With the new dawn, my dread and worry has me almost running to the bathroom to throw up several times.

I have to find him. Find out what happened for him to have left so abruptly and become unreachable. I force myself up as Shadow whines.

"I know, boy," I croak, fighting back tears, but I don't know what they're for.

Downstairs I hear quiet chatter from my father's office, and if there's any news from Rhett, perhaps he told him instead to keep his job post safe. I knock and enter after he calls through. Everyone is standing, and disturbance pinches my parents' faces.

I can't pay them any attention when all I can take in is the daunting sight of the two police officers.

"What happened?" I ask, feeling the ground softening under me. It's like I know what they're going to say. My head is shaking before they even speak.

"There was an accident yesterday afternoon," one of the officers says.

My vision sways. "Where's Rhett?"

"Ana, please sit—" my father tries gently.

"Where. Is. He?"

"It was a fatal vehicle collision, and we tracked the registration here," the other officer explains.

My heart stumbles.

Fatal.

I cling to my denial, believing the story is a fable, something sick and twisted to keep us apart, until a newspaper is slid across the desk and an officer lifts it before extending it to me.

My blood runs cold.

There's no mistaking the car we've used together so many times. It's completely wrecked, flipped onto its roof. My hand covers my mouth as I blink my vision clear, imagining Rhett inside such devastation.

"We haven't been able to identify the male inside, but from our understanding with the senator, it's very likely to be Rhett Kaiser. His uncle has come forth to confirm this afternoon."

My whole body flushes at that. His uncle.

"He did this!" Those words slip from me through struggling breath.

"Ana, dear," Mom says. Her hands are on me, but I can't feel them.

Rhett isn't dead. He can't be.

"His uncle did this," I say, louder this time as rage begins to overpower the pain, because I *refuse* to believe there's no Rhett in this world anymore. "You have to arrest him!"

Mom stops me from stepping up to the officers, who barely flinch at anything I say. As if they don't hear me.

As if they already know.

His uncle is a very powerful man and he's managed to elude Rhett for all these years. Does he have the strings to puppet the police force too? My eyes burn. Rhett was right: there's no righteous path when corruption cracks through the glass of any moral compass.

"Ana, come sit, please," Mom pleads.

I can't. Shadow barks and then growls as if he can feel my tangible anger. The officers shift, wary of him.

"He's not dead," I grind out.

"That's not all, Ana," my father cuts in gently. I slice him with a look. "Rhett Kaiser is not who he claims to be."

My body stiffens. "What are you talking about?"

"His credentials are forged. I'm looking into it further to find out what he intended. Perhaps this is a blessing in a grim disguise if he meant you harm."

"Rhett isn't the danger here." I dare to target the officers. "He never has been."

"He's gone, honey," my father says, sharper now, and that only grows on my anger. "I will get to the bottom of it, but I can't say I'm not glad he can't be around you anymore."

I'm on the verge of snapping, and I don't know what kind of ugly could unleash from me in the wrong company right now. So I say nothing as I spin on my heel despite my parents calling after me.

My world is crumbling.

The weight of what they implied starts sinking me slowly, and I run down the halls until I burst back into Rhett's room . . .

Then I shatter.

Grief like nothing I've felt before tightens in my chest as I sink to my knees. It pours from me in chokes of agony.

Shadow nudges me, but I can't take comfort in him when he serves as another reminder of what I've lost. I cry until I can't breathe. I don't believe I'll be able to rise from the floor. I don't want to.

I think of his beautiful face and how I'll never see it again. How I never got to tell him I love him.

I love him.

I love him.

I love him.

And I never will.

At some point I turn hollow and the ghost of me opens drawers until I find one of his all-black hoodies. I break all over again when his scent embraces me, and it's like a knife won't stop twisting in my heart and tearing through my stomach at the same time. I curl into his bed and give up on time, not caring what passes when Rhett isn't in the hours I lie there. He'll never be in another.

I try calling his number, over and over, until the *beep beep beep* breaks my heart into too many fragments and I drift away to the echo of my hollow chest.

CHAPTER 38
Anastasia

Seventy-two hours pass without Rhett and each one feels like my life is draining slowly. I only know this from Riley, who came over yesterday when she couldn't get a response from me and stayed the night.

I don't have it in me to tell her I'd rather be alone.

It's not that I don't appreciate her attempt of comfort. I just can't, *won't*, absorb any of it.

My parents are worried. Maybe my father is even regretful of how he spoke of Rhett. I don't care, and I'm not ready to forgive him.

I've hardly left Rhett's bed. Staying curled up in his hoodie is my reassurance he's coming back. I'm tormented with everything I never got to say to him. Everything we'll never get to do. Rhett's gone, and he deserved to know how much he means to someone, how important and special he is, that he's not the monster he believes he is. He deserves to be loved.

I let him down.

"You need to shower," Riley says softly on the bed beside me. "Start taking care of yourself."

"I didn't tell him I love him," I croak, curled away from her.

"I bet he knew."

"That doesn't matter. He never thought he deserved it, and I should have told him."

Riley tucks up behind me, squeezing my arm. "I'm so sorry, Ana. I know that doesn't mean shit for what you're going through, but he wouldn't want to see you like this."

She didn't know him. Not really. There's no one in my life who knew who Rhett truly was, and that only cleaves in me deeper.

My tears won't stop falling, but I no longer sob until I choke. My denial is turning to anger and I've been reeling with what I want to do with it. How I can avenge him with the serpents I still wear and will forever.

"Okay," I say.

It's a beacon of hope for Riley. It will be for my parents. But as I stand in a state of mind-stilling numbness under the waterfall of the shower head, I craft my plan. Maybe it's the echo of Rhett that lives in me now pushing the grief and loss aside to make room for what needs to be done. No matter how long it takes or what morals I have to sacrifice for it.

There's a monster on the loose, and I'm nothing if not part of Xoid, and Rhett Kaiser's girlfriend, ready to stop him.

So I dress in all black and I leave his room for the first time.

Eating breakfast is my first challenge, but I need the strength. My parents' voices are mostly a hum to my calculating thoughts and I nod enough to appear present. They leave that afternoon for some speech my father is giving at a hotel in the city, and I don't waste a second, infiltrating his office, intending to find anything I can if he's still looking into Rhett. I've already plucked the keys from his bedroom for every locked space in here. When my child-self first discovered them and found nothing but boring paperwork, I never had reason to steal them again.

The first filing cabinet turns up nothing. Neither does the next. I go to his desk, sitting in his prominent chair and leaning down to sift through his drawers. Then I find it. His name sprawled in eleven beautiful letters, and I have to force back my threatening grief. *Focus, Ana.*

My father has been looking into him like a criminal. My resentment grows.

Sifting through Rhett's file, my fingers brush his face from his forged secret service identification, and all that clenches in my chest are words unspoken and feelings that will forever kill me slowly.

There isn't much inside, to my relief. His birth name, Everett Lanshall, isn't anywhere, but I'm only looking for one thing. I pull out the police report of the accident and I'm slammed with anger that trembles my hand. He uses Rhett's alias, and I want to carve the name he had no right to: Alistair Kaiser. The bare minimum about him, likely mostly false, is in here as part of the police accident file when he identified Rhett.

He's lying.

My mind won't stop tormenting me. Denial circles with vicious accusations to spin any possible alternative that Rhett is still alive. Alistair has him.

I will never be able to rest until I find out for myself.

I'm admiring the sea view of the restaurant I'm sitting in. The winter sun glitters on the surface of the calm waves, soothing my senses, which are razor-sharp.

The chair opposite me finally pulls out, and I slide my eyes to meet those of my greatest enemy.

Alistair Lanshall is everything I pictured. His hair is a far darker blond than Rhett's silvery hue. He's very tall like him, though not as broadly built, and his eyes are a darker blue. He regards me with a delighted feline smile as he unbuttons his suit jacket and sits. I give him nothing in return.

"Anastasia Kinsley, it is an absolute honor to finally meet you," he says, his voice as slow and cruel as I imagined.

"I can't say the same."

That only curves his wicked mouth further.

"I was most surprised to receive your message. I'll admit I thought it a setup at first, so I'll advise you, I have many men surrounding us should you have anything planned."

I shake my head calmly. "Nothing yet."

His blue irises sparkle at that. "I followed you and my nephew in the tabloids and papers. A *very* convincing couple, I must say. Even if it was false, I imagine you grew at least somewhat close with it all, so I'm sorry for your loss."

I have to take a pause to collect myself, if only to stop me from running my idle fingers up the stem of my wineglass to grip it and smash it over his head. I'm not used to these violent thoughts, but something in me is chanting them for Rhett.

"Did you kill him?"

He makes a show of seeming *wounded*. Alistair leans back in his chair, looking over the water as if he's reflecting on fond memories with his nephew. "Rhett was everything to me," he says, trying to sound sincere. "I am devastated."

"You can cut the bullshit," I snap. "It's just you and me here, and we both know there was nothing fake about what was in those papers. You don't get to claim you had feelings for him when all you did was hurt him."

He drops the mask, flicking his eyes to me with cool amusement.

"I said he was everything to me, not that I had a pathetic weak heart for the boy." He leans forward as if taunting me. "I saw something in him that no one else did. Certainly not my brother or his coddling, insufferable wife. I saw someone worthy of succeeding me—leading an empire."

"Of crime and corruption. He never wanted that."

"Sometimes we don't know what is best for us until we're shown."

"You gave him no choice."

"He had a child's heart to grow out of, that's all. He would have come to understand if he'd stayed. He would have tasted the riches, felt the power, and he would have slept like a damn babe at night."

"You're wrong."

"You want to see something good in him. It's adorable."

My jaw tightens, and whatever else I expose in my expression makes him tilt his head, watching me curiously.

"Maybe you were suited to each other after all," he says with a vacancy that reveals he's thinking far more than what he speaks. "I could keep you safe, you know. I could offer you the world on a platter and the moon on a string."

He can't be fucking serious.

"I'd rather take a knife to my own chest."

"There's not just a price out for you, Miss Kinsley—you're already sold, and it's only a matter of time before that debt is collected. I am the only person who can protect you. It is why I came. For Everett. He would want this."

"You don't know a thing about him," I hiss. "You murdered his fiancée."

"Ahh, yes, it was one the most unfortunate collaterals in all my years, but it did exactly what I needed it to do. It made Everett Lanshall everything I saw within him even as a child. The anger that was calm and waiting to be given a purpose, the way he could analyze people and things, the control he had despite the darkness he harbored. If left to his own devices, they would have said he was a volatile, troubled kid, a lost cause. They never would have appreciated all his worth, but I did."

Alistair wanted Rhett since he was a child. My mind is racing, nagging with something that feels just shy of being put together. Until it dawns on me with bone-trembling clarity.

"Rhett's parents died in a car accident," I whisper, hoping my thoughts are reaching. Alistair couldn't be capable of killing his own brother and wife just to have Rhett.

Yet by the way he watches me, almost impressed . . .

I'm going to be sick.

"You killed them. The same way you killed Rhett."

Alistair leans back with a sigh as if it's something I can't possibly understand. "I can't have children, Anastasia. I've never pictured myself the fatherly type, but I longed for someone to share my empire with—someone with the potential to succeed me. To continue the legacy I built from the fucking ground up. Then Rhett came along, my first nephew, and it was like he was born to the wrong person when he was just like me. I saw my younger self in him, and just like when we were kids, I knew my brother would never understand or appreciate Rhett. I did it for him. His parents would have made him believe there was something wrong with him. His fiancée would have held him back. *I gave him the freedom from all of them to be everything he was destined to be. I let him think he was the hunter for years while I watched and waited. I would have come for him eventually, and now he'd done unspeakable things I was willing to spend as much time as it took to show him we would be unstoppable together."*

I can hardly breathe I'm so unprepared for this kind of world-shifting revelation. I knew he was a twisted, evil man . . . but all he's orchestrated . . . all he's taken from Rhett . . .

"Will you walk with me?" I ask calmly, not waiting as I stand and slip into my coat.

I need the air, a moment to think.

We head down a deserted boardwalk and I try to keep my stomach at bay as I look over the sea rather than at the vicious being next to me.

"He might have been some of the things you said, but Rhett was good. Why couldn't you just let him go?" I ask.

"I've always thought of him as my son. I could never give up on him."

"He wasn't yours," I say, finally stopping, and my heart is beating out of my chest. My hand shakes in my pocket, but my anguish and agony is ready to do what I've come here for.

There's no taking it back when I spin and aim a gun at Alistair Lanshall's head.

"You took him from me," I say, voice quavering.

He doesn't seem at all fazed by my threat. It's Rhett's gun. I found it tucked away in a drawer in his room. I can do this for him.

"You're no killer, Anastasia."

"You don't know what I am," I hiss through the pain tearing me apart and blurring my vision.

With gritted teeth I click off the safety.

I have him right here under my gun, the person who abused, tortured, and ultimately killed the only man I've ever loved before I had the chance to tell him.

"Neither of us will walk away if you pull that trigger," he says, so calm, not believing I'll do it. And what pricks my eyes and trembles my hand is that I don't have the confidence I'll do it either. "It would be such a waste."

"Why did you do it?" I ask. An angry tear slips down my cheek and I *despise* myself for it.

Alistair steps closer until the barrel touches his forehead. "I think I severely underestimated you, Miss Kinsley," he says, so gentle, like he's approaching a storm to tame it. "You're in grave danger and my offer still stands. I see why my nephew was drawn to you. You're not like Sarah Carter. She would have always been too good, too quiet, too safe. But you . . ." He reaches a foul hand to my face, and that's when I break, stepping back with a sob and lowering my gun. "You are an absolutely stunning creature of potential. You, my dear, would thrive in our world. Let me help you, Ana, before it's too late."

My lip wobbles, angry with myself that I couldn't follow through. I lured him out here, I came face-to-face with the man Rhett hunted for years, and I was too cowardly to end it for him.

"Burn in hell," I say venomously.

"Oh Ana, people like you and me are forged from those fires."

The way he speaks of us as the same—*you and me*—riddles me with so much disgust I have to get out of there. Away from his eyes that start to thread a claim around me.

Over the past three days there have been two clashing, damning forces that won't allow me to accept such a finality as death. No matter that I saw the paper with the wreckage no one should be able to survive. Even now I'm standing in the presence of his killer who plays the part so well.

I can't let go of the doubt laced with hope.

Because he isn't no one. He isn't anyone. He's Rhett fucking Kaiser, and he can't be dead.

Not like this.

"I want to think about it," I say. Bile rises in my throat. *I'm so sorry, Rhett.* He would tell me not to do this. But this is the only way to get close enough again and muster the strength to kill Alistair. And only then, if I don't find Rhett in all I have to do and all I might become, will I accept that he's gone forever.

"I'm afraid you don't have the luxury of time, my dear."

"One night. Can we meet tomorrow?"

His lips purse, contemplative. "I really hope we get the chance to. Stay in your home tonight. Don't even go into the garden without your guards. If they come for you, it will be too far out of my hands then."

"Who is coming for me?"

He scans me over as if curious. "Your buyer, of course."

"My . . ."

Realization hits me like a bullet.

The missing jewelry Rhett was trying to find. The ruby, sold for a sickening amount of money that night, yet they never found the woman it correlated to.

All this time. I've been walking around with a fucking sale tag on my back, and now I'm furious with no face to direct it toward.

"Jacob?" I ask.

Alistair takes a deep breath, sliding his hands into his pockets. "Go home, Ana. Don't leave until you come to see me again tomorrow. I'll send for you."

I nod, letting Alistair escort me back to the restaurant, and I don't protest when he says he'll be following me home. I drive with my thoughts racing by faster than the road. I've never felt so lost and alone and scared. I yearn so deeply for only one person, but he's not coming for me this time.

If he's still out there, I have to come for him.

CHAPTER 39
Anastasia

Eighty-one hours have passed without Rhett, and each time my phone pings it dissipates another piece of my delusional hope that it'll be him.

I sit tucked up against his headboard with Shadow when sleep won't find me. I don't know what tomorrow will bring. Will I ever see my parents again? I'm sure Alistair has the means to make me disappear. I'm hoping to negotiate, but if that's what I have to do, I'm ready. Perhaps whatever I become at the hands of Alistair Lanshall will make me strong enough to pull the trigger the next time I hold a barrel to his head, and it'll come with the pleasure of knowing he trained his own murder weapon.

Shadow alerts me to an approach moments before a gentle knock sounds against the wood. I never answer, but it's never stopped the intrusion I don't want to face. This time I'm too in shock to immediately cast them away.

"What are you doing here?" I ask Adam, who's closing the door and walking in like he's testing a minefield.

"I heard what happened and I . . . Shit. I don't know. There's not a lot of bullshit you haven't already heard, but I've been thinking about you."

He sounds nervous. I get it. Grief makes people awkward when condolences sound like insults. That's because they are. There are no words that can even soothe the wounds of loss. No gifts nor actions nor comforts. I know people mean well—they don't know what else to do. No one wants to believe I'd rather they left me alone.

"That still doesn't answer why you're here," I say coldly.

"I thought you could use someone."

"You're the last *someone* on this earth I want to see right now. Come to gloat, have you? You never liked him."

"Of course not," Adam says, doing a good job of appearing genuinely disturbed.

"Go away. You're not wanted here."

He eyes Shadow carefully before coming closer. Shadow tracks Adam with unnerving attention, but he won't react unless I command it. Which is too fucking tempting right now.

"I know."

Except he proceeds to sit on the edge of the bed. I'm too exhausted to fight him, so I try to pretend he's not there. When that doesn't work I simply glare at him, though he's not looking at me. He almost looks . . . nervous. Picking at invisible threads of the duvet like he's trying to arrange his thoughts before they spill wrong.

"What is it?" I snap.

His green eyes flick up to me then, and the bastard is suppressing amusement. "I should have been honest with you from the start," he says, and his tone takes on an edge of vulnerability.

My brows knit together. "About what?"

"I care about you."

I huff a laugh, but his expression remains serious. "I never would have guessed. You've been nothing but an arrogant asshole."

His mouth quirks. "Yeah, I have."

"Why?"

Adam takes a deep breath, staring off as if he's accepting this moment had to come at some point.

"I didn't know how to tell you. Lying and pushing you away seemed easier."

I fold my legs as I sit forward, curious as to where this will lead.

"I told you I slept with another woman. It was lie. I went to a party and I met a guy. I guess I've always known I've had an attraction to men, but that night . . . I couldn't stop my desire to explore it. I told you right away, but I lied and said it was a woman when I wasn't ready to come out. His name was Henry, and we only hooked up a couple of times after you and I ended."

I'm slammed. Stunned. It was never something I would have considered, and now my mind is reaching back, trying to figure out how I could have missed it.

"It doesn't matter that it was a guy. I still knew it was wrong that one time when I was seeing you. I still hurt you, and this doesn't change that. But with my father's campaign, I didn't know how he'd take it. So I told Henry I couldn't see him anymore. I was a dick to you because, yeah, I was jealous. I saw you with Kaiser and you looked so fucking good together. You looked happy in ways I'd never seen you with me, and I resented myself. Both for being unable to love you that way and being unable to gain it in return. I did love you and I think you're hot as fuck. But there was always just something..."

"Missing," I whisper.

How could I not have seen his turmoil all this time?

"Yeah."

"Shit," I say, running a hand over my face. "I'm sorry you didn't feel like you could tell me the truth."

"It wasn't that. I knew you wouldn't judge me. But I just wasn't ready."

I look at Adam now in a new light. Yeah, he was a huge ass all year, but he owns that. Perhaps I think I can relate in some small fraction—being afraid of what his parents or the world will think of his true self.

"I'm here for you whenever you are," I say, and I mean it.

He hooks a brow at me. "You're letting me off that easy? I came prepared for your wrath."

"Are you hiding a bulletproof vest?"

He pats his chest. "Around you? Always."

I chuckle and he joins in. For a second it splits through my misery. But grief is like cutting through water; it crashes back together all at once.

"He was a great man. I'm so fucking sorry, Ana."

I think I smile, but I'm not sure it makes it to my face. "Me too."

My chest feels like it's on the edge of imploding. I sniff, trying to hold back the tears flooding too fast in my eyes by biting my nails into my palm.

Adam wordlessly, carefully moves, and I can't stop him. His arms touch me and I crumple in a complete mess of sobs and heartbreak. It's unfathomable that there will never be a cure—

that this agony will have residency in my life forever and the only thing that can fix me is a reversal of the cause. To have Rhett back.

"What can I do?" Adam asks softly.

It's still jarring to be sitting here with Adam Sullevan, the thorn in my side all term. But at the same time it's a relief I didn't know I needed. To have the animosity broken between us.

"Nothing," I say, not leaning off him. "Just being here is enough."

Collecting myself, my mind is temporarily distracted thinking about Adam's confession. "The guy with you in Cali . . ." I trail off. I won't mind if he doesn't want to talk about it, but his mischievous smile is a relief to see.

"Nathan. He was hot, right? Yeah, we hooked up."

I smile at that, dumbfounded at how oblivious I was.

"Just a hookup?"

Adam lies back with a sigh and I join him. "I can't commit to anything more."

"Why not?"

"I think I'm still hung up on Henry."

I roll onto my side to watch him as he stares at the ceiling. "Does he live nearby?"

"Only an hour away. He's entirely out, though, and I don't know when or if I'll ever be ready for that. He knows what he wants and is only interested in guys. I like women too, and I guess maybe there's a cowardly side of me that thinks I'll meet the right one and never need to have the conversation about my bisexuality with my parents."

Something about that hurts inside.

"You don't have to hide that part of yourself. No matter who you end up with. If part of you remains in a cage, you'll never fully be free."

The silence that stretches between us isn't awkward. It's thoughtful.

"Thank you," he says quietly.

I don't respond. It isn't needed. Something else weighs on my mind. I didn't expect Adam to come, and now I think he might be the only person I can say this to who won't freak out like Riley would.

"If something happens to me–"

Adam's head falls to the side to look at me with a firm brow. "Nothing is going to happen to you."

He doesn't know what I mean. Perhaps he's worried I'll do something to myself in my grief and, *shit*, I should have kept my mouth shut.

"I just mean . . . Never mind."

"Ana," he says, rolling onto his side too. His hand reaches for mine, and I don't retract. "We're all here for you. Whatever you need."

I nod. "Thank you."

It's all I can say. How will I be able to explain Alistair and what I might choose to do tomorrow?

I'm so tired I allow my eyes to slip shut. I never expected this turn of events, that I would be taking comfort in an unexpected friend. But I don't want to hold onto grudges when I know how precious time is.

My phone rings, lurching me from a deep sleep.

It's dark as I scramble, squinting for the bright light of it across the bed. I'm alone, and I remember I fell asleep next to Adam, who must have slipped out.

Lit up on the screen is Nina's name. I question with a note of dread why she'd be calling long past midnight.

"Hi," I croak.

"Ana?" Nina's voice is hushed with fear.

Suddenly I'm wide-awake, pushing myself up. Shadow leaps off the bed in alert.

"What's wrong?"

"I think someone's in the house."

"Your safe house has security watching the whole building—are you sure it isn't one of them?"

"I-I don't think so. They haven't rung the buzzer or called out like they usually do, and I'm hiding in a closet."

"Have you called them? Or 911?"

I'm already pulling on my boots and tucking Rhett's gun into the waistband of my leggings.

"I could only reach you."

That sounds an alarm in my mind. Alistair warned me to stay home tonight.

"I'll call them for you—"

A loud slam through the phone, followed by Nina's scream, sends my legs running before my mind can think logically.

"I'm coming," I tell her.

She doesn't answer, and all I hear are her cries. They pump adrenaline through my blood.

"Better hurry, little bird," a voice taunts.

The phone cuts off as I slip into the car, and I have to pause. Only Rhett ever called me that.

I don't have a choice with my friend in danger as I speed out of the garage toward Nina's safe house only ten minutes away. I try to dial 911, but I keep getting cut off, and I swear, slamming my hands to the wheel.

Pulling up, I cut the engine and get out with my heart drumming in my ears. The night is so still and quiet. Normal, but my anticipation finds it eerie. There's a black car that should host two officers on watch, but it's empty. I ring the buzzer and it only takes a few seconds for the entry to unlock. Expecting company. Expecting me.

I don't call out; instead my footing is light as I strain my hearing to pick up on any sign of movement. Down the hall the kitchen light is on, and I head for it tentatively.

My tension slams to shock when I round the corner.

"Matthew?" I say, but it sends chills down my spine to acknowledge his presence.

"Hello, Ana," he replies coolly.

I want to be relieved he's here, but what should be a friendly face chills me with fear.

Nina sits at the kitchen island, shrinking into herself with a tear-stained face.

"She looks so much like you," Matthew says, tipping Nina's brown hair over her shoulder, which causes so much terror to cross her face that I turn sick with it. "Or at least she used to."

"What are you doing here?"

Bile rises in my throat. I don't recognize this man who looks over Nina like she's a glass doll, so familiar to him.

"Let her go," I say vacantly.

He doesn't know Nina. They never met.

"I have every intention of letting her go," he says, straightening and slipping his predatory eyes to me instead. "Now I have the real thing. I've waited too long for you, Ana."

I can't believe what he's saying. My mind fits together pieces, but they're so grim and wrong, the most outlandish conclusion for the brother of one of my best friends, the son of my father's vice president. . . yet it's so glaringly obvious with what's right in front of me.

Matthew leans in close to Nina as if he relishes in the whimpers he lifts from her. My fists begin to tremble tightly at my sides, itching for my gun.

"I want you to run to Ana's home, but don't let yourself be seen. Go to Archibald Kinsley and tell him he has two hours to come for his daughter before she starts arriving to him in pieces."

"No!" I object.

"Yes, my dear."

I gasp at the new voice to enter the kitchen through another gap in the wall.

Gregory Forbes walks in with a remote expression I don't recognize. Not the warmth of a father I'm used to.

"Why are you doing this?" I ask in defeat.

This can't be happening. Not Gregory Forbes, my father's most trusted advisor. His vice president who'll be sworn into office with him. Nothing makes sense right now.

"You have a lot to understand, Anastasia. This is between your father and me. Truly, I am sorry you had to be used for this. I hope you believe me when I say my fondness for you is genuine. But your father stole everything from me, and I am not going to live in his insufferable shadow."

Nina whimpers by the door. "I'll stay with you," she says, so brave and timid, and my heart cracks for her. She's been through enough at the hands of these horrid men.

I step over to her tentatively and Matthew watches me like a hawk. I don't know if he has a gun, but he allows me to reach my friend, and I pull her into an embrace.

"Go. I'll be okay. Don't go to my father, Nina—get to safety," I whisper.

"But—"

"Please don't make my father come. He'll kill him."

"He'll kill you."

I squeeze her, praying she'll do as I say. "I'll be okay," I repeat.

Watching Nina run out of the house is both a relief and a frightening dawning that I'm alone with the vultures at my back.

"Sit, Ana," Matthew commands.

"You fucking sit, you sick bastard."

His eyes flare wildly, and I'm seconds from pulling my gun with the near lunge he takes for me.

"Matt . . ." Gregory warns.

That halts him. I've never heard his name shortened before.

"Matt," I repeat.

Because I have heard the name before. Rhett spoke of it.

"Matt Heizer," I whisper with the weight of the world crushing me.

His slow smile is twistedly amused as I figure it out. Though it doesn't make sense . . . Is it just a prop name to sway the likes of Xoid off his tracks?

"You're a smart girl, Anastasia," Matthew marvels.

"Why use Balenheizer's name?"

"Because he's my real father."

I wish I'd taken the seat he offered now because the ground doesn't feel so steady beneath me. My mind starts to go back. It scrambles to try to figure out how I could have missed it. He had a different hair color from Liam, but that didn't seem like enough when his mother has the same red hair.

"My father, the infamous Damien Balenheizer, married my mother and had me. But when I was ten he met someone new, better. Balenheizer doesn't like loose ends and planned to kill us both to start a new life free of burden. My mother managed to escape with me."

"And I found them," Gregory cuts in. "Gave them new names and fell in love with my wife. Then we had Liam."

So corruption runs in Matthew's blood from his real father. It doesn't explain Gregory's vendetta against my father.

"You put the hit out for my father all along?" I ask him.

Gregory says, "It was for you, in fact. Your father was always going to be surrounded by too much security and eyes, but you were wandering freely. Going to school, out to parties. It was too easy, but the timing was everything. Now, with your father elected, it's time for him to be put down and let me take his place."

"That's all it's for? Power?"

"Power is everything. There is no man who doesn't strive to hold as much of it as he can. You know he went to college with Rolf Sullevan. I was in their classes too, you know. I was the kid who never got invited to those parties they bonded over. I watched them at the university. They were so alike it was easy to see they'd both chase the same paths, but I never could have predicted how closely. I followed Kinsley to D.C. I admired him greatly and wanted to prove to myself I could be as good as him. Yet he continued to best me. We both ran for senator, you know. Of course, the people voted him in and he laughed it off with me, joked I could be his vice when he took office one day. That arrogant asshole deserved to be put in his place, and so I languished on the idea. Got close to him until his comment made in superiority became our reality."

I can't believe it. But keep your friends close and your enemies closer, right? I'm thinking of doing the same damn thing with Alistair. Same gamble, different game board.

My father never would have suspected him. Rhett did at some point, but the Forbes excellently swayed the trail onto the Sullevans. The competitor with an obvious motive.

Gregory was fueled by jealousy and power.

"So the Heizer alias was just to cover up your despicable affairs," I spit at Matthew.

Matthew's smile is viciously proud. "Of course. I took a lease from Sullevan under that name. He never knew it was me nor what the house was used for. Then Gregory came to me with a request . . . if I would be able to set Sullevan up to take the fall for what he wanted to do, and if I could get my real father to take the job of assassinating him. But, you see, Balenheizer isn't into this kind of shit. He wouldn't have a gain in getting his hands dirty assassinating the president when he's wealthy beyond his means for generations to come. But I knew of someone else."

"Alistair Lanshall," I say. I'm so cold where I stand.

He nods. "I work for Alistair. I'm in charge of getting his cargo to their buyers. So I went to Lanshall first, and he put a hit out for you on the dark web that turned up a few eager takers for the job, but none of them made it close to you. Then when Rhett Kaiser was known to be by your side we didn't have any more interest. Turns out this guy has made something of a reputation for himself. Alistair said he was taking on the job personally from then, but he practically kicked me out of my own plan to use you to lure out Archibald Kinsley. It made me curious, and you can imagine my surprise realizing a criminal like Kaiser had managed to infiltrate the strict defenses your father had in place already. It is no small or easy task, and I guarantee anyone else who tried that route would have failed. I knew Kaiser was trying to find out who was behind the hit and I had to get him off my trail. It was perfect, really, as I was already planting what I needed for Sullevan to take the fall for your father's assassination. So I planted the papers in Sullevan's hotel room at the debate, which led Kaiser to the stop house. I didn't expect him to find Nina and kill two of my men. That was an unfortunate, irritating mess I had to clean up. Alistair would have come after me for the losses, so I burned that house to the ground so Sullevan could claim insurance, and I had to come up with another plan. Another powerful alliance."

I know who comes next, and this is like some fucked-up dark horror story featuring everyone I know. Everywhere I've been. For the past few months.

"Before that, I couldn't help having a little fun with you. I didn't mean to cut off all your stunning hair, though I might like this look on you better. I sent what I cut to your father. He's been aware of the threat this whole time, but I hoped he'd let Kaiser in on it too when I left a special message for him. He didn't see it for weeks. A shame."

I already know most of this, but Rhett didn't tell me about the hair, which drops the idea in my gut that he could have kept more from me.

"After Alister fell through, my next option was to set you in the sights of Jacob Forthson. Alistair's biggest rival. I knew he had a trafficking auction coming up and I told him I could make sure you were there and plant the sum of money he could garner from you. Of course, you wouldn't have come for me, so I had to make Liam get you there. You were the grandest prize all along, Anastasia. You sat in that casino unknowing of the fact you were being watched, devoured, around so many patrons who became desperate for you. Some were ready to sell all their assets just to afford you. The twisted part? Some even wanted both of you, only to have Kaiser watch as they fucked you and then make you watch as they killed him. But I watched so many bid for you and I couldn't stand the thought. You were always supposed to be mine, Ana. I thought I could live with having the next best thing when Nina was taken, and when I couldn't afford her, I told Lanshall I could work for him for her."

My head is shaking. Everything I know of the world and life around me feels like a lie. A twisted, horrible lie.

"Does Liam know?" I dread to ask.

"Not everything. He knows who I am, what I've done. He knew about the goings-on at the Gala, but not exactly why I wanted you there. He thought it was to get Kaiser."

It's part relief, part absolute agony, to find out Liam isn't entirely innocent. Yet I want to reserve judgement from him. Just until I hear it from him as he looks me in the eye.

"Why me?" I breathe. Oh god. He kept Nina all this time because of me.

"I've wanted you since the moment I laid eyes on you. I can't explain it, only that you're perfect for me, yet you would never see it. I tried to treat Nina well, but she had a spitfire personality that had to be broken. I would have taken her out of state eventually, but I stayed because I couldn't leave you. Even if I only got to watch you from afar and see you when Gregory saw you. I thought I'd have the strength to leave you for good. Then everything changed. It seemed so perfect, like fate had a plan for us after all and my patience was about to be rewarded. My father would be president and the country would mourn the tragic death of Archibald Kinsley and his beloved daughter."

Matthew comes close to me, and I can do nothing but sit now, disgusted by the hand he reaches up to my face.

"It doesn't have to end entirely like that though," he says tenderly. He has to be fucking insane as well as sick. "If you agree to be mine, I won't have to hide you away. You can still come with us to the White House. I can pay off my debt for you to Jacob and we'll be happy."

My hands plant on his chest and I push him with a cry of anguish. Slipping off the island stool, I'm seconds from pulling my gun.

"I rejected you all those years ago. Most would take the fucking hint, you twisted bastard."

His hand connects with my cheek with enough force to snap my head to the side and make tears well in my eyes. Then I see white.

Reaching behind myself for the gun, I gasp when fingers close over mine and an arm pulls me into a firm body. My gun aims at Matthew by another's hand.

"Always knew there was something slippery about you."

It's Adam.

He aims lower, and a short scream leaves me at the sudden ringing of a gunshot followed by Matthew's wail of agony.

Gregory swears, and I can do nothing but clutch Adam's forearm still pinned around me as we swivel. My heart stops at the barrel pointing to my head in Gregory's hand.

"You don't want to lose her this way," Adam warns. "I'd kill you before your bullet hit her."

"You have no idea what you've done, stupid boy," Gregory hisses.

"Perhaps not, but it felt fucking good."

I have no idea what the fuck is happening. Why Adam is here and risking his life to save me.

Matthew is still groaning, his face panic-stricken, and my stomach churns at the amount of blood pooling from the wound on his leg.

"What is the plan now?" I ask him, having no choice but to put my faith in the only person who seems to be helping me when before now I would have put money on Adam Sullevan *enjoying* this twist of fate.

"Honestly, I didn't really think that far ahead."

"How did you know I was here?"

"I've had my suspicions about that asshole for a while. Even when we dated, his fixation on you was creepy, and you were totally oblivious to it."

I cringe at that. Matthew has always been around, but how was I to sense anything like the depravity that lies beneath his skin when Liam is one of my best friends? I couldn't see his brother being capable of this.

"Do you know where Liam is?" I ask.

"He's been missing for about a week, actually," Adam answers. "Because when I found out what Matthew was up to, my first thought was to check if Liam was in on it too, but I haven't been able to track him."

"My son always had a weak heart," Gregory spits. "I wouldn't be surprised if he found out himself and decided to cower from it all instead of look you in the eye and show you the bloodline he comes from."

"He's not like you," I say with the confidence that returns to me in defense of him. "He's always been afraid and disgusted by you, and I'm only sorry to him I never pushed to know why."

"He's a worthless boy who flees at the first sign of responsibility."

"He's a better man than you could ever be."

"I'm all for team Liam," Adam drawls. "But right now we need to get the hell out of here."

"Nina's headed for my father."

"I intercepted her outside. She's safe. Your father won't know any of this."

I don't know how we'll take down the Forbes later, but right now all that matters is getting out of this house alive.

"No one is going anywhere," a new voice cuts in, smooth like the shadow he emerges from.

Familiar. So dauntingly familiar that I wish I was wrong—until the sleek hair of dark blond catches my sight.

Jacob Forthson reveals a wicked dimple with his smile. He strolls into the kitchen as if he's wandering into a summer party, looking down on the quivering Matthew Forbes like he's the disappointing entertainment.

"There are two ways to pay off debt, darling. And with what he owes me for you, I don't think I'll ever be seeing it in bills."

I don't get to blink nor take a breath, because Jacob moves so fast I don't see the gun he produces until a ringing fills my ears with the firing of a bullet that shocks me still.

"So blood it is."

CHAPTER 40
Anastasia

I don't feel gravity weighing me anymore and I can't tear my sight from Matthew's lifeless form. Blood now pools from his head, and his green eyes turn to haunted glass. Adam's tightening grip is the only thing keeping me from buckling, but I heave, doubling over, sick from the gruesome, brutal murder I witnessed.

The sound of the gunshot still rings in my ears, and I'm slashed back in time. But this isn't like when Rhett held me to him and exacted his revenge. Rhett was good even when he didn't want to believe it. The man he killed had wronged him so despicably.

Jacob is not Rhett.

He is one monster slaying another.

My whole body trembles tightly, but Adam doesn't let me go. At least not by choice.

The first sound to return to me is the agonizing cry of a father. No matter what, Gregory is mourning his child. I think

I'm in shock. Nothing seems grounding and everything seems chaotic. Adam is ripped away from me at some point. More men flood the room. Two take down Gregory, and I glance back, terrified for Adam as they bind his hands behind him, but I can't move.

"It'll all be over soon, darling," Jacob says softly, so close to my ear I don't know when he approached.

"Tie them together for now. I have to deal with this."

I sit in a chair and don't fight. They tie my hands behind me, and Adam and I are back-to-back. I'm facing Matthew and I risk throwing up again as they drag out a fighting Gregory.

"Close your eyes, Ana," Adam says gently. His fingers brush mine—the first contact of something that feels safe, and that lashes me back to this nightmare of a reality when my mind had drifted away in denial that any of this was real.

"Oh god," I whisper. Tears prick my eyes and flow down my cheeks.

"You're going to be okay." He tries to console me.

Maybe I don't want to be anymore. I've seen things that will forever haunt me. I've lost Rhett who I yearn for more than anything in the world right now, and that breaks me. I sob, unable to hold it back. I can't be strong like Rhett.

Be brave, little bird, he would say.

I try to absorb the echoes of his presence that wrap around me now. The only thing that will get me to survive this.

"How did you know I was here?" I ask weakly, closing my eyes like he instructed.

"I must have fallen asleep too. But I didn't think you'd want to wake to me there, so I left. I saw Matthew Forbes lingering in a car outside your house, but he didn't see me. I've always had a bad feeling about him. The way he looks at you, stalks you, and it's like you've never noticed his creepy fixation."

"He . . . he's Liam's brother. Or I thought he was . . . He's always been around." My cheeks burn at the enlightenment to how naïve I've been.

"I don't blame you for not seeing it," he says softly as if he can feel my humiliation. "He put up an excellent front, but I guess, having a deeper care about you, I was more observant to those around you. I followed Matthew tonight, which led me here, and then I had a really bad fucking feeling. I watched him kill the two police that were guarding the safe house after Gregory lured them out. I was about to call the police until . . ."

At his pause of silence I conclude, "Jacob found you?"

His voice quietens. "No, actually—"

Jacob returns, which silences Adam and turns me stone-cold with fear. He doesn't look frightening. In fact, he's so charmingly beautiful that it's chilling to know what all the wealth and the pretty face hides.

"Anastasia." He rolls my name around his mouth as if he's sampling fine wine. "You caused quite a lot of trouble for me in New York. Or at least Rhett Kaiser did in taking my girls."

"They're not property to be sold, you piece of shit," I hiss.

I'm boiling with rage at his audacity. How he can talk so easily about selling people. Women. With families and friends who'll be searching for them. Mourning for them.

"I don't expect you to understand the business, so let's not waste our breath. I hoped I would get the chance to kill Kaiser myself, but I heard of the unfortunate accident. The notorious leader of Xoid, gone in a mere blink from a car crash. It's so disappointing, really. I could have made it far more fun."

"You're a sick, twisted bastard."

"Perhaps. But you don't get to pick your monster this time, Miss Kinsley."

"What do you want from me?"

"I don't want anything *from* you. I want *all of* you."

"Fuck you and go to hell," Adam spits.

I squeeze his fingers, my anticipation shooting at his boldness. I can't watch Adam die too. "I'll go with you," I say quickly.

"Ana—"

"Just let him go, please?"

Jacob regards us, looking over Adam curiously as though deciding whether his bullets should take another life tonight.

"A friend?" Jacob ponders.

"Yes. Just a friend."

"What will you give me to spare his life?"

Jacob's eyes flick sideways with a silent command that has one of his men untying my bonds. I rub my wrists, heart thundering to keep track of all his movements that could become unhinged at any moment.

"Am I not enough?" I ask, trying to keep my voice from wavering and straightening with confidence.

"I don't think you're willing to do what it takes to be enough. To be mine," he says, his voice so arrogantly smooth. Coming close enough, he tips my chin up with the barrel of his gun. Adam struggles, and I clamp my fists and my teeth against my trembling.

He's a fucking sadist.

"Then what do you want?"

Jacob's smile slithers down every notch of my spine. Tears prick my eyes when I don't know what he's going to do, and a man with no morals exposes my mind with a million fears.

"An alliance," he says.

His hand is so smooth circling my waist. He's surprisingly gentle, but he presses me to him and I bite my lip against a whimper. This closeness feels so wrong, and I prepare to fight him if he tries anything further.

After scanning my eyes, my face, like he's admiring every surface of a diamond, he leans in close.

Not to kiss me.

His lips come close, but they brush over my ear. Then he speaks. Every word races my thoughts. Faster and faster. My heart is going to explode out of my chest.

Then he pulls back, gives one wicked smile, and lets me go.

"Sir, we're about to be surrounded," one of his men says to him.

Jacob hovers around me, stopping only to graze his fingers under my chin, and maybe he does contemplate kissing me then. But a crash erupts and he's broken from his trance.

"Until we meet again, Anastasia."

I shiver at that promise.

Then he's gone, but his presence lingers like a ghost that will follow me.

"Uhh, wanna help me out so we can get the hell out of here?" Adam's voice snaps me back from my reeling thoughts.

I twist and scramble to undo his bonds.

"What the fuck was that about? He just left?"

"We're not in the clear yet," I say through my tight throat.

Adam takes my arms when he's free, scanning me over like Jacob could have harmed me during the seconds I was in his hold.

"Darling Ana."

The sound of Alistair Lanshall at my back makes my next inhale shudder.

"Didn't I tell you not to leave your home? We'll have to work on your obedience first."

Adam's expression hardens, his grip tightening like he's about to push me behind him, but my hand goes over his to stop him. He pins me with a look of incredulity.

I turn to Alistair. He's all dark, haughty confidence in his black coat and slicked dark blond hair. Older than Jacob, but it's easy to see they're cut from the same blood-soaked cloth. They both feed from the same roots of poison.

"You missed Jacob," I say, slipping into the detached person I need to be. "Would have been quite the show to see you go head-to-head."

Alistair smiles wickedly. "You would like to see that, wouldn't you? You really are starved for violence, darling. We'll fix that soon enough."

He holds out a hand and it's my ticket to the devil's playground.

"What are you doing?" Adam hisses.

I have no choice. This opportunity won't come around again.

There's a war in the underworld, and I'm going be the reason they both go down in their battle. I'm going to find out myself what happened to Rhett, because in my heart he's still out there, waiting for me just like he was on that bench on a snowy Christmas Eve.

To the people I'm Anastasia Kinsley.

For the people I'm Anastasia Kaiser.

So I take the hand of one evil, with the hope I can defeat it, not become it.

CHAPTER 41
Rhett

I wish I could say this is the first time I've awoken beaten and bloodied, strapped to a chair. My head feels like a boulder with another hundred ramming into as I lift it. My neck is stiff and it takes all my concentration not to black out from the pain. My eyes flicker open, adjusting to the low, warm light. The room is small and empty. There's a screen opposite me and on either side of me. That's all.

Every breath spears my insides with knives, but as I examine my hands I see someone has bandaged me. There's a cannula in my arm and an IV drip next to me.

The door opens, and the grinding of metal against stone makes me sick. The sight of my uncle makes me lurch in my chair despite the restraints and the agony piercing through me.

"Take it easy, Everett. Don't want to delay your recovery. You have a long road ahead."

My anger is coursing hot through my veins, and maybe my

willpower alone can break the bonds strapping my arms and legs to the seat. But two men stand at the door, and I'm too incapacitated from my injuries to take out everyone I would need to take out in order to make it out of here. And I *have* to make it out alive. For Ana.

A timid woman comes in holding a glass of water. She raises it to my lips and I have no choice but to drink it as my throat is dry as fuck.

"I've waited a long time for you, nephew," Alistair says, pacing in front of me. "I watched you all this time. I studied everything you built, and I'll admit, I'm impressed. You've genuinely caused a lot of trouble for me and cost me a fortune. But part of me believes it was all worth it, for who you became in your vengeful search for me. You let yourself be everything you were destined to be."

"I'm going to fucking kill you," I seethe at him.

It's a promise. I made it the day Sarah died, written in as much blood as I had to spill to get here.

"I don't think you will," he says calmly.

When he moves from the screen and a picture floods the black, I hope to hell this is a nightmare. That I'm still lying in the wreckage of the SUV or even fucking *dead* if it means she's safe. If it means I'm not staring at Anastasia Kinsley in the worst place I'd ever want to see her. A room so familiar it makes the cowardly child in me shrink away. It's dark and tastefully old fashioned, but it's all a guise for the wickedness that lurks in every corner of Alistair Lanshall's office.

"Let her go," I snarl. *I'm going to kill every man in my way to her.*

"I'm not holding her," Alistair says.

I know his tells even after all this time. He's telling the truth, and I can't decide if that makes this so much fucking worse.

"Anastasia came to me. She took my hand. I see why you're drawn to her. Like calls to like, and your darkness has awoken hers. Now it will be my pleasure to craft it."

"Please," I say—it's all I have. A miserable, pathetic plea to spare Ana. "I'll do whatever you want, just leave her be. She doesn't belong in this."

Ana wanders around his office observing the décor, until she lingers by the fire pit that blazes against her silhouette. She's wearing all black. I've never seen her so passionless and dark.

"You know she does."

"What have you told her?"

"Nothing but the truth."

"Did you use me to get her to come?"

"No. Anastasia saw the wreckage of your car. She's since believed you dead. So, you see, her being here is entirely of her own volition. She's not restrained, not resisting. Not like you. Perhaps watching her grow into all you could have become will make you see sense. You could be reunited. Imagine the two of you working for me. The power we would have."

"Never," I snarl.

"We'll see."

Alistair leaves along with the woman who checked all my wounds, but I'm numb to the pain now, fixed only on Ana, wishing the screen would change. That it's some kind of trick. Her hand runs along the back of the tall seat I sat across from Alistair in so many times before. In front of a raging fire pit. It haunts me to see her there now, like my past awakening, and eerie laughter rattles my mind.

Then Ana looks up, right at the camera, and I want to scream, shout as loud as I can, and by some miracle have her hear me. I need her to know I'm alive and that she doesn't have to do this.

I can't figure out her mind, what she's thinking as she walks into the mouth of the viper.

Oh, little bird, what have you done?

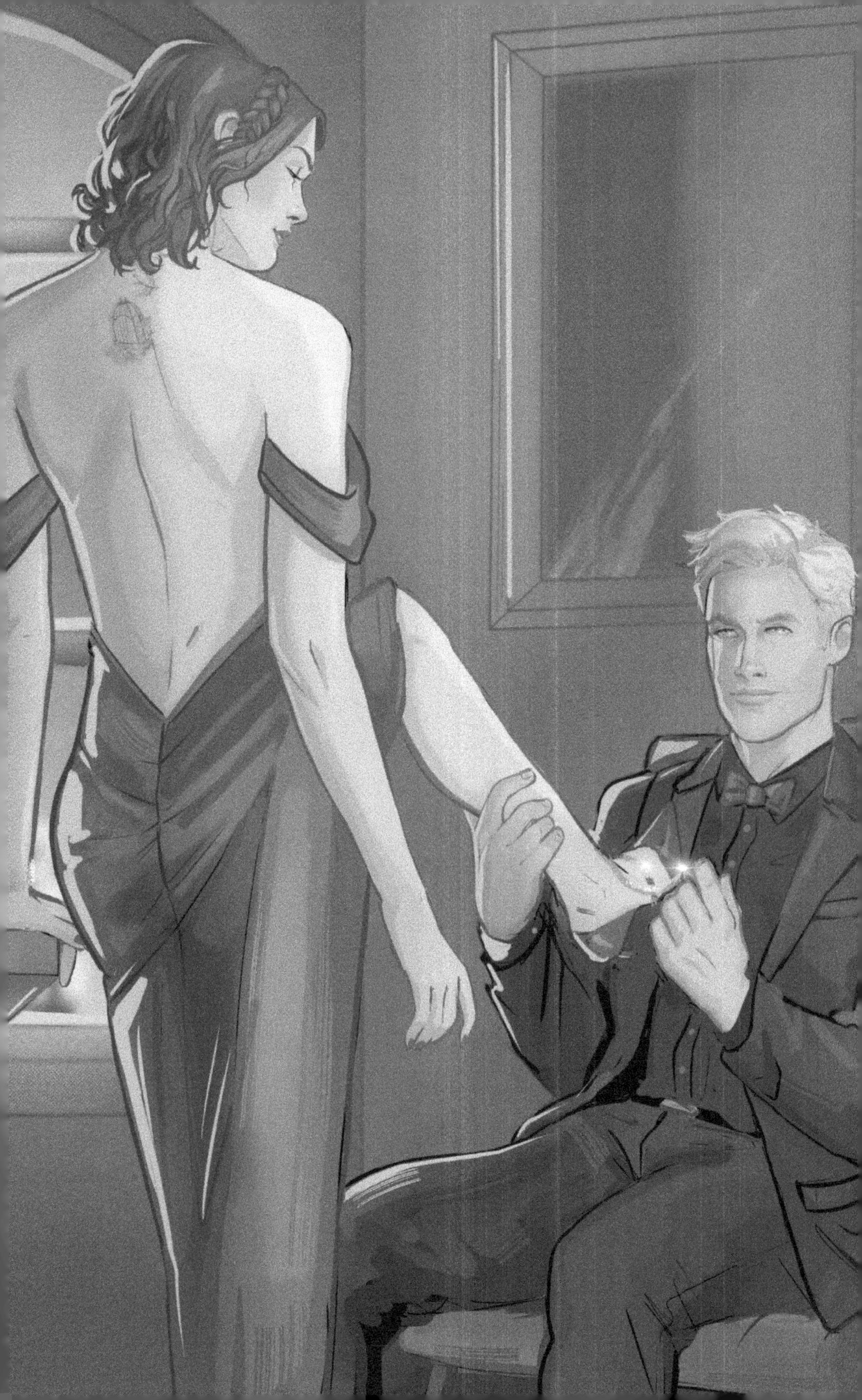

RHETT AND ANA'S STORY CONTINUES IN...

INSIDE THE
Wicked

BEHIND DARKNESS DUET BOOK TWO

USA TODAY BESTSELLING AUTHOR
CHLOE C. PEÑARANDA

Also by Chloe C. Peñaranda

An Heir Comes to Rise series

A New Adult slow burn high romantic fantasy with strong found family, chosen one, fae & dark fae, royalty, fated mates. (Third-person, multiple POV)

An Heir Come to Rise

A Queen Comes to Power

A Throne from the Ashes

A Clash of Three Courts

A Sword from the Embers

A Flame of the Phoenix

The Nytefall Trilogy

A New Adult star-crossed, villain gets the girl tale in a darkly whimsical world. (First-person, single to dual POV)

The Stars Are Dying

Untitled book 2

Untitled book 3

Behind Darkness Duet

A darkly heart-wrenching, and scorching contemporary bodyguard romance.

Behind The Broken

Inside The Wicked

Acknowledgments

Endless thanks to you, always, for deciding to pick up and read my book. I started in fantasy, but as an avid reader of many genres, I was so excited to put my own book out for the contemporary romance community. Rhett and Ana's story turned into so much more than I anticipated and carved a special place in my heart. I really hope you fell in love with Rhett and Ana as much as I did and I can't wait to share the next side of their story in book two.

To Lyssa, my chaos coordinator and emotional support human. I don't know where I'd be without you. Thank you for being the strongest believer, biggest enabler, and someone who's always there to rant, laugh, and cry to. You rock!

To my wonderful editor Bryony, thank you for following me on this new venture into contemporary romance! It's always an absolute pleasure to work with you and your magic worked on my books is invaluable.

To my mum, keep fighting strong, you have so many more golden years to live. Thank you for being you.

To my ever supportive family, I kind of hope you're not reading this book. But even still, your belief in me despite not knowing a lot about it always means the world.

To my dogs; Milo, Bonnie, and Minnie. It's us against the

world most days from our solo living. Still promising the house with the garden—soon!

Until the next book!